# THE TREES
# BEYOND
# THE GRASS

*The Trees Beyond the Grass* is a work of fiction. All incidents and dialogue, and all characters with the exception of some well-known historical and public figures, are products of the author's imagination and are not to be construed as real. Where real-life historical or public figures appear, the situations, incident and dialogues concerning those persons are entirely fictional and are not intended to depict actual events or to change the entirely fictional nature of the work. In all respects, any resemblance to persons living or dead is entirely coincidental.

FIRST EDITION
Published in the United States by The Spartina Company, Ltd.

ISBN 978-0-9898549-0-0
eISBN 978-0-9898549-1-7

2013915521

Cover photography by Kathleen Gill
Cover design by damanza.com

*To family and friends who have always supported me,*
*especially my mother who instilled in me that there is nothing*
*you cannot accomplish if you truly try.*

# THE TREES
# BEYOND
# THE GRASS

– A NOVEL –

By ROBERT REEVES

# PROLOGUE

*"Mother was a meth-head and I was currency for her next hit. My father had long disappeared. There were other men, though...lots of them. They would smile at me, petting my hair like they would their daughters I went to school with. Then they would take my hand. Momma's face would glow. 'Go on, baby, you be real good and do what he says.' In the back room of our trailer they would lay me down in my mother's bed, kissing my neck, running their hands up my shorts. The first few times I screamed, confused as to why it was happening, what I had done wrong? Later, I learned it was the weakness of men for all things red that drives them into dark places. But they were undeserving. I can still hear Momma calling from the other room, 'Be strong, my sweet flower... my sweet, sweet red flower.'*

*P"*

POINSETT HIT THE 'submit' button. It was important that everyone know... She needed *him* to know. The final hunt had arrived.

# DENVER

*Day six-eighty-nine.*

A DEEP GASP for air could be heard as Cole Mouzon broke the surface between sleep and consciousness. He had been drowning in fear for over a month, taunted by a dream long believed to have been lost somewhere in childhood. Its return had been without warning or reason, hunting him every time he closed his eyes, submerging him in dark places.

His eyes still pinched closed, he shook off the residual fear like a wet dog and then instinctually slid his arm across the bed where only the cool underside of a pillow was found. He exhaled a long breath. Dream or no dream, he dreaded mornings. Not in the 'it's time to go to work' way. No. Waking meant remembering he was alone. The feeling had grown thick and viscous since Atlanta and left him drenched in the tannic feeling of a solitary life.

Slowly, he opened his eyes, still damp from the piercing emotions. It was six-thirty a.m. and the sun was already beaming saffron through the narrow bedroom window when he finally brushed off the remaining hollowness and swept his long legs off the bed. His toes reached the chill of lacquered ponderosa pine floors, wishing to recoil to the warmth of his down duvet. *Get your ass up!* Slowly, he moved until he was completely standing, still rubbing the sting of salty sleep out of his eyes.

Dixie jumped off the high bed with a heavy thud, her thick board of a tail now smacking Cole against his right leg, whipping him forward into another day. "I'm going, you dog. I'm going." Dixie acknowledged him with a tight wag of her tail before bounding into the hall and beyond with her heavy paws, towards the kitchen and its dog door. Cole shuffled across the floor, half-blind from his missing contacts, into the single household bathroom, which was too small for much more than a shower and wiping down. He flicked on the switch behind the bathroom door and leaned into the ceramic pedestal basin, looking at himself in the mirror.

The face staring back at him had begun to show some wear from his years, with fine lines spreading out like webs from the corners of his eyes and one too many freckles blotting his pale skin. Telling himself he needed a tan, he pulled at the thin skin at the corners of his eyes to smooth it and lift the otherwise dark purple bags. His second spring in Denver had been unusually cold and long, making attempts at color futile.

He had looked worse, he knew that. But in the years since Atlanta, he felt the damage had been done. The scars of his thirty-three years had finally begun to settle in, like fog nestled in a cool mountain valley, and no amount of care could burn it off. The high desert dryness of the Rockies emphasized the creases of too few hours of sleep and the tight eyes of pain.

Running his fingers through his sandy blonde hair, he wondered how he had survived his life so far. He had lost his mother at two and festered privately ever since then. His will to endure seemed to spite his deep longing to fade to black. "Just get over it," he would tell himself. But he couldn't move forward. Attempts at therapy had resulted in one revelation: he was stuck. This was a play that he rehearsed every morning, like a Shakespeare tale that never found a commoner crowd to listen to it. He kept it to himself. There was no need to burden his family or friends; they had their own issues. Untold, his grief languished, restlessly knocking at his solid facade in hopes of being heard.

It was in these early morning moments that he was weakest. Slowly, he raised the dense wall that kept it all in, that stored his suffering in some out-of-the-way place in his mind so that he could function. He couldn't think of a time the wall wasn't there, at least since losing his mother. But he kept it hidden well. Staring at himself, he could feel the wall's presence stabilizing his mood, his thoughts, as he moved about the cramped space of the white-tiled bathroom until it was completely raised and all thought of pain, longing, and sadness dissipated into the morning.

POURING YESTERDAY'S COLD, bitter coffee into a speckled yellow stonecraft mug and then pushing it into the microwave, he hit two minutes. Its fan hummed as he leaned back into the rainforest green marble counter and watched as Dixie first looked up for approval and then approached her now-full morning bowl for breakfast, her bat of a tail wagging with excitement. Transparent images, like slides, flashed before his eyes to reveal his thoughts in vivid color. There were always images. Those this morning were just of things needing to be accomplished during the day. The image of luggage packed. The image of walking out the front door. The image of being in a deposition. They each came one after the other, until he consciously pushed the mental projector off to the side of his mind to focus on Dixie.

"Well, I'm glad you're perky, Dixie Carter Mouzon. Daddy is draggin' this morning, between your ruckus in the middle of the night and that damn dream. Why do you always have to bark at the wind? You know it's just that. Daddy needed his sleep for his flight later, while you, lucky dog, get to chill with your boyfriend Luke-e-Luke up in the mountains for the next week." Dixie looked up from her half-empty bowl with sparkling eyes as if to say, *yep, I know,* before turning back to finish. Cole shook his head at her pleasure and then turned to pull the stale coffee out of the microwave using an oven mitt, the mug now way too hot to the touch for bare hands. While blowing on its top in a weak attempt to cool it off, his mind drifted back to his night.

The nightmare had come back. It had been almost twenty years since he'd last had it, but now its return gripped him in the darkness of his sleep, pulling him into the trees and palmettos of his childhood. The same sequence, the same images. *Why now?* Whatever the reason, it couldn't have come at a more inconvenient time. Work had consumed him for the past few months, and the lack of sleep only compounded his already drained energy. He brushed off his thoughts, refocusing on Dixie who had stepped back from her bowl to sniff out random pieces of dry dog food that had escaped her mouth.

"Okay, missy. You finish up and let yourself out while Daddy gets dressed. Aunt Maggie should be here by lunch to pick you up, and you better have not made a mess of the place, you hear me woman?" Morning conversations between the two were the reality of a single man living alone in a small Craftsman-style bungalow with no one else to cater to in the early hours of the day. But for Cole there was the larger reality that Dixie had offered some relief from the hollow created back in Atlanta.

Dixie looked up again as Cole walked out of the kitchen in his white V-neck t-shirt and grey pinstriped slacks towards the bedroom. Maggie was a friend, not an aunt, but Cole loved her like a second sister and so had bestowed the honor of aunt-hood upon her when he'd adopted Dixie a year earlier. Little did she know that the honor came with puppy-sitting responsibilities.

A MIST OF PERSPIRATION coated Cole's forehead as he walked out of the bathroom to finish packing for Charleston. It was May and a mild heat wave had descended on Denver; yet the city's high altitude meant double-digit cool-offs at night, making open windows a very cheap and effective alternative to running up the power bill with the A/C. This unfortunately invited trouble. Cherry Creek was an affluent neighborhood, and summer was the season for bored teens to raid homes in hopes of scoring while their owners were away for the season. Cole could count three homes just on his block that lay empty while their inhabitants enjoyed the Caymans, Brazil, or some other exotic place. The idea of leaving his home empty for a week unnerved him, but if anyone wanted to steal something they were just as likely to do it while he was at work as when he was out of town. Dixie's nighttime barking had added to that concern. *What if someone was outside?* Cole ignored the concern, zipped up his overstuffed blue carry-on bag and worked to gather Dixie's overnight bag of food and a pink pig dog toy long-emptied of stuffing. Maggie would swing by around lunch and collect the bag and Dixie while he was away.

Ten minutes later, he said good-bye to Dixie and loaded his tattered carry-on and a large pale blue canvas beach bag into the trunk of his silver Audi A4. Slowly he crept into the morning traffic towards the Denver Tech area of town, an alcove of medium-height towers that hosted insurance companies and corporate headquarters away from the tourists and tight corridors that choked the pedestrian-friendly concrete of downtown Denver. A winner-takes-all deposition needed to be taken before he could board his two-thirty flight to Charleston.

The seated form of courtroom interrogation was being hosted at the plaintiff's attorney's office, which adjoined a Chipotle in a small, aged strip mall. Home turf was always desired. Too many times lawyers and doctors cut off the heat or air in the often-tight room in an effort to unnerve and hasten the unpleasantness of being cross-examined, analyzed, and their credibility being called into question, even if rightfully so. No one desired to be called, and often shown to be, a liar to their face—such realities were best left to the silence of dark places.

It was in dark places that lawyers lingered. As civil defense counsel with Johnson, Roberts & Steele, it was Cole's job to discover not only the truth to a plaintiff's claims, but to analyze his or her ability to credibly and convincingly convey that truth. Where they were able to tell a compelling, true story, the case settled at a reasonable value. But if the plaintiff lied, or was ineffective at telling the truth, the case was subject to being attacked by paper hyenas, picking off the weak from the strong. The reality was no less true on the plaintiff's side, thereby creating a balanced system of hunters and supporting a justice system based more on skilled advocacy than the seeking of truth.

Pulling up to the old shingle-sided building in the mall and putting the car into park, Cole looked into the rear-view mirror and stared into his own green eyes. The mental wall that held back his turbulent pain was still firmly in place as he prepared himself to enter the hunter's den.

# CHAPTER 1

*Dallas, a week earlier...*

*"He was sweet enough when we met. His wide lips and brown eyes made me feel safe. But, safety was needed, not found in him. His first strike left only the slightest bruise along my brow line, the second a cut in the corner of my mouth. I told myself he loved me, that I had deserved it, with every blow. My third rib was broken by a fall in the shower, or so I told my friends. But I could see in their eyes they knew just how weak I was to take each blow. Escape was no option. Slowly, very slowly, I gathered the strength to survive. He lingers no more.*

*P"*

The post was submitted.

POINSETT SAT IN her rented cream-colored Accord outside Wild Salsa in downtown Dallas, watching with shaky trepidation—waiting for her next kill. Looking down, she re-read the message she had typed Wednesday night while sitting alone in her Dallas hotel room. She then glanced over at the photos resting in the leather passenger seat of the humid car. *Tony Patrick*. With his shaved head, thick, muscular physique, and standing at six-five, he had been easy to locate upon arriving in Texas three days earlier, once she'd determined where he worked.

And now she sat, her body tingling with the exhilaration of what was about to occur. Other than the hum of the engine and slight whistle of the A/C running through the car's vents, there was silence—no radio played—as she reflected on how she had come to the place where she killed those she had never met. It hadn't been so easy, so invigorating, the first time. Fear and her internal conflict tore at her, making her feel like a fumbling little girl on a dark first date.

The self-interrogation was common enough. *You're an educated woman, have everything going for you. Why do you have to do this?*

But the response came swiftly and sternly from somewhere deep in her mind. *Because they don't deserve to live— didn't deserve the years they have stolen. How could he have let them live at the price of your happiness? You must kill them, all of them. Take away his prizes.* Reflecting on the chastising voice's sting caused Poinsett to recoil slightly into the headrest and close her eyes.

The warm heat of red anger and jealousy overcame her body and made her brow damp with pearls of perspiration as she tried to regain control. She could feel them slowly pulled down across her face. She was used to hot and humid places; she lived in one. But she would not let this place drag down her Southern-laced beauty. Opening her eyes, she dug into a bright orange Gucci quilted-leather handbag and withdrew a Bobbi Brown compact.

Flipping it open, she grabbed the sponge, dabbed it into the powder and then onto her forehead.

THE ONE-SIDED CONVERSATION continued. *You can do this,* she told herself as she looked into the small circular mirror. *He's like the girl in New York, weak and undeserving. He must die. You have to do this.*

It was a compulsion, and though she tried, she ultimately failed in attempting to resist it. She took trips to Fiji and did Bikram yoga, hoping that through peaceful doings it would dissipate. But all the quiet did was foster it and allow it to grow uncontrollably in the deep crevices of her mind. Like a horrible dieter's hunger, it refused to be ignored, growling and scratching at her insides until she finally opened the door and gave it attention. That's when it consumed her fully, taking any will to fight against its determination to seek retribution. Her career, her life, now existed purely to disguise her movements to feed her hunger.

There were moments of lucidity where she wondered if the deaths, the risks were all worth the reward of seeking revenge against her pained memories. In her youth she'd told herself to grow up and move on. Yet those moments came so rarely now that she could barely think beyond her focus on retribution and planning the next kill. The venom of her childhood had taken hold and poisoned any rational thought beyond revenge.

*He left you because of them. He chose them…*

She'd cried when she thrust the first, killing stroke of a ceramic knife deep into Whitney Havex in New York. At first she was ashamed of the tears—*what a fool*—but now, she saw them for what they were, the pouring out of weakness, a purging of the soul, giving her strength to move on to the next kill. So she now sat in her rental, waiting for Tony Patrick, the reason she'd come to Dallas. He had been marked almost thirty years earlier in Houston, a prize of sorts, which she now intended to claim as her own.

From the side mirror she caught sight of Tony's old white Ford F250, which she had seen him leave for work in early in the morning. Like the killing before, Poinsett had watched, documenting Tony's every move, before ever approaching him for the kill. She researched and located him. She arrived several days earlier in the week and then observed his life. He was a line-worker manager at Coca-Cola, eight a.m. in, five p.m. out. He had little social life, based upon her observations—was never seen with a date or woman, though she had learned he was once married, as a teen. That clearly didn't pan out, as the man she saw was a barfly who sat alone at the bar, hoping to garner some sugar from the drunkest woman. So, when it was his time, it was easy for her to figure out the best approach. She would be careful to avoid any cameras. *Can't be making it easy for the cops.* Male weakness would take over from there, as he would attempt to sniff up her skirt like a stray dog.

She had waited thirty minutes in her car, letting him grab a drink as she had learned he always did after work. He hadn't noticed her in the shiny Accord as he drove by it to the Coca-Cola bottling plant west of town, but he would notice her now. The time had begun for another kill, and Tony was the prey. *Let the hunt begin.*

# CHAPTER 2

B Y THE EMPTY booths and bar, Thursday nights were clearly not the night to be at Wild Salsa. Poinsett walked into the bar and quickly located Tony at the counter, two empty shot glasses before him and a beer in his hand. His red polo shirt, blue jeans, and thick brown leather belt screamed *boring* to Poinsett. A black cap covered his close-shaven head. She quickly noticed him flipping a white linen paper card between his fingers like a quarter. *My card.* She had mailed it to him from New York several days earlier after finishing off Whitney Havex. He looked down at the card and Poinsett could tell he was re-reading it.

> *Dear Tony,*
>
> *You cower in life as you will at death. I am here to reclaim what has been taken.*
>
> *I am beside you…*
>
> *P*

She watched as he laughed to himself and then moved to step away from the bar. *Time to introduce myself.*

Before Tony's foot could reach the floor, Poinsett pulled up beside him, sitting on the wooden swivel stool and pressing her chest against the counter to gather the attention of the bartender…and Tony.

"I'll take a skinny margarita." Her accent, perhaps from Alabama or Georgia, was noticeable. Feeling his gaze on her breasts, now firmly pressed against the counter's edge until they looked like there were about to pop free of her dress, she glanced over to him. By his look, he was loving this. It was clear it had been some time since he'd gotten laid, and it certainly wasn't with any woman who looked like her.

"Where you from?" Tony smiled his toothy smile.

"Oh, Birmingham originally. But I work in Tulsa now," she lied.

Tony was intrigued and wanted to know more. "What brings you down this way? Business or pleasure?"

She smiled as she answered, "Business, but I'm not adverse to pleasure." Her eyes rolled up and down his body before returning to his gaze.

Tony's face flashed clear moments of hot sex before she could even finish saying 'pleasure.' His light mahogany eyes glanced across her half-exposed breasts and the deep, layered V formed by her pink and green floral-print sundress. His gaze then ran down her body to her white leather sandals and returned to her breasts before he looked back at her eyes.

"Well, you're in luck, ma'am. I happen to be a very pleasurable guy." His cliché line was met by a slight come-hither look in Poinsett's blue eyes, one brow slightly askew. With her left hand, she swept her long, blonde hair off her face and over her shoulder. A wig, purchased before the killing in New York.

"Oh? Do tell, cowboy?" *Two can play at this game*, thought Poinsett. By this point she was two-thirds through her drink.

HE LEANED IN toward Poinsett and placing his empty glass on the bar. "How about a shot?" Tony was trying to speed up the process. Time was wasting and he was clearly ravenous to play. He pushed for requests. "What would you like? A lemon drop, chocolate cake, what's your poison?" He placed his right hand on the back of her wooden stool and rubbed her exposed shoulder with his thumb in small circular movements, the grin still firmly on his face.

Poinsett looked at his hand and cringed internally. She wanted to kill him right there in the middle of the bar. She would break her now-empty glass against the edge of the bar and slash his throat with the shards if she thought she could get away with it. The thought played out for a few moments in her head before she spoke. "Tequila!" she announced, matching his grin with a slight smile. She wanted him dead, and now.

A deep, hollow-chest "Ha," came out as Tony pulled back in excitement. "My kind of girl... I mean, lady." He tipped his faded black cap in apology. She smiled back as to say, 'no offense taken.' Looking around her, he waved the bartender over and ordered two shots of Jose Cuervo Silver. The bartender grabbed two shot glasses and the bottle, pouring the shots in front of them. Poinsett caught the slight look of *what the fuck* cross the bartender's deeply tanned face. He clearly didn't understand the attraction playing out at the otherwise empty bar. Running his hand over his black fauxhawk haircut, he returned to the opposite end of the bar to apparently discuss with the ample-breasted waitress with the daisy-duke shorts and tight white tank top what they were observing.

Poinsett turned back to Tony after seeing a giggle from the waitress. Tony promptly raised his glass at her gaze, which she followed with her own. "To business and pleasure," he said.

They both downed the stinging shot without involving a lime or salt. By the look on his face, he approved.

Poinsett wondered if he had any clue what was about to happen. With Whitney in New York, there had been no interaction until the first blow. Before Whitney got home to her Astoria Park condo, Poinsett had arrived and convinced the front desk security guard to give her access to the building.

The story was simple. Her new boyfriend lived in the building, and it was his birthday. She intended to surprise him with a bit of a peep-show: "He loves strippers, after all." The deal was closed with a slight flash of her red bra, which sent Jeff the doorman over the top. His face went flush as he nodded in understanding. He walked her to the elevator bank behind his circular stand and let the door open. At the twelfth floor she stepped off and looked around for the stairs. As a precaution, she selected a floor other than that of Whitney's so as to not immediately raise suspicions when her body was ultimately found. Fire wells couldn't be locked under the local fire code, giving her free access to each floor. She opened its door and walked another three stories up to get off near Whitney's sixteenth-floor condo.

It was an old building; any renovations done focused on the aesthetics of the hall, not on the mechanics of the doors. *They clearly relied too much on Jeff the doorman.* A quick slip of a credit card and a small screwdriver and she was inside Whitney's apartment, where the fun began when she arrived twenty minutes later.

# CHAPTER 3

"ANOTHER?" SHE SAID with a sweet Southern smile still beaming at him. Poinsett snapped back to the present, determined to get the hunt moving along. This time she placed her soft hand on Tony's thigh, close to his groin, to emphasize her implications. He stared at her hand for a moment and then raised his head. "Of course!" He waved over the bartender, who tore himself away from the waitress and walked over to pour the second shots, and as quickly as the first, they were gone. He was halfway back to his post when he obviously heard Poinsett say, "Let's get out of here."

The look on his face was pure shock when he turned to walk to the register beside Poinsett. He shook his head slightly in disbelief as the bill printed out and he delivered it, folded down its spine and placed in a shot glass.

Using the opportunity for closer interaction, Tony leaned in to grab the glass and softly said, "Sounds like a great idea. Where's your hotel?"

The slight grin returned to Poinsett's face. "Awh, can we go to your place? I'm here with co-workers and I'd rather not be seen bringing a boy home. Sorry...a *man*." She intentionally mimicked Tony's prior remark and then pulled her left hand from her lap, tapping her ring finger to flash a diamond.

Tony's face flashed shock, then pleasurable trouble. "Sure." He was attempting to muster an 'I understand and am a mature man' voice, but what came out was 'gleeful kid who's just received a new toy.' Poinsett smiled. She had him hooked.

After Tony paid the tab with cash, they walked out to leave their admiring audience to discuss. Poinsett could feel Tony's gaze on her cross-fit firm backside as she walked to the Accord with him behind in obvious ecstasy. It was after nine and the parking lot's streetlights dotted the street parking with small circles of creamy light. She looked up from her five-eight frame to Tony. "So, I'll follow you to your place?"

"Yeah, I'm in that white pickup over there. It's maybe a fifteen minute drive. Just stay close. Wouldn't want to lose you." Poinsett smiled. *Oh, you won't lose me.*

Following behind Tony, Poinsett's mind again flashed back to New York. Whitney was taken down with nightshade. Much like its rumored effects on Romeo, Whitney was helpless on her bathroom floor—aware of everything, but unable to move. Poinsett had worked slowly with a steady hand until Whitney lay slowly dying from the cuts. Peeling off a pair of polyester gym pants and a top that had been coated with blood, Poinsett looked down at the body, satisfied with her work. Her heart pumped heavy with the thrill. She wanted, *needed*, that thrill again. Tony was her next chance.

Minutes later, Tony pulled up to his A-frame home off Angelina Drive with Poinsett in tow. It was nine-thirty p.m., and the street was quiet but for a few kids several blocks down on skateboards under a street lamp.

Tony was visibly giddy with anticipation as he walked up to her car door. "Come on in." She stepped out in a grand sweeping movement like she was about to walk the red carpet, and extended her hand for him to assist her up. She then closed the car's door and proceeded to the nondescript white-painted home. Entering through the door, she glanced at Tony and said softly in her genteel accent, "Let the fun begin."

# CHAPTER 4

TONY FELT A slight prick in his neck as he swung closed the red-painted wooden front door. "What the...hell?" He turned to see Poinsett with an empty needle in her hand. "You fucking bitch! I'll kill you."

Poinsett had acted too soon. He swung around with his right arm and backhanded her with his broad right hand. She fell to the brown shag carpet floor and tried to crawl away. Leaning down, he grabbed her left leg and pulled her from beneath an aged yellow table.

Poinsett panicked at the idea that she could become the victim. Standing over her, he whipped off his cap, throwing it to the floor and revealing his shaven head. "So you like it rough, huh?"

He unbuckled his belt and yanked it free of his jean's loops when she kicked and spat back. "Go to hell."

As he bent down to grab her legs again, he stumbled, falling hard to his knees. Poinsett pulled out a scalpel she had hidden in the strap of her bra during the car ride earlier and sliced the air, landing her last swipe across his left cheek. Tony screamed in pain and rolled to retreat. She jumped up and was on him, stabbing him below the ribs and in his stomach. He grabbed her right wrist, bending it back and forcing the blade to fall. He chased and within a second he had a hold of it, jabbing it like an ice pick into her. Then his body failed him.

Tony was helpless within a minute of being stabbed by Poinsett's needle. He felt his body go lifeless and tumble down like a large tree that had been chopped low at its base. His head caught the corner of his glass-topped coffee table as he fell, causing a throbbing gash that consumed his head.

Standing before him, Poinsett stared down, grinning. He wasn't dead. It was worse than death; he was alive and trapped in his body like in a dream. He could see and hear everything Poinsett was saying. He could feel everything, he just couldn't respond. "Sorry Tony, you won't be getting laid tonight. Guess you kind of figured that out by now." She shrugged her shoulders, pinching them at her neck. "I know you can hear me. You've been given a very strong tranquilizer, a muscle relaxant used by hunters to take down their prey." She held the grin tight and narrowed her eyes. *That's what Tony is, prey.*

"I told you that you weren't worthy of life, of the stolen years you lived, Tony. And now it's time for it to end. I'm here to take back what is mine." Tony watched in horror as Poinsett cleaned the scalpel with the bottom of her now-disheveled sundress and dropped to her knees to straddle his body at his hips, pinning him between her thighs. Slipping her smirk to one side, she told him, "Tony, I'm not going to lie. This is going to hurt." Tony's eyes welled up with fear, tears cresting their inner frames. Pure hatred could be read in them as Poinsett used the blade to slice vertically up his red polo shirt in rough repetitive movements until it was completely cut, lying in two limp pieces on either side of his frame. His eyes revealed his racing thoughts. *What the fuck is she doing? God, please help me, please!*

POINSETT'S LEFT HAND ran up his solid stomach, her eyes admiring his six-pack with its slight tuft of hair at the navel. "You know, it's a shame I didn't get to enjoy you. I'm sure that you would have at least been good at that." Pulling back and sitting erect, she added, "But...perhaps not. Looks can be deceiving, can't they?" Grinning, she cut a swath of his shirt off and wrapped her arm, creating a red bow.

She waved her finger at him. "Tsk, tsk, Tony. You shouldn't have done that." Poinsett thought to herself that he was sexy in a 'dirty mechanic on some lonely road' type of way. His face was covered in salt-and-pepper scruff and chiseled, slight smile marks created brackets on either side of his broad lips. But she had no interest in his attributes. She was on the hunt and it invigorated her. It was far better than any sex she'd had. Her heart pounded as she drew the scalpel across Tony's upper groin; she was enjoying this power over him.

Tony looked on in horror, then pain, as she drove the blade deep into his left ribs, close to his sternum. She was carving. Unlike Whitney, Tony was conscious and Poinsett enjoyed the panic playing out in his eyes. The fast pulsing of her heart was a high; the feeling euphoric and addictive. Tony likely wanted to scream out in pain, but his mouth wouldn't move. She smiled as more tears filled his eyes from the pain and shock of it all. He was dying, and the sight of him coming to this obvious realization excited her.

After a long top-to-bottom and rounded stroke, she

stopped. Blood flowed everywhere. A pulsing artery had been hit and blood splattered across her face. Poinsett leaned back and down to admire her work, wiping her upper lip with the back of her hand and smearing some of the blood. A grin. A very large grin appeared on her face. Tony lay there watching and gasping for air. One of his lungs had been punctured and he was slowly downing in his own blood collecting in his lungs..

Poinsett pushed herself partially up to roll Tony onto his stomach and the brown shag carpet that covered his floor. Bubbles of blood burst from his mouth as the internal puddle of blood sloshed around and out. On his left lower back she found what she was looking for. Pronounced and clear, the mark had been put there and made small enough to not be seen in day to day life, but obvious to those hunting for it.

It was a brand, like a cattle brand. A square with a 'P' in its middle. Poinsett carved along the edges of the square, then underneath the skin to remove the tag. Tony was obviously still alive, as rasps of panicked air came out as she cut. She had no concern; he would be dead long before the toxin wore off.

Poinsett sat up from Tony's flaccid body. Stepping over him, she noticed his breaths were all but nonexistent. After several minutes of watching, she found a large serrated knife in the kitchen and continued her work on his body before snapping a photo with her phone and walking to the front door. "Hunter and prey, you just pulled the wrong stick," she exclaimed as she closed the door behind her. As with Whitney, a photo of her prize would be placed on Tony's Facebook page within the hour. It announced to the world her success and the failure of the prey. His friends would be shocked, the police would be called, and some lowly police department would work to capture the killer. But they would never succeed in stopping Poinsett.

# CHAPTER 5

*TULSA*

"AGENT LEAS, LET me repeat the question. Did you or did you not strangle my client immediately before he gave you the taped confession that you now hang your hat on for his guilt in the death of Pam Rubert?"

Agent David Leas couldn't recall how he had ended up in Judge P. Jenson Rhode's Tulsa County witness box on this Friday morning as Hal Grady, David Flint's hired gun of a defense attorney, worked to have the recorded confession of Mr. Flint excluded as being coerced out of him by fear and force. At forty-three, *I'm too old for this shit*, blinked in his mind. He lifted his left hand and ran his fingers through the shaggy coal-black hair that accented his Latino features.

If he was honest with himself, he had been a little rough with Flint. A bloody nose and dislocated jaw was the least he deserved. He had murdered Miss Rubert and her two children after slipping into their house dressed as a UPS man. The reason was still unclear, but he had three other murders previously, all done the same way: tied with a phone cord or other wire, gagged, and then their throats sliced from jaw to jaw. He made the mother watch as the two children were killed first... That was his high—their fear.

Leas had pieced together the pattern, the method of the victims being selected. Flint used laundromats to discover them, then followed them home and returned the next day in uniform. So, Leas had staked out the most logical next locations for Flint's selection. He had gotten lucky on his second location and noticed Flint, following him as he similarly followed his next selected victim, and then laid a trap. As he waited in the spare room of Rita Drankle's home the next day, Flint came knocking, claiming he had a package and needed a drink of water, if possible. As soon as he slipped into Mrs. Drankle's home and attempted to pin her to the ground, Leas was on him.

"Yes, but..." Leas wanted to add, *but the bastard deserved it*. He'd killed children...a mother. The anger in Leas had collided with his personal anger and spilled over into his work. It hadn't been the first time he swung one too many times on a suspect. And he suspected it wouldn't be his last.

The attorney pushed again. "So you admit that you physically assaulted my client, and then and only then did you 'beat' that statement out of him."

"Now wait a damn second. I did not beat him." Leas' temper flared.

*Okay, maybe I did just a little. But, Miss Rubert...and Maria deserved to get a few stings in on a cold-hearted killer like Flint.*

"Then you strangled him, deprived him of oxygen and made him fear for his life if he didn't say exactly what you wanted him to, correct?" The attorney grinned, obviously enjoying the cross-examination.

Leas squirmed at the direct verbal assault. "No! That

man over there killed Miss Rubert, her kids, and three others, and he knows it. Hell, you know it, you snake! That's why he confessed!"

"Objection!"

Just as the venomous attorney spat out his objection and coiled to strike again a ringing came from Leas' tan slacks pocket, buzzing against his side. Clasping his hand over its location he looked up to the disapproving eyes of the judge.

The judge spoke in slow words. "Sustained. Agent Leas, one more outburst like that out of you and I will put *you* in jail, do you understand me? And didn't I tell you to turn off your phones? Bailiff, collect Agent Leas' phone and don't give it back to him until we are done here." A large officer in a black uniform with a holstered pistol swaggered up to the witness box and put out his hand. Digging deep into his navy blazer pocket, he withdrew his phone and handed it over, still buzzing from the call. The judge continued, "Now answer the question."

Looking across the room to see the bailiff switching the phone off, Leas spoke as he stood halfway up and leaned out of the witness box. "He confessed...and he laughed when he did it, laughed at their deaths and their pain." Leas settled back into his seat.

The attorney turned to the center bench and the large black-robed judge behind it. "Your Honor, as you can see the confession is coerced. I respectfully request that the statement be suppressed based upon the admission of Agent Leas that it was obtained by force, fear of injury, and that because of that, it is unreliable."

The judge looked to his side to peer at Leas and then turned to address the lawyer standing before him. He rubbed his chin. "I don't like this, but I have no option under the testimony presented in this hearing today. The evidence is clear. Mr. Flint was strangled immediately before giving the statement. Under those circumstances I find the statement unreliable and it shall be suppressed. Trial is scheduled for a month from now, counsel. I expect real discussions on trying to resolve this case prior to it proceeding. The court is adjourned."


DEFENSE COUNSEL HAD done his homework, twisting a tale of a FBI drunk suffering from the death of his young wife into the defense, and it resulted in the loss of the defendant's admission to killing multiple women. Leas could still see the DAs' faces, bowed down as he testified, clearly not liking what they heard. His drinking had not interfered with the investigation of Flint and his five roadside murders. *It hadn't.* But the loss of his admission meant the jury would be less likely to convict at the trial next month.

Halfway through the courtroom doors, the local prosecutor grabbed the jacket sleeve of Leas' right arm and spun him into the wall, preparing to hit him. Before Leas could respond, another young suit interjected, tearing the two men apart and pushing them into a side room of the courthouse. Agent Leas was looking down, straightening his black jacket's lapel, when the attorney began speaking. "Do you have any *fucking* clue what you have done? If this shit gets loose he's going to kill again and that blood will be on your hands. What the hell are we supposed to do now?" The narrow-faced prosecutor shoved his finger into Leas' face, pacing the room as if he actually wanted an answer.

Leas gave the man a stern stare and said, "Here's

something novel, you could do your job and prove he's the murderer just by using the evidence that links him to it." Leas' thick black eyebrows were raised as he delivered the last few words.

The prosecutor looked over his glasses with disdain at Leas' response. "No, you... You shut your fucking mouth. Do *my* job? That's ballsy coming from you, Agent. You know, they warned me about you. A fucking drunk. That's what they said. All fucked up since your wife's murder back in D.C., taking it out on every suspect you come across. I'll have your badge for this royal fuck-up." Leas' thick arms tensed under his too-big jacket as he fought to restrain himself. He knew he had screwed the pooch on this one, but he couldn't control himself. The guy was a killer, and he could prove it, with or without an admission.

"Just get the hell out. I'm done with you. Go pour yourself into one of those bottles of whiskey that you reek of. And if I ever catch you sniffing around one of my cases again, so help me God, you'll be the one getting the shit beat out of you."

"Actually counsel, he has to get on a plane." The other suit piped in and handed the prosecutor a stack of files with what appeared to be a plane ticket on top of the rubber-band bound collection. The attorney looked at the top document for a moment and then turned to Leas again. "Well, lucky fuck. They want you down in Dallas, *tomorrow*. You're someone else's problem now." The files shoved into his hands, Leas looked down briefly at the ticket and promptly walked out of the courthouse without a word.

Jumping into his rented blue Kia Sofia, Leas went directly to his dank first-floor hotel room. He hated motor lodges because rooms that opened to the parking lot always posed a danger in his line of work. Opening the door, he discovered the whiskey he had desperately needed since stepping into the courthouse was gone, consumed just hours before he took the stand and forgotten. The silver-grey and brown pinstriped wallpaper and thin-sheeted bed demanded whiskey if they were to be endured one more night. He had eyed an old bar on the corner of the block three days earlier when he arrived for his testimony, but the suits stuck around like flies on a steaming pile, leaving no opportunity to restock the single bottle he'd grabbed on the way from the airport.

Outside again, he was immediately miserable. For May, it was unusually hot and steamy in Tulsa. He had worked the case against Flint five months earlier when snow dusted the ground and heat was the last thing he needed to worry about. But now, his clothes stuck to him, grasping at his slight chest and arm hair with every movement down the sidewalk. *Damn it's hot.* D.C. would have its heat, but not for another month if the city was lucky. Leas just wanted to be back there, where getting a drink didn't require a steam bath and a dusting of red clay. Tomorrow couldn't come soon enough, but for now, he needed that drink.

Stepping into the empty corner bar, he grabbed the red-cushioned stool closest to the door. His placement was a habit from his days working the beat in Philly for seven years, before the FBI picked him up because he had made a reputation for himself as the 'hunter of hunters.' It was Philly where he met his wife Maria, who loved him even if his job required him to work off hours and never see her. When he was around, he was still mentally working the case, trying to get into the minds of killers. But she never complained.

It was one of those killers who took her life, and he hated himself for it. Alcohol helped numb the pain of loss—he could live, even if there wasn't much to live for, so long as he was in a consistent state of intoxication. In the past few years the alcohol had taken over, and with it, his temper against killers.

"Hey sugar, buy a lady a drink?" A crane of a woman with what appeared to be a Dolly Parton wig piled upon her head had moved in on the stool beside him, placing her hand on his knee and repositioning the shoestring strap of her red top onto her shoulder with the other.

Leas decided to play along. "What would you like?" The woman was nothing he would have chased after before Maria. But, now… Knob Creek told him he needed to get laid, and it didn't matter how or with whom. Anything to make him forget. The script played out for thirty or so minutes before he escorted 'Bridget' back toward his room.

They diverted their path slightly to hit a small liquor store in the direction of the hotel. Looking over at the woman as the Indian clerk behind the counter rung up the fresh bottle of Knob, he thought, *She doesn't look like a Bridget—maybe a Betsy or Mercedes, but not a Bridget.* The saggy skin under her arms suggested she had lost weight by trading one oral fixation for another, further evidenced by the two Virginia Slims she puffed down between the bar and the door to his room.

He was grateful for the dense mallard-green velveteen curtains at the windows, permitting him to imagine something much better than what Bridget was. *All things are beautiful in the dark.* The only indicator of her true lacking was when her raspy smoker's voice tried to add drama to the event, moaning an "oh baby" that sounded more like a demon crowing from a small child's mouth than any seductive measure.

The deed was done in less than ten minutes. He placed a fifty on the night stand after flicking on the bedside lamp, giving her the clue it was time to go. She was smart enough to gather her things and take the money as he walked towards the bathroom, leaving without question.

Alone, he sat naked at the edge of the bed. Leas wondered how he had come to this place of murder, cheap sex, and booze. The thought of Maria seeing what he had just done made him sick in that moment. He swung back two more chugs until the whiskey took the pain away with its dry sting. A shower and half a bottle later, he was passed out for the night, wishing it was him who had died.

# CHAPTER 6

*DALLAS*

H IS PORES STILL emptying themselves of the whiskey onslaught from his Friday night, Leas passed through airport security at DFW trying to remember how he had come to hunt those who killed. As a member of CIRG, the FBI's Critical Incident Response Group, he had been told that his time in Tulsa was done. The reprimand would come, but he was still one of the best they had. So, they were sending him out to investigate a death that matched one recently in the Tudor City neighborhood of Manhattan. He had talked with New York's Detective Lefler on his way to the airport and been filled in on the investigation in that case and another potentially related killing outside San Diego a month and a half earlier. There was a loose pattern and that was never good. Boarded, the plane's seatbelt made a point of reminding him of his few extra pounds from too much whiskey and too many fries on the road, digging against his government-issued black blazer.

A blonde, middle-aged flight attendant with too much drugstore makeup came to his cramped coach seat and asked if he needed a drink. Thinking it was best for now to hold off, he ordered water. As she walked away she gave him a big smile framed in deep red lipstick over her shoulder. Except for the deep black circles under his eyes, his black hair and creamed-coffee skin would have disguised his forty-three years. "Being Hispanic has its advantages," he would say when someone feigned shock at his age. "...Of course, there are disadvantages, too." The prejudice of color still lingered like a cat hanging by its claws on a window ledge. Yet, he had benefited from the gravity of time taking its effect on the issue, slowly pulling down some barriers.

Leas had joined the FBI to satisfy his need to understand killers. In high school he'd read Kraft-Ebing's 1886 study of homicide, *Psychopathia Sexualis,* which introduced him to the study of serial killers. In his opinion, other than the occasional movie at the castled El Raton Theater, growing up in rural Raton, New Mexico, he had few options but to read. Today, his reading choices would be flagged by the school as a potential threat to other students and the school. But in the mid-80s, he was just called 'dark.' He had to agree that 'dark' was a good description for that pimple-faced boy in New Mexico. His teenage bookshelves were loaded with fiction and non-fiction, all on one subject, serial murders. He couldn't say when he acquired his taste for the crime, but it had stuck early and he had never let it go.

The 'punk' movement overshadowed his obsession back then, with bands like Flux of Pink Indians and X singing of riots and standing up to organized government. The Reagan years were great for those voicing anarchy, violence, or just hatred of any issue. The government was too busy with the USSR to consider threats in schools.

Today, it was a very different situation. With 9/11, a new focus was placed on domestic sources of violence. This was only compounded by the recent events at the Aurora Theater in Denver and Sandy Hook Elementary in Connecticut, which put a clear focus on threats in our own backyard. His lifelong fascination would rightfully raise flags in school today and land him in counseling, at a minimum, if for no other reason than to ward off liability for the school should he act on his interests.

But he didn't act. He never wanted to murder, but he did want a front seat to the psyches of those who did. And he hadn't been involved on either of those recent events. Mass killings, where four or more people are killed at once, weren't his specialty. At forty-eight, Leas wasn't 'the expert' on serial murders, but he was pretty close. It was still unclear whether there was a new serial killer on the loose. Technically, a serial murder is defined as a series of three or more killings, not less than one of which was committed within the United States, having common characteristics such as to suggest the reasonable possibility that the crimes were committed by the same actor or actors. In layman's terms, someone who killed three people in separate and distinct events.

Looking down at the stack of manila files on his lap, he wondered if he was dealing with another serial killer. From the outside, there wasn't anything special about the murder he was now flying to Dallas to review; well, at least for someone who investigates such things. What was unique was that he was being assisted back in Quantico by Units 2 and 3 of NCAVC, the National Center for the Analysis of Violent Crimes. *What interest would Unit 3, Crimes Against Children, have in a thirty-four year-old dead guy in Dallas?*

With Mr. Patrick, he now had three bodies. *Were these murders linked?* He still didn't know. What he did know was that if they were linked, the murders were occurring at a much faster rate; the killer had become impatient. And, impatient knives produced more bodies.

# CHAPTER 7

ARRIVING AT TONY Patrick's Angelina Drive home just west of Dallas's downtown area, Agent Leas immediately noted the lack of any evidence of forced entry. *He knew his killer.*

"Captain Monroe, the FBI's representative is here. What did you say your name is again?" A young local detective, no more than maybe twenty-six, with a large camera around his neck, ushered Leas through the doorway of the home and into its living room, where several other detectives stood discussing indecipherable matters.

Leas had learned from one of the files that the body had been found at six a.m. Friday when a co-worker had arrived to give Patrick a ride to work. When there was no response from honking the horn, he knocked on the door and it opened, revealing the bloody body of Patrick lying in the middle of the living room. The officers had been on the scene a full day by the time Leas got into Dallas. It was now six p.m. Central Time and the officers were worn and tired like an old rag.

"Agent Leas, Quantico. Nice to meet you, Captain Monroe." Leas extended his hand to the black officer and they shook as the captain took stock of the man before him. Leas similarly took in his host, noting Captain

Monroe had some obvious years on him. *Sixty-eight?* His classic double-pocketed, deep blue short-sleeve shirt and matching pants were accented by the large egg-shaped badge with a star at its center that was brandished across his left chest. On either side of his collar were pinned four gold stars, to signify his experience and importance. From the busied movements about him, it was apparent the captain had full control of the scene, and Leas had no interest in stepping on his toes.

"Agent, can you tell me why you're here and what you have to do with my guy?" The look on the captain's face conveyed the clear message that he was not happy to have to tolerate the FBI's involvement in his case. Another agent came up behind him, and the captain occupied himself with signing a form while Leas answered.

"Captain, your guy caused a few red flags to pop up in our system. Seems some of the injuries match another recent crime in New York City, and perhaps one in San Diego. So, of course, I'm here to see if there's any relationship between them, and if so, I have a lot of restless nights ahead of me." Leas looked down at the small plastic numbered tents scattered around the room.

"Indeed." The captain's face soured but his interest was clearly peaked. "Do tell. Agent Leas, you say? What about my guy has the FBI spending my tax dollars to fly in a high-class shrink to tell me how to do my job?" The younger agent walked off, satisfied with the signature he had collected.

Leas looked around the room. "Captain, I'm not a shrink, just an investigator like you. And I'm not here to frustrate your investigation, and certainly not here to tell you how to do your job. In fact, you are very much respected back at Quantico. Your work on the Charles

Albright case was impressive, to say the least." Leas was referencing the Dallas Ripper, also known as the Eyeball Killer, who killed three prostitutes between December 1990 and March 1991. His signature was shooting the victims and removing their eyes. But for the hair found by Captain Monroe's team on the last victim, Albright would have walked because the jury did not convict him of the first two.

The captain huffed, "Agent, don't blow smoke up my ass. Dallas is still in the South and we are very much astute at recognizing a snow job. You still haven't answered my question. Why. Are. You. Here?" The captain was clearly losing patience in playing host.

Turning his direct attention to the captain, Leas continued. "Of course, Captain. It seems some of the elements of your scene caused a match in ViCAP." ViCAP, the Violent Criminal Apprehension Program, was the database where all violent crimes in the country were cataloged and collected so that they could be analyzed for potential patterns. "In this case, the cut patterns seemed close enough to another crime to cause 'taxpayer dollars' to be spent to ship me to Dallas."

"Yeah, like what?" The captain's Deep South Texas accent oozed out.

"Well, to be certain, I'll have to take a look at the body back at the coroner's to confirm; but your officers documented a square cut on the victim's lower back that may match that New York case I mentioned."

The captain looked at Leas and said, "When was that death?" Leas had the captain's attention now. He needed to provide enough information to keep it, and his cooperation, but not enough to risk a leak by any of the captain's crew. It was too early to put whoever this was on notice that the FBI might be on their trail.

Leas continued, "It was a week ago, Wednesday. The body was found a day later…after a photo surfaced on the internet. Facebook. Evidence of a struggle, no forced entry, but a square patch was removed from the body."

The captain lifted one brow and looked up slightly as if peering over a pair of glasses. "Are you saying someone is hopping planes and killing people? TSA stops a granny for carrying a butter knife on a plane, but can't stop a cut-happy doctor from jumping on and slashing all over the country? A waste of my taxes, again." The captain looked away with that last statement; he clearly didn't like the fact that he paid taxes.

"You said doctor… Where did you get that?" Leas was surprised; there were suggestions of surgical precision in the Havex case in New York.

The captain twisted at the hips to look over at the door where the young officer who had met Leas upon arriving now stood. "Hendrix, get over here." With his large, worn hands he waved the man over. The skinny, bony-framed man of maybe five and a half feet scurried over, grasping his camera in one hand. "Yes, Captain?"

"Show the FBI guy those fancy pictures you get paid to take." Hendrix moved between the two towering men and flicked on the black Nikon d600 that hung around his neck. The screen glowed in the dimly lit room. Elbowing the short detective in the shoulder, the captain barked, "No, no. Go to the injuries to the back." Hendrix flicked through as the captain had ordered and then twisted the screen towards Leas.

ON THE SCREEN was a photo of someone's bloody back. The body was face down on brown carpet, its arms spread to either side. A small swath of skin on the right hip had been removed, forming a perfect square. Lifting his head, Leas looked around the room and noted the same carpet in the living room where they were standing. "See there, Mr. FBI Agent, that cut is too precise to be some fool's deer knife, or even a steak knife. Look at those edges. You mentioned the Charles Albright case. I learned in that case that when someone uses a very sharp, surgical-grade blade, like that crazy did on those poor woman's eyes, the edge of the cut is smooth and crisp. When I look at the cut on this guy's back, I see Albright all over again. Whoever cut Mr. Patrick here used a scalpel. I'll bet on it."

Looking back down at the camera's screen, Leas nodded his head in agreement. The captain was as good as his reputation back at Quantico suggested. Indeed, from the picture at least, it looked like someone had used a scalpel to remove the skin patch. Of course, that did not mean a doctor was the killer. But it certainly narrowed the field.

Leas said, "You got any pictures of the front of the body?" Hendrix leaned the camera closer to Leas after first locating the frontal shots. Mr. Patrick was on what appeared to be clear poly plastic from the police crew's processing team. His hands had been cut off with a much rougher blade, an act that would have taken considerable time and patience. The contusions around the edges of severed wrists suggested he was still alive when the sawing commenced. The hands were missing from the picture of the body. A close-up of the face showed several deep cuts, suggesting a knife fight. Several shots later the hands were displayed, resting on some table, palms down, as if they were waiting for dinner to be served.

Leas took a deep swallow and looked over to the captain. "Yeah, that looks like the work of a scalpel on the cut, but not on the hands. But I'll wait to confirm when I see the body. Have you estimated time of death?"

BUSY AGAIN WITH another officer, the captain spoke without eye contact, "My people say sometime last night. From the looks of things, he knew the lady."

"Lady?" Leas was twisting his head around to gain access to the captain's eyes.

Feeling the gaze, he looked back to Leas. "Yeah, some kids down the street say a white Toyota pulled in right after this guy sometime around nine last night and a woman got out. Couldn't really describe her other than to say she was tall and slender. White or Hispanic, with long hair. Other than that it was dark, and them being under a streetlight made it difficult to see two blocks over."

Leas knew what he was talking about. The phenomenon of light pollution turns people into silhouettes when the viewer is in an area lit more brightly than the area being looked into. The eyes get overloaded and can't adjust to see the details in the dark area. Leas had been taught the principle using the example of trying to see stars in the city versus the country. Lots of stars versus little to none. They're there; the viewer just can't see them because of all the other light. All the kids could likely see was the person's outline.

The captain was good, bowling strikes left and right. First the scalpel, now a woman. Detective Lefler had seen the same signs of a female being involved in the Havex case. The captain continued, "He must be six-four, two-hundred pounds at least. We suspect from the puncture in this guy's neck that she drugged him or something to be able to deal with him."

"Tranquilizers? Poison?" Leas pinched his eyes, causing a furrowing of his brow as he processed this information.

"No clue yet, that's in the coroner's hands. I'm just here to coordinate and investigate once we figure that out."

Leas looked back down at the white outline on the floor as he pondered this information. The use of poison was usually a dead giveaway of a woman's involvement. Men tended to be violent in their killing, using brute force and weapons to take down their victims. Woman almost always used poison. Here they had a hybrid, poison with violent force to finish them off.

There were tons of theories for the disparity of methods between the sexes, but Leas had come to find that with the rare occurrence of a female serial killer, she needed an advantage over the muscle and bulk a man usually possessed. Women also tended to murder for money, not passion or control like men. The rare exceptions included Aileen Wuornos, made famous by Charlize Theron's portrayal in the 2003 movie "Monster," and the couple, Gwendolyn Graham and Cathy Wood, who killed for sexual pleasure. All three came out of Florida. But Leas wasn't in Florida, and statistics suggested it was highly unlikely he was dealing with a female passion killer.

# CHAPTER 8

"AND THEN WE HAVE THIS..." Officer Hendrix motioned Leas over to an old Gateway tube-monitored computer sitting on a yellow table being used as a desk. Its screen was dark.

Walking over, the captain interjected, "Yeah, we don't know what to make of this yet. It appears the vic was on the computer at the time of the murder. But we aren't quite sure. The evidence is conflicting at this point. The hands were found on either side of this, placed there after their removal. Like the killer was trying to send a message."

Leas looked down and saw the evidence markers placed in dried puddles of blood to the left and right of a worn keyboard and then looked at the computer. "What do you have?"

Hendrix pushed his small frame between the two men to stand facing the screen. It was obvious to Leas that Hendrix was used to having to push his way around the world to compensate for his height. With his slightly squeaky voice, Hendrix said, "Well, we know someone typed on the keyboard at the time the first blow was struck or during a struggle thereafter. Look at the keyboard—there's a small amount of blood on the back side of the "z" key. We are all but certain the ultimate stabbing took place over near the door, some eight feet away. So it's highly unlikely it's splatter from that. So, either the first cut occurred over here, or the perp used the computer *after* the vic was down. We think Mr. Patrick lingered for a good thirty to forty minutes before ultimately dying of his injuries, bleeding out and all."

Leas pulled his black half-frame glasses out from the inside pocket of his loose blazer and then slipped on a pair of latex gloves offered by Hendrix.

At forty-three, his sight had long since started to diminish from all those years with his head buried in murder books. The keyboard was dirty from being used by greasy fingers. Years of dirt and oil left a paste of black smudged on the tops of the most frequently used keys. The standard QWERTY design used in America and most of the English-speaking world placed the "z" key on the lower left row of the keyboard. Leas examined it closely. The area was dim even with the ceiling fan light in the center of the room on, its loose ticking echoing throughout the room. On the side of the table there was a cheap black desk lamp and a pile of what appeared to be bills. They were free of blood splatter. Leas grabbed the lamp, clicked the button on the base and it came on with its yellow light. He lifted the lamp and turned it toward the keyboard.

The captain and Hendrix watched in silence as Leas completed his inspection, clicking off the light, returning it to its spot and standing back up to face the two men.

Impatient for his insight, Hendrix pushed, "Well? What do you think? Perp or vic?"

Leas was careful to speak. This wasn't his turf and he didn't want to intrude. Bloodstain pattern analysis, known as "BPA," used physics, biology, and other fields to determine what blood spatter shapes and sizes can tell about the violent event that caused their release. Leas had seen enough of the reports to understand that experts in the field can determine from the shape of a splatter mark everything from velocity, angle of impact, and source. If you have enough of these blood markers the experts can determine the "Area of Origin," a fancy term for where the murder occurred in a space and possibly how it went down. Undisturbed splatter has relatively clean outlines on hard surfaces like the keyboard. When it doesn't it means someone has disturbed it after being deposited. "Have you had a blood splatter analyst look at this yet?"

The captain responded, "Not yet. He got called out on another investigation around lunch and is due to hit here first thing in the morning."

"I'm no expert but, and Captain I'm sure you'll back me up on this, you learn some things when you've been at this game long enough." The captain nodded his head in agreement with what Leas had just said as he took a glance behind him where there was a loud distracting conversation between officers occurring.

Leas continued, "From what I see, that isn't blood splatter. Rather, it looks like a smear, as though the blood was on the user's hands and accidently wiped off onto the key while typing." Leas motioned the captain over to the keyboard and pointed. "See those edges? Splatter would not present that way; they're too rough. Also, notice the top edge, there's a 'tail' on the left-most top. Someone tried to wipe off the blood. They probably didn't see that they missed a spot because this bit was on the back side of the key. If you don't mind?"

Leas walked across the room to grab a photo evidence

marker and placed it on the keyboard. Hendrix instinctively took several shots from different angles and then stepped back for Leas to finish. Withdrawing a white pen with some random hotel name stamped on it, he removed its plastic cap and placed its clip under the "z" key. A flick of the wrist and the key face popped off the keyboard. Leas carefully grabbed it as he clicked back on the lamp used earlier. Inspecting it for a moment under the light, he raised to face the two men waiting for him to speak.

"I'd say that the perp used the computer after stabbing Mr. Perkins, over there. So, the question is, what was the perp looking for? What did she want us to see?" Leas looked pensively at the computer's black screen.

The screen had been dark since he arrived. Hendrix nudged in again, grabbing the mouse with his gloved hand and moving it around its worn pad. The computer popped and crackled as it awoke. Slowly the tube warmed up and revealed its yellowing screen.

In the center was an internet browser open to Facebook. It was on a man's profile page, not the vic's newsfeed. The profile was for 'Cole Mouzon.' From the looks of the page, the vic and Mouzon weren't Facebook friends. The profile was locked, only showing his picture and name. *Who is this Mouzon guy and how is he related?*

# CHAPTER 9

SURROUNDED BY SEVERAL other lookers-on to the crime scene across the street, Poinsett thought the computer was a nice touch. And cutting off Tony's hands was deserved, after he touched her. *No one touches me.* She already knew Mouzon lived in Denver and that was her next stop.

Focusing back on the crowd of officers across the street, the presence of the man in a black blazer suggested the FBI had finally gotten involved. She didn't care if they tried to stop her. They wouldn't, couldn't stop Mouzon from dying next. She needed the police and FBI to spread the word, to announce the deaths, if she was to ever get the Taker's attention. He had lain quiet for almost thirty years and she needed him to reveal himself if she was to ever get answers. If that meant killing his prizes, she would kill all of them. Mouzon was the last, her last chance to draw him out. She salivated at the thought of her next kill. It was like dousing herself in scalding hot water, causing her skin to burn. She loved it.

She walked by the taped-off roadside like an innocent on-looker, to an area outside Tony's house. It looked like an even bigger dump to her in the daylight. He was so excited to get her into his home that he never thought about whether he deserved it. She suspected he knew in the end that he deserved to die like the rest of them. Mouzon would soon have that reality, too.

She would return to her life in due time, but for now, she couldn't avoid the deep need to kill them all, each and every one of them. What she would do when they were all dead, she didn't know. That was to be figured out once retribution for the pain they had caused her as a young girl was delivered. She dreaded the idea of stepping back into her old life.

*Why did it take me so long to come to this wonderful place where I am in control, not them?*

She asked herself that every time she saw the fear in their beady little eyes and felt the last pump of their heart through her blade.

*I have sacrificed too many years of my life being captive, submissive to what they had caused. But no longer.* It was their turn to feel what pain truly was, to fear their last breath escaping from their mouths.

She watched as the boys under the streetlight from the night before walked over to the officers. *I've been careful, right?* She'd covered her face that night, only allowing them to see her silhouette. She wanted them all to know it was a woman, not a man, who had taken down Tony. They looked around as Poinsett hid behind another spectator, acting as though she was talking to a nondescript woman in a red tee, jeans, and baseball cap. Poinsett had 'dressed down,' now wearing khaki capris and a yellow V-neck fitted tee, the sundress burned in a dumpster behind a warehouse. The blonde wig was still affixed to her head, just in case, and large Jackie-O sunglasses covered her gaze. She didn't look like anyone surrounding her, but she didn't care.

A few minutes later the boys were gone, apparently unhelpful in the officer's investigation.

The FBI agent working the scene was Latino, and looked like he should be operating a bar in some Western town rather than managing the federal government's response to what Poinsett had just done. *Is he going to figure out my next step?* She had all but written it out for him and the others. The large bags under his eyes told her he lived his work.

As she jumped in her rental and headed to the airport, she wondered. *Perhaps things are about to get more interesting.*

# CHAPTER 10

LEAS HEADED STRAIGHT from the crime scene to the medical examiner's office, located at Dallas's Institute of Forensic Sciences off North Stemmons Freeway. Dr. Grant had already performed an autopsy and sent fluid samples to the office's toxicology lab by the time Leas arrived. Waiting on the results, Leas inspected the body with the doctor.

As suspected, the bruising along the wrists was consistent with the removal occurring while Mr. Patrick was still alive. *Why didn't he fight?*

The doctor picked up on Leas' suspicion. "I suspect some type of drug, possibly a very strong muscle relaxant or sedative. I can think of no other way in which the killer could have held down this man and removed the hands while he was alive." The pudgy man had a strong widow's peak across his white hairline and rubbed the back side of his wrist across his forehead as he talked. Though the air could be heard rushing into the room, it was still steamy-hot. The white lab coat was clinging to the doctor and worked to enhance the man's poor girth-to-height ratio, making him resemble an awkward ghost. A slight limp could be detected as he waddled around the sparse brushed-steel and white-tiled room.

Overlooking the body, Leas asked, "Doctor, have you seen any signs of bondage or injuries beyond the obvious?"

The doctor waved him over toward Tony's head before responding. "Come here. See that? That's a needle prick. He was injected with something. This was not voluntary drug use here. Someone took this man down and I suspect with something that worked fast. We are talking about a six-four, two hundred and twelve-pound man here."

Leas eyed the slight purple pin-point mark to the back of Tony's right ear. He didn't recall any injection site in the Havex or San Diego cases.

Leas wondered if the cases were linked at all or was this just a very similar case by accident. "When is that toxicity report due back, did you say?"

Pulling the crisp white sheet back over Tony's body, the doctor said, "Anytime now. Let me go check."

Leas felt the twitch of whiskey hunger deep inside. It had been almost a day since his lips had tasted its amber sting and he felt the sudden need for a drink. *Shit, let's get this on, doctor.*

Trying to distract his hunger, he focused on the sheet-covered corpse that lay in the middle of the room, wondering who the killer could be. *Three bodies. Three types of killings. The last two missing a swath of skin from their lower backs placed there as children when they were all kidnapped. They are linked, but not in death at this point.*

Halfway through his analysis, the doctor slowly wobbled back into the room, looking down at several sheets of paper that looked more like computer printouts then any report. As suspected, Mr. Patrick had been poisoned. Something called *curare*.

Leas immediately reached in his pocket and called Quantico; he needed insight into poisons and fast. If the killer had switched to poison for taking down men, there was a chance she would do it again. Half an hour later he had a contact. Leas left the ME's office in haste, leaving more questions than answers for the Dallas Police. He would send another agent to complete the FBI's investigation into the Patrick matter. For now, he needed to get to Atlanta and talk to his new contact, a Dr. Winters, about the poison they found, before Mouzon died.

# CHAPTER 11

*ATLANTA*

L EAS HAD SOME experience with poisons. He had
learned some time ago that poisons are handled by
several different federal agencies. The Department of
Agriculture studies them with an emphasis on livestock
deaths, the Food and Drug Agency is charged with of
warding off exposure pathways arising from food and
pharmaceuticals. The Center for Disease Control and
Prevention in Atlanta covers the rest, usually acting as a
central hub for poisonings nationally and internationally.

Dr. Beth Winters held an impressive curriculum vitae;
a fancy name for a resume in any other field. At thirty-
five, she was the youngest person, much less woman, to
ever head the National Center for Environmental Health/
Agency for Toxic Substances and Disease Registry within
the CDC. Her expertise, poisons, required her to be an
expert in botany and toxicology. Working in conjunction
with the FDA and its detailed poisonous plant database,
she had become a 'go-to' expert where plant poisons were
involved. Leas had been instructed to head to Atlanta and
meet with Winters about what the agency was seeing in
the murders.

He had flown into the busiest airport in the world on Sunday night and checked into his room at the Residence Inn on Peachtree Street carrying nothing more than his carry-on, originally packed just for Tulsa, and a fresh bottle of Knob he'd grabbed from Mac's liquor store in the heart of Midtown, Atlanta. With the luggage thrown to the corner of the room, the bottle was promptly opened and tipped back as he loosened his tie. He passed out half-dressed, saved from the darkness of the memories that had returned in his sober state.

First thing Monday morning he jumped into another rental and weaved through the winding roads of the affluent neighborhood of Ansley Park, headed to the CDC on the north end of Emory University's campus in the North Decatur area of Atlanta.

"Did you know, Agent Leas, that adults aged twenty-four to fifty-six are more likely to die of poisoning than in motor vehicle accidents?" Leas was still slightly in shock from Dr. Winter's youth and beauty as he was escorted into her office. She immediately grabbed a stack of files and opened a grey metal filing cabinet, and began thumbing her way through the drawer until she'd placed each manila folder. This placed her backside front and center into his view. By his calculations, she was five-eight; five-ten with her powder blue heels that perfectly matched her eyes. Her dark hair was collected in a ponytail and stood out against her white lab coat. As she busily moved around the room while still talking, the coat flashed open here and there to reveal what appeared to be a billowed black linen shirt and deeply-cut white blouse intended more for a cocktail party than a lab. This impression was only enhanced by the large string of pearls she wore around her neck.

Trying to refocus, Leas spoke. "Really? That's a statistic you don't hear a lot about. How many of those are intentional?" Leas observed several cultural masks and paintings on the walls of the otherwise white drywall of the office. From the corner of his eye, he thought he caught a picture behind her desk of the doctor with Obama.

Still moving about the room, she responded. "Well, that's hard to say. Ninety-one percent of all poisonings are caused by prescription drugs. As it relates to murder, which is why you are here, the statistic has been for centuries that woman are more likely than men to use poisons to kill, which explains to some degree the fact that men are twice as likely as woman to die from them, though they also have a higher exposure potential to poisons because of their workplace conditions. A recent study by Shepherd at the University of Georgia actually reviewed mortality rates for homicidal poisoning. His findings were very interesting, showing that though poisonings accounted for less than one percent of all homicides, there is a clear up-tick in such deaths over the past decade or so. And, this really doesn't help you, but homicide by poisoning is usually reserved for children and the elderly, not the age bracket you indicated you are dealing with in your case when you called."

Leas didn't know what was sexier, her body or her mind. She clearly was more intelligent then he would have imagined if he saw her on some Atlanta street. She continued babbling facts like an encyclopedia-fed brook. "Now, from what I understand from your guys at the FBI, there is a strong suspicion that poison is involved more often than documented in murder cases generally. There is a great deal of support for that suspicion. Coroners and their labs rarely consider homicide by poisoning unless the bottle is sitting right in front of them. Even where a poison is identified in the deceased's system, there is an eighty percent chance the manner of death will be deemed 'undetermined' because poisons and their pathways are so misunderstood. Seventy-six point six percent of poison exposures are through ingestion. Other pathways include breathing in poison gas, bites and stings, and exposure to the eyes or on the skin."

She paused for a second to catch her breath and look up from the fresh batch of files she had been shuffling around the office since Leas arrived. Smiling, she said, "I'm sorry, I can rattle on forever about this stuff. If this were a date, you would already be out the door. But tell me, Agent, why are you here again?"

Leas grinned and then described to the doctor the three murders he was investigating and the belief that more were to come. If the murders were related, the first appeared to be a test of sorts, and with each new murder the perpetrator was refining his skills and trademark. The last had signs of poisoning. The last two had the same mark of removal of a small patch of skin on the victim's lower back. That patch contained a mark, a brand left there when all three of the victims were young. It appeared someone was collecting those who had been kidnapped all those years ago, and she was moving fast.

With Winters now seated behind her desk listening intently, Leas walked further into the office. "Doctor, in this case, it appears that the most recent victim was poisoned, injected with *curare*. Is there any significance there?"

She turned her head to the side like a parrot as she pondered what had just been disclosed. "Interesting. A plant poison...highly lethal. *Curare* is nasty stuff. Because it mimics total lock-in syndrome, where paralysis impacts every part of the body, including the eyes, it's impossible for someone poisoned to signal they are actually alive. It's the 'trapped in your body' drug."

Leas shook his head in horror as Winters turned to a particle board, thrift store-looking bookshelf, withdrew a teal covered book and handed it to the agent. "You may want to take a look at Fronhne and Pfander's book just to see what you are dealing with."

His mind was still on the visual of someone being tortured while trapped in their body when he looked down to read the back of what had been handed to him and then turned it to reveal its cover: "Poisonous Plants: A Handbook for Pharmacists, Doctors, Toxicologist, Biologists, and Veterinarians." Just the thought of reading a book made him sick, much less some scientific manual.

Nestling back into her black cloth office chair, she told him, "It's pretty straightforward book on plant-derived poisons, and can at least tell you what symptoms and etiology you can expect. I would give you my own book, but I've been told its sedative effects rival that of Ambien. It's a bit technical." The doctor flashed a smile to reveal teeth as white as her pearls, breaking her otherwise focused appearance.

Leas smiled back in kind, looking up from the book to respond. "No, no... 'Poisons for Dummies' will do for now. But I might have to hit you up on that book if my insomnia keeps up."

She playfully tightened her eyes and said, "Fair enough. But, as I was saying, the use of raw plant poisons is extremely rare today. I say raw because a large percentage of our pharmaceuticals are derived from plant chemicals. In fact, some chemicals like digitalin—which comes from the flower *digitalis*, also known as foxglove—are high highly poisonous in even small doses. But when used in minute amounts the chemical helps with cardiac conditions such as atrial fibrillation and congestive heart failure. And that's just one example."

Leas shook his head as he leaned into the wall beside him. "Wow, when I was told you were the person to talk to down here, they weren't lying. And, again, thank you. My understanding is you just came back from some trip to collect samples or something. The Amazon?" His eyes caught what looked like a hand-held GPS under some files.

Noticing his glance at her desk, Winters leaned back into her chair and crossed her legs, revealing firm, tanned legs. "Ha, yeah. I may appear like a simple *Southern belle*, Mr. Leas, but inside, I'm a warrior and certified witch doctor." She flashed a playful 'don't mess with me' face when she emphasized the words 'Southern belle.'

"I was down in the Balsapuerto area of the Upper Amasonas region, deep in the headwaters of the Amazon, studying the use of plant-derived poisons used by the indigenous people. My research was focused on *strychnos*, a plant whose resin is used in dart hunting by the local tribes. Think poison dart frog, but this one is plant-derived." Winters looked to her desk and the still remaining files.

"It's a shame really. I had another month of research planned down there, but in the middle of the night about a week ago, there was a raid by a Protestant fundamentalist group who've been killing the shamans, local witch doctors, for years in the area, accusing them of being 'possessed by demons.' My shaman survived, but he lost his wife and a son to axes by the time it was all over. His son's head was ravaged, just *ravaged*, by the blades." Winters grabbed her wrist. "I was pretty lucky; I had a metal bracelet given to me by a woman in the tribe on at the time that prevented a machete from completely slicing right through my arm." She pulled back the white tape and gauze to show a clean cut with several black stitches. "It took two days to get me up the river to Yurimaguas for medical care."

Leas stood in awe, eyebrows raised. "Wow. Warrior indeed, Dr. Winters. I'd say that would go head to head with any story I could offer in my career."


SHE LOOKED UP. "I doubt that, Agent." There was a slight pause before she continued.

"You know, it's interesting that you mention *curare*. Like *strychnos*, it's used in hunting. It paralyzes the body, while the prey remains conscious until suffocation kicks in. The thought of dying that way; well, that's just rough to swallow."

Leas agreed. "Yeah, as you mentioned, the patholo-gist couldn't rule out the poison as the cause, but with the cuts, it was hard to say."

Winters stood up from her desk and began slipping off her heels before maneuvering her feet into what looked like cheap white nurse's shoes. With her back still to him she said, "Let me do this, Agent Leas... I need to step into the lab and complete some tests and check on the progress of research I have neglected while in the Amazon. But, I'll think on this and what you've told me. If I come up with anything, I'll let you know. Here, let me give you my cell phone number. I'd be interested to see how this plays out. So, call me anytime, day or night. I'm at your service."

Leas couldn't resist focusing on the shortness of her charcoal skirt and how it formed a perfect outline of her obviously firm ass as the doctor bent over her desk to write the note on a yellow sticky. A bit too slow in refocusing, he was caught. The doctor smiled as she smoothed out the back of her lab coat.

"Be careful out there, Agent Leas. Poisons are dangerous business. I look forward to our next meeting." After a quick flash of her smile she exited the office and disappeared down the hall. Leas regained his focus and turned to leave. *Yep, Obama.*

# CHAPTER 12

AGENT LEAS MADE prompt use of the number Winters had handed him and by six-thirty he was on his way to meet her for drinks. He was surprised she had said yes, but he wasn't going to complain.

She arrived at Wisteria in the Inman Park area of Atlanta in the same dress as before, but this time it was uncovered and more completely spoke 'Southern lady.' Meeting her at the door after just arriving a minute before her, they immediately agreed to extend the night into dinner. The host walked them to a corner table of the dark-lit brick and natural palette colored space and took stock of the couple. It was apparent from his face that he did not understand the mismatch between the sophisticated lady and Leas, who had swapped out his standard black blazer and tan slacks for dark indigo jeans and baby blue button down, rolled at the sleeves.

"I have to say I was pleasantly surprised when you called, Agent. I thought you would just leave town without any further contact." Winters smiled wide as she turned to look at Leas, while slightly cutting her eyes. "I mean, it has been a while since I've had drinks, with the Amazon and all…"

"Well, I had the night here and it's never fun to eat

alone. And, company like yours is a rarity. Have you ever eaten with a group of cops? It isn't pretty. Plus, the table talk is less than appropriate on most occasions." Leas spoke a bit too loud, trying to compensate for the background noise of the completely packed restaurant.

Unrolling her cloth napkin and formally placing her silverware, Winters continued the conversation. "I would think so. Serial murders, huh? How did you get into that?"

Leas explained his fascination at an early age with the subject and his need to understand the criminal mind. Dr. Winters listened with deep interest in the conversation. It was obvious to Leas that she had never discussed the subject, though she admitted at one point in the conversation that she had some interest since a child. She'd read the thrillers of Patterson and her imagination always went wild with how someone got to that point of actually killing. "What makes them do it?"

Leas was enjoying the switch in roles; he now being the expert being questioned. "That remains the question—why? Serial killers usually come from rough backgrounds of abuse, neglect. But the sad fact is that a large percentage of our country is exposed to the same treatment without ever being triggered into the psychopathic mindset. There is a theory that if the 'triad' of symptoms is present: that is, setting fires, torturing animals, and wetting the bed, there is an extreme likelihood that the child will advance to killing others. Like myself, they are fascinated with the police and authority. They may have even worked, or attempted to work, in the security field."

He took a sip from the cold glass of sweet tea perspiring on the table before continuing. "Their psychopathic nature hinders them from feeling sympathy for others and they must learn to mimic 'normal' behavior. Driven by a need to perform, to control and succeed, they create traps for their victims. Once fallen into, the killer exerts authority over the victim, taking pleasure in making them submissive. But the pleasure wears off at that point, as he has already won. So he exerts more authority, by killing. I say 'he,' because women are rarely serial killers, but it does happen occasionally."

Leas could tell Winters was letting it all sink in before she spoke. "Wow, in my world you are usually dealing with knowns. If 'x' then 'y,' that type of thing. It really is interesting, not to say I would ever want to cross paths with a serial killer. But it is amazing. Don't killers usually have trademarks?"

Shaking his head, he responded. "Some do, yes. Others just kill. But, the majority take pride in their work, and going back to the pride and public recognition aspect, they want to make sure everyone knows they killed. So, they usually leave a mark or handle the body in a certain way."

Winters scooted in closer and slightly whispered. "And this one? What is the mark?"

"Ahh, I know you are a consultant and all, but since this is an active investigation, I better just leave it at there does seem to be a major link between all three."

"Oh my god, to die that way. Who deserves that?" There was a pause as the doctor contemplated what she had just heard, shaking her head in disbelief.

As the waiter placed a plate of fried chicken on a bed of cornbread and collard greens in from of him, Leas continued to explain his theory as it related to the poison and the possible motives. He knew the victims were linked from a common past, information not made public to date. So, he suspected that same past was now coming to hunt them. The reality was that his only lead was a Facebook page of some guy named Mouzon. It wouldn't be hard to find out where he lived, but whether he was alive when Leas arrived was another concern.

By midnight Winters had had her fill of the case and left Leas at the restaurant's door, wishing he didn't have to head back to D.C. But unless they located Mouzon, he had no other choice.

# CHAPTER 13

B Y TEN-TWENTY A.M. Friday Cole Mouzon had been deposing Ray Wier for over an hour, pressing him on the details of his alleged injuries when a semi-truck carrying oil was sideswiped and spilled petrol. Wier, his lawyer, and a court reporter were crowded in a small white-washed room in the lawyer's office, where the A/C had clearly been turned off in an effort to rattle Cole, who was defending Folsom Petro United, an oil transport company. Beads of sweat appeared and were quickly dropped, like torpedoes, off Cole's chin onto his red silk tie.

Taciturn by nature, Cole had developed the ability to channel the limited words he said into stealthy comments and interrogations. So far, he had caught Wier in multiple lies over his claimed injuries, and he was just getting started.

Cole shook his head in disagreement as he spoke. "No, sir. That is not what I asked. Now, answer my question."

Wier slyly grinned. "Colin…"

To Cole, a deponent using a lawyer's first name was a clear red flag that the guy was a crook. Whenever a deponent attempted this he was trying to gain power, to dominate the questioner. Cole had seen this too many times in his six-year career as a lawyer. It was a desperate act that signaled Cole was getting under this guy's skin and close to showing the guy for what he was—a fraud.

Wier looked sadly down at the wood table and wiped it with his hands as he spoke. "You see, my life has been devastated. I can't do my job. I'm behind in my child support...all because your client dumped a tanker of oil in my front yard." He was avoiding eye contact. "It's really quite horrible, Colin. I had a great life before this, but now...well, I've lost everything." Mr. Wier's gaze on Cole deepened with his last words.

Cole turned and reached into his red well file holder to withdraw a document. He didn't need to look at it. Its image had been saved, like every other document in the case, safely in his head. "Let me show you what's been marked Exhibit 13. Do you..."

Before Cole could get out his question, Wier interrupted. "What the... Those are my Facebook pictures. How did you get those?" Mr. Wier's face now matched his lawyer's, red and inflamed. He shot Cole a look full of hate.

Cole glanced over to the court reporter who was apparently enjoying the show as she typed. It was her turn to get in on the action. "Sir, I'm going to remind you again. I cannot take down two people talking at the same time. Please let Mr. Mouzon finish his question before you answer. Okay? ...OKAY?"

Wier gave a half-hearted, "Yes."

Cole continued, this time speaking slower. "Mr. Wier, is that your picture, a picture of you snowboarding just two months ago in Vail?" Cole gave a Cheshire cat smile. He had this guy and he knew it. Cole's intensely green eyes glowed with excitement from the heated exchange. Wier lurched across the table to attack, but his lawyer caught him with his right arm extended.

"Objection! Now, sit your ass down, boy. Just sit here and hush while I say something to Mr. Mouzon." That seemed to have awoken Wier's lawyer, Henry Babbick, a large, red-faced man with bulging pale blue eyes and bad skin. His butter-yellow dress shirt was unkempt, and the layer of dandruff on his shoulders could pass for snow, but for it being the middle of May. In his late 40s, the lawyer came across more as a first-year associate than the experienced partner his wrinkles suggested.

Cole pushed on, ignoring the objection. Wier's skin was turning 'oh shit' red, signaling that he knew his story of having the perfect life just before this accident, only to have it come crumbling down, was falling apart. "And you lost your job, not because of respiratory failure as you claim in this case, but because you got your butt kicked when you picked a fight with your boss on the job, then showed up with the cops and tried to press charges. All because you called him...a 'fuckwad?'"

Babbick tried to slow down the interrogation. "You're badgering my client. Asked and answered. Lack of foundation."

Cole smiled again as he turned to the lawyer. "I think the only objection you forgot was 'calls for speculation.' Would you like to add that one? Your client is here claiming $500,000 in damages because my client got in an accident and five gallons of oil, *five*, leaked into a ditch two hundred feet away from his front door."

Wier stood to lurch again. "You're an ass! That bastard had it coming to him. Just go fuck yourself, I'm done here." Defeat covered Wier like smoke settling in, choking his ability to play victim any longer.

Looking up to the still-standing man across the table, Cole responded. "Is that a yes?" In an effort to put the final nail in the casket, Cole pressed forward. He knew this case would settle for nuisance value in a month if not sooner, but he had to have the admission on the record.

"Yeah, that's a yes, and yeah, you can go fuck yourself. I'm done!"

Moments later, the red-faced lawyer trailed behind Cole as he walked out of the old office. Cole wasn't paying attention to the man's pleas and proffering of why Wier presented so poorly in his deposition. "Mr. Babbick, save it for a jury. You and I both know the claim is bad, your client is worse, and your reputation will be left stinking unless you convince him to get reasonable. I'll be sending over an offer of judgment tomorrow. I'm thinking three thousand dollars. It will cost me that just to draft a motion to dismiss this case. Decline it at your client's peril. My clients love it when you pay their fees." Cole opened the glass door and left.

# CHAPTER 14

B ACK AT HIS Sixteenth Street office, Cole walked into a half-empty space—everyone seemed to have had out-of-office work to do. *Perfect,* he thought, *I can get out early and be at the airport with enough time to grab a Fat Tire.* Between work and the bad dreams, he needed his vacation and the sooner it started the better.

Kathy, the office assistant, came walking into his office with her hands full of documents just as he was settling down in his chair. "How did it go?"

Cole threw his jacket over the back of one of his guest chairs and loosened his tie. "Ah, it went… Same story, different day. He gives injured parties a bad name. Draft an Offer of Judgment for three thousand dollars and let's get that out. That way if they decline it and the jury gives them that or less, he has to pay our costs."

"You got some mail. That crazy Mr. Kreepers filed something again. Looks like he's been reading Peanuts this week." Mr. Keppermoore, Mr. Kreepers to Kathy, was *pro se*, representing himself in a case outside Atlanta against one of Cole's clients. His claim was that the laying and spreading of woodchips had been toxic to his sensitive system and he demanded justice. "Respect my a-thor-a-tay," as Cartman from South Park would say, popped into Cole's head every time he thought of good 'ol Kreepers.

Kathy yelled from the front desk, "When's your flight to Charleston?"

Looking down at the stack of mail in his in-box as the image of his ticket flashed across his mind, he shouted back, "Oh, two-thirty. That should get me in by eight p.m. or so with the connection through Atlanta. It's Friday after lunch, so it shouldn't be too busy at the airport." It had been five months since he'd been home and Cole was excited to return to see his family, even if that meant subjecting himself to their form of cross-examination about all things Cole. He didn't know why, but the constant turmoil in his head was always better when he was home. He always brushed it off as just being around family.

Walking out of his office into the reception area with the piece of mail Kathy had just handed him, he laughed. "Ha! I love Kreepers! Look at that, he cut and pasted a mini version of the Magna Carta in this brief. I guess I better get licensed in the U.K. if we're going to start arguing English law." Kreepers' pleadings were always a mosaic of cut and paste. A Xerox copy of some criminal code pasted here, the judge's signature pasted there, with just the right touch of lawyer comic strips sprinkled throughout—all in support of his opinion that justice was being denied him. The court in Cobb County, Georgia had a handle on the situation, having dismissed all claims and found Kreepers in criminal contempt for his continued filing of frivolous pleadings against the court's order. Apparently he hadn't got the memo that his case was dead.

BRINGING HIS ATTENTION to a box full of emails, he saw little of importance. He double-clicked on the Google Earth icon on his computer's desktop and a large image of the world popped up and spun. It was obvious to Cole that someone at Google believed Kansas was the center of the world by the map's default center always landing on the state at start-up. He typed in 'Charleston, SC' into the search box and hit enter. The globe spun and zoomed in to his hometown, grey with development on his screen. As he moved the mouse around the map, numbers at the bottom of the screen changed to note the longitude and latitude of the marker. He zoomed in further to note the distance between his hotel and the Dock Street Theater, where he had tickets for Saturday night. The map was saved in his mind. *That's walkable.*

Closing out the program and turning, the capital building outside his window caught his eye. He took a second to enjoy a mental break. He had come to Denver almost a year and a half earlier after living in Atlanta for six years. He loved Atlanta, but it housed too many bitter memories. He accepted that a move would be best and Denver offered a 'life with a view.' That it was a state that provided the opportunity to get licensed to practice law without taking the dreaded bar again was an added bonus.

Looking out the window and thinking about his past pushed up against his inner wall. He took a deep breath and shifted his thoughts back to work. Cole shot off a few more emails and decided to get out while the getting was good. Grabbing his jacket, he said, "Okay, I'm out of here. I'll see you in a week and a half."

Kathy looked up from the pile of documents she was indexing and responded. "Have fun! I'm so jealous,

I've heard Charleston is just beautiful. I bet it's very romantic."

Cole grinned. "It is, though when you're from there it gets lost on you." Cole was only half serious. No, he didn't walk around the cobblestone streets of the Holy City, as Charleston was known, looking like some crazy tourist. But he did take pride in the city, its history, and all its eccentricities. And it had an ample supply of those. "Later 'gator, just email or call me if you need anything. I have my iPad and I'll be doing some work." The sad reality of being a lawyer—you're never completely off the clock.

# CHAPTER 15

COLE TORE OFF his suit in the building's first floor gym, crawled into his gym shorts, and hit the pavement outside for a short pre-flight run. Shirtless, he noticed his recent busy schedule was wreaking havoc on his six-pack. From his view, two beers were missing. Traveling down Lincoln Street, he picked up the pace in an attempt to reclaim those beers as he merged onto Speer Boulevard and the Cherry Creek bike path. This routine cleared his mind daily, and the cool wind off the creek that ran down the spine of the path provided needed relief from the heat wave that had descended on Denver. In his 'running zone,' Cole thought of his trip. It had been months since he had been back to his hometown, and the trip was a reunion of sorts for his friend Ann and himself to enjoy Spoleto.

Every year at the end of May the Holy City hosted an international arts festival which showed off the most exclusive, preeminent musical, visual, dance, and other art displays. For seventeen days, operas, art installations, jazz bands, and artistic dance descended on the peninsula, clogging its streets and buildings with crowds from around the world salivating at not only the art but the city stage it was being hosted in. As a child, his Granny would take him and the rest of the grandkids to one event, each separately. Each child got to pick his or her event and then go alone with Granny. She always called it 'our' time. Cole tended to pick big productions with singing and dancing over any music concert or art display.

Like the city itself, the event wasn't without secrets and controversy. It had come to Charleston in 1977 when Pulitzer Prize-winning composer Gian Carlo Menotti decided to start a counterpart to his Festival dei Due Mondi, or Festival of Two Worlds, in Spoleto, Italy. Menotti chose the city for its charm and the plethora of venues. His lack of understanding of Charlestonians and their innate sense of defiance immediately placed the event in financial and interpersonal turmoil.

Menotti was accustomed to exclusive control of the company's limitless expense account. Much like the city perceived the North's actions, Menotti's attempts to dictate and spend the city's money was met with a long, heavy thud, followed by revolt. By 1993, Menotti was run out of town, but not without attempting to take the festival with him. Seeing him as a carpetbagger, Charlestonians armed themselves with muskets loaded with lawyers and drove him off, never to return. The festival endured, and had grown ever since.

Thinking about his trip, Cole realized he missed his hometown deeply. Images of his family, Charleston and its marshes flickered in transparencies across his vision of the sidewalk he was jogging. His family was a mix of love and pain like most out there. But he always sought to focus on the love and craziness that made them his own brand of family.

*She said 'romantic.'* Kathy's words had unintentionally popped back into his head mid-step. The Peninsula, another nickname for Charleston, oozed romance that rivaled Paris or Venice. Add the tropical, palmetto-studded atmosphere and you had the makings of a Hemingway romance. Cole hadn't thought much of romance since Atlanta and he had no interest in starting now. He could feel the mental conversation once again crashing against the wall that kept him stable. *Stop thinking about it. You're damaged goods.* Visualizing his emotions as a dirty rag, he manipulated it in his mind, shoving and packing it into the crevice from which it came until the emotions were back behind the wall. He took a deep breath and focused on the last mile back toward his office.

Seven miles completed and showered, Cole arrived at DIA with ample time to check in and grab two Fat Tires. It had been a long week of depositions, and a couple of beers helped him transition into vacation mode. He ultimately plopped down into the cramped blue fabric seat of the United Airlines flight and set his iPod playlist to 'Trip.' He was in the habit of making playlists for every event worthy of music. Hitting play, Empire of the Sun blared, deemed by him as appropriate travel music since discovering them while road-tripping between Sydney and Cairns. He lay back and closed his eyes.

# CHAPTER 16

B LADES OF MARSH grass prickled the tips of his
fingers as he walked the line between mowed and
undisturbed marsh. Perhaps two or three years old, judging from his size, the darkness engulfed him as he stared
on along the artificial line that defined nature from man.
Thick, salty air filled his nostrils with the damp, organic
odor of the sea. A cinderblock building rested yards to
his right, with the marsh grass inches to the left. This
place was strangely calming to him in that moment. For
being alone, the place was noisy with life in the darkness.
Cicadas buzzed in the distant Spanish-moss draped live
oaks and top-heavy pines. He took in the busied noctur-
nal life around him.

His mind was too preoccupied by the nature to hear
the approaching steps from behind. As his hands brushed
the tops of reed and grass, a sudden need to run came
across his body, brewing in his shoulders before lightening down to his feet. *It was too late.* A hand had grabbed
his outreached arm and pulled him down, into the
marsh. He could feel his throat clench as he involuntarily
attempted to scream. No one came.

Pulling, pulling; there was no escape. His eyes turned
ahead to see what, who had grabbed him, but all that

could be seen was a hand, nothing more. The rest was a blur, like he had entered a dark underpass. It pulled him deeper into the marsh, leaving him looking back to see the brick facade of the school building drifting away. Reed and oyster cut, their sting emphasized by the salty marsh water. Pain and pressure conjoined in his shoulder as he was dragged deeper into the darkness. "Stop. Help, help!" His voice tensed and resisted being heard, as he was swallowed by the blackness and into the trees. "Momma!"

# CHAPTER 17

IT WAS EASY enough to break in. The home adjacent to Mouzon's hid the view of nosy neighbors. A slip of a knife under the window's edge and Poinsett was in the house. She had visited the spot the night before to watch as she had done with the others, but his dog barked, requiring her to cut off her observation prematurely. Standing outside again, she had returned to issue her warning, to commence the game with Mouzon, but by looks of the vacant dog bed and the Amazon package on the front porch, he was gone.

Slowly stepping across the pine floors, Poinsett looked for any sign as to where he could have gone. A quick inspection showed no signs of a phone or answering machine. Pictures of him were spread throughout the house, with scenes of the Iron Lung in Sydney, the Gherkin in London, and others with tropical beaches in the background. The thought of him enjoying life at her expense sickened her. *How dare he*. Her rage simmered deep inside her, threatening to boil over into chaos. She hated him. His permitted existence had caused the damnation of her own life. For thirty years he loomed, torturing her without her ever knowing. But now she did know, and the time had come to show him the damage he'd inflicted, to show him how his existence destroyed her childhood and life. Only by ridding the world of those taken and released by the Taker could she find peace.

Poinsett's heart raced as she ran a hand across an old walnut desk onto the keyboard of Mouzon's computer, causing it light up. Opening the Safari internet browser, she typed in Facebook.com. *Bingo*. The computer was still logged in. Several clicks away, a picture of her prey filled the screen along with his wall of posts. The latest entry was, "DEN => CHS."

# CHAPTER 18

COLE AWOKE DRENCHED in sweat again, his heart racing with panic, still seated on the plane. Faint tears lingered in his eyes. It took a few seconds to recall where he was and where he was going. "Fuck," Cole murmured under his breath while trying to regain his bearings and resituate in his cramped seat. His refusal to pay full ticket price for anything frustrated even him at these moments.

He had unfortunately brought two carry-ons, his bag and that stupid dream. *Too bad United didn't shove that shit into check-in.* He liked the idea of leaving it on the carousel and never claiming it. The dream was on a repetitive loop lately, replayed every night for the past three weeks with no off button to hit. If he fell asleep it was there.

It wasn't the first time. It had haunted his dreams as a child before being all but forgotten in recent years. Between the ages of three and ten it was a given whenever he slept. The routine was fixed. Fall asleep by nine p.m. Wake up in a panic by two a.m. Then get up and watch black-and-white reruns of *Lassie* and *Dennis the Menace* on Nickelodeon until it was time for a shower and school. That is, if he showered...

Then, like his mind had outgrown it, it stopped

without warning. His sleep went undisturbed for years, until three weeks ago when it reappeared in all its dark vividness. *Why? What was causing him to dream like this? And why now?*

Visits to home had never triggered this response. The dream always ended like a scratched DVD with darkness at the same point. Sometimes he would get out the last scream for help, sometimes not. He was always left with the consuming feeling that the darkness was death.

*What kind of fucked-up kid dreams like that?* The horrific possibilities of where the dream could go were endless in Cole's mind. Molestation, torture—or worst, being left alone to die a solitary death. None were thoughts or images Cole wished to dream and certainly didn't think his juvenile mind should have thought up. Yet, awake, he mutilated his thoughts with the imagery of those possibilities.

His limited time in the criminal defense arena had provided fodder for the old dream. The sad reality was that his worst thoughts were supported by the reality of just how cruel and evil humans could be toward each other. He had seen those possibilities played out as a public defender in Douglas County, Georgia. Too many child-molestation clients had burned him out in less than two years. It was a final case, child-on-child molestation, that sealed the deal and expedited Cole's planned exit.

IN A STRANGE way, he was grateful for the dream. It had unknowingly hardened him to those situations long before he was personally faced with the very acts he daydreamed about whenever he awoke from the dream's 'what happened next?' In that way, it was a gift of sorts, giving him strength and the ability to shield himself from the allegations, more often than not true, of horrible things done to children. His mind had partitioned itself from the harm of emotion, compartmentalizing the analytics of his daily life from emotional interference long before it was exposed to real horror. He wondered if somewhere deep down it knew he would need a shield, the 'wall' to survive in the future.

Prior relationships suggested that the benefits of keeping one's emotions under lock and key came with the serious disadvantage of coming off cold and calculating personally and professionally. *What was the word used? Not mean, but...simply disconnected, aloof.* He liked the word 'reserved' better. It just seemed more prestigious. He couldn't ever recall that word being used as a negative; rather, it was used to suggest intelligence, success—things he aspired toward. The mental image of him pompously raising his chin flashed before his eyes, making him quietly laugh at himself.

But three therapists had agreed with 'aloof,' advising him that contrary to what he had come to believe, one should not stare a crying lover in the face and ask for rational, objective justification about why something had happened. Intellectually, he understood rage, disappointment, and panic, but he felt they were wasteful emotions, unproductive in resolving whatever actual issue existed.


IT WASN'T THAT he didn't feel emotions; he did, otherwise he would be classified a sociopath—an idea that certainly had its attraction, *but all that blood...* No, his random bloody noses were enough for him.

It was the wastefulness of it all for him. The forty

minutes or an hour of crying could be avoided, and problem would be analyzed and resolved more practically and promptly. Permitting himself to feel freely, letting emotions wash over him like the waves of a sandy tide, subjected him to danger and harm. He couldn't afford that again, even if his team of therapists demanded 'homework' exercises in emotional freedom.

Dixie the dog was his current emotional muse. Her ability to just live without the torment of too many emotions was inspirational. He knew her ultimate death in old age would test the therapists' credentials, but in the short run the worst he could suffer was puppy eyes when she didn't get her peanut-butter filled Kong. *Baby steps*. If happiness was measured in empty Kongs, he was set.

Stop it, Cole. Stop. The wall was back, demanding to be raised. His mental exercises in emotion tormented it. You are starting a vacation, going home. You've needed this for a while. Salt air and home cooking is just what the doctor ordered to clear your head and return to Denver refreshed. Mind-fucking yourself was not what the doctor ordered. He said his safe words to push out the emotions. *Sweet tea, sweet tea, sweet tea…*


PLANES HAD LONG become a disappointment when airlines started shaving inches from not only the width, but the leg space between the seats. For Cole, trying to fit his six-foot, three-inch frame in economy meant knees pressed hard against the seat in front of him. Travel was utterly miserable if the person in the seat before him tried to lounge his seat. Somehow in this tortured configuration he had figured out how to grab a nap, and a nightmare, on the two-and-a-half hour flight to Atlanta for his connection to Charleston.

An hour later he was back on a plane. He closed his eyes again and tried to ignore the fact that the man next to him reeked of cheap cigarettes and was pouring inches of his flesh into Cole's personal space. Skin contact with a stranger sucked. Well, at least contact with one he didn't want to sleep with... His slight buzz from the Fat Tires had worn off, leaving him groggy with irritated emotions and anticipation. The idea of sleeping again on the short connection to Charleston was even more unappetizing when he realized that his fellow traveler's drool had just dropped on Cole's striped baseball tee, leaving a growing wet spot in its navy blue fabric. He busied his mind with thoughts of home in hopes of not purging at the sensation crawling over his body as the moistness reached the skin of his arm. *Coach sucks.*

# CHAPTER 19

## CHARLESTON

"HEY BABY! DAMN, you are looking good." A woman's voice caught Cole's attention.

Landed and walking out of the guarded exit, he glowed as he looked for words to respond. "Well, you are too, sexy. Atlanta is treating you well I see." Cole's coastal drawl was emphasized in hearing the much stronger version before him.

"Damn straight! And I treat Atlanta just as well." Elizabeth Ann Fray, Ann as she was called, did indeed look good. Curvy in all the right places and gorgeous. Her long, brown and blonde-highlighted hair brushed Cole's cheek as they hugged. Ann was safe harbor, providing Cole one of the few opportunities to be himself without judgment or fear that she would try to 'cure' him of his aversion to feeling.

"Damn, woman, I've missed you." Cole pulled back, his hands on her shoulders, and admired the view. The pistachio green and brown paisley maxi dress accented her carefree appreciation for life. The thought of her in Boulder or San Diego flashed across his mind.

She flipped her long hair over her shoulder as she

responded, "Me too, babe. I'm so excited to be back in Charleston with you."

He channeled a pompous broadcaster's voice. "Uh, it is the number one tourist destination *in the entire world* according to Condé Nast Magazine, thank you very much. And the best in the U.S. by Travel Mag. Oh, did I also mention *we* are from here? If that doesn't mean something, I don't know what does." The two laughed. Cole continued, "So, I think it should be a blast. I can't wait to catch up and just enjoy you. How long have you been waiting?"

"Well, I flew in yesterday to hang with my old sorority sister, Patsy, you remember her, and she just dropped me off about thirty minutes ago. Your flight was late, mister. So I grabbed some nasty-ass Yellowtail while waiting on you." Ann's tendency to animate her words with head gestures had not been lost over the years with it swinging left to right several times as she talked.

Cole's eyes widened playfully. "Look at you, already getting the party started. Yellowtail? I thought you were too much of a wine snob for that bottom-shelf brand? Well, let's get out of here so you can gargle it out and fix the situation, boozehound."

Warmth filled Ann's face as she spoke. "For sure! It really is good to see you. I've missed you."

"Good, that means you'll carry my bags, right?" Cole pushed his old carry-on towards Ann playfully.

She swiped it away with her leather-sandaled foot. "Ha, not a chance, Jack." Together they walked out of the airport to find Cole's rental car.

COLE DROVE AS ANN filled him in on life in Atlanta.

They had met in high school and pretty much been inseparable since, or at least until Cole's move to Denver. She was the strongest reason to stay, but ultimately he reconciled that she was just a telephone call and plane ride away. There were tears in Ann's eyes when he broke the news of his move almost a year and a half earlier. He gave her six months lead time before the move to emotionally prepare herself, but it didn't help. It strained their relationship for a time. Yet, things were definitely back on track and the distance actually seemed to bring them closer together.

"So then he was like, 'but you told me you didn't want a relationship.' What the fuck, do you guys really buy it when us girls say that? I mean, seriously, when has a woman ever just wanted to have sex without there being an expectation of more?" She clapped her hand on the car's seat to emphasis her feigned frustration.

Smirking, Cole replied, "It worked for Madonna."

Ann gave him an 'I can't believe you just said that' look. "Madonna? Please. Please don't compare me to Madonna. It clearly has not worked out well for her lately."

"So what did you do?" Cole had been through this conversation before. Ann, for all her beauty and intelligence, seemed to be on an endless cycle of dead-end relationships. Each was with a similar guy. Handsome, yet totally lacking in success. *Window dressing for a large pile of shit… with a half-chewed Barbie arm in it.* But they had aspirations of success. Just, bills, kids, ex's—fill in the blank— kept them from actually dedicating the time and energy into chasing success. The latest was an aspiring doctor with nothing more than his GED. But for his consistent need to get drunk and waste all his money, he would be the next Dr. Travis Stork *ala The Bachelor* and *The Doctors* talk show. Like a first-time home buyer, Ann saw only the potential for a palace and not the long, expensive road through remodeling, bills, and withdrawal from society, in her men.

"Well, I told him I had changed my mind. That I cared for him and thought he cared for me. Oh, and this is where it gets good." Ann bounced in her seat like a kid excited to be heading to Disney. "He looked at me with those beautiful brown eyes and said, quote, 'you're nice and all, but I have a lot on my plate and really can't handle a girlfriend right now.' Can you believe that shit? The man had been in my bed every other night for the past month, me cooking him breakfast—and you know I suck at cooking—and then, when I want it to be legit, he says he's too busy. *Screw him.*"

Filling in the momentary pause, Cole added, "You know how to pick them."

"Don't you start." She smiled as she cut her eyes away. They knew they could tell each other anything without judgment. Cole exercised his right to make observations of Ann's choice in men and relationships often. Only once did it result in him being on 'probation,' without hearing from her. And that only lasted a week, until she needed a sidekick for a Christmas party at work.

Exhaling loudly with a huff, she started again. "Yeah, I know. I sent mixed messages, *yada yada yada*. You've told me before, and I agree, I have acted stupid in the past. But I really *did* change my mind this time. I entered it just as friends with benefits. Then we started seeing each other every night or so and it just grew. Or, I thought it did."

"Ann, the men you date are good for one thing and one thing only. *Sex.*"

Ann looked down to her lap, deflated, arms limp to her sides. "Ugh, and it was *good* sex. I mean, earth-shaking, body-trembling good sex. My only complaint was that he was too lean."

Cole turned his head from the road at Ann's comment and took the bait. "Huh?"

She grinned knowing she had successfully drawn him into talking about sex, something he did not like to do. "I mean he had like *no* body fat. His body was smoking hot, don't get me wrong, but his penis was like cold steel."

"Oh my god. Please sto…"

"Just think of having sex with an iron rod and you get the point. How that damn Bella chick does it I will never know. Cold steel touching my girl with my feet in the stirrups once a year is enough for me, thank you very much." Her head was weaving again.

"…op". They both burst out laughing. There were few limits to their conversations and she demanded that sex not be one of them.

Playing along, Cole added, "Well, look at it this way, Ann, you now know what it's like to have sex with an android or robot. The first woman in the world who can say that."

"Sure felt like it. But, man, did he know how to use that robotic dick." The laughter returned harder as they arrived at Charleston Place, or the Omni as Cole knew it from his childhood. They checked into rooms that had been unintentionally booked on separate floors, both overlooking Meeting Street and the Old Slave Market. There was no time to waste, drinks were to be had and they were not apt to disappoint.

# CHAPTER 20

L OOKING AT HIS watch, Cole noted it was half past eight. *West to east travel sucks.* He was no fan of losing time, especially when he was on vacation. Ann and he had rushed to their rooms to change and were to meet in the downstairs lobby of curved staircases in front of check-in. Cole ran to Godiva first, one of many shops attached to the interior of the hotel.

As a kid, he had always loved Godiva and frankly, he needed the caffeine to keep up with Ann's spastic energy. As he walked across the beige marble-tiled floor of the shops into the small store, he recalled being told once when he was a kid that Elizabeth Taylor ate Godiva and ordered it exclusively from Charleston. He would learn in college that Godiva was a chain, like McDonalds or anything else, and that there was better chocolate to be had in the world. But visits to the store evoked enough memories of his childhood that he would routinely stop by and grab a piece. Memories, good or bad, comforted him, make him feel in control. Now, his analytical side suggested that it was chocolate's impact on endorphin levels in the brain that caused that reaction, but whatever the reason, he did it purely out of tradition—something Southerners revered.

Halfway through a white chocolate truffle he lifted his head and noticed that he must have been making a spectacle of himself enjoying it because a lady was staring at him from across the interior garden of the Charleston Grill as if she was thinking she wanted a bite, too. His contacts were too dry and blurry from travel to fully make her out, but she was definitely admiring the view. He suspected it was a bite of the truffle, not him, because he certainly wasn't channeling the Diet Coke guy at the moment. He popped the last bit in his mouth and casually returned to the lobby, chuckling at himself. He was always his own best entertainment.

Ann was running late as he bit into the dark chocolate truffle with milk chocolate center. It melted in his mouth and tasted of cream and sugar. Ann being late was like the moon rising. It was expected and routine. Sometimes it was quiet, sometimes it flooded everything in sight with lunar tides. Cole always added thirty minutes to a planned meet-up time in an attempt to avoid disappointment. Moments after the second truffle was gone, she finally appeared.

Casual dress had no impact on her beauty as she stepped out of the elevator in skin-tight blue jeans and a sparkly silver V-neck tee that hugged her in all the right places. She was stunning no matter the attire. This had led to a lot of suspicion among friends and prior co-workers about their dating status. Cole and Ann had made a run at dating for a very brief moment several years before he left Atlanta. It ended as quickly as it started when they both realized they were much better for each other as friends then they ever were as lovers.

Cole realized that the great advantage of friends is that you don't have to sleep with them every night. You can listen and live through all the crazy shit they do, say, and think, without personalizing it or attaching a 'how does this impact me' to it. Love is defined by those 'impact on me' moments. Avoiding that question just isn't possible when you date, much less marry someone. If they piss off their employer, the first thought is how will 'we' deal with this. When a friend pisses off a boss, you think and say, 'well, that sucks, let's go grab a drink' without another thought. When a lover buys an overly expensive car, you wonder how 'we' are going to afford that. When a friend does, you encourage them to drive it like it's stolen and go partying to celebrate.

The risks and consequences of Ann's decisions accumulated fast for Cole. On one side she was intelligent, successful, and driven. Yet, on another, she made poor, contradictory decisions, told one too many people off on a daily basis, and lacked the stability that he had long since discovered was a personal requisite. The feeling was mutual for Ann. By the end of the three-month trial, she described Cole as 'bossy,' 'cold' and his personal favorite, 'boring.' She resented his control and restraint as a lover. She needed excitement, risk, and the careless nature of a dandelion parachute, adrift in the wind.

The process had strained but not broken their friendship. It would take two years before it was healed. In that time both Cole and Ann came to respect and revere each other for the very differences that made them incompatible as lovers. Several events in each other's lives thrust them toward each other, forever strengthening their bond as friends. Had Cole known that it would make him fair game for conversations about her sex life, he might have rethought, but secretly he loved that they each felt so very comfortable that sharing even those conversations felt natural.


ANN WAS READY for a drink. "Okay, babe, where to? I haven't been out here in ages. What's hot?"

Cole reached in to pull a stray hair off Ann's shoulder and responded, "Jackie says that Tommy Condon's is still a great spot for a pre-dinner drink." Jackie was Cole's older sister and a local police officer in the Town of Mount Pleasant, right across the Cooper River, or the 'Cooper' as locals called it. "And, you know if there's a person who knows what bars are hot, it's a police officer."

"Sounds perfect. You know how I love Irish pubs. Ha." Ann was referring to last year's summer trip to Ireland where she and Cole drank at every pub they could find, sampling the local beer and 'supporting the local economy,' as they told themselves. The beer made the reality that the euro was almost two for one a little less painful.

Cole laughed to himself as he recalled that Ann also loved the Irish men. "Yeah, I think it's time for a revival of our support for the Irish and their beer."

Stepping out of the hotel, Ann walked in tight, four-inch heeled steps. Heading eastward down South Market Street and alongside the Slave Market, they continued to catch up. Cole interjected into the conversation as they crossed Church Street. "Ahh, horse shit. Welcome to Charleston." Ann laughed and pinched her nose. The downtown sector of Charleston was clogged with all sorts of transportation. Cars and bikes? Boring. Rickshaws and London-style black cabs, novel. And then there were the horse-drawn carriages. Stereotypical, yes. But very much a symbol of Charleston, nonetheless. Pats of horse manure could be found along any street in the historic area, i.e. the whole peninsula. They were unavoidable. Like the smell of the salt marsh, the random smell of horse symbolized home and evoked memories.

Cole and Ann walked into Tommy C's and immediately pulled up at the bar. The scruffy bartender rested his eyes on Ann and asked what they would have, clearly wanting to place his own order. *One glass of Ann, please!*

"I'll take a Palmetto Pale Ale."

"Make that two," Ann piped in. The bartender's eyes had yet to leave Ann, and a grin crossed his face. The idea of a woman who drank beer clearly agreed with him. Ann turned to Cole to continue their reunion conversation, wherein the guy took the message and walked away to retrieve their beers. Moments later he was back, popping off the caps of both beers with an opener attached to the underside of the bar.

"Here you go." His concaved-faced grin was back.

"Thank you, darlin'." The *g* in Ann's darling was dropped in typical Charlestonian smooth-talk fashion. Charlestonians' lyrical speech caused words to merge together at their ends, with few hard consonants or vowels, only inflections. Vowels were held longer here. Their jaw-jutting made them pronounce house as 'hoose,' and their proclivity to add syllables caused words like state to come out 'stey-it' and boat as 'bow-et.' The bartender's up-state Carolina roots were evident in his slight twang, something Charlestonians lacked. He took his cue and left with anticipation.

Having paid attention to the two accents play out, Cole sat back. "Awh, I miss you and the South. And I really miss the accent."

"What do you mean?" Ann leaned in to hear more.

"You know what I mean. People here just have a certain manner in the way they talk and communicate. It's like everything is a big flirt. Even an insult comes across as a compliment unless you know better. Just add a 'bless your sweet little heart' to 'you're an ass' and it's like turning vinegar into wine. And then there's the style. Bow ties and bright colors are the norm for men and woman. It's like a spring festival every day. People here love to look good and outsiders clearly agree that they do look good. Didn't Charleston get named fourth for most attractive people in America, behind Miami and Puerto Rico, last year by some magazine? I think it got first one year."

Cole thought to himself that indeed the city was colorful, the result of trade with the Caribbean in the city's early history. Its colorful nature extended to its people, too. Pink gingham, yellow polka-dots, and lime green sundresses filled the streets. Palmetto-lined cobblestone streets stood out amongst all the color and only added to the city's charm and beauty.

Ann smiled as she spoke. "Lord, you know this city collects accolades like a dog collects fleas. Most beautiful people, most mannered, top destination, best restaurants... the list goes on and on. We have this love-hate affair with our Southern roots and characteristics. We cherish them, holding them tight like the damn Yankees are coming to rip them from our arms, while also parading them around with pride as though to say, don't you wish you had some of this crazy?"

They laughed at that thought. By no means was crazy unique to the South, but it sure did love to parade it around on the front porch, give it a drink and welcome the world to stare. YouTube had made them video stars for all to see. And, God knows if there was a hurricane anywhere between here and Japan, some Weather Channel or CNN caster would be coming to town to elicit a fool to talk about trailers, beer, and Granny like a good'ol country song.

Cole responded, "Well, I love your crazy. You need to get out to Denver soon so we can show it a thing or two."

"You know it! Before I head back to Atlanta we'll have to compare calendars and see when will work."

"Excuse me, I think you're in my seat." Cole's back was turned when he felt a tap on his right shoulder. Looking up from his beer, Ann was smiling at the person standing behind him. Cole swung around and looked up, way up, to see Daniel Page grinning. At six-five, the young Denzel Washington look-alike towered over Cole, who was still seated at the stained-oak bar. "Daniel! Wow man, how are you? It's been like forever." Cole stood up and gave him a male hug. One of those 'we're cool enough dudes to hug, but world, we are not jumping in the sack together at the end of the night, okay?'

"Life is great, Cole. What brings you back to town? Didn't you move even further away from Charleston to...is it Denver or Portland or something?" Cole felt his phone vibrating in his pocket as he went to respond. Years as a trial attorney, in and out of courts, had taught him to keep it on silent.

Disregarding the vibrations and looking back to Daniel, he replied, "Yeah, Denver, but don't you worry. I'm always just a plane ride away from harassing you, little man. I think we still have to have that basketball match. It's one and one right now, right?"

"Ha. In your wet dreams, man. It is two and oh; and you cried." Daniel and Cole had been close friends since elementary school and giving each other grief was part of the job. Ann laughed at the competitive exchange.

Cole reached up and placed a hand on Daniel's shoulder. "Man, I have missed your ugly mug."

"Same here, Cole. So, what brings you to town?"

"Just visiting the family and taking in some Spoleto, nothing big." As Cole talked, a woman in a tight-fitting dress crowded her way between Cole and Daniel to place an order at the bar. Daniel moved his eyes up and down the woman's slender back and then back at Cole with a grin. He liked what he saw. Cole bent his neck to look around the blue-and-red striped summer dress obstructing his view to continue his conversation until she ultimately left, but not without her returning a flirting look at Daniel. Following the woman with his eyes, Cole said, "I can see you haven't lost your mojo there, mister. Always popular with the ladies."

"When you got it, you got it. And, when you don't, you don't. And, boy you got it. That's what Momma always says." Daniel flashed a pursed smile and lifted one brow while pinching his chin with his right hand, reminding Cole of the bad poses forced upon teens and adults at the old Glamour Shots photography center at Northwoods Mall.

Cole laughed. "Awh man, I better pull up my pant legs, it's getting deep in here. Hey, what are you doing tomorrow night?"

Daniel looked over at the woman from earlier as he responded. "No real plans, why you ask?"

"Dinner…at SNOB…six-thirty?"

"Sounds like a plan! Ann, are you joining?"

Ann leaned into and over the bar to see around Cole. "Oh, and miss seeing you two testosterone-filled men keep pissing on each other like blind tick hounds? Wouldn't miss it for the world." The two men laughed, shaking their head at Ann.

Getting up from his stool, Cole said, "Okay, Ann, are you about ready to jet? This boy is worn out. I slept like shit last night and we have a long day tomorrow."

Ann stepped off the stool and shook out her dress. "Sounds great to me. See you Daniel."

Cole looked back as he was about to walk out the door. Daniel had turned to the lady from earlier and was giving her the charm. *Yep, he's still got it.* "Damn."

# CHAPTER 21

WALKING PAST WASHINGTON Square, Ann looked over at Cole. "What is it?"

"Someone is calling me again. Didn't they get the memo?" Cole shook his head as he looked down and began digging into his back pocket for his phone. He pulled it out after some struggle, *damn tight jeans*, and saw it was Jackie calling.

"Well, speak of the devil," he announced into the phone as he brought it to his ear. Jackie was speaking softly; it was almost eleven p.m. on Friday night and she was likely trying to avoid waking Billy, Cole's four-year-old nephew. A crowd of people passed by, making it difficult to hear exactly what Jackie was saying so he pressed his ear tighter to the phone. Being Memorial Day weekend, coupled with Spoleto, the streets were busy and loud with strays and couples.

"You need to talk to me? Huh? Can't this wait till tomorrow?" Cole yelled in hopes that Jackie could hear him. "No? Why not? I'm out with Ann. I'm supposed to see you at brunch tomorrow to pick up Billy, right?"

From the comments Ann could tell that the conversation was serious. She looked at Cole in his jeans and his snow-cone blue gingham shirt and mouthed 'dashing.'

Cole smiled and bowed with large accompanying hand gestures.

Ann whispered, "Is everything okay?"

"I don't know." Cole responded while covering the receiver of his phone. "She's acting weird. Something's up. She's demanding I go to Mount P tonight." A quizzical look came over his face as he pondered why his sister was being so insistent.

Cole spoke into the phone. "Mount Pleasant? Tonight? Why?"

After a few moments of listening, Cole whispered back to Ann. "She keeps saying she'll fill me in when I get there."

Shaking his head in defiance, Cole responded to his sister. "Listen Jackie, I'm out with Ann and we've already had a few drinks. You've said no one's is dead or dying, so let's do this in the morning. I'll come over earlier, say ten? But for now, Ann and I are going to close out the night."

Jackie had relented. Cole ended the call with a rushed, "Yeah, I love you too."

Ann's eyes were big as she pushed for details. "What's up?"

"Ugh, no clue. She was like in a panic but refused to say why. But she said it could wait till tomorrow. So it's clearly nothing urgent. Funny though. She told me to watch out and make sure to watch out for you, too."

Ann and Cole puzzled over the call for a minute more before brushing it off to wander the streets of Charleston, passing by cobblestoned streets and private gardens on their way back to the hotel. A horse-drawn carriage passed by without clients as it headed to the stables. Away from the main drag of Meeting Street, the thick air dampened sounds and made the city seem empty. Gas lamps lit their way with a warm glow usually associated with some European town. Reaching the hotel after their slow saunter through the side streets of the Peninsula, they parted to their respective rooms.

BACK IN HIS room, Cole picked up the phone and called Jackie back; he needed to know what in the world was going on.

Jackie pounced to answer the call, ultimately disclosing the reason for her earlier panicked call. "Yeah, some FBI agent, that's all he would say."

Cole saw his face narrow into a puzzled look in the mirror that sat across the room, as he wondered why an FBI agent would want to talk to him. The FBI didn't scare him. He had worked for the Department of Justice in Washington, D.C. the first two years out of law school, where he interrogated FBI agents, Department of Defense personnel, and others. But that all related to environmental cases. Them calling now out of the blue, well…that was new.

*Why would the FBI want to talk to me?* At age three the FBI collected a copy of his fingerprints from a safety fair he attended at school. Since law school he had been fingerprinted at least half a dozen times in relation to school and licensing requirements in various states. Each event flashed in his mind with vivid accuracy. Trying to get away with a crime was the stupidest thing he could ever do.

Cole's mind immediately went to the image of a typed document, a pending application for admission to practice in New Mexico. *Damn those people are detailed.* It had been one of the most difficult and prolonged admissions he had gone through, and he had been through ample, with four states already under his belt. His clients were all over and they didn't want to use anyone but him. It was flattering and good for the wallet, but getting admitted to any state was a pain, with background checks, credit checks, and all sorts of checks. New Mexico had all but asked for a cavity search.

"Awh, Jackie, that's just in relation to me getting licensed in New Mexico. They've been calling every place I've lived, worked, and obviously now been born, in the past few weeks as part of my application."

"No Cole. This was an FBI investigator, not some bar association. He was looking for you. Detective Phil Betrous over in Charleston put him in contact with me. Agent Leas?" She paused on the line as if to see if Cole would respond. Hearing no response, she continued. "I told him you didn't live here anymore, that you lived out in Denver. He said he knew that but he also knew you were in town. He refused to tell me why he needed to talk to you, just saying I needed to get you in touch with him, pronto."

"You think one of my old criminal clients has gone crazy?"

"Cole, don't joke about such things. Georgia is just a hundred miles away to Savannah and if one of your crazies comes here looking for you, the only person he is going to meet is my friend Mr. Glock 21."

Cole regretted the guy that pissed off his sister now. She had always been tough, and if she hadn't been in love, she would have introduced her ex-husband to Mr. Glock. But she was, and she didn't. After, she was stronger than ever, with a splash of attitude in there that made her dangerous.

Cole chuckled. "Okay there Dirty Harry, I'm sure whatever it is it isn't serious. How did he know I was here? I'll call this when I hang up. I bet he called my office this morning. They wouldn't have seen it as serious. The FBI calls me frequently on my cases and I use ex-FBI agents on occasions as investigators. But this is clearly different. Those guys don't fly cross-country to give me a surveillance report." The puzzled look returned to his face.

"Give me his information and I'll call him tonight or in the morning." Cole was concerned but didn't want his sister to worry. He assured himself that whatever the FBI wanted it was nothing big and didn't directly involve him. It likely was one of his crazy criminal clients back in Douglas County, or so he chose to believe until he heard otherwise.

Moments after getting off the phone with his sister, he called the number she had given him. *Damn voicemail.* He left a message and tried to forget it. He was on vacation and didn't want to deal with whatever the FBI wanted.

# CHAPTER 22

*Day six-ninety.*

A S WITH THE LAST thirty days or so, the dream had come, waking Cole in the middle of the night. The morning routine that followed was the same. Slowly he forced the wall to go up while staring at himself in the hotel bathroom's black-framed mirror to create the facade of having it together.

Seated in the passenger side of Cole's rental Ann waved her hand across her bare legs. "Can I just tell you, I am so in need of this beach day. I mean, look at me...ghost!" They had taken it easy their first morning in Charleston, having a quick breakfast at a dinner in Mount Pleasant to meet his sister and grab Billy for a beach day. To Cole, Billy was pure entertainment; almost always happy and very inquisitive, things Cole loved to be around... needed to be around. His ability to swing from tantrum to crying to bliss and come out completely unscathed instilled hope in Cole.

Jackie had pressed about the FBI call during their brief exchange at brunch, but Cole brushed it off. He had no desire to mess up his Saturday at the beginning of the day. Things that could potentially go bad were always best left to the end of a day, in his opinion,

Reconnecting to the present conversation, Cole said, "Yeah, I was going to talk to you about that. It's bad enough you didn't shave those Frankenstein legs, but if I'm going to have to look at them you should have warned me to put my sunglasses on earlier." Cole smiled an 'I got you' look.

Ann looked with wide eyes, her mouth open. "Why, I oughta…"

Leaning away and placing his hand in the air to avoid a possible swat by Ann, Cole laughed. "Careful. Children…" Billy looked up in the rear-view mirror and laughed. "I told you we could have run to the Super Piggly Wiggly to get you some stronger sunscreen so you wouldn't burn, but, noooooo… you said you wanted to get some sun. So don't complain to me when you are as red as a lobster." Ann stuck her tongue out at Cole and then turned to peer out the window.

As they approached the old Ben Sawyer Bridge between Mount Pleasant and Sullivan's Island, Cole's mind flashed back to the image of the bridge knocked down, one end submerged in the water below, by Hurricane Hugo twenty-four years earlier. He could still see Oprah walking the streets in her TV special, surrounded by homes sifted into the streets and boats washed ashore.

Passing over its grated supports, Bruno Mars started singing about being locked out of heaven on the radio. Cole reached for the knob and turned it up to join in. Ann followed the chorus as Billy covered his ears in feigned pain. In an attempt to make Billy laugh, Cole switched up the words to 'locked out of Chucky Cheese.' Billy broke out in a high pitched squeal of a laugh.

Moments after the impromptu concert, they parked the rental on the sandy lot of the Sand Dunes Club where Cole had lifeguarded in college. Owned by the local power company, it was run like a country club for employees until the island residents complained enough to gain access in exchange for quelling their disputes about traffic and noise.

Billy immediately ran under the elevated pool's deck after being set free of the seatbelt he had struggled with for the entire drive to the barrier island. Pressing his face against the glass, Billy peered into the round underwater windows to catch a glimpse of the legs in the water. "Billy, come on, this sand is hot, boy!" Seconds later Billy ran past them, taking the lead to the beach on a narrow, sticker-laden path running between the pool and a large white stilted home. "Hey, you know that's Mark Sanford's old house, right?" Cole pointed to one of the homes along the beach drive.

Ann nodded. "Yeah. Can you believe he's back in politics? At least his wife got the house."

His eyes squinting in the bright sun, Cole let out a loud single laugh. "That's no surprise. It's South Carolina. We like our givens, even if we don't like what is being gave. Strom Thurmond was like a hundred before they let him leave office. We have over three hundred years of history with sex, guns, and religion. Can't mess that up now…it would be bad for business."

"Spoken like a true South Carolinian." Ann laughed at Cole's nonchalant attitude.

He nudged her side with his hands full of beach

towels and a cooler as they walked toward the beach. "Don't talk, you're one, too."

"Ouch!" Cole looked over to watch as Ann balanced her load of beach chairs and then lifted one foot to pull the sticker that had just become embedded in her foot. Free of the burr, she responded. "Yeah, but unlike you, I wised up to the fact that things are not always what they seem in this fried-shrimp and sweet-tea paradise. Like here... The idea that forty percent of all slaves in this country came in right here, right where we are standing on this island, is just shocking if you looked at it today. It's the Ellis Island of blacks."

Cole added, "Let's just be happy we didn't grow up in that and weren't raised that way. My granny would have cut my ass if I treated MeMe any differently than a white. I can hear Granny now, "You better get your white ass out there and apologize. Granny don't play."

"Oh, you don't have to tell me! Remember when she caught us smoking behind her house in town? I think she had made a run to the drive-through margarita place on Coleman and busted us running off the back porch when she returned. That crazy woman made us put a bucket over our heads, covered it with a wet towel and then made us smoke a whole carton of cigarettes. I don't think I've ever puked so much in my life."

Cole shook his head as he dropped the cooler on the beach. "Ha! Good'ol Granny. You have to love that crazy woman."

"Indeed."

Billy had already reached the frothy waves and kicked off his sandals to get in the water. Cole shouted against the wind for him to go on, but stay in eye-sight while he and Ann set up the towels. Moments later they joined him in an effort to wash off the sticky sand that had already caked their skin, kicking and splashing upon reaching the water. Billy was lifted on Cole's shoulders and all three waded waist deep until they found a sand bar several yards out, Cole and Ann still discussing their youth, which had been filled with days like this one.

"Billy, hold on…here you go, don't drop it." Cole had found a sand dollar and, using his toes, sandwiched its flat disk between his toes and drew it up for Billy to see. "You know there are angels inside of sand dollars, right?"

"What?" Billy inspected the light brown disk now in his hand and its small million red-peach colored feet still fighting to find something to grasp.

"Yep, we'll let that one go, but if we find a dead one, I'll show you." Billy turned his hand and let the animal fall, rocking back and forth as it fell back to the murky bottom.

Several minutes of flipping Billy through the air and into the water, they were all back on shore. Cole took in the moment to watch Billy make a sand castle a few yards away.

# CHAPTER 23

"SO, COUGH IT UP, mister. How's the dating life?" With Billy out of earshot, Ann had decided to finally press for details on Cole's life in Denver.

"Ugh, are we really going to talk about that? There are so many better things to talk about, like *your* dating life. What was his name again, Jose? Columbian, if I recall...."

Ann's eyes went up and rolled. "Brazilian, thank you very much. But we're not talking about me. Seriously... How's your bed treating you?"

"My bed is treating me very well, thank you very much. Probably because the only person in it is me. Well, and Dixie."

"Sounds lovely.... Are there any potentials? Give me the scoop." Ann leaned in as though something exciting was about to be said.

"There are a few, but I really don't have time for that right now. My job keeps me pretty busy, and then otherwise I am enjoying exploring the West. Plus, you know all the good ones are taken by the age of like twenty-eight, anyway."

Disappointed at the lack of anything juicy, Ann leaned back into her seat and stared at the waves. "Yeah, but in reality the great thing is we are all royal fuck-ups. So the game plan for those of us who haven't landed a keeper by thirty is to wait until someone messes it up with one of the good ones or gets really stupid and dumps them. Then...like sharks, we smell the blood in the water and grab that sucker before someone else does, praying that we don't repeat the first guy's mistake. That's the key, mister, don't mess up." She reenacted someone capturing a fish with their hands.

"Wow, you and Dr. Phil should write a book together. I'd like to think love is a little more romantic than sharks fighting over a bite into the next tuna. Plus, I think I'm done with all that for now. Let some shark find me."

"Cole, you can't hide behind your job forever. You have to date."

"Ann, I'm not hiding behind my job. I'm just busy, okay?"

"Look, I love you, you know I do, mister. And I just want the best for you. It's been two years, don't you think it's time to try again?"

Cole's mind went to Atlanta. He had let down his defenses for the first time ever and been damaged. The pain wasn't fresh, but it did linger and he secretly had no interest in trying again. Cole didn't know if keeping it in, refusing to feel, was good or bad, but it was the only way he could exist and function for now. In the mornings, when the wall was its lowest, the emotions came flooding in, blinding him and reminding him of just how helpless he now felt. To him, being unable to save someone he loved meant he deserved the cold side of the pillow every morning.

Over the past year an internal fight had developed between the longing to be loved and feeling unworthy of actually having it. He felt helpless against his own yearnings. With the wall, the two feelings were forced into their corners like fighting little boys, held there only so long as he was awake. In sleep, they were free to wield their punches, tearing away at the scar that had been created in Atlanta.

Closing his eyes in an attempt to wipe the blackboard of his thoughts clean, Cole lied. "It isn't that, promise."

"Bullshit. You left Atlanta to get away, and now you're burying your head in your job. You aren't getting any younger, Cole."

She had pushed too hard. Cole looked up from watching his toes dig in the sand and yanked off his sunglasses. "Look who's talking... I know, I know, you're right. And I have gone out on dates. But how do you teach yourself to trust...yourself? To feel again? H. E. double L, I was barely feeling before. I can't stop seeing it, Ann. It's like it happens all over again every time I think about it. You know how I am, Ann. Images get stuck in my head like a bad movie on loop. And the only thing I can think is I failed. If I had done more or said more, it wouldn't have happened. A cocaine overdose, Ann, cocaine. With me in the other room. I had no f-ing idea of the drugs, the hurting. What kind of boyfriend does that make me? That's not good for the 'ol heart. And it sure as hell isn't good for the self-confidence that you can provide what your lover needs."

"God man, you are..." Ann looked over to Billy a couple yards away now digging a moat around his sand castle, having taken note of Cole's spelling of certain words. "F-ed, up aren't you?" Ann smiled at her attempt at levity, apparently realizing she had crossed a line.

"Cole, you are an amazing man. You deserve someone just as amazing in your life. But you can't have that if you don't try. It wasn't your fault. Some people are just damaged beyond repair and there is nothing you can do about that. You asked how you learn to love again, to feel again? Well, you can't learn those things if you don't extend love."

Cole relaxed back into his chair. "And my head agrees, but my heart hasn't found the person it wants to attempt that with yet, that's all I'm saying. I'm enjoying my unfeeling world. You can't be hurt by what you don't feel. Come on in, it's nice and comfy." Cole spread his arms in his imaginary hot tub.

Ann relented. "Fair enough..." There was a long pensive pause, then Ann spoke again. "Just make sure I'm invited to the wedding." Cole smiled at Ann, the sun shining in her face and wind sweeping her hair.

"I can't imagine it without you... Someone has to be the drunk fool; it might as well be you."

By two the sun had drained them of all their energy and their stomachs ached in hunger. "Billy, you about ready to go grab some lunch before we have to drop you off?"

"Yes, sir."

"Will you grab Miss Ann's towel and see if she needs help with anything else?"

Billy rushed over to Ann now standing to brush the sand off her legs. "Miss Ann, do you need help with anything?"

"Oh baby, I'm good. If you will grab that towel, that will be enough."

Arriving at the pine green-sided Dunleavy's Pub just down the main street of the island, they slid into an old picnic table outside and promptly placed orders for sandwiches. Cole was starved and dehydrated, never a good combination for Billy's boundless energy. Dread passed through his mind for a moment as he recalled having to ultimately deal with the FBI agent. *Why was he asking to meet? And why is he coming to Charleston?*

# CHAPTER 24

TOTALLY BEACH-DRAINED, COLE met his sister at the police station to drop off Billy and ran back to the hotel for a quick nap. It was almost six by the time he snuck in a forty-five doze and then showered. There was a voicemail from the number he had called the night before. Agent Leas' heavy voice indicated he needed to talk to Cole as soon as possible and was flying into town tomorrow. He would contact Cole when he landed. *What the hell?* The mental wall went up, cutting off further consideration of why the FBI would be chasing him down. His evening was planned and he didn't want to worry.

Cole was no spendthrift, but he did admire nice clothes. So, when Gilt had a sale on Armani suits, he'd pounced. The dark grey striped two-buttoned suit fit like a glove, thanks to a tailor back in Denver. He matched it with a crisp white spread-collared shirt, leaving unbuttoned the top two buttons. He almost always rolled his sleeves, the result of shirts never fitting the length of his arms, and also a style dictated by humid, warm nights. But that would have to wait until after the Spoleto event scheduled for later in the evening.

"Holy shit, you look gorgeous!" Ann had swung the door to her room open in a grand, sweeping move, revealing her in a gown that would demand any man's attention, even the Pope's. With a gold fading to grey base, it was studded with all sorts of gems that emphasized the extreme V which cupped her overflowing breasts. It was off the shoulders, and short. She had put her hair in some type of bun and Cole suspected the use of a 'bump-it' to create the extra height. "Why, thank you. Do you think this will get me laid tonight?"

"Tonight? Hell, I can get you laid right *now*!"

"Ha ha, I've learned my lesson. I don't think my tickets are accepted on that fun park ride." They smiled playful, growling smiles at each other and walked out of the room to head to the main entrance of the hotel where a stranger held the door open for them. The friendly nature of Charlestonians was always apparent to Cole. The city's inhabitants went out of their way to say hi and look you in the eyes like they were on the set of *Gone With the Wind*, promenading about. If you tried that in any other city, you would cuss yourself because people would either look at you like a creep or put out their hand for your spare change.

Walking a few blocks from the hotel into Slightly North of Broad, or SNOB as the locals called it, Spoleto's energy engulfed them and poured through the city's streets. Ann and Cole had barely arrived when Daniel walked through the door, with a guest.

"Wow! Y'all look amazing. I am clearly underdressed."

"Thanks man, and who is *this*?" Pulling back to take in the woman to Daniel's left, Ann pressed him for information.

"This is Janet." They exchanged pleasantries as Cole admired his friend's obvious date. Her light brown eyes glowed against the green and black cocktail dress she wore and her auburn-red hair. He had immediately recognized her from the bar the previous night, the image of the event flashing before his eyes. The hostess walked up just as he was about to play dumb and ask Janet how she met Daniel.

Janet leaned around her and whispered, "We just met last night." Cole smiled at his old friend and admired his confidence. *You dirty dog*.

Sitting, the introduction continued, with Janet telling the table she was a local anesthesiologist. "Oh, I've handled a few cases with them. An interesting bunch…" Cole stopped himself before insulting their guest with a harsh generalization of such doctors being pill and needle poppers. Ann and Cole followed with their introductions, disclosing their professions and how they knew Daniel. Janet seemed deeply intrigued by their careers and prodded Cole to tell story after story of his legal experiences.

"Janet, have we met before? I don't mean last night. I swear I have met you or seen you somewhere recently."

"Nope, I don't think so. I haven't been to Denver in years." The thought frustrated Cole. Ordinarily his memory was precise and crisp. But, if he didn't pay enough attention to the event or image he was observing, it came in fuzzy, ragged at its edges like an out of focus camera. He let the frustration pass as the continued to talk.

REMNANTS OF FILET with crab sauce remained on his plate when Cole disclosed the strange message he had received from the FBI agent the night before. Daniel and Cole had known each other since kindergarten and knew each other's teen secrets like brothers.

"So, he said in the message that he was curious if

anyone had tried to contact me or had made any threats against me. Listening to it, I thought to myself it was always possible that I could be threatened; after all, I was a trial lawyer and certainly have pissed off a few people in my cases...but nothing serious. The worst I have ever seen was that crazy murder case when I worked in Georgia and I pointed the finger at the sheriff's office. I got a personal warning from the sheriff saying that he couldn't control his boys if I kept pushing. Nothing ever came of that though."

Daniel asked, "Did he tell you why he was asking?"

Cole shrugged his shoulders. "No, man. That was the entire message. Just 'I got some questions for you' and then that he would be in contact. How cryptic is that?"

"Did he say how he got your name? How scary!" Janet piped in, concern showing on her face.

"I bet he got your name from one of your old criminal clients. I wouldn't worry about it. Plus, if someone is coming after you, they would have to get through me first." Daniel pounded his chest, causing the two ladies to laugh.

Cole had only seen Daniel in a fight once, during a basketball game, and the victor wasn't the other guy. Daniel also played receiver for the Wando Warriors in high school and he didn't dodge people, he plowed through them. Though he was a tech start-up guy now, Daniel hadn't lost his bulk, and looks alone said to not mess with him.

Cole playfully elbowed his friend. "Awe, love you, too, man."

"But if you would like me to look into it, let me know. I have some contacts in D.C. who I bet can get me some information."

"I appreciate that man. I'll let you know if I need anything."

Looking across the table to Ann and Janet talking, Cole interrupted, "Drink up ladies. Ann and I have a show to see. *An opera!*" Cole threw his hands in the air in a theatrical loop.

"It's been great seeing you Cole. You too, Ann. Don't be a strangers, you hear me? I've missed that ugly face of yours Cole."

"Hey man, better than that bull-dog of a mug you call a face." Daniel put Cole into a loose headlock as they exited onto the sidewalk. "Oh, it's on now!" Cole smiled as he walked backwards with Ann, looking back at his friend.

# CHAPTER 25

OVER A WEEK had passed since her last kill, but Poinsett's final kill was close, driving her to into frenzy like a starved dog over food. She could taste death in the damp air; the unworthy would die. Mouzon would die. Sipping her Earl Grey outside the Slave Market across from the Charleston Place hotel, she wondered if he knew that he was about to die. She had found him in this old city…hiding. Did he sense his hunter closing in, her hot breath breathing down his neck? Or would he be ignorant until the very moment she announced her presence?

Putting away her pen, she stared at the square note card sitting on the black wrought iron table where she was seated. The notes were the prefect touch, in her mind. It told them everything they needed to know. How they were never intended to live. That by living they had deprived her, robbed her of her life. And that they would die for what they had done. The process was about enjoying herself, after all. Some people had cars, others played cards. For her, it was the hunt of retribution.

If they knew what she went through as a little girl, the pain, the abuse of it all…they would understand their guilt. They might actually have welcomed their fate. Those before had died not knowing just how miserable they had made her life. Mouzon would be different. She needed him to *feel* her pain.

She thought to herself that it was pretty easy to locate him really; she'd called his office in Denver after leaving his house Friday morning and told them she was his sister and wanted to surprise him with a bottle of champagne for his visit. His assistant coughed up the information with glee. She giggled as the phone hung up. *Stupid little girl.*

TO HER, THE HOTEL had Charleston vomited all over it. The furniture, the walls, the decor all screamed the Holy City in the late 1700s, early 1800s. Mahogany four-poster beds, beige linens, historic oil paintings of birds and long-dead people hunting foxes and rabbits adorned its walls. The buildings surrounding the hotel's tan brick facade were painted what most would consider black at first glance, but was actually a color called 'Charleston Green.' Poinsett had learned in history class that the paint was the very colorful city's revolt from using the Union-issued black paint after the Civil War; so the locals added yellow and blue to create the deep black-green still used today. A short walk around the city exposed any visitor to homes which, if they weren't pink, robin blue, or yellow, were white with Charleston Green.

Inside the hotel, she wandered its hallways looking for this room. Stealing from housecleaning always got results in her experience; and according to the guest list found in the cart, his room was on the fourth floor, facing east. She watched as he left the hotel that morning with some tall brunette with big Texas hair. *Girlfriend?* Doubtful, since they weren't staying in the same room. *Sister?* That was definitely possible, but from what Poinsett knew his sister lived here. Either way, she figured this was her opportunity to taunt him.

As she exited onto the fourth floor she noted this hotel tried to mix traditional fare with a high-end hotel. To her it was Hilton meets a bed and breakfast. Poinsett found the room and slid the stolen white access card she'd picked off of housekeeping into the door. A green light; *we are in.*

The room was tidy. A carry-on was splayed open between the bed and window, with shoes and a belt sitting on the floor in front of it. Poinsett opened the closet: some pants and shirts, hung way too tidily for her taste. *OCD much? Hugo Boss, Armani Collezioni, nice.* There were no personal items otherwise, only an iPhone charger on the nightstand next to the bed.

She pulled out a sealed white envelope exactly like the ones she'd used with Whitney and Tony. A red wax seal worked to hold the folded ends together as she placed the note on the tan and powder blue-striped stool at the end of the bed for Mouzon to find. Exiting the room, her phone buzzed in her purple leather purse. Work was calling.

# CHAPTER 26

MATSUKAZE WAS THE U.S. premiere of a Japanese opera about a monk who comes across two sister spirits bound to earth until they can be released from their lover's spell. The irony of the conversation earlier in the day about not being able to let go of the hurt of the past was not lost on Cole as they read the handbill. He had demanded they attend because the sets looked amazing to him on the Spoleto website, and it was a reunion of sorts. The last opera he'd attended was Madame Butterfly, with Ann at the Sydney Opera House several years earlier, so it seemed only fitting their next should be Japanese-themed as well. But he now wondered if subconsciously his mind was telling him to move on.

It was venued at Dock Street Theater, the oldest theater in America, having originally been built in the early 1700s, only to be destroyed several years later in the Great Fire of 1740 that took half the city. According the brochure in Cole's hand the hotel was built on the site at the heart of Charleston's French Quarter by the early 1800s. But the 1800s were not kind to Charleston. Between the Civil War and the 7.3 earthquake of 1886, the Holy City was left worn and damaged. It would be another forty-nine years before the theater would reopen in 1937, after the hotel was gutted and remodeled in London style from the architectural remnants of the nearby Radcliffe-King Mansion. Though DuBose Heyward was named writer-in-residence at the theater and together with Gershwin, wrote the opera Porgy and Bess on nearby Folly Beach, it would not be until 2012 that his opera would play at Dock Street. Charleston was changing, but like grapes to wine, it was a slow process.

The theater was wide and shallow, with dark wood everywhere. Walking into the theater, earlier Cole and Ann were escorted to their lower level seats only a few rows back from the stage. Cole liked aisle access, otherwise he felt claustrophobic, his long legs often hitting the seat in front of him. The curtain was still covering the stage as they continued their conversation about work at Ann's previous employer.

"I'm telling you, they are crazy. You would think with a million senior managers they would have it figured out. But no. All they do is piss off their employees and cash the checks." Ann spoke with terse words.

"I'm so glad you got out of there. I mean, I know you loved working for that Douglas guy, but he wasn't able to shield you from the other partners."

"I know." She grimaced with disappointment.

"Well, I can say you certainly sound happier now than when we last we talked about all this."

"Oh my god, it's so much better. I love working for PWC. It was just meant to be." Ann had switched to PricewaterhouseCoopers nine months earlier.

At that moment the theater tone chimed like an old doorbell, warning everyone the show was about to start. Cole leaned back in his seat and Ann slipped her arm between the bend in his, taking his arm. Cole loved their 'date nights.' To him, it had been too long.

The lights went dim and the curtain was pulled back. The stage itself was bare. In the middle of the set stood a giant artistic tree that looked more like an icicle dragon. The lighting was dramatic, and emphasized the stark contrasts in the Asian-inspired costumes. Rich blues, greens, and reds were balanced against white.

As the production unfolded, Cole's mind wandered back to the dream that had been dominating his sleep lately. Unlike the geisha-like faces of the spirits on the stage, his demon remained faceless. There was that hand, just that hand. *What did it all mean?* Cole's thoughts were distracted by the pulsing of his phone; someone had just texted him. He ignored it and pushed his thoughts of the dream out of his head, forcing the wall higher. Watching the opera, he accepted that his mind was trying to say, *Let it go, move on.*

The opera impressed, as both Cole and Ann had expected. Ann commented on the final few acts and the spirits' pain as Cole and she walked out of the theater.

Halfway out the theater Cole's pocket buzzed again. Digging around in his suit jacket pocket, he withdrew his phone and half the powder blue silk lining, but that was enough to see the caller's ID. He flashed the phone's screen at Ann. "Look: Jackie. She's calling about what that damn FBI guy had to say, I'm sure of it." The phone was shoved back in his pocket.

"Okay, total buzz-kill." Ann responded.

"I know, right? How about this… Let's go back to the Omni and hang at the bar at Charleston Grill. They have those comfy leather chairs, and we can drink till close and crawl into our rooms without hassle."

"Ugh, boring. But I think you're right. Plus, if we still have energy after closing down the bar we can just watch porn." They both erupted into laughter. Ann was referencing a prior trip to Puerto Rico where they'd landed in a hurricane and had only porn, protein bars, and booze to subsist on for a day. He grabbed her hand and took a step off the grey slate sidewalk onto the cobblestone below. "Yes, my darling, there will always be porn."

# CHAPTER 27

POINSETT WALKED INTO the Rooftop Bar at the Vendue Inn in a low-cut white blouse and navy pin-stripe pencil skirt wherein she promptly grabbed a free chair at the bar next to a guy probably ten years younger. Tan boat shoes, khaki shorts, and a purple check shirt with the sleeves rolled up to his elbows—*typical Charlestonian style.* His friend had on burgundy Bass penny loafers, no socks, khaki shorts, and a pink polo. Poinsett caught the glimpse of one of those South Carolina belts with mini-monogrammed versions of the state's flag of a navy rect-angle with a white palmetto and crescent moon.

Turning her attention to the bartender, she ordered a glass of pinot gris. Even for late May it was humid, and a warm wine wasn't going to cut it. The salt in the air made her feel damp and sticky, but a coastal breeze blowing through the bar offered some momentary relief. From the roof Poinsett could see the steeples that dotted Charleston's skyline. The bar offered a visitor the perfect vantage to see the sights and for a hunter to eye her prey. While in the lobby of Charleston Place, she'd overheard Mouzon and his girl discuss their plans and intentions to hit the Waterfront Park after some 'fancy-schmancy' show. It was a little past ten and any show should be getting out soon. She could wait and watch.

Frat-tastic closest to her had his back turned, deep in conversation about some boat he was drooling over earlier in the day. Poinsett heard the word 'Scout.' Something about doubled hulls, *blah blah blah*. She couldn't see his face but youth wasn't being wasted on him. His body was firm; even in the dark she could see his individual muscles under his shorts. One left Poinsett with the impression that Mom had been a very lucky woman if father was like son.

She had been caught lingering a little too long; his buddy had seen her staring and was seen filling him in. He did that under-sloop look to his left to inspect his stalker. There was a huge grin on his face as Poinsett turned away, intentionally a bit too slowly. Her quick impression was this guy got laid, *a lot*. Sun-bleached shaggy, curly hair crowned a square and tanned, chiseled face. His lips were juicy and red from too much sun.

"Tourist?" He engaged her.

Turning on her stool to face him, she replied to his weak attempt to start a conversation. "In town for the weekend to catch some of the Spoleto shows and events." She said, while taking a casual look around the room as if to say, 'you're not important enough for all my attention, *yet.*'

"Nice. Where are you from?" Frat-tastic was intrigued.

"Mobile. It was supposed to be a girls' weekend, but my friend had to bail at the last minute. My ticket was non-refundable, so here I am." She gave a half-hearted frown.

"It's a perfect time a year to be here. It's not too hot and you've seen all the azaleas and wisteria."

*Was this joker really trying to carry on a conversation about flowers?* He *was* correct on that point. The flowers matched the homes, matched the people, on fire with color. "It really is beautiful. Are you from here?"

"Grew up on the IOP, that's the Isle of Palms, just north of the city. A senior at the College of Charleston now."

Poinsett feigned interest, leaning onto hear more. "Oh? What are you studying?"

He smiled and then continued. "Economics, but I'm really hoping to get recruited by the Braves."

*Ah, that explains the thick, muscular arms.* A vision of him shirtless over her, propping up his chest with those arms on either side of her, flashed across her mind.

"Doesn't Charleston have a team?"

"Nawh, not a major league team. We have the Riverdogs, but they're affiliated with the New York Yankees, new blood and all. Bill Murray from the movie Caddyshack owns the Dogs, and you see him down here at a game every once in a while. So that's cool I guess. But I'm a Braves man." His accent got thick as Poinsett played dumb. She knew the city had a team that was once called the Rainbows, an apt name, she thought, for the colorful city.

"Wow. Very nice. I'm sure you're a great hitter." With this she brushed his forearm as she returned her empty wine glass to the bar top. He grinned in invitation.

He pulled back in an effort to puff his chest. "I've been known to hit a home run a time or two." The sunglasses that had been previously placed on the back side of his neck fell, pulling the Croakies snug against his Adam's apple.

"I bet you have." She returned a playful grin as she

watched him tug the black neoprene strap down his chest to resituate his glasses.

"Would you like another?" he said as he turned on his stool to face her completely, thoroughly engaged now. His friend was working hard in the corner on some blonde with a glittery top and cheap heels.

"Sure, that would be nice, another pinot please." She waved at the bartender.

"By the way, I'm Jackson. I don't think I properly introduced myself."

"Katie here." Poinsett pulled the name out of her ass; it sounded like some sorority girl's name Jackson would think was hot. It was also the name she selected to use with her girlfriends when they wanted to be naughty by alias. The conversation continued on, with 'Katie' glancing over the railing to spy Mouzon if he came. It wasn't important that she see him. She just liked observing her prey a few times before taking them down.

# CHAPTER 28

"Y OU KNOW WHAT? Fuck the hotel, let's hit the park
for a walk and then a night cap at Blind Tiger like
we originally planned."

"There's the Cole I love! Now we're talking." They
were halfway to the hotel when they took a left onto
Queen Street towards the harbor. Queen would turn into
Vendue and intercept the park, but only after passing the
Rooftop Bar.

As they approached Waterfront Park they could
see one of the newer icons of the city, a giant pineapple
fountain. The pineapple had been a symbol for the city
since colonial times. Some man said pineapples represented hospitality and welcome, everything Charleston is
known for, and the city said count us in for one of those.
So it obviously made sense to place a giant one in a park
in the middle of the tourist area.

This one was concrete. With a circumference of
about fourteen feet, it resembled two round waffles, one
tiered higher than the other, and their edges curved up.
If it wasn't for the large ribbon-leafed head at the center
top, one might be led to believe Charleston invented the
Belgian waffle. And Cole wouldn't put it past his hometown to make a run at yet another accolade.

"Isn't it a great night?" Ann was locked arm-in-arm again with Cole as they walked lazily toward the pier that overlooked the Wando River, which separated Charleston from Mt Pleasant and the Patriot's Point battleship museum with its massive aircraft-carrier turned-museum. As a kid he had played in the tight, grey corridors of the ship while his aunt and adopted mother, Ava, worked the ticket booth at the front gate. Cole could see it all as if he were walking the tight corridors just then. He and Jackie got lost routinely trying to locate the best spots to hide aboard the old aircraft carrier, connected to the real world only by a long, thin pedestrian bridge that traversed fifty feet of water and swarms of bull sharks.

"Damn, my feet are killing me. My ankles aren't conditioned for heels on these cobblestone streets. I'm glad the four-inch heel thing hasn't caught on in Atlanta like it has here. I would die." Ann slipped off her heels and put them in her right hand as she maintained her left arm's tight wrap around Cole's. Now walking in her bare feet upon the wooden plank pier, she asked, "Cole, do you miss the South?" He knew what she really meant to ask— *Do you miss me?*

As Cole and Ann reached the end of the pier, he grabbed her hands to dance. "Brown-Eyed Girl" was playing in some distant bar. Hand in hand, Cole stepped back and brought their hands together in front of them, then twirled Ann inside and back out again. They were Shag dancing, the local dance.

Unlike the Charleston, which had fallen out of favor some time ago, the Shag had maintained its hold on locals. It made sense that a swing-style dance which encouraged bare feet in the sand and holding a mixed drink would arise from the lowcountry of the Carolinas. The dance was born up the coast from Charleston in Myrtle Beach, quickly spreading and fostering a generation of music and ultimately a movie. Groups such as the Drifters, Embers, Catalinas, and the Temptations, along with the likes of James Taylor and Van Morrison, all had songs considered "beach music" suitable for Shagging. There were books highlighting the dance, including Pat Conroy's *Beach Music*. The Shag was bred into Charlestonians and percolated up whenever a beach song caught their ears.

Ann's cheek rested against Cole's as he brought her in tight, with his arms wrapped around her and hers around his. They swayed as Morrison spit out some "la la la's." They were reunited, even if it was just for a weekend. As the music wound down, Cole let himself momentarily feel just how much he missed Ann and Charleston. It truly was a wonderful place to be for him. As they always did, Cole and Ann pretzeled, an intricate move of hand tying that ended with him deeply dipping Ann. They laughed as she stood and then they hugged. He had never responded, but she was satisfied with his answer to his question. The city's charm had penetrated and now washed over them like the salt breeze.

# CHAPTER 29

POINSETT HAD SEEN it all from her rooftop vantage from across the palmetto and live oak-studded wind-scaped park. Mouzon and his girl had been twirling like seniors in a Viagra commercial for several minutes. It repulsed her, and she liked the idea of ending that in a bloody mess. *Run down there and just do it.* Perhaps she would make Mouzon watch as she took down the girl first with one quick slash of her scalpel. She longed for a more engaging hunt. Regardless, she had seen enough for now.

"Would you like to get out of here?" she said as she turned to Frat-tastic again.

"Uh, definitely." Poinsett got the impression that he had just said 'score' in his head.

Jackson was clearly loving what he was seeing as he sat on the edge of her bed admiring her flowing red hair. 'Katie' had an incredibly flat stomach that rivaled his own ripped abs. She stood in front of him, between his legs. His shirt had been removed as soon as the door closed and he was now lifting off her thin white blouse. Earlier in the night he had enjoyed that he could see that Katie was lacking a bra. He didn't know how much older she was, but it clearly did not reflect in the perkiness of her breasts.

He cupped them as she finished pulling her blouse over her head, having not bothered to unbutton it. They were firm and ample. He rolled his thumb over her right nipple; she moaned with her eyes closed and threw her head back. He moved in and cupped his mouth over her left nipple, lashing it with his tongue. She was obviously enjoying herself as she placed her hands on his head and began to curl her fingers in, pulling him in closer to raise his arousal. He moved his left hand slowly around her body to her back and began feeling for a zipper on her skirt. Once found, he patiently pulled it down until it stopped.

POINSETT WAS IMPRESSED; this guy knew what he was doing, and he was doing it well so far. Her skirt fell to the floor and revealed her bare skin and black lacey panties. Jackson pulled back to admire the view and then looked up at her, with a soft, "Wow." She grinned back and admired her view.

As she expected, Jackson was built like a brick house. He was lean, but not so lean as to be a pencil. He had muscle in all the right places. His shoulders and chest were thick and defined, with just a little tuft of hair connecting his pecs and collarbone. Like the hair on his head, his chest hair was bleached from frequent shirtless days, whether from the yard, beach, or that boat he longed for.

Removing her hands from his head, she pushed his chest down and he complied, laying his back on the bed. She moved in slowly to kiss his chest as she leaned over him, first his sternum, then his nipples. She worked her way down the line that separated his eight-pack. His navel had the slightest bit of hair that led further down. She followed with the tips of her fingers like she was reading a Braille map. She moved her hands to the aged brass buckle of his woven leather belt and unlatched it. The buckle of his khaki shorts was next, spreading apart the opening to reveal what appeared to be black boxer-briefs with a silver top band. The light from the bedside lamp accented shadows that defined his devil's horns, the abdominal V formed by the meeting of his abs and groin. A tingle of anticipation flashed across her skin.

He lifted his butt from the bed to facilitate her attempt to pull off his shorts, and she crawled on top of him. He rolled her and twisted their bodies to place her head at the top of the still-made bed. With her legs bent and him between them, he sat up to again admire the view. He ran his hand down her firm body until he reached her panty line and then moved it to her left leg to return to the lower panty line. He leaned back in and pressed his broad chest against her. His tongue acted with intention as they kissed, chasing hers playfully around her mouth. He withdrew and moved down her face, neck...

She leaned her head to the side as he reached her neck, first at her collarbone and then up toward her left ear. She moaned again, as if to tell him, 'more.' He continued while slipping his hands around her lower back and under her panties to cup her ass. He closed his hands around the cheeks as if to pull her up. In response she pulled her knees in more and wrapped her legs around his firm buttocks. He pumped his hips in a serpentine motion, using his frame to knead the dough of her hips. His moans were clear but light. He was enjoying himself. "You are so sexy," he whispered in her ear. Slowly he pulled down her panties. She unlocked her legs to let them slip off.

He moved again down her body, stopping only when he reached deep between her legs. His tongue was evil, in the best sort of way. He lashed her with the firmness of its tip. This made her body involuntarily curve back, thrusting her hips into his face and leaving a hollow under her back. He continued his moist assault for several minutes, coming up for air only once. Every few moments she would open her eyes and peer down her body to see the mop of his sandy hair between her legs and his arms wrapped around her hips on either side, maintaining a firm grip on his focus.

As he crept back up along her body, she used her hand to pull down his tight boxer briefs. Pressing his hips into hers, he was inside. His chest met hers briefly as they kissed, then he lifted himself up to look at her and occasionally lean down to kiss her neck, all while maintaining his connection to her. Her body went flush, warm and tingly. Heat swelled up from her hips, slowly taking over her whole body. Inside her, he felt even more than average, as she had suspected. She hadn't seen, but it certainly was hitting all the right places and had substance. She was no size whore, but she certainly wanted to know she was getting laid. Over and over again he kneed his hips into her, penetrating deeper and deeper. He moaned in that deep way that let her know he was fully enjoying himself. Looking down his body on top of hers excited her more—he had a perfect ass for a man. His tan line, low on his waist and halfway to his knees, just made it pop even more. He grabbed her hair and pulled her head back. *Someone has clearly read the manual.* Pump by pump, a slight dizziness and tingling snuck up on her from below until her entire body was on fire. Her moans made his body respond and he pumped deeper and deeper and then stopped, laying his body on hers, trembling.

*Ugh, I needed that.* She pushed Jackson off of her after waiting the mandatory minute or two for him to enjoy the after-effects of his work. *Who said she wasn't a giver?* He remained lying face down, naked on the top of the comforter. She was beside him, trying to figure out the best approach for getting him out. After all, he wasn't prey, he was a distraction, a needed distraction. She no longer had a use for him and needed to get her rest for the hunt.

"So babe, I really enjoyed this and all...but I need you to get out." He raised his head after hearing her, a look of sleep and confusion on his face. "Huh?"

She looked at him with pity. "Yeah, I kinda need you to gather your clothes and leave. It was hot, very hot. But you aren't staying the night."

He was obviously thrown off. "Uh, okay. I mean, that's cool. I respect that." As he gathered his shorts and put them on he asked for her number. "Maybe we can get together again while you're in town."

She looked away to place her watch on the nightstand, "Hon, that isn't going to happen. You're a great lay, but I have other plans."

"Sure, sure. Well, if you change your mind, I work at FIG tomorrow night, feel free to drop by."

She looked back sternly. "Jackson, I need you to get your ass out of here before you piss me off. You don't want to piss me off." She was losing her patience with Frat-tastic. *The kid couldn't take no for an answer.*

"Fuck, *okay*." Jackson quickly gathered his things and

headed to the front door. Still naked on the bed she heard him mumble under his breath as the door was closing, "Crazy-ass bitch." She thought to herself, *damn straight.*

# CHAPTER 30

*Day Six Ninety-One.*

THE CLOCK WAS SHOWING seven forty-seven a.m. when Cole woke, groggy, on Sunday morning. As with every morning for over two years, he woke up engulfed with the angst of sadness, loneliness...cold. He was usually a morning person, but his circadian rhythm annoyed the hell out of him on mornings like today where he had stayed out too late, but involuntarily woke up at sunrise. He and Ann had hit the Blind Tiger and grabbed a few beers before calling it a night. He couldn't recall when they got back, but the last time he looked at his watch it was two-thirty a.m. That wasn't a big deal, but waking at seven in the morning was like waking at five for him with the time change between the cities. He rolled back over and pushed his head under the pillow to ward off the light streaming into the room.

After tossing and turning for another thirty or so minutes, he sat up and attempted to text Ann. His eyes were crusty and coated from sleeping in his contacts. Blinking hard and then closing one eye like he was looking through a gun scope helped.

"U up yet chica?" He liked to mix his small grasp of

Spanish with English in his daily life. There was no immediate response to his text, and he hadn't expected one. With five international trips and too many years between them, he had come to know that Ann was anything other than a morning person. He had learned the hard way in Columbia when he'd delivered breakfast in bed in an attempt to get her up for a tour bus waiting outside full of other tourist to take them on a zip-lining expedition. Like a crazed, rabid raccoon or badger, she snapped, and food went flying to all parts of the room. Many 'what the fucks,' 'who the hells,' and 'fuck offs' later, she went silent and didn't speak another word to him until the she had finished the first zip-line.

While waiting for a response to his text, he checked another from Pam, another friend who lived in Atlanta. She had texted earlier in the morning to just wish Ann and Cole a good time. Pam was an early, early bird, getting up at like four every morning to work out and then get back home to see her husband off to work before heading out herself. She was a workout nut and Cole loved her for it. It kept him motivated to not fall too far behind.

"Hey sexy! Thx for the wishes. CHS is perfect and we r having a blast. How r u and the man?"

Within seconds of popping off the text a response was delivered. "We r great. Missing u bunches. Grab a drink for us at Magnolia's."

"Will do! Ttyl, jumping in the shower."

It was only after opening the shower's door that he recalled the panicked call and texts from his sister during the night. *What was that all about?* He had already seen her twice the day before when he picked up and dropped off Billy. What had happened since?

It wasn't like her to be dramatic anymore. She was

pretty even-keeled since having Billy. When her ass of a husband walked out with a fellow addict, it was a maturing experience, and he was proud of the way she had handled it. Cole turned on the shower after opening iTunes on his phone to sing off-key to some song he could barely hear over the water. He would call her after he got out of the shower, but first he needed to wake up and get some caffeine in him.

Showered and having fully killed the lyrics to James Taylor's "Steamroller," he went in search of coffee. He still hadn't seen or heard from Ann. It was almost nine in the morning. It wasn't unlike her to sleep till noon, so Cole had no concerns. *Best to let the beast lie.* Slipping on some lightweight blue seersucker shorts and a yellow V-neck tee, he walked out of his room into the hall.

The closest coffee was at the Charleston Grill, but Cole was too fragile to consider a sit-down restaurant for just coffee. As he wandered through to the King Street exit, he noticed the same woman from the morning before. There was no reason for this to stand out to Cole, as far as he was concerned; she was just another guest of the hotel. Several blocks later he found a coffeehouse and grabbed the used paper from the adjoining table to catch up on the local satire.

# CHAPTER 31

"ANN? ANN? ARE you in there?" There had still been no response from Ann and it was hitting eleven by the time he decided to go to her room and see if he could rouse her. Cole was getting concerned by the lack of response, but only because he promised he would head to Mount Pleasant and visit with Jackie before heading to the rest of the family. He had already texted Jackie and his parents to let them know he might be late. Jackie had simply responded, "b careful."

"Ma'am, did you happen to see the lady leave?" Housekeeping was outside the door when he arrived to check on Ann. The small Latino lady shook her head. "No one is in there."

"What? Are you sure?"

"Yes, I just turned down the room."

A puzzled look crossed Cole's face. Ann never got up early and it was certainly unlike her to not respond to a text at least by now.

"When did you get here?"

"Oh, uhm, about fifteen."

As Cole turned to look in the direction of the elevator he thanked the lady for her assistance.

*Where the hell could she be?* Ava had raised a good son

and that meant walking a lady to her door. He had seen the door close before he headed back to the elevator. *Shit.* He pulled out his phone and called her number. It went straight to voicemail. *Double shit.* "Hey, this is Cole. I don't know where you are or what you're doing, but I'm getting worried, woman. Your flight is at three back to Atlanta and I thought we were going to hang for a little bit before your sis came to pick you up for the airport. Give me a call." He headed back to his room, now completely worried about what could have happened to her.

Upon entering his room he shot off another text to Ann. "Dammit woman, where r u? ;-)" He added the winky face to ward off pissing her off. *No response.* He started to pick up the room some before heading to Jackie's, gathering his socks and dress slacks from the night before. He didn't immediately notice the envelope under his jacket when he first picked it up because he was still looking around the room. When he brought his eyes back to the bed, the bright white envelope caught his attention.

*Huh? What is this?* Its exterior was blank, with no indication of what it contained. It was a small, square, wax medallion-sealed envelope. Slowly he slipped his thumb under the gap at the edge of the medallion and slid it down the seal, separating it. He unfolded the letter, noting that it was made of fibers, linen it appeared, that had been pressed together. A note card was inside, its edges slightly frayed, but square.

He flicked it open with one hand, his coat still on his other arm. It contained several lines of handwritten, cursive words.

*Dear Cole,*

*Escape once, shame on you. Escape twice, shame on me. I will have what is mine.*

*I am before you…*

*Poinsett*

*What the fuck? Poinsett?* Cole puzzled over it for a few moments. "Ann? Are you here? Did you leave this?" There was no response. *Where did this come from?* He would have assumed he'd accidently picked it up last night somewhere but for it having been addressed specifically to him. *I don't have time for this shit. Ann, where the hell are you?* He shoved the note and its envelope into the pocket of his shorts.

Cole's worries were getting serious. Should he call Ann's sister and see if she had any clue where she was? He didn't want to raise concerns. He needed to leave, and he couldn't imagine Ann just taking off without saying goodbye.

From the door came a series of loud knocks and banging, in rapid succession. Someone wanted in and now. Cole cautiously went to the door and looked through the peep-hole. No one was there. "Hello?" There was no response. He repeated, "Hello?" Again, his greeting was unanswered. Slowly he turned the deadbolt and cracked the door. He peered through the crack to an empty hall.

# CHAPTER 32

"BOO!" COLE ABOUT shit his pants in surprise and fear as he opened the door to look out.

There before him, Ann stood wrapped in a towel, hair in a wet ponytail, grinning in her success in scaring Cole half dead by jumping around the corner.

Staring down, still trying to recover from the shock, Cole slowly looked up. "What the fuck, Ann? Shit, I almost hit you. And where have you been? I was about to call your sister."

Jumping up and down like a sparing boxer, she bounded into the room, still smiling and giddy. "I know, I know. I got your message, Mother. Seriously, I am sorry. I couldn't sleep. Not even the Xanex was working last night. So I hit the sauna about seven a.m. and totally passed out. Next thing you know I'm waking up and this turd was like, staring at me. My towel had fallen down and one of my nipples was showing. Should have charged the creep. I had no clue it was so late. I didn't look at my phone until just ten minutes ago when I left. I ran up here because I knew you had to head out soon… Here I am!" A huge smile was on her face.

"Yes, here you are," Cole said grudgingly. He had calmed down. There was no way for him to stay mad at

Ann. "Well you are just lucky, sister. This man was about to leave your ass. I gots places to goes." Cole jumped into thug talk just to show he was fine. He returned to picking up while talking to Ann. She had stopped bounding and was sitting on the edge of his bed watching him.

"I'm going to miss you, mister." She pursed her mouth to the right as if it pained her to say it.

"I'm going to miss you too, woman. But I'll be in Atlanta later this summer for work and we can hang. 'Ritas?" Long ago they had established a habit of sharing a few pitchers of margaritas, without salt, and catching up. Even when they lived a few miles apart they had to at least catch each other up on their dating lives. And, with Ann, there was always plenty to talk about.

Lying down across Cole's bed, Ann said, "Okay, I guess I can hold out till then. But promise me you'll consider my offer." Ann was referencing her recent offer to let him stay with her for his visits to Atlanta rather than stay in a hotel.

"Let me just see. I don't know how much I'll have to do while in town and don't want to be a bother."

Throwing up a limp arm like a drunk, Ann responded. "You are never a bother, so just hush."

Cole relented. "I'll think about it."

She sat back up. "Well, I'm just glad I caught you. I was scared I had missed you. That would have sucked a big one." Ann made large cow-sized chomps on her gum, clearly enjoying the moment.

"You had me scared, too. Next time, stop letting old men have free peep shows and answer your damn phone."

"Awh, but Cole, you know how I do love to give a good peep show." She pretended to offer a peep, grabbing the top of her towel and bringing it slowly down almost to her nipple while trying to recreate a Marilyn Monroe moment.

"Woman, ain't anything I haven't already seen." Cole smiled playfully. Ann acted in kind and covered back up. She knew he was right and she loved it. "True man, true. I wouldn't want to tempt you into being my baby's daddy." They both laughed. "Okay Jack, I'm out of here. My sister is picking me up in forty-five and we're going to the Charleston Tea Plantation to pick tea. That's right, she wants me to pick fucking tea on Wadmalaw Island. I drink that shit. I don't pick it; even if it's the only place in the country that grows it."

Cole laughed out loud. "Oh my god, what I wouldn't do to take pictures of that. I'd rather pick tea than subject myself to the interrogation I'll receive at the folks'."

"Your folks rock, shut the fuck up. Anyway, I better go. Thank you so much for the invite. The show last night was amaz-a-balls. And seeing you was okay, too, I guess." She was playing with Cole.

"Always a pleasure, ma'am. Anytime your hooves of feet want to stomp on my Bing Crosby's, you let me know." Cole continued to busy himself with picking up his loose belongings and piling them into his carry-on.

Ann looked down to her feet. "I got these toes all prettied up for this trip, thank you very much."

Looking up from organizing a pair of shoes, Cole asked, "What is that, one or two gallons of paint on those clodhoppers?"

Ann responded with feigned shock, "Ahh, bite me!"

"I would, but you would enjoy it."

Ann looked down at her feet again with a big smile

and looked back up as if looking over glasses. "Hehe, I would." She flashed a cheeky smile in acquiescence.

"Okay, woman. Get out of here." With that they hugged and parted. Cole threw the last of his belongings in his bag so the cleaning lady wouldn't have to pick up behind him. Within twenty minutes he was out the door and in his rental headed to Mount Pleasant.

# CHAPTER 33

THE FBI CLEARLY had a leak. The national news had all the details...the letters, the mutilations, even the kidnapping-murder connection, plastered on their websites and broadcasts. Poinsett was loving all the press. The victims' names were safe, for now, but the journalists had been ringing Leas' phone off the hook wondering who would be next. Extra scrutiny had descended on the investigation and the news was now interfering with Leas' ability to conduct his work. FBI profilers had made of list of likely characteristics: male, white, 30s, likely from an abusive background. 'Male' was struck off the list immediately based upon the video collected in Dallas. Within hours Leas would be on a plane to Charleston and hopefully start actually getting some real answers. Until then, Mouzon was on his own.

POINSETT SAT AT A TABLE in Starbucks thinking about what she just heard on the news and about how she had come to this wonderful place. She had escaped her mother when child services took her at twelve years old. But she hadn't escaped the heavy cruelty of her past. She was only in the foster home for a week before her foster dad snuck into the room and crawled into her bed with her, ignoring that two other girls slept just feet away in the same room. It would happen over and over again until she was eighteen.

Her only sanctuary was school, where she made straight As, which allowed her to go to college. Her first boyfriend, Sam, liked showing his love in openhanded servings. Her second boyfriend was always breaking things around the house, including her arms and legs.

Poinsett went back to the television. The news had it all wrong. According to them, the killer was likely a white male. The FBI was clearly not sharing all they knew. Two talking heads were on the screen discussing the murders and how the FBI handled such cases. If what they were saying was true, and she highly doubted it, the FBI would be swarming the next target now.

Soon, Poinsett would show them all that she could not be stopped, that they were helpless to save the unworthy, those who had thrown her into the abuse. The news was needed, even craved. She needed the Taker to know that they would all die. Mouzon was like all the others, a poster child of worthlessness in her eyes. Outside appearances would suggest he was the perfect Momma's boy, with success and good looks. But behind his blondish hair, tan cheeks, green eyes, and perfect teeth, he was weak and useless to this world.

To her, that was apparent from his taking over thirty years ago. *He should have never been allowed to live. Why? Why did he do that?* He was marked like cattle for the slaughter. But a nail to the head would be too good for him. No, his death would be slow and painful like the others. He would plead for his life. He would beg her to stop. But, slowly, the coldness of death would wash over him as he watched her take his life. He would feel her pain.

# CHAPTER 34

A S COLE DROVE over the massive new Arthur Ravenel Jr. Bridge, he recalled the 'old bridges.' The Ravenel was beautiful for sure, as the longest cable-stayed bridge in America with its double diamond shape, but nostalgia took over as Cole crossed over into Mt. Pleasant.

In his opinion, anyone who drove over the old bridges deserved a medal of honor for valor in service to this country. The experience would have brought the strongest and bravest to their knees. Before their removal, there were the 'old' and 'new' bridges. Traveling the 'old' meant really placing your life at risk for driving straight off into the Cooper River. The two-lane Grace was narrow, built with Model Ts in mind when constructed in 1929. Cole had always had two hands tightly on the wheel when crossing Grace for fear he would hit the car in the other lane, separated by maybe two inches, and propel himself into the depths of the Cooper. The cantilever steel bridges were so old the potholes were hollow, with nothing but the Cooper's waters at their bottom. There was no avoiding them, which meant always having to correct for the resulting force that seemed designed to throw you off the bridge. Rust was everywhere, and thick. Cole's folks always joked that but for the rust, the Grace would have fallen down many years earlier. All of this made it the perfect location for Bruce Willis to jump off a bridge in *Die Hard with a Vengeance*, though New York, not Charleston, got the credit.

Mount Pleasant, like the bridges, symbolized resilience long before Cole was born. Lying directly across from Charleston, over the Cooper River, it was home to the Sewee Indians until the English landed in the late 1600s. Almost immediately its new settlers were at war, fighting off the Spanish and French multiple times. The secession convention of Charleston on December 20, 1860, was a continuation of one held in Mount Pleasant three months earlier, which first recommended leaving the Union. The town would ultimately host the training ground for the crew of the H.L. Hunley, a Confederate submarine that was just recently located off the coast, and serve as its launch point via Breach Inlet, which lay between Sullivan's Island and current day Isle of Palms, directly off the coast of Mount Pleasant.

A FLOOD OF MEMORIES poured over Cole as he exited the bridge onto Coleman Boulevard. Palmettos lined the town's roads. The South Carolina tree, they grew like weeds in the lowcountry, but were prized ever since the Revolutionary War, where they were credited for saving Charleston from the English because their 'trunks' bounced incoming cannon balls like a military bed was supposed to bounce quarters. Locals have always been unwilling to part from those growing locally. That meant somewhere in the swamps of Florida, a land owner was being paid to ravage his land to deliver the plethora of cabbage palmettos which had been planted in the medians and along the sides of every street, making the entire area resemble a beach postcard.

Cole reflected on his childhood. Before he was born, his family lived with Granny on the IOP, or Isle of Palms. That ended when his father was injured working a construction site and the family fell on hard times. Between around three and twelve years of age, Cole and his parents lived in a trailer up the coast on Highway 17, an area nicknamed Eight Mile off of Rifle Range Road. Ultimately, his parents bought a piece of property further out on the marsh of the Wando River and built a stilted home there, where they still lived. Until recently, his Granny stayed in the city after having to sell the island house to help the family. No matter where Cole had lived, Mount Pleasant stood out to him as quintessential beach-town suburbia.

His use of the term 'parents' was relative. He was technically referring to his aunt and uncle, his mother having died in an auto accident when he was around two and there being no father around. They were the only parents he had known, and frankly, it was just easier to say parents instead of aunt and uncle, as it tended to avoid the mud bucket of questions that otherwise would arise. In his mind, they adopted him and he had long ago resolved his issues with not knowing his mother.

As he approached the bend in Coleman, he continued straight onto Whilden Street towards the 'Old Village' where Jackie lived. A few right turns landed him on Pitt Street where he saw the old pharmacy, where he would go after his pediatrician visits for a homemade cherry Coke. The storekeeper Annita must have been seventy, but worked behind the counter serving up malts, floats, and the best cherry Cokes. She would pour a glass-bottled

Coke from the thumping vertical bottle refrigerator under the counter and then dip a spoon into the maraschino cherry bin, pulling out a few spoonfuls of the syrup and a cherry. A stir and a straw, and it was ready to be slurped down on a hot summer's day. Her chocolate malts were the best malts to cure a poor kid's cold. The antique butter yellow rose vine from which Cole had picked flowers for Ava after finishing his malt still grew on the corner of the building, loaded with flowers like always.

The Old Village was a mini-Charleston, complete with shotgun homes, which got their name from the idea that you could shoot a shotgun from the front door into the long, narrow home and the shot would exit the back door. Almost all had piazzas, or what the rest of the world would call a porch.

With each turn Cole's mind spewed images of random facts about whatever he was seeing, things he had learned. His mind was constantly flooded with the flow of information it had stored since he was a child, occasionally bogging down his ability to think. *Stop!* His brain went silent.

As he turned right onto Center Street, Cole saw his sister's 'modest' home. In any other neighborhood the relatively new two thousand square-foot nondescript beach-style home would certainly be modest and a third the price. Its plantation shutters and aluminum roof were as common to the area as the nasty biting sand gnats.

But this was Mount Pleasant, and, like Charleston, the city was in demand, having doubled its population between 1990 and 2000, still being one of the fastest growing cities by percentage in the nation. His sister had 'married up' and she didn't deny it. For her part, she had been in love. She didn't accept until little Billy was born and almost two that William Sr. was a drug addict, and a mean one at that. Motherhood gave her the clarity she'd lacked as merely a woman. Being a mother and a police officer, she wised up fast and kicked him out of the million-dollar home, wherein he'd disappeared with some woman he met in rehab, losing custody of Billy even if he had wanted it. Cole was proud of his sister for standing up to the guy. Had he known what was going on, Jackie wouldn't have had to worry—William would have been chum for the swarms of bull sharks that swam off the edge of Jackie's marshy backyard.

# CHAPTER 35

A S HE PULLED up, Billy ran out of the house to Cole's car, screen door slamming behind him. He could hear Jackie inside the house yelling for the door.

The car door opened to Billy's face trying to squeeze in. "Hey 'lil man. Look at you! Is your mom feeding you Miracle Grow again? I swear you've grown two inches since yesterday." Billy laughed a kid's laugh, medium-pitched but full.

"Oh Uncle Cole, you know I only eat mac and cheese." He had grabbed a hold of Cole's leg like one of those toy monkeys that clasps on to a pencil, legs, arms and all.

Trying to walk toward the porch with his newfound ankle weight, Cole laughed and replied. "Mac'n cheese? That's it? What about shrimp'n grits?"

"Mom doesn't make that anymore. She's on a *diet*." Billy looked up, still attached firmly.

"What? Diet? I better talk to that woman. I can't have her starving my lil'man."

Billy let go after Cole took the first step onto the front door. They climbed the steps of the stilted house onto the wood plank porch hand-in-hand.

Like most homes on the town's edges, the house was stilted to ward off damage when the area flooded from the frequent lunar tides and storms. Cole had never seen a basement until he moved to Columbia for college. The water table was just inches down, making such things foreign to the area.

His sister was walking towards the screen door with a dish rag in her hand as Cole walked in. At five-ten, she was tall for a woman, and curvy. Her sweeping blond hair was raked over one shoulder and down her seersucker skirt and tucked white blouse. Typical of Jackie, she had no shoes on. "There's my favorite sister," Cole exclaimed as though the room were full of people. He was going in for a hug when she reminded him, "I'm your only sister," and shook her head.

"The only one we know of." Cole winked. It was a script he and his sister—technically his cousin—went through every time they were reunited. Though cousins by blood, they never recognized their relationship as anything other than brother and sister.

Jackie swung the dish towel at Billy. "Now what did I say; get those toys cleaned up before we head over to Nana's and Pop's in a bit."

Billy put his hands on his hips. "Uncle Cole interrupted me, Mom." He then walked over to the small living room displeased in being removed from the meeting.

"I interrupted him." Cole looked at his sister with a sideways smile and inspected her as he mimicked his nephew. She looked good, real good. Better than she had in some time. He wasn't around to see the damage William had done to her before she decided to stand up to him. But he'd flown into town immediately thereafter for a week, and she was a mess. The bruises would heal. But she'd just looked broken internally. Cole secretly hated himself for having not picked up on what was happening. Yet the two years since had obviously been good to her; she had color and life back in her.

With Billy out of ear shot, Cole pressed. "Okay, woman, what the he…" he stopped himself after remembering he was in the presence of a child. "What is going on? What was up with those calls and texts?"

Her face immediately showed pain. "I'm sorry. I knew you were out having a great time with Ann. How is she, by the way? I ran into her sister the other day."

"She's fine. Now, your calls. This can't be about the FBI agent….is William back?" Cole whispered the last part so Billy couldn't hear. Billy's father had all but disappeared after the divorce, but only after the court had made him hand over half his trust fund. With the blessing of the court, Jackie set up a new trust fund, with payments to cover the mortgage and living expenses of him and his mother. So William had no reason to stay in their lives. There were no child support or alimony payments to hand over. Billy was almost three when the divorce was final, and other than the occasional birthday card or random Christmas gift, he hadn't since seen since.

Jackie interrupted him. "Everything is fine. No, he isn't back and I hope he never comes back." She shook her head in disbelief at Cole's assumption. "No. I got that call from that FBI agent who was referred to me by the Charleston County Police, so…"

Throwing his hands to his sides, Cole reacted. "So what, Jackie? Oh my god. I called him back. He left a message and said he was coming to town tonight and would give me a call. That's all I know. God. Relax. You know I'm in no trouble because I can't recall the last time an officer called to say they were coming to arrest you.

I mean, that would kinda defeat the purpose, don't you think? So chill the fuck out, okay?"

"Well, fuck me, lil'bro, for caring. I'm just worried about you." The hushed use of cursing made Cole laugh at his sister's last statement.

"I know, I know." Cole cooled off, knowing she was just being his big sister. But he really didn't want to deal with this issue right now.

Jackie scrunched her nose and smiled to suggest she was calm now, too.

Still standing in the doorway of the home, Cole asked, "Now, are you going to let me in this house or are you hiding bodies somewhere?"

"Ha, I'm sorry. I totally forgot we were standing in the doorway. Yes, come in. Want some tea? Billy, that mess better be picked up in ten minutes or you aren't going to Nana and Pop's, hear me?" The argument passed fast, like the routine four p.m. thunderstorms, without any residual harm.

"Yes ma'am," came from the other room. Cole could hear Billy 'zrooming' with a toy car in the living room as they passed. *Billy wasn't afraid of his mom and her Glock.*

They walked into the kitchen and sat on stools at a large granite island, Jackie leaning in from across its yellow and brown speckled top to watch Billy in the other room while catching Cole up on the life and family drama he had missed out on since his last visit. After a few minutes his sister leaned around him to face the foyer and the living room. "Billy, you ready to be spoiled? You got that mess all picked up? It's time to go." Billy joined them as they walked toward the door. Cole looked into the living room to inspect the cleanup—*all clean. Perhaps Billy was scared.*

# CHAPTER 36

JACKIE AND COLE piled into separate cars. Billy had negotiated the honor of riding with his Uncle Cole and stepped into the front passenger seat. Cole looked over with surprise. "Uh, mister, are you thirty years old already?"

"No." Billy flashed a faux puppy frown as he slowly reopened the door.

"Well, then I think unless you want me killed by your mom, you need to sit in the back. Seatbelt…mister."

"Okay." Billy sauntered to the back passenger side and jumped in, and began latching his seatbelt.

Cole worked swiftly to mine Billy's brain for an update once the door was completely closed and they were alone. Turning his head to the back seat, he said, "Okay, it's just us men now. So, what's the story, mister; how many girlfriends you got?"

Billy was still fumbling with the belt as he spoke. "Uncle Cole…" Billy blushed as the conversation continued from there without a second of pause for the remainder of the trip. As they merged onto Highway 17 North Cole spied a sweetgrass basket stand. Remnants of the slave era, the hand-sewn marshgrass baskets existed only on a five-mile stretch of the highway. Nowhere else in the world could you find the yellow and brown striped baskets, except at the Slave Market in Charleston. As a child, the stands were plentiful and their baskets relatively cheap. But development and interstate widening had pushed the random scrap-wood framed stands to the edge of town, pressed against Francis Marion National Forest. Prices had skyrocketed exponentially as a result. His nanny, MeMe, had showed him how to make them during a visit to her house as a child, and he thought of her every time he looked at the basket they made, now back in Denver.

Pulling up to his parents' home, he admired how it had withstood the years without much exterior wear. Its pink, wood-sided frame had some mildew, but otherwise looked new. The heavy iron stains from the sprinklers were present at its base, but pretty much any house in the lowcountry that used sprinklers had the same stains, old or new. Randall Mouzon, his uncle and adopted father, was sitting in a rocker on the front porch with his pale jeans and typical patterned shirt. He could be in a Norman Rockwell painting. *A drunk Norman Rockwell*. The Thanksgiving one came to mind, with a drunk of a father stammering around with a very large knife, demanding a prayer be said. The entire table would acquiesce out of fear of igniting an outrage. Cole had lived that painting over and over again, Thanksgiving, Christmas, Easter… Monday through Sunday, it didn't matter. Jackie took the blunt of it, protecting Cole and Henry, her little brother, from the verbal rage of Jack Daniels. Cole took a deep breath as he started to walk toward the home.

Jackie pulled up behind his green Ford Focus with her dirty black Volvo SUV as Cole was assisting Billy in crawling out of the back seat. They reunited and walked up the long brick and moss covered pathway to the front porch.

"Dad, how goes it?" Randall stood up, standing almost as tall as Cole at six-foot-two. For the last ten years his father had been dry, and for that, Cole was proud. But he couldn't push off the fear and memories that had filled his life from early childhood until his father's new-found peace with the bottle. He never struck, but there was always the fear that would change. Cole had no clue what had brought on the condition, but from what he understood Randall had never had a problem when he met Ava, Cole's biological aunt. It was only when kids entered the picture that booze seemed to have eased the stress of life. Cole had always felt partially to blame, a burden to the family, though there was absolutely no support that anyone other than him felt that way.

Cole looked at Randall and noted old age now hung on him like a branch with too much Spanish moss and too little fortitude. Since going dry he had aged...a lot. They embraced as Randall responded. "...Oh, I've seen better, but can't complain."

Cole laughed. "Seen better? Better than this?" Cole waved his hands up and down his body, mimicking a *Price is Right* show girl, with a big smile.

Settling back down into the rocker, Randall joked back, "Boy, I've certainly seen better than those sticks you call legs. You better get in there and get some of your Mamma's hummingbird cake before you start trying to compete with this Adonis." He repeated Cole's movements over his now seated body making Cole laugh in a deep, heavy voice. His father had never lacked for a sense of humor, a trait conveyed to Cole.

Randall swatted at Cole's legs. "Boy, get on in there before your momma has a conniption fit."

Cole turned and entered, noting the home hadn't changed much since it was first built some twenty years earlier. The folks had obviously upgraded the furniture, but the colors and pictures were all the same. He liked the consistency of it all. It was home.

"Hey, hey baby. Hold on a second while I put down these potatoes." His aunt and adopted mom, Ava, was wearing a sundress of yellow and pink. Even at sixty-nine she held her beauty, the beauty that had made her Miss Shrimp Queen sometime in the early sixties down in Sanibel Island, Florida. She had on her 'kitchen slippers,' as she called them, pretty much glorified socks with some grip material on the bottom. Cole bought her them every year for Christmas at her request. Her dyed blonde hair showed black and grey roots. An apron prevented an obvious ketchup glob from getting on her floral summer dress.

Ava moved in for a hug. "Hold up Mom, you have something on your apron." She looked down, stuck her finger in the red smear and returned her finger to her mouth. Looking up, she proclaimed, "Ketchup," and smiled. She promptly removed the apron to hug Cole.

At the same moment Billy ran into the old yellow kitchen at the back of the house where Cole and Jackie were standing with their mother. Cole was released and Billy took his place. His mom leaned down, suffocating him with her fleshy arms.

"Nana, I found a frog!" From behind his back he revealed his treasure, a fat green frog larger than a cantaloupe. Ava immediately released him, her hands flying into the air, and looked in amazement.

"Oh, that's a baby bullfrog. Probably getting ready for that storm coming next week. Angela, Andrea, hell if I know…some woman who pissed off a weather guy." The aged, raspy voice had come from behind Cole.

"Granny!" Cole moved in fast for a large hug. At five-five, she hugged his waist while he was left trying not to implement a choke-hold on her neck.

"Hey pumpkin." Her arms tightened. In the past year his grandmother had moved into a mother-in-law suite off the back of the house. Randall and Ava were getting up there themselves at sixty-eight and seventy-two, and taking care of Granny was certainly taxing them. Jackie had stopped taking them up on baby-sitting for over a year because their plates were full babysitting Granny.

As Cole looked at his grandmother he laughed to himself. Granny was, well, Granny. She was full of spirit, spunk and energy…more energy than even Billy. But she had fallen and hurt her hip a few years back and her mobility was failing. Her weathered, deep-wrinkled skin reminded Cole of some historic photos he had seen of Native Americans from the 1800s—sturdy, defiant, and noble.

"Pumpkin, you want some tea. Billy wants some tea, don't you?" Granny's sweet tea was famous with kids and dentists, both thankful for her ability to cram as much sugar into liquid form as possible without making it syrup. Granny looked down at Billy like she was luring Hansel and Gretel to take a bite of her candy house. Granny was a spoiler. As she put it, "It's retribution for all the grief you gave me when you were growing up." She always said that with a huge smile and ended with more of a cackle than a laugh, whether from her decades of smoking or her intent, it was unknown. But, it was known the woman was wonderfully evil and slightly crazy.

Cole decided to tempt her. "Granny, how the men treating you? Find a sugar daddy yet?"

Busy pouring Billy a tall glass of 'insta-hyper,' she responded. "Ha, sugar daddy? I've got enough sugar for me and five others! The question is have *you* found any sugar lately?"

She had successfully turned the focus on him. He threw up a hand as if to say 'no more' and said, "Uh, no. And, if I had, I wouldn't be telling you, dirty old lady. Don't make me put you in a home." They both laughed. Being in the Mouzon family required thick skin and a lot of humor.

Billy rushed out the door with the frog, leaving an empty glass on the counter. Cole turned back to hear Granny speaking. "I was going to go out to the dock after dinner and go gigging for fish. You want to come with the old lady? I promise to not out-fish you." An evil grin crossed her face and her eyes went slender. She always out-fished you. "Nah, I've got plans after dinner, but perhaps before I leave. But only if you cook up some of those flounder." The planned meeting with Leas was still on Cole's mind. He dreaded whatever the FBI agent was coming to discuss.

Granny smiled at Cole's response. "Deal."


COLE STEPPED BACK to take in the moment. With everyone but Cole's dad crowded in the kitchen, it felt like home. Cole's dad was the strong, silent type, and so he was often left to his own thoughts in reunions like these. During his drinking years that was a welcomed habit. But

Cole secretly desired that for one sitting, the family could be that Rockwell painting. When his father did open his mouth, it was to either scold or to joke. Over the years the ratio had switched in favor of joking. He had always been a good father, but not necessarily the most emotionally available. That had changed when he went dry. Cole and his sister agreed he had gained a new appreciation for family and happiness that he'd never showed before that change.

Granny came alongside Cole and grabbed his hand. "Sit, sit, baby. Let the old lady grab a tea, too. Ava, you finish that coleslaw, that boy looks starved. Don't they feed you out there in Colorado? See, that's what happens when you move somewhere that doesn't know how to cook grits. I bet they only bake their chicken out there, don't they?" Granny was being playful—she knew full well they had KFC like the rest of the world.

Cole sat on a stool on the far side of the white marble counter and continued talking to Ava while Granny ran about here and there. When she delivered his tea and Cole looked at her she went in for another hug. The warmth of her love washed over him as, still seated, Cole wrapped his arms around her with his head landing squarely on her very large breasts, or 'baboombas,' as she called them. They felt like a pillow.

Released, Cole turned to Jackie. "Sister, what happened to you?" Cole asked, referencing the clear discrepancy between his sister's breasts and the other women's in the room.

Jackie looked down and back up. Before she could respond, Granny piped in, "Pumpkin, you know I always told you that 'more than a handful is a waste.' See this? Waste." She waved her hands over her breasts. "Back in the day, your grandpa and I would go scooter pootin' around the the ba'try, and stop to watch the submarine races at night when no one was around. You know, I never did see a submarine." She winked impishly.

"Granny!" Ava exclaimed, playfully appalled, her hands now full with a mandolin and a bowl of shaved cabbage. Cole just shook his head. Yes, his grandmother had said that many times and he loved it each and every time.

Jackie had her hands on her hips. "Well, I get no complaints."

"Indeed, sis. How *is* your dating life?" Cole felt comfortable throwing his sister to the wolves. His mother and Granny would focus their attention on her and avoid him at least for thirty minutes or so.

# CHAPTER 37

L EAS HAD ONLY BEEN back in Quantico a few days when he was notified the FBI had located Mouzon visiting in Charleston. After attempts to locate him by phone had failed, he was instructed to get there fast and make personal contact before anything happened. *Who is this Mouzon character and what is in Charleston?*

It was Sunday and his mind was racing as he boarded his three forty-five p.m. Delta flight to Charleston. The city was foreign to him. He knew it had started the Civil War with shots at Fort Sumter and was an original colony. He'd learned in college that it had its share of violence, too. In fact, the first documented American serial killer was a woman, Lavinia Fisher, who poisoned and killed numerous men and woman in Charleston between 1810 and 1820. From what he could recall, Fisher and her husband were part of a gang of highwaymen. Together, they operated Five Mile and Six Mile House, along the Ashley River in current day North Charleston and just south of Middleton Place Plantation, a spot then called Ashley Ferry. *The Charleston News and Courier*, still operating today, reported on the events with enough excitement to rival the likes of CNN or Fox News.

The reporting detailed how the gang, including Mrs.

Fisher, was frustrating Charleston's trade routes with their thefts and murders. Locals, dissatisfied with the authority's response, implemented 'lynch law.' A cavalcade of horses and riders descended on the property, and advised the residents and guests that if they did not depart within minutes, they would be lynched. All left, only to return and attack the watchman left by the citizens. Mrs. Fisher, for her part, was first to attack, choking the watchman Dave Ross and shoving his head through a window. Ross would ultimately be saved from his otherwise impending doom by a passerby. With this the authorities acted, capturing Mrs. Fisher and a majority of her gang.

The Fishers were never convicted of murder, though numerous bodies were found on the inn's property. But the sentence for highway robbery was a public hanging, because such a crime was a capital offense in early America. On February 18, 1820, the hanging was convened and Mrs. Fisher impressed and insulted the crowd into silence with her large collection of expletives. She cursed Charleston, its government and its citizens for 'letting a woman swing.' Her last words were the most memorable, telling the crowd, "If you have a message you want to deliver to hell, give it to me—I'll carry it." Though certainly not as wicked as Aileen Wuornos's final words to her jury, wherein she said, "May your wife and children get raped, right in the ass," Mrs. Fisher's remarks were certainly shocking for the time. The *Post and Courier* described to its readers that Mrs. Fisher died almost immediately. Mr. Fisher wasn't so lucky, struggling, gasping, and swinging for minutes before death consumed him.

Looking down at a file labeled 'Mouzon,' Leas

didn't know what to expect when he finally landed in Charleston. But whoever was killing those who had been taken thirty years earlier was moving fast. Mouzon appeared to be the last of those survivors. Everything in the background check his office had pulled together said the guy was highly intelligent, having aced law school at Emory. The CIA had actually tried to recruit him in law school but he'd declined. Leas thought that move alone showed 'smarts.' Mouzon was going to need his 'smarts' if he was going to survive.

# CHAPTER 38

COLE WALKED OUTSIDE with the potatoes Ava had previously washed, joining Randall, who had come around to the back of the house to start dinner, frogmore stew. Randall heated the water in a giant pot over a gas burner and added a pouch each of Old Bay and Zatarains seafood spice bags to form the base for what the rest of the world would just call a seafood boil. Cole craved a beer. In the ten years since his father got dry, Cole had avoided drinking alcohol around him out of respect, even though his father was clear he would never touch the stuff again.

"So, Dad, what have you been up to since retiring?"

"I got me a job at the new Royal Hardware on Highway 17; I think my official title is 'customer liaison.' That's a fancy way of saying bag boy. Keeps me busy though and out of that hen coop." His father looked behind him to the house to reference the women inside and grinned. He continued for a few moments talking about the tools he sold and the crazy customers that walked through the door on a routine basis in a flustered attempt to finish a home-improvement project they should have never started. Cole could see his father enjoyed the escape from what would otherwise be a quiet life in the marsh backwoods.

"Where's Henry nowadays?" Cole said.

Replying without looking up from the boiling water, Randall responded, "Oh, he's down in Ft. Myers with Ava's sister Fran. Got some t-shirt business or something down there. You know how he is."

Cole nodded. Henry, Randall and Ava's son, had always been independent and aspiring for the next big thing. Though only twenty-three, he had already started a gourmet pancake restaurant, been a partner in a para-sailing company and tired his hand at a tax return prep shop—all ultimately flopping hard to the ground like his pancakes.

"So, you dating anyone?" His father had decided to pick up where the ladies had left off. Dating and relation-ships were things Cole never really talked much about and moments like this flustered him deeper into silence.

"Nah, not really. Well...at least nothing serious." Randall dropped the large bowl of washed potatoes into the pot—now a rapid caldron of hot, spiced water.

"Well, you know we love Billy and all, but your mom and I would love to see you with some children, son. You would make a good father. But, more importantly, we aren't getting any younger—so you best get to it and soon." His father smiled, showing his playful side while looking up, his head tilted towards Cole. His father rarely gave compliments, so when he did; it was known to be heart-felt.

Cole was shocked for a moment before he spoke. Rubbing his forehead, he said, "That is certainly on the list. I need to find someone who will marry me first, though. But, don't you worry; I'll make sure the kids drive you utterly crazy like we did." Cole patted his dad on the back and Randall looked up with a large grin. Cole knew retribution for all his childhood shenanigans was in store when he had kids.

With the sausage and onion already dropped in, Cole's father added the shrimp, shells on, into the pot and let them boil until just pink. Cole called his family as instructed by Randall and the entire family ran out, Ava in the rear with a stack of paper plates. Billy was pushed back while Cole and his father lifted the large pot, almost overflowing with water and its load, and poured it out onto newspaper that had been placed on top of the old wood picnic table. Scalding water went everywhere, spilling to the ground as the rest of the family held their plates at the edges to act as a lip to hold the bounty on the table. Once the water had completely run off, Billy scooped up the first plate as the youngster. He was followed by Granny and the rest of the women before Cole and his father dove in, Cole focusing on the shrimp and sausage.

The adults now sitting around a glass patio table on the screened-in back deck of the house, Granny said, "Bet you don't get this out there in Colorado?" Granny was dipping a shrimp in homemade cocktail sauce with one hand and holding a Bud Lime in the other. She clearly didn't subscribe to Cole's line of thinking about booze around his dad. "No, ma'am. No roadside-fresh shrimp or crabs to bring home, and certainly no boils."

Granny smiled at his response; it was obvious that she saw potential for continued visits home in Cole not having such things. The family was quiet as they looked out over the marsh, enjoying its fruits. Consistent with its meaning in the South, dinner was served at three p.m.—the term supper was reserved only for a late, final meal of the day. In Cole's youth, that meal was served Monday through Saturday, around nine pm. It was too hot any sooner than that to get in the kitchen to cook where the night temperature might drop ten degrees in an average ninety-five degree, one-hundred percent humidity day.

SUNDAYS WERE ALWAYS special days in the Mouzon family. Until Cole was a teenager, the routine was fixed. Granny came over in her giant gold Cutlass Supreme at ten a.m. from her home behind the Red and White in the heart of town. Sticking out the window were three fishing rods, one each for Jackie, Cole, and her. Jackie and Cole would pile in the back after Granny caught up over coffee with his dad and mom. Henry, their always-reclusive younger brother, wouldn't join until he was four and Cole fourteen. Until then, Cole and Jackie would head off to some pond up in Awendaw, over the Wando River, and unpack and wait.

Sunday was God's day in Granny's book, and you were not allowed to drop in your pole into the green-dyed water until twelve noon on the dot. Until then, you were on 'the Big Man's time,' whether you went to church or not.

With God's approval to clock-in after twelve noon, Jackie and Granny would use bread balls on their cane poles, created by spitting on a small piece of bread and molding it around the hook into a ball. Then, with a glorified, overly-long stick with fishing line tied at the top end, they would swing the hook and attached bobber out. Their bobbers would dip, dip, dip, and then go under before Cole had a chance to dig a fat worm out of the rusty tin can his Granny had placed them in while gardening the day before. The score was never in Cole's favor. Whether by numbers, size or kind, Granny always won. Even when the kids challenged her and she agreed to sling an empty hook against their bait, she was the victor within ten seconds. By three Cole and his sister would usually be tired and starved, the Lance cheese toast and peanut butter nabs Granny gave them having worn off some time earlier.

Like today, Cole would long for dinner and all the food his Ava would have prepared during the cool morning hours. And like then, the remainder of today would consist of lounging around the house, with occasional small bites to eat. Little was done on Sundays back then. Cole's Sundays in Denver were drastically different: cross-fit at Red Rocks Amphitheater promptly at seven a.m., followed by errands, then a brunch or some other social event with friends, and closing the day with a long run after sobering up from too many bottomless mimosas or beers at brunch.

In this moment, surrounded by his family, Cole missed the simplicity of his youth. His mind fought, trying to linger on the FBI agent coming to town, but he pushed it out, telling himself there would be ample time to deal with that issue later. But, for now... *Let the warm salty air flow over you and relax, Cole.*

# CHAPTER 39

AVA WALKED BACK in the house to refill the sweaty pitcher of iced tea, when someone knocked on the front door. From the back deck, Cole could hear Ava greeting someone. "Well hey there Blueberry! What brings you here?"

"I just saw the car in the drive and recalled you saying Cole was going to be in town, so I figured I'd stop bye and say hi."

"Well, of course, come on in. He's just in the kitchen." The entire exchange had been overheard by Cole and his sister, who along with the rest of the family had followed Ava and were now standing in the kitchen. As soon as the invite had been issued, Jackie mouthed a 'shit.' They had history.

Cole had walked into the house through its glass doors and joined his mother in the foyer. "Hey there, Blueberry. How's life?" The six-foot, three-hundred-pound man clogged into the kitchen with Cole and Ava while Jackie tried to hid behind her brother. "Jackie, is that you back there?"

She peeked her head out from behind Cole. "Oh hey. Sorry, I dropped a fork. How you doing, Blueberry?" Her tone suggested Blueberry Mildred's visit was no big deal.

Cole looked humorously perplexed at his sister and then back at their guest. His faded jeans and yellowed t-shirt were a bit too loose, and but for a giant belt wrapped around his waist his pants would likely fall to the floor.

"Doin' good, Jackie, doin' rear good." His Moncks Corner lazy-jawed accent sounded thick like sorghum served on biscuits. Cole could swear he had a wad of dip in the pocket of his jaw.

"I heard you was in town. How's the fancy life in Hotlanta?" Cole had no clue how Blueberry got his name, but he'd had it when he landed at Wando High School his sophomore year.

"Have a seat, Blueberry. Make yourself comfortable." Ava was playing host as Jackie tried to pretend like she was washing tea glasses in the sink.

The large man shook his head. "Oh, Mrs. Mouzon, I can only stay for a bit. The wife's in the car." Cole and Jackie simultaneously looked out the kitchen window and its slatted plantation shutters to view a large silver pick-up with someone in the passenger side. *Double shit.* Jackie wasn't happy to see the company but her mother didn't pick up the clue. "Well, invite her in, by all means."

Cole attempted to steer the conversation back to their guest, hoping Blueberry didn't take Ava up on her invitation. "Awh, man, I moved to Denver two years ago. It's beautiful out there. Ever been?"

"Me? Nosiree, farthest I've been is Stuttgart, Arkansas for some duck hunt'n. But I've heard it's real nice out there. Real nice. What took you there?"

"Man, just needed a change, that's all. Atlanta is nice and all, but I like being outside year-round and the Atlanta summers are just too damn hot and the winters just too cold for me."

Blueberry chuckled, "Colder than Denver? You're crazy."

Cole heard someone walking in the foyer as he spoke. "No sir. With no humidity, it's amazing how comfortable thirty degrees is. Plus, we rarely get snow that lasts."

"Barbra-Ann, get you ol'ass in this house and say hi." Granny decided to stir the pot. Cole looked over to see Ava's head down in embarrassment, clearly appalled at the means of invitation. From what Cole could gather, Granny was at the front door yelling across the lawn. "Hell girl, you doing that Paleo diet or something? You're looking real good." Granny was holding the door as she walked in.

"Thank you Mrs. Mouzon, I was burning up in the truck. Some people have *no manners*." A stern look firecrackered across the room to Blueberry. Resting somewhere around five and a half feet, Barbra-Ann was almost as wide as she was tall. Her attempt at style made Granny's outfit of pink sweatpants and a Christmas t-shirt look in vogue. A torn t-shirt that said "got pork," a clear pun on the milk commercial overhung Barbra-Ann's tattered, stringy daisy dukes, suggesting to the casual viewer that she had no shorts on at all. Lumps of cellulite could be seen fighting for air at the shorts' lacking hem.

"Jackie." Barbra-Ann nodded her head at Cole's sister like two enemies playing nice. In high school Jackie had momentarily swooped in on Blueberry and snatched him from his then and now lover. Not appreciating the action, Barbra-Ann sliced the tires of Blueberry's gold El Camino. Two days later, they were back together. That was twenty-five years and several pounds ago, and Jackie never looked back. She started dating Billy's father a year later and inherited a whole 'nother bag of earth worms.

Cole was no fan of Barbra-Ann's either; she had been his childhood bully. Around the same time in school, all four of them plus Barbara-Ann's sister Wanda and her boyfriend Poon were playing spin the bottle out at the Moon, an old sand quarry at the edge of town that got its name from its moon-like landscape. After losing horribly to the girls, the two older boys went skinny-dipping and the girls joined. While watching from the edge, Barbara-Ann got out of the pit, snuck up behind Cole and pushed him in. When he attempted to swim, she jumped in, pinning him with her large buttocks to the sandy floor. Half-drowned and crying, his only savior was Jackie, who pulled him from his otherwise impending death by lard.

Cole cut his eyes to Jackie, scrubbing the same glass she had picked up when the conversation started fifteen minutes earlier. She wrinkled her nose back and turned to focus on Billy playing in the front yard. Several minutes of conversation passed before the tension in the room was too much and the Mildreds decided to leave.

With the guests gone, Cole said, "I think I better go, too. I'm supposed to meet a friend later and want to get this shrimp smell off me." Cole lied. He wanted to head back to his hotel and prepare for the FBI meeting. Throughout the day he hadn't forgotten about Agent Leas, which he and Jackie had agreed not to mention to the family. Worrying them was not something he entered into lightly.

# CHAPTER 40

BACK AT THE HOTEL, Cole jumped sideways on the bed and closed his eyes for a second. *What does the FBI want?* Finally he reached into his pocket and pulled out the small slip of paper his sister had given him, flicked it open and read the number. He dialed it slowly, pausing before he hit the last number. The phone rang several times without an answer. Finally, a recording came on. "You have reached Agent David Leas of the FBI's Critical Incident Response Group. Please leave your name and number and I will return your call promptly." The 'beep' came quickly and Cole had to clear his throat before talking. It hung up on him. *Shit.* Now he felt stupid, like a boy who calls a girl but is too nervous to speak. Worse yet, he felt it made him look *guilty*. Guilty of what, was the question. Perhaps the movie execs had discovered that bootleg movie he downloaded last week. *I didn't watch it, promise!* He punched in Leas' number again and caught the beep with a clear throat, leaving his name and number, inviting him to call when he finally landed in Charleston. *Well, the waiting is sure going to suck.*

Cole turned back into the bed. He didn't have to wait long. Fifteen minutes after Cole's message, Agent Leas returned his call. He was finally in town. When questioned, he refused to speak over the phone about the reason for his calls, wanting to meet in person. They arranged to meet at six p.m. across the street at City Lights Coffee, the hipster coffee place Cole had passed by earlier. That gave Cole thirty minutes to prepare himself for the likely interrogation.

# CHAPTER 41

COLE WALKED INTO City Lights and admired the retro décor of old jars and 50s mugs. It reminded him of hipster spots in Denver and Portland. He had no clue who he was looking for. Agent Leas said he would find Cole, as he knew what he looked like. *Great, the FBI has my pic,* ran through Cole's head when that was said. Not a surprise, but still... The recent news of the NSA tapping phones and internet was no big surprise to him. He had long figured that anything typed, mailed, or spoken over the air was fair game whether they wanted to admit it or not. It didn't mean it didn't still make him uncomfortable.

"A cappuccino, please." The tattooed cashier turned to the machine behind her to make his order when he heard his name spoken. He turned and was greeted by a man, maybe six feet tall, average build with creamed-coffee skin. He was older, perhaps early forties. "Agent Leas?" Cole twisted his head up at a slight angle as he spoke.

"Yes, David Leas. Thank you for your time, Mr. Mouzon."

"Of course. Would you like anything before we sit

down?" Cole turned back as the tattooed girl was returning with his coffee.

"Coffee, black for me." Cole placed and paid for the order. He never minded picking up the tab, especially for servicemen and officers. After collecting Leas' coffee, they found a small couch and chair in the corner with a retro coffee table between them. Taking opposite sides, they sat.

As Cole was getting settled on the old red velvet couch, Leas inquired, "Mouzon? Is that French?" He was 'creating rapport,' a 101 trick for cross-examination that Cole himself used in his cases. Small talk typically permits a witness to relax and spill their guts, good and bad, or at least make conflicting statements.

Cole nodded his head after taking a sip. "It is. French Huguenot to be exact. My family came from Ville de Mouzon during the persecution in France, back in the late 1600s, and settled in Charleston. Ultimately, they possessed large parts of South Carolina, with a great-grandfather or uncle mapping the state so well, the map was used until just last century."

"Oh, wow, so your family had been here some time?"

"Indeed, Agent. They fought with the Swamp Fox, as in the movie *The Patriot,* in the Revolutionary war, and to some extent in the Civil War. Though, much like my French pedigree, that property was lost some time ago. My dad was a poor farmer's kid. To listen to him tell of seeing chickens through the living room floor is something to hear." Cole's words were crisp as he spoke very formally. He wasn't willing to get casual with Leas.

"Huh, but you came out okay. I mean, you're a lawyer right? And a good one, from what I hear."

Cole gave a short laugh. "I don't know who you've

been talking to, but I like poor rumors like that. But, yes, I did come out okay. I have a great family. Now, Agent, are you going to tell me why you've flown to Charleston to interrupt my vacation, or what?" He'd had enough idle chatter. It was time to discover the agent's interests.

"Mr. Mouzon, I'm here to talk to you about Tony Patrick. How do you know him?"

"Who?" Cole's faced squinted into an obvious question mark.

"Tony Patrick, in Dallas, Texas." Leas patted a short stack of files laying beside him to emphasis his statement.

"Agent, I have no clue who you're talking about."

"Are you Facebook friends with him?" Agent Leas played dumb, knowing that the status on Patrick's account in Dallas said they weren't.

Cole reflected, mining his head for any reference to a Patrick. Images of his account flickered across his eyes. "I'm not seeing it, but I can't say for sure. I mean, it's possible. I have several 'Facebook friends' that I have never met, have never talked to. Hold on a second..." Cole took out his phone and opened the Facebook app. As he typed in P-A-T, it auto-filled to Leslie Patmeric, nothing else. "It looks like I'm not." Cole looked up at Agent Leas. "Let me pull up this guy's profile picture and see if I recognize him..." Several 'Tony Patrick' listings appeared. Scrolling through them, Cole said, "Nope. Not anyone I've met."

"Hmm, you have never met any of those guys?"

Cole shook his head. "Sorry, Agent. If I have, I certainly don't recall, and it wouldn't have been anytime soon. I haven't been to Dallas in a couple of years. Why do you ask? Did he say he knew me?"

"No, no he didn't say that, but he isn't saying very much anymore. He's dead."

Until that point Cole had been coasting. He was an interrogator himself, and little shook him. *But, dead?* That got his attention. *Shit, shit, shit... who are my alibis? Ann will suck at this.*

Cole choked out a few more words. "Excuse me? And how am I involved in that?" His eyes tightened again as he waited for the answer.

Leas leaned in some. "Well, it seems your profile was open on his computer at or immediately after the time he was killed." The term *killed* stuck in Cole's head.

"You mean to tell me that Mr. Patrick was Facebook-stalking me when he was killed?"

"No. Not exactly. We actually think the killer accessed your profile *after* killing Mr. Patrick."

Cole's mouth dropped. "What! Who the hell would want to look at *my* profile? I mean, I'm not a Facebook whore. It's pretty rare that I post." Cole was getting anxious and confused. The idea of some killer checking out his profile was unacceptable. "Do I need to call my credit card company or something? I mean, are they trying to steal my identity?" A much darker possibility had crossed his mind but he was hoping it wasn't true.

"Mr. Mouzon, there was also a travel site pulled up and..."

Cole's mind raced. *Shit, shit, shit...*

"Whoever it was checked flights to Denver the same night Mr. Patrick was murdered."

*...SHIT.* Cole covered his eyes in disbelief of what he was hearing. "Officer... Sorry, *Agent*, are you telling me that a murderer is in Denver looking for me?" He had no clue why he whispered the last few words.

Agent Leas leaned across the coffee table, his coffee still in both hands. "Mr. Mouzon, we can't rule that out.

*And...* we can't rule out that they found out you are here in Charleston. We've pulled the last-minute bookings between Dallas and Denver, Dallas and here, from the day of the murder till today; and we will keep monitoring those until we figure out where the person is. That should help us narrow suspects in that murder."

Cole took a big swallow of his cappuccino and quickly realized it was still a bit too hot. The roof of his mouth blistered. *Great!* But the distraction helped him calm down. The mental wall went tightly up. A cold, unemotional state passed over his body. His brain went into silent overdrive, thoughtless but humming, ready to process the next piece of information it was given.

It was a coping mechanism he had always possessed; from what, he had no clue. He once again envisioned all his personal feelings, emotions, and thoughts being crammed into the crevice from which they had seeped and it 'cleared the room' for his cold, analytical side to work highly efficiently. As a lawyer it worked perfectly for Cole to 'zone in' on a case and its facts, which he then could release when he got home. But at times it had become hard to release, leaving him isolated from everything around him...trapped by his own protector.

"Agent, you being here tells me there is more than one body. I did criminal defense and represented a few alleged murderers, including a serial murderer or two, in my day. The FBI thinks there is a serial murderer out here, doesn't it?" Cole's words were parsed like some newscaster...too formal for the setting.

He knew, contrary to popular belief, serial murderers rarely kill across state lines. They have a territory or 'comfort zone' defined by an anchor point, usually their home, place of work, or another similar place. When they do kill in multiple states, it is usually a product of confidence through past success or from fear of being caught. And when they do, the FBI steps in. Otherwise, the local police handle it all with maybe some advice from the FBI.

Agent Leas looked down and then into Cole's eyes. "I am here to make sure that there are no more bodies. Do you get that? And that means I need your help."

"What can I do? Until just now I had never really heard of this Patrick guy. Who are the others? Can you connect them to me in some way?" Cole waved his arms in frustration as he asked.

Agent Leas shook his head. "Directly, no. But, well… let me ask you this. Do you have a scar on your right lower back?"

# CHAPTER 42

H OW DID HE know about my scar? Cole was still staring at Agent Leas, running this question through
his mind. He put his large mug down on the coffee table
and moved his right hand around his back to touch it.

Speaking in skeptical words, Cole asked, "Why do
you ask?"

"From your look and the fact that you just checked it
with your hand I'll take that as a yes. The others, all three,
had scars in the same spot. I'm going to take a wild guess
as say it's small, maybe an inch high and wide, with what
appears to be a 'P' inside the box. Am I right?"

There was a long pause before Cole answered. "No.
Mine's a large gash, about the same size as you mentioned, but there is no box. I've had it for as long as I can
remember. I was playing with cousins at my Granny's.
We were horse playing on a tall pile of top-soil for her
garden and I fell against her joggling board."

"Her what?"

"It's a Charleston thing; think yoga ball from the
1800s. A very long, flimsy board suspended at two ends,
painted Charleston green. You sit and bounce on it. I
think it turned into some dating tool or something; but
like most things Charleston, it sticks around because,

well... it's old and we like old. Granny's had a broken corner, so when I fell against it, it cut my back. But why are you asking about my scar?"

"Mr. Mouzon..."

"Please, call me Cole." Cole felt weak in permitting the Agent to call him by his first name. It went against his rules of engagement. But he justified it since the guy appeared to be here to actually save his life.

"Thank you... Cole, do you remember that happening?"

"Well, no. I was like maybe one and a half, two when that happened. I can't recall that far back. But my mom can certainly tell you all about it. From what I understand, she about killed my cousins and my Granny switched them good from what I recall." Cole's childhood is where his memory failed him. He had tried to access it many times as a teen. But, it was just black until he was maybe three or four. He could never remember a time Ava wasn't his mother. The only image he had of Libby Mouzon, his birth mother, was that of her picture in an old gold frame in his grandmother's home.

"Mr... Cole, the other three, they had similar scars. None of them knew each other and they came from different parts of the country. I read some files on the plane that indicate, well... They indicate all three were kidnapped somewhere between the ages of one and two and disappeared for up to a week before being found. When they were found, they had a scar, the same scar you have, though it sounds like yours was removed."

Cole shook his head in disbelief. "Dude, are you fucking crazy? I wasn't kidnapped as a kid." This was more than he had ever expected when he scheduled this coffee date, and he was just trying to digest it. He leaned back into the couch as Leas turned slightly to pull something out of a pack of folders held together by a red rubber band. He withdrew a folder with some Post-it flags and passed it to Cole, who immediately speed-read through the pages.

Just pages in, Leas added, "Cole, you *were* kidnapped when you were two. It's all in there. It took some digging at the Mount Pleasant Police Department by our guys, but, at least from what it says in there, you weren't injured by horseplay. Someone snatched your mother and you and you both disappeared for five days. Like the others, you had been branded with a 'P.'"

Cole's head hurt. *What was he saying? Kidnapped?* But he had no memory of that...just blackness.

Leas kept going. "The scary thing, if it can get any scarier, is that your mother and you, and the other kid, appear to have been the first kidnapped, branded, and then released across the country between 1982 and 1983. Your mother was tortured and died, but only after escaping with you and one of the boys. In all the other cases, the parent or parents were killed, slaughtered. And it was only here, with you, that more than one kid was taken at the same time."

*Kidnapping, branding, release...escape.* The words circled in Cole's head like flies. No amount of mental swatting would knock them down so he could think. He placed his hands on either side of his head, looked down, and closed his eyes in deep thought. The wall was partially down and he was trying to push it back up.

Agent Leas was patient, letting Cole take it all in. He had been here before in other cases and learned that the best approach was a slow one.

Cole's steely persona, momentarily shaken, was back.

He looked up and placed his hands on his knees. "So, what are we going to do about this? From the sounds of things someone is out to collect what escaped thirty, thirty-one years ago? Well, I'll be damned if I'm going to go down like that. Point me in his direction and then get out of the way." Cole's anger was seeping out.

"Hold up, Mr. Mou... Cole. The worst thing you can do is go off half-cocked and seek out this person. From what we know so far she acts slowly and either watches or studies before she acts. I doubt she has had enough time to get here and do that sufficiently to feel comfortable acting. Comfort is a big deal to these fucked-in-the-heads. So, let's just think about this. Have you noticed any suspicious people, has anything suspicious happened lately?"

COLE LIKED HIS idea better. He had represented enough criminals to know how to take someone out successfully and get away with it. But for now he would agree to work with Agent Leas. Cole rested his chin on his left fist, which was being supported by his knee, and shook his head. Unfolding his fist and running his fingers down his five o'clock shadow, Cole thought harder. His mind flicked through images of the last few days like album covers in iTunes, each hour a different image that he could process in microseconds. His photographic memory wasn't always perfect, but if he paid any amount of attention to something, that image was locked in his brain for life. Great for arguing treatises and law, tragic consequences for his personal life. Being right rarely resulted in the best outcome. So he had learned to play dumb, *a lot*.

He said 'she.' His scan of memories uncovered

nothing significant. "No. I haven't picked up anything. Can you tell me anything about the others, I mean as to their final day or days that might be playing out with me right now? No, wait!" Cole remembered the note that he thought Ann had sent. He turned to his right hip and started patting. Agent Leas was getting interested in what Cole was feeling for as he dug into his front pocket. "Is this related? I found it in my hotel room this morning. It just says... SHIT! It says, 'I'm before you.' He's here, Agent, isn't he? He's here and has been in my room. Admit it. You've seen this note before. And, a woman?"

Leas let out a deep sigh and then looked up, having seen inside the linen letter just handed to him. "Yeah. Both victims had similar notes. And video from the second confirms that the last person to be seen with Mr. Patrick was a woman...blonde." Cole rubbed his head; it was throbbing as Leas spoke.

He took a deep breath. "So is this the sign that she is about to act? What's the M.O.?"

"Honestly, we have no clue. You say you got this one this morning?"

"Yeah."

"Well, from what we've been able to determine, it was only at the time of death that both of the previous notes were delivered to the prior vics, so this is a change."

"What the hell? So I'm being played with? I'm supposed to wait like I'm in *The Ring* or something, anticipating my death? *FUCK YOU!*" The whole café went silent and looked at Cole for leaning his head back and howling that out in public. The tattooed waitress gave him a 'eat shit' look and then went back to wiping the counter. *Clearly it wasn't impressive to her.*

"I'm putting police protection on you. And I know

you're here only for vacation, but I don't recommend you go back to Denver. You're already here. I'm here. And it appears that Charleston may have been where this all started."

Cole rubbed his eyes; all this had worn him out. "What do you want me to do, Agent?"

"Where are you staying tonight?"

"I'm staying next door in the Omni. The killer clearly already knows that since he...I mean, she, left me a note."

"You can't stay there. Can you stay with family tonight? We can sneak you out tonight and she will lose your trail for a while until we can figure this out."

"Agent, I can't expose my family to this. If this crazy is coming to kill me, I don't want my family in the fire."

"You have to trust me; it would just be for a night or so. Your sister is a cop, isn't she? A pretty damn good one from what I've heard so far. Stay with her."

"She has my nephew; that is the worst option."

"Cole, she's already agreed. I talked to her before walking in here. I didn't fill her in on all this. I just let her believe what she had already thought, that some ex-client was on the loose and your name popped up on a hit list. She is cool with it and you are NOT staying in that hotel again."

Cole crawled off the couch, whispering "Fuck you," in Leas' ear as he passed by on the way to the counter with his empty mug. He knew that if his sister had gotten involved he had already lost this argument. But it didn't mean he had to like it.

FROM THE GUCCI store across the street Poinsett had watched it all, and she didn't like what she had seen. The

FBI agent from Dallas was here, in Charleston, and was clearly trying to mess up her plans. She'd wanted a challenge, and, more importantly to let the Taker know, but she had gotten more than she had planned for.

Whatever he told Mouzon, it wasn't taken well. And Mouzon had shown the guy her note. It wasn't that she didn't think an investigator would be looking into her vics, but that he got a jump on her and frustrated the hunt pissed her off. *Make lemonade out of lemons.* She'd wanted a challenge and it looked like she had just been given one.

# CHAPTER 43

COLE HAD MADE IT to his sister's home in the Old Village, with Agent Leas introducing himself at the door to Jackie before leaving. He had booked a room at local hotel for his stay and agreed to meet in the morning. Cole had intended to go boating to Bull Island with his college friend Victor Sweeney, or 'Vic.' Once a pirate hideout, the only pirates it served now were Captain Morgan's sauced boaters who could make it to the secluded national wildlife reserve island for a day in the sun. But Cole's desire for a PBR and coconut rum day wasn't possible with all the events of the night. So he texted Vic during the drive to let him know he needed to cancel and would owe him big, perhaps beer before he left. Vic had texted back that he understood and to just check back in later in the week. *If there is a later in the week.*

His sister wore concern on her face as Cole walked into the house. She was quiet as Agent Leas left, waiting for Cole to start. Cole went up to the spare room, threw his bag on the floor and came back downstairs. "I need a drink, and then we are going to talk. What's your poison?" Because of her history with William, she didn't keep much in the form of alcohol in the house. He opened the cabinets one by one until he found a half-empty bottle of gin and a new bottle of tonic water. He held the two bottles in the air. "Gin and tonic it is." As he mixed the drink, he looked up at his sister, who was still silent. "Kidnapped? Kidnapped, Jackie? And, my mom... Libby was murdered?" He let the words float out there. He was bordering on rage, disappointment, fear...swirling like a whirlpool in his mind.

Her mouth dropped. That was clearly the last thing she'd expected to hear out of his mouth. "Oh my god, Cole. Is that what this is about?"

"You knew. *You knew*? And you and Mom and Dad didn't think to tell me? I mean, isn't that something you would think is important? Hey, Cole. So you know when your mom died. Well, actually she was raped and tortured. Yeah, like a bad movie. And you may be a little fucked in the head because of that. Don't worry, we have insurance for therapy."

Jackie rounded the corner of the kitchen counter to get closer. "Cole, please understand. You had no memory of it. I was seven and from what I recall there was a therapist, he...he said that it was best to just leave you without remembering. That it was your mind's way of protecting itself." She was sobbing. "...He said it would help you heal."

Logically, he understood that and the choice. But he couldn't be logical right now. He had been kept in the dark for over thirty years, played by his own family. "And this brand thing? Is that what this scar is?" He pulled up his shirt, flashing his back to his sister.

She looked down to his back, her eyes wet from the tears. "Mom and Dad hated that thing. It reminded them of the horror Aunt Libby went through. Dad and Libby were close, crazy close. So they had it removed while you were still in the hospital. What's happening, Cole? I thought that this was about one of your ex-clients in Georgia. How does that have anything to do with what happened thirty years ago?"

"Dammit Jackie, someone is back...killing those who were kidnapped like me. She's back and she wants me dead." Cole trembled as he said it out loud; his wall was unintentionally down. Jackie ran over to him and clasped her arms around him, sobbing harder.

COLE'S EYES WERE red from fresh tears as he looked up to the ceiling and faked a smile. "But you're a bad-ass cop with a Glock 21, right sis? You'll kick his ass." Cole tried to add levity to the moment. It was a way for the wall to be raised again. His sister released and punched him in his arm, still upset. Cole had an aversion to being serious for too long. And his brain tired quickly without a break from the seriousness of life and always processing it in high-definition. This moment was burning his brain. "Do you have any Tylenol? My head is killing me." His sister rushed to a cabinet and poured out three pills from the bottle she had grabbed. Swallowing them down, he chased the pills with his gin and tonic.

His sister spoke more calmly now, the tears controlled. "I don't understand, Cole. Who is back...to kill you?" She choked on the last words.

Over the next hour Cole filled his sister in on everything: the others, the murders, the note. He was still mad about the secrets. But he was even more pissed that someone dared to think they were going to take him down without a fight.

# CHAPTER 44

*Day Six Ninety-Two.*

IT WAS FIVE-THIRTY Monday morning and Cole was sitting on the back porch of his sister's home, his arms wrapped around his knees with his feet tucked under him, seated in the rocking chair he had crawled into several minutes before. The sun was slowly peeking in, beckoning another day. Though her home didn't sit right on the water, he could see it thirty yards off, through a separation between the homes directly behind hers.

The dream had come again, followed by the hollowness of longing when he woke. Sitting in the chair, his mind was now silent as he stared at the ripples in the distance. The tide was moving out. The soft sound of the lapping waves filled the silence otherwise left by those around him sleeping. He took it all in, zoning on the buzzing of energy around him. His body mimicked the waves as he rocked. He could feel the inertia and ebb through his body. It was like this for a while. *Silence. Peace. Healing.*

Jackie could be heard rustling in the kitchen by six. The thick, chocolate-laden smell of coffee wafted Cole's way and a few minutes later Jackie came out to the porch with two cups, catching the screen door with her hips so it didn't slam shut. She sat next to him and began to rock. No words were spoken until both had taken a few sips of the coffee and the marsh view.

"Okay, so according to my scanned reading of the file materials Agent Leas gave me, I was taken in March of 1982, along with a Mark Calhoun and my mother, by a fake cop. Four or so days later, I was found in the marsh, behind the Academy, by one of MeMe's boys." There was a long pause. "...Mom dead, the Calhoun boy and I huddled around her." Cole took a deep breath. "Branded, dead mom. That about sum it up?" Cole looked over at his sister, who had her head down, clearly holding back from crying again.

"Cole..." She spoke softly and slowly, "...I really don't know. I mean, I remember the event. I remember you being found and that you had that mark. I remember a lot of crying and screaming by Mom and Dad. And then...well, you didn't remember and so I remember Mom and Dad making it very clear that I was to never speak of it unless you did. You never did, Cole. *You never did.*"

"Sis, I'm not blaming you. It wasn't your fault I was taken. Hell, I hope you haven't been carrying that all these years. Have you?"

"I know that now Cole. But..." The tears had returned.

Cole reached over to his sister and grabbed her forearm. "Sis, I am so very sorry if you ever felt that way. If you do now, stop. As a cop, you know better than anyone that it was not your fault. What's happening now is *not your fault.*" He spoke the last three words slowly. She nodded her head.

*Of course it all made sense now. The dream, the*

*nightmare...it was my mind trying to remind me. And I was stubborn and refused to see it as anything other than a stupid, disruptive dream. The marsh, the field, the hand, it was all real. Shit.* Cole had come to this conclusion sometime after waking up at three a.m. and being unable to fall back to sleep.

Cole took a deep breath. "Jackie, I don't want you involved. You've done enough. I will not have you and Billy in danger."

"Cole, you're my brother and I'm not going to let some fucker mess up that pretty face." Like Cole, Jackie liked to disrupt serious moments from taking hold. "Plus, I've seen you handle a gun, it's not pretty."

Cole let out a singular laugh. "Oh, please. You know, Little Miss Annie Oakley, I can take you any day." He made a finger gun and shot it sideways, gangster-style, adding the sound effects.

She pinched her mouth tight on one end to show her skepticism. "In your wet dreams!"

Cole almost spit his sip of coffee out with laughter. "I love you, sis. You *truly* are my favorite sister."

Jackie stuck out her tongue and turned back to the marsh view. The sun had risen and orange had turned to blues and greens.

# CHAPTER 45

"COLE, PLEASE DON'T take this out on Mom and Dad. They were just being parents and wanted you to have a normal life. As far as anyone knew, the creep just liked marking and releasing kids. No one knew he was going to come back." The conversation had moved to the kitchen where liver puddin' had been fried and poured over speckled grits, still steaming on Cole's plate. Aptly named by some as liver mush, the rich, grey concoction of liver, random pork parts, rice, and spices native to the lowcountry had been sliced from its soft sausage form and fried until it turned into something that resembled a meaty sauce more than any solid meat.

"I know, but I have to talk to them. I'm not going to just sit here and wait. I need to figure out what's going on and, at a minimum, I need to talk to this Calhoun guy. He's probably next."

"Did Agent Leas say anything about him?"

"No, nothing. I didn't learn that till I read the file. But you know what I'm saying."

Pouring another cup of coffee, she continued. "Yeah, and as much as I hate it, I tend to agree. Let's get this fucker."

"Mom!" Billy was now seated next to Cole, playing some kids' game on his iPhone after Cole had turned off the signal to avoid any one of his immature friends' texts from flashing across the screen. One friend in particular had a certain proclivity for sending random internet photo discoveries that Cole believed a child should never see.

He cocked his head in feigned shock. "Language, woman." Cole was mocking Ava who, like all Southern ladies were taught, didn't cuss, and had utterly failed to pass that on to her daughter.

"Uh, you started it, insulting my frail female sensitivities with your harsh language, dear sir." Jackie fanned herself with an imaginary fan and batted her eyes.

"Lord, what I would give to see you in hoop skirt."

"If I keep it up I'll be as big as a hoop skirt." Jackie looked down to her stomach.

"Woman, you are *crazy*. What are you, maybe one-thirty? You look amazing. I'm sure all the sugar daddies are lining up for you. In fact, didn't you tell the biddies yesterday you had a date tonight?"

Walking over toward the built-in kitchen desk, Jackie said, "I'll need to cancel that. I have an investigation and it's important. I'm going to shower and get dressed. When I get to work I'll pull everything I can on that Calhoun kid and let you know." Pausing, she added, "Cole, when you see them, please...please remember they were doing only what they thought...what they were told was best."

Cole looked up from his empty plate with a pensive face. "I know...I do. And I promise I won't yell at them. But I have to know. And more importantly...I need to get them somewhere safe. I'd ask you to get out of town but I really don't feel like getting shot by you. My card is already full." Cole flashed a smile at Jackie as she grabbed a cell phone off the desk and walked up to her room.

# CHAPTER 46

"COLE, WE THOUGHT it best not to tell you about your mom, about how she died. What would have been the purpose? It was horrible enough that she died, but...but to tell you she died...was *murdered*, trying to protect you... Well, that just didn't seem the best way to have you remember her. She went through horrible things to save you and that other boy." Cole listened while Ava trembled with overflowing emotions that boiled over and caused her words to sputter. He'd dropped the bomb within minutes of arriving at the house. Between the tears, she was trying to justify the impression he had always been left with, that his mother had died in an auto accident when he was two years old. The truth splintered off from there.

Cole's meeting with Leas had torn that story wide open like the violent pop of a bag of chips, leaving the flakes of Cole's childhood flying in multiple directions. The residual effect of this revelation was almost as frightening as being hunted. He could no longer trust his memory. For as long as he recalled, if he saw it in his head, it was true. No 'if's, and's, or but's.' But now...he was scared to trust anything he saw in his mind. It had betrayed him.

Libby Mouzon was a single mom, Cole's father having disappeared as soon as the news of pregnancy hit his lap. According to the files supplied by Leas, sometime after Cole's birth, his mother took a job as a housekeeper and sitter for the Calhoun family, including taking care of Mark, their only son at the time. According to the final police report, on March 16, 1982, she left to take Mark to kindergarten but never made it. The car was found abandoned off Rifle Range Road, everyone missing. Witnesses described seeing a car that matched the description of hers pulled over, an officer at her window. No officer could ever be identified as working the area, much less issuing a ticket.

Using the coroner's report and limited evidence, the police had pieced together the next few days of Cole's life, which read like a bad dream.

# CHAPTER 47

LIBBY MOUZON LOOKED at her baby boy Cole through her rear-view mirror. She smiled as if to say, 'How you doing, Buster?' as he played with his Cheerios, seated in his car seat. Mark Calhoun was seated next to him in the back seat, coloring in an old Disney coloring book, faded from sitting in the rear window of her wood-trimmed, red Ford Country Squire station wagon. "Good morning, Officer. Can I ask why I was stopped?" Libby knew she had been speeding down Rifle Range, but if she delivered Mark Calhoun late to kindergarten one more time, she was going to be fired. Playing coy worked well for her in these situations.

"License and registration please." The thin-faced man with a salt and pepper beard stared down at her. His uniform was wrinkled and worn. Libby bent over, popped open the glove compartment and started digging for the registration. *Shit.* From the passenger's side mirror she noticed the officer admiring the view of her bent over, then looked to the back seat and grinned at the boys.

"Here you go, Officer." He inspected the materials the peroxide blond had just handed him for just seconds. "I'll need you to step out of the car, if you don't mind."

"Are you sure about this? I mean, what did I do?" Frustration entered Libby's voice.

"Ma'am, just step out of the car, please." Libby clasped the car's interior handle and took a quick look back in the mirror to see that the kids were safe as she opened the heavy, squealing door. It closed with a heavy latch. "Ma'am, did you know your license was suspended?"

Libby looked down at the documents in his hand, shocked. "What? When? That can't be possible."

"Ma'am, I'm going to have to arrest you. You can clear it up at the station. But I can't leave you on the road with a suspended license." He reached behind his cuffs as she protested.

"Please, please… my house is just a few miles away. My kids, I can't leave them, what will I do with them? I can clear this up if you will just give…"

"Ma'am, place your hands behind your back." Tears fell off Libby's sunburned cheeks as she looked at the two boys in the back seat, Cole still playing with his cereal. The officer moved her quickly into the back of his sedan. She watched as he reached his hands through the driver's side window, still rolled down from the stop, and pulled up the latch to the back door.

"Hey buddy, we are going to move ya'll to my car, okay? That's right, jump on out."

Mark stared at Libby as the door was opened and he was pushed into the backseat. "Miss Libby, are you okay? Why are you sad?"

Trying hard to not show her panic, "Oh, baby, I'm okay. It's going to be okay. I promise." Mark slid in next to Libby and looked back at Cole, still in the back of the wagon. He joined them moments later, still in the car seat, giving his mom a large smile. She forced one back.

The navy sedan was driven several miles before Libby looked up and immediately noticed something was wrong. The police station was in the center of town, in a mostly commercial area. But all Libby saw were residential homes zooming by. "Where are we going? This isn't the way to the station. ...Hey, do you hear me? Please answer me!" His only response was to speed up. Libby looked out the window to the occasional person on the sidewalk. What was he doing? She looked down at the two boys at her side. "Officer, please tell me where we're going. You are scaring the kids. Hell, you're scaring me." He remained silent, turning onto a wooded lot. From the look of the white sand drive, it was along the marsh. Libby started pleading. "Please sir, stop the car. Please." The tears had returned as she pled for the officer to stop, gathering in thick streams across her face. The car came to a stop in the middle of some forested lot with a small dark brown painted cabin.

Libby fought, screaming, yelling, as he dragged her by her cuffed hands through the sandy soil into the cabin. The boys would come easier...anything to be close to the safety Libby represented. Mark and Cole had picked up on the horrified energy pouring out of her and started to cry. Mark asked for his mom, prompting Libby to attempt to hold back her tears, but they continued to break through in small explosions of emotion. "Shhhh, shhhh, it will be okay. It will be okay." But it wouldn't.

# CHAPTER 48

FROM THE MEDICAL report, Libby was cuffed to a cot in the corner of the square cabin and raped over and over again as the boys were tied in the corner, left to watch. The ragged lashes on her back, buttocks, and legs told of routine whippings by what was later identified as a horse crop.

The boys were branded at some point, like cattle. Libby would have to watch as they were burned, left to scream for her help.

On the night of their escape the captor had apparently left, supporting the police's theory later that he lived somewhere nearby, coming to the cabin during either the night or day for his next session of torture. It was then that Libby slipped her left hand free from the cuffs, but not without removing most of the skin and leaving the hand dangling limp, broken. From the looks of the rope found in the cabin, she broke a coke bottle and slowly cut through the children's ropes. From there she had apparently made it the half mile through the marsh, carrying the boys until she collapsed in a thicket of trees and palmettos surrounded by marsh...

It was unclear how long they had been hiding under the palmettos and sea wind-beaten pines of the hammock, but when found, Libby was dead, Cole and Mark holding her as though they were taking a peaceful family nap. Cole was unconscious from dehydration, but stable. Mark was weak, but alert and calling for help. They had been missing five days before being discovered by MeMe's sons.

Cole's mind ran crazy with the imagery of the report when he read it. It pieced together the horror of his childhood, over a month-long investigation that never resulted in an arrest. They had no leads. The fake officer had disappeared as quickly as he appeared. There was DNA, but it was a dead end, no match.

From what Agent Leas had told him during their meeting, the Charleston abduction was one of four that were too similar to be anything other than the act of one killer. The dates of the missing suggested Charleston was the first. The other abduction, in White Plains, Fort Worth, and Vegas, matched in every detail—a police stop, disappearance, and ultimate death. In each one, the children had been left to live, to bear the mark of their captor and endure the grief of the torture and death of their parents. Libby had escaped, only to die in the marsh... having sacrificed her life to save them. The other parents didn't fare as well. Leas had shared their police reports, too. Burnings, bleedings, and strangulation were the intended deadly climaxes for Libby, based on the others' ultimate moments.

He closed his eyes to try and black out the pain of what he had just learned. Whoever it was seemed to have decided the children were ready to be killed. He had no idea who was after him, but he knew he was next.

# CHAPTER 49

THERE WERE TEARS, lots of tears, at the Mouzon house. Cole had explained it all. He was unemotional and almost cold in his rendition. It wasn't from anger or distrust. Rather, he was locked into that side of himself that handled everything matter-of-factly, with steely precision. He knew that this probably made his parents' concern and pain worse, but he couldn't help it. He tried to assure them that he wasn't upset, that he just needed to understand and figure everything out as fast as possible before something happened to him, or worse, his family.

His mom couldn't get much out. Randall was silent, very silent. Just years before, this would have been a warning for a drunken rage brewing. The quiet made Cole uncomfortable at the prospect. Like the silence of the eye of a hurricane, such quiet meant you better run and seek cover because hell had arrived on earth and all would be in its path. He had never blown up beyond yelling at his children or wife. But he still clearly recalled his father exploding on the poor guy who refused to move from in front of Cole and his siblings one Fourth of July on the old Pitt Street Bridge. Randall had made sure they got there early for the Charleston harbor fireworks. When a latecomer took up post directly between them and the show and refused to move when asked. *Pop*—the man was down with one punch, leaving his wife to pull Randall off of him. Ava's only response was, "What will the neighbors think?"

"Well, I can tell you this, Rambo Momma isn't going anywhere. I will take that man out if he messes with one of my babies again." Cole had just instructed his parents to go down to Fort Myers and stay with Ava's sister and Henry. They begrudgingly agreed, but Granny was being a harder sell.

"Dammit Mom, we are going and that will be the end of it." Randall broke his silence. Granny mumbled under her voice some words probably best not heard.

Cole intervened to quiet both sides. "Leave me the keys and I'll check in on the place. I've called work and told them there's a family emergency. They didn't ask any questions."

# CHAPTER 50

"COLE, BABY, COME help this old lady pack for this forced trip." Granny gave a sly look at his father as Cole extended his elbow to her to assist her to her apartment. Walking outside with her on his arm, the memory of Jackie's wedding and escorting his grandmother down the aisle flashed before his eyes. At the time he could think of no happier moment for his sister. But he knew now that image was a fraud, with Billy's father having slept with one of caterers just moments before the vows. The drugs would be revealed to his sister for the first time that night, the same night she would be introduced to his open hand when she objected. His sister's constant strength was put to the test over the next few years, but as always she came out the victor. He admired that ability in her, to survive.

Cole pushed off the thoughts of his sister to ply his Grandmother for information. "So, it said...the report said that MeMe's boys found me?"

"Yeah baby, she deployed those boys like an army when she learned what happened. They walked more marsh and forest than all the police involved. They were on a mission. Man, that woman was good." Granny chuckled to herself. "No one was going to mess with one of her boys."

Still walking alongside his grandmother, Cole looked down at her. "How did they know where to look?"

Granny stopped to respond. "Hon, her people have been here as long as ours and probably worked most of it at one time or another. They just *knew* the best spots."

They started walking again as Cole said, "I haven't seen MeMe in forever. Is she even still alive?"

"Well, last I heard they were still on that property next to ours, off Rifle Range and Porchers Bluff."

Cole sat down on the edge of his grandmother's bed and looked off, outside the back window of the open room. He would need to visit MeMe and find out what she knew.

"Hand Granny that luggage over there in the closet." Inside the small separated apartment his father had constructed on the property several years ago in anticipation of Granny's need for closer care, Cole couldn't help but think it looked a lot like her place in town. Same furniture, same decorations, same musky smell of dank, old places. It was just all in one square room with a small kitchen in one corner, a bed in another and a makeshift living room making up the rest.


THERE WERE ROOSTERS everywhere, as though a traveling rooster salesman got rich unloading his entire stock on his grandmother. She had always been a collector, but in this small space they seemed to stand out more than he recalled. The entire reason he went to the University of South Carolina was because his first exposure to anything college-related was his grandmother's black coffee mug with a chipped, gold-leaf gamecock embossed on one face. It took him several years just to figure out the image was that of a fighting cock and not some Japanese emblem.

Peering over the collection, he noticed what appeared to be a new addition. Bright red, with some white and black streaming feathers painted on the ceramic body, the bird looked fierce and intimidating at almost two feet high. The cockscomb alone added five inches.

"Looks like you got a new one, Granny." She glanced over and back to Cole. "Yeah, QVC was having a sale one night and he's a big one, and I thought 'a house isn't a home without a big 'ol cock in it,' so I ordered him. Who knew cocks came delivered with free shipping."

Cole about choked on his laughter, attempting to shake off the imagery that had just flooded into his head. Granny was never one to hold back, something that scared the shit out of him in public or social settings. He could still recall her breaking into a safe sex lesson during a kids' sleepover she hosted. His friends loved it. Their parents, on the other hand, couldn't figure out what they were more pissed about—that she demonstrated the best way to apply condoms on a banana or that she handed out Playboy and Playgirl, *because Granny didn't judge,* for illustrative purposes. Later she would confess she'd planned it all just for her own entertainment. *A clever old lady.*

Leaned over head deep into her luggage trying to shove some type of nightgown in, Granny said, "Cole, can you promise this old lady something?"

Cole cocked his head like he had seen Dixie do every time she struggled to understand what he was saying. "Of course Granny, what you want?"

Dissatisfied with her packing, Granny walked over to Cole and sat beside him. As her hand smoothed out a wrinkle in the pink rose pattern of the duvet, she turned to him. "Baby, you know everything is going to be okay, right? I mean, we have had some crazy times in this life and you have more than any in this family. But we're strong people, Cole Mouzon, and you are the toughest. When your momma Libby died, this family pulled together to protect and nurture you. You was in horrible shape. Don't be mad at Ava or Randall for not telling you what happened. We all agreed that it was better you know how wonderful your momma was and not how horrible her death was." Cole had only seen his Granny cry once and that was when Poppa died fifteen years ago. Otherwise, the woman was steel. In this moment, that steel was flimsy. Her eyes went moist as she continued. "Baby, I don't know why...how you survived. But you did, and you will again. Just promise me that you will call me when you get whoever it is that did this to your momma."

Cole wrapped his long arms around his grandmother and whispered in her ear, "You know I will."

# CHAPTER 51

COLE HAD WAITED around until after lunch to see his folks off to Ft. Meyers. His stomach ached from one too many ripe tomato sandwiches and a slice of hummingbird cake. He hoped that would last him the rest of the day, because he didn't have time to waste. Moments later he hopped into the Focus and drove over to the old homestead where MeMe had lived. He hoped she was alive and still where he last visited her.

MeMe Jenkins had been Cole's nanny from birth until he was twelve, though the term 'nanny' conveyed a drastically different meaning than would be implied. When he was first born his mother fell sick for several months. MeMe's family property bordered theirs, so Libby hired MeMe to care for Cole when she was working. Cole's existence had been modest; after her death and Randall was injured, the family moved to the property and its triple-wide off Porchers Bluff. MeMe stayed on, taking care of all the Mouzon children. He could still feel her large, engulfing hugs whenever he thought of her.

He drove to the property off dead-man's curve on Rifle Range Road. A historically treacherous bend in the road that converted Rifle Range into Porchers Bluff Road, it was a hot spot for deaths in the 60s from drag racing.

When he and his family lived on the end of Porchers Bluff, numerous accidents occurred from the unwitting, risk-taking, or just drunk drivers attempting to ride the almost ninety-degree curve. But the greatest casualty ever seen was a mammoth boar that festered along the side of the curb for weeks until ultimately claimed by nature. The local paper celebrated the death of the curve in 2006, announcing it had 'a date with the executioner.' In its place was constructed one of the many round-about intersections that now dotted the lowcountry landscape like dizzying chickenpox, causing confusion to the locals used to driving in straight lines.

A few miles off the curve, Cole approached the property. Other than one new structure and a few extra cars, the place appeared just as he recalled. Cole parked directly outside the newest building as a small child and a man crossed his path with skeptical eyes.

He had been here many times. His childhood days routinely consisted of waking to MeMe cooking shrimp'n grits or cornbread. While he ate, she cleaned the house and laundry. By noon, she was done and they would walk along Porchers Bluff to MeMe's property. The large white sand circular driveway with several once-white wood buildings following the exterior of the arched drive remained unchanged. These buildings were similar to the housing in the recent movie *The Help*, but were certainly less well-maintained, with green moss and pine straw coating the roofs and ground around the structures. The white had long succumbed to grey from dirt and the sap of the overhanging loblolly pines and live oaks, their branches weighed down by Spanish moss. Peering across the property, he could see where he'd played with MeMe's grandchildren around the makeshift homes.

"Can I help you?" A tall, slender man with mocha skin approached to determine if Cole posed any threat. It wasn't an issue of race; it was an issue of belonging. And a white man in the backwoods of Mount Pleasant on a black family's property spoke loudly of not belonging. Cole began to speak cautiously, "I'm here to see Mardean Franklin... MeMe."

The man asked, "Is she expecting you?" His eyes narrowed.

"No Sir. I'm Cole Mouzon; she took care of me as a child, and I was in town and thought I would..."

"Cole? Cole Mouzon? Wow, man, you have grown. I mean, I expected you would have, but damn. It's been forever. It's me, Jeffery. We use to play around this yard when you were little; we were tight as brothers back then."

Cole's mind raced, settling on one image in particular. "Oh, man. Jeffery, how are you doing? You're looking pretty good yourself. Was that your kid that I just saw walking past?"

Jeffery threw his right arm back in the direction of where the girl had gone. "Yeah, that's my baby girl, Abby. She's my world. So, what brings you out here? Oh, Grandma, damn man. Let me get her." As he walked toward one of the larger buildings Jeffery turned back, "Cole Mouzon, who would have thought." A minute or two passed as Cole stood next to his rental before Jeffery leaned out the front door and waved him in. "Come on, she's up."

# CHAPTER 52

WALKING IN, THE space was clean, old wood floors and walls with a light coat of white paint. The mallard greens and golds suggested the decoration had remained relatively the same since the 70s. Pictures—almost too many pictures—filled the walls, likely prized moments with all of MeMe's family.

"Come'n." She shouted from the single side bedroom directly behind a very small galley kitchen closest to the door. Slowly she cracked open the door. Cole glowed as the black, wrinkled woman was revealed. "Wehl, don't jus' stan' der, gib MeMe a hug." Cole happily obliged, catching MeMe as she squeezed his upper waist. MeMe was a thick, solid woman, almost as tall as Cole, and wider. She had a slight limp that Cole did not recall.

Her arms tight around him, Cole spoke into her ear. "I'm here to collect that slice of banana cake you promised me."

"I don't have no 'nanna cake, but I got peach cobbla if ya wan' some." She released and flashed a broad smile.

"No, no, I was just kidding. I'm here to see you, not let you get me fat all over again." Under MeMe's care Cole had been what the rest of the world called fat, but MeMe called 'healthy.' It wasn't until her care stopped at age thirteen that he slimmed down and discovered a gym.

Looking him up and down, she said, "Bebe boy Mouzon." MeMe was in awe of her visitor. "Look at dem green yey. Hmm, lub dem yey...Where my manner, seddown, seddown." She motioned him to a small couch in the far corner of the room.

MeMe was Gullah, and Cole's ears strained to remember how to understand the throaty, African-English language he had grown up with, but hadn't heard in almost two decades. Outsiders foolishly equated the language with ignorance, a lack of education. Cole experienced the same prejudice from his own accent, though certainly to a lesser degree. Yet, Granny was Geechee, a white speaker of Gullah, and had taught him early that the Gullah could match wits with anyone. *You didn't get anything over on a Gullah woman, especially MeMe*. Those smarts had obviously come to fruition in locating him in the marsh.

"You look good, real good boy. What chu been doin'?" MeMe moved over to a green Lazy Boy that had seen its days and some.

"I'm a lawyer now, in Denver; moved out there a couple years ago from Atlanta."

Cocking her head to get a view, she said, "I don't see no ring, you married, got bebes of your own?"

"No, ma'am. Single, no childs, yet." Cole could hear is own accent getting thick on the tongue when he said 'childs', fighting to be echoed because it was hearing a kindred voice.

After only a few minutes of catching up, MeMe leaned in and touched Cole's knee. "Smattah, bebe?" Her large, leathery dark hand felt warm and comforting.

Cole had been paying attention to their banter but his

thoughts had drifted off to his immediate concerns while he spoke. Caught, he filled her in on learning about his kidnapping as a child and that now it appeared someone had returned to complete the task. MeMe hesitantly told him what she knew of the event.

"Dey tol' me, 'somebody gone and stole the bebe boy Mouzon.' A tief. Cole, your grand-momma was bad somethin' horrible, ill about it she was. She couldn't function. My people had been on tiss land almost as long as yours and if someone had you, we would find'm. So, I get me boys to go look. T'ree days yous had been gone. 'De police tried, but couldn't find you. 'Dem boys check every crik and maa'sh they knew. Two day later, dat's where they foun' you. Side of the ol' school. 'Dem police had look t'reetime dere. Dem boys foun' you, dough, under some palmetto tree in deh maa'sh. I was so thankful, t'engk'gawd!" She raised her hands in reverence to the Lord.

"Your momma was good people, Cole. Real good. And, boy did she love her some bebe Cole. You was attach to her hip like em' oyster. When you was born, she just stopped all she doin' and decided to be a good mother. It be horrible what happen' to her, just horrible. 'Dem boys tell me she holdin' you, even dead, watching over you and em' boy. Her love is in you, Cole. And with it, her strength. 'Dat man may taken her life, but not the strength she gave to you."


COLE REFLECTED ON MeMe's words. He had never thought about his mother's death much. He was too young when it happened; it impacted him as much as reading a sad story in a book, in a detached way. He had been told she was lost in a car accident. But now, that connection was real, with the reality of the truth of what happened; the emotions welled up in his face, forcing him to isolate them so that he could function and push forward.

"'Dey never foun' de man, I wonder...wonder where he go. T'ief'n chill'un like 'dat. An, that t'ing on yah back." MeMe looked behind Cole, toward his hip and the brand she clearly recalled being left by whoever had taken him those years ago. Her head shook as she returned to face him. "Had to be a buckruh, (*white man*) cuz uh know no black folk do such a 'ting."

Cole laughed and agreed. Yes, it was likely a white man back then. Everything so far matched the stereotype, even if the stereotype was usually wrong. Cole had learned as a public defender that plenty of studies had gone to this issue, all coming up with their own theories. The most commonly accepted was that because serial killing is usually carried out by males, and white males outnumber black or Hispanic males by almost seven to one, there was roughly a seven to one chance a serial murderer was white.

Leaning in, Cole asked, "MeMe, did I say anything? Did I talk about what happened?" MeMe sat back in her plastic-covered lounge chair as if she were deciding if she should speak. "Cole, digging around in da' past is dirty business. Bess leave t'ings as they are."

"MeMe, someone took me all those years ago and now, well...it looks like someone is back. If there is something in the past I need to know about to save my future, please tell me." The softness of her face dissolved into a fortified mask of anger, daring the world to attack something that she cared for, loved.

With a stern voice, MeMe barked, "Jeffery, go get

Penney." Jeffery had been sitting quietly on the floor against the door the entire conversation, absorbing it like a sponge. He quickly got up and ran out the door, leaving MeMe and Cole alone in the dark home. Silence crept in while they waited.

Several minutes later, Cole could hear the heavy steps of Jeffery on the front porch and behind him a second, lighter pair. The door opened to reveal a woman in a dirty purple t-shirt and jeans. In her hand was a book bag that had weathered too many hurricanes. Jeffery was out of breath as he introduced to Penney. She was soft-spoken, smaller than MeMe and probably several decades younger. When MeMe began to talk her authority was recognized by everyone in the room, who all lowered their heads in deference.

"Penney, Mister Cole has come with questions 'dat shouldn't be answered. But, it seems 'dey muss if he to get 'dis evil after him now."

"I understand. Give me your hands, boy. Jeffery, get the lights." The room went pitch dark, with only a gap of light streaking under the door as Cole extended his hands. Slowly, a chant exited Penney's mouth. It was hoodoo, the nicer, kinder sister of voodoo practiced by the Gullah along the coast. Cole had grown up around it with, MeMe saying random chants and applying herbs to his cuts when he was little. A blend of Christianity, herbalism, and folk magic, its roots were in the slave times, when medical care for slaves was rare at best.

Penney was obviously a root worker, or conjurer of these spells, each with their own color. White for protection, red for love, green for money, purple for success, and black to harm. As Penney chanted, Cole listened to her lighter accent and mentally joked that he needed to order a white and a black for now, though green or purple where attractive options, too. *Red will have to wait.*

"Pay attention, boy!" Penney had caught Cole's drifting thoughts and knocked him in the head with his own hand to snap him out of it. He had learned long ago to respect people's religions and practices, but he felt this was getting him nowhere.

Herbal smoke filled his nostrils just as he was about to protest. "Breath deep, breath real deep." Cole wasn't a smoker and the smoke burned as he inhaled. Small flecks of light slowly started to burst into his eyes and he felt dizzy. His head felt like it was being weighed down by a soft, heavy pillow. He closed his eyes to try and focus, but it wasn't working. His mind went deeper, until all was black and silent.

# CHAPTER 53

I T WAS UNCLEAR how long he was out before Cole kicked as he woke, still fighting off his captor in the marsh. He was surrounded by MeMe and the others when he opened his eyes. "I saw!"

"What you see, boy, come'on now and tell us." MeMe's words were rushed.

Cole was still groggy as he spoke. "There's a mark, a tattoo or something on his forearm. Like a bird, maybe like a crow's head?" The look on MeMe's and Penney's faces read fear and surprise. "Crow you say, dat's a bad omen, Cole. Carry death it does. Did you see anyt'ing else, did you see 'ehm?"

Slowly shaking his head and pushing himself up, Cole responded. "No, ma'am, just his arm still. But that's more than I have ever seen." The image came with fear and excitement. Perhaps Cole was getting closure to his childhood capture. But, he knew from the files and his meeting with Leas that the killer was a woman. *Who is the woman?*

"Here, eat some bennie wafers, you need the energy." Jeffery was lifting Cole up from behind as MeMe shoved a plate of thin caramel-colored wafers dotted with sesame seeds into his hands. Cole knew the offer was special.

Sesame seeds, or bennie seeds as old Charlestonians called them, were said to have been so prized by the Nigerian and Angolan slaves that they buried the seeds in their hair when captured and brought them to Charleston to grow. Cole had eaten more than his share of the cookies every time his family went to his Granny's home. Taking a bite, he felt the sugar do its quick work.

MeMe clapped her hands on her knees and sat back in her Lazy Boy. "Ha, 'dis remind me of when we foun' you. You was rabbish, I rememb'r that. 'Bout ate me out of house and home, I tell ya." MeMe's kinder spirit was back.

"Never seen someone eat so many bennie wafers, as you." MeMe laughed in memory. "*E teet da dig e grave.*" *(You were overeating.)* "Like a gay'da, you were."

Smiling back at her, he thought 'God, I loved this woman.' Being reconnected to her, he missed her even more. She had been a second mother to Cole and but for her, he might have died in the marsh.

Half an hour later, Cole bid his farewells to MeMe so she could get to some event at the center.

"Tek'care, bebe. *Mus tek cyear a de root fa heal de tree.*" He recalled that she said that old Gullah proverb often when he was a child. 'Take care of the roots in order to heal the tree.' *Indeed.* It seemed perfect for the situation; if he was to ever survive this, he would have to deal with his childhood and being marked for death. MeMe's confidence that all would be okay helped. She made Cole promise to write, to let her know of his travels once this was all over. He accepted the promise in hope that he could fulfill it many times.

# CHAPTER 54

B Y THREE COLE had still not heard from Jackie about what she had discovered on the Calhoun kid. He texted and then headed to Melvin's Bar-B-Q off Highway 17, to get some something to eat. It took only two sentences for the weathered waitress with a white apron to pour out several 'darlings,' 'su'gas,' and 'babies' while delivering his drink. "I'll have a coke, ma'am."

"Of course baby, what kind?"

"Sprite, please."

"Sprite comin' right up, su'ga."

Cole missed Melvin's. There was nothing like it in Denver. Like most things in the South, bar-b-que caused feuding as much as land or family, and Melvin's was no exception. Melvin Bessinger was the older brother of Maurice Bessinger and together they had cornered the market on all things mustard sauce, dividing between them the Palmetto State; Melvin taking the lowcountry and Maurice taking the other three-fourths of the state.

Maurice's in Columbia was always the larger franchise. But that all changed when he decided to stand for the Confederate flag, hoisting massive versions over every restaurant he owned during the height of the 'great flag debate' over placement of the flag above the state capital building. Cole's family, like most of Charleston, put their backs behind the politically correct, or more likely politically silent, Melvin's and had Maurice's sauces removed from every Pig and Bi-Lo in the lowcountry to make room for Melvin's sauce. But the blacks still revolted, believing that Melvin was bottling Maurice's sauce to keep it on the shelf. That's when a black minister, James Johnson, inserted himself into the dispute, at the request of Melvin, and brokered a deal no less contentious than a Middle-East treaty, holding a press conference to assure all that he had witnessed the bottling operations of Melvin's and that all could rest assured that Melvin's sauce was indeed different and in no way associated with Maurice's, causing the balance of tangy sauce power to shift and never truly be regained by the little brother.

A few minutes later the waitress returned with his drink and a red plastic basket overflowing with thick-cut fries and a hamburger bun stuffed full of mustard-yellow slathered shredded pork. One bite and Cole felt revived from the heat outside. The spicy mustard and vinegar-based sauce oozed out the corner of his mouth, and he caught it with his tongue before it dripped onto his tan linen shorts. He learned in a 'geography of bar-b-que' class at the University of South Carolina that the state was divided into four distinct bar-b-que sauce regions, with Charleston split between the vinegar sauce of North Carolina and the more local mustard-vinegar sauce. To him, bar-b-que was one of the two. The other, tomato and ketchup sauces were just too sweet and were unknown to him until he went to college. Popping a fat garlic-salted fry into his mouth, his longing for Southern things washed over him. He was home.

At a quarter till four Jackie finally called. "Hey, sorry

for the delay. This place is crazy with all this going on. My chief has decided I can just communicate with you seeing as how the FBI is already involved and...well, you're my brother and all. I located that Calhoun guy. Cole... He's dead." There was silence as Cole processed the information.

"He committed suicide. It looks like he jumped off the old bridge like ten years back. From what I know so far he was pretty messed up after you and he were found and never really got over it. Sorry bro."

For the first time since learning of his kidnapping he was thankful for the secret his family had kept from him...that his mind had blacked out. *That could have been me.*

"Does he have any family? Maybe they know something."

"Already on it. Seems he had a brother. He's a professor or something over at the College of Charleston. Another officer here already talked to him and set up a meeting this evening. Captain was hesitant , but has agreed that you can attend. You can thank your buddy Leas for that."

Agent Leas wasn't his buddy, but Cole was thankful, nonetheless. Cole wanted to understand this craziness that he had just been clued in on and that meant talking to everyone that had anything to do with it, or knew of it.

Slurping down the last bit of his Sprite, Cole asked, "When and where, sis?"

"We're to meet him at the college. Meet me at the house, say six, and we can ride over together. Hanna 'the miracle worker babysitter' is at the house with Billy and says she can stay on till later if I drop off some dinner. God, I love her."

Cole interrupted, "Well, I'm at Melvin's if you want me to grab their dinner and then head over there."

"Perfect! Anyway, I need to run. You being in town has kicked up a shit storm here and I need to get back to work if you are ever going to pay me back."

Cole laughed. "Okay sis, see you in a bit."

# CHAPTER 55

I T WAS ALMOST seven thirty by the time Cole and his sister reached the history complex on the C. of C. campus. Cloaked under giant live oaks and moss, the two-hundred and thirty-three year-old school with its red clay and brick exterior looked more like well-preserved Spanish ruin than a university. The emptiness of school being out for the summer only emphasized this. No wonder it was often the backdrop for movies like *White Squall*, *The Notebook*, and *The Patriot*. "What was all that traffic about, sis?" Cole was looking over his shoulder as he exited the SUV.

"Uh, don't get me started. Ever since they started filming that *Army Wives* show here, trying to get around this campus has *sucked* every other weekend. Then there is some reality show shooting here, too. That show has royally pissed off some of the houtie touties. I'm glad I stay on the other side of the Cooper."

Cole knew the show. One of those on Lifetime, the 'men suck channel,' Cole would always say. Granny had her TV locked on that channel whenever he visited her at her old place. After an hour or so of the channel, he didn't know whether to hate himself or be thankful he wasn't old enough to be poisoned, stabbed, or run over by a raging woman out for revenge of her daughter, son, or just because she had been wronged. Cole attempted to shake off this mental conversation as they walked up the steps of the old building, but Jackie kept it going.

"But I think I'll try out as an extra for that new CBS show *Reckless* that they're starting to film here. That evil Twilight vamp Cam Gigandet is too damn hot. Did you see him in *Burlesque*, half-naked? That eight-pack? *Yum*. He can wear my Lululemon spandex yoga pants anytime he wants. He just rented a place around here somewhere for when it shoots, and it's a legal show about cops. Uh, hello! I'm perfect!" She flipped her blonde hair as though she were on some imaginary red carpet in Hollywood.

Cole smiled at his sister as they hit the top step. "Just invite me to the wedding, lady. You can do like Ryan Reynolds and Blake Lively just did and have it down the road from Mom and Dad's at Boone Hall Plantation. If it was good enough for them and also inspire Twelve-Oaks for *Gone With the Wind*, then it should surely be good enough for you and Cam." The thought of seeing his sister in a hoop-skirt flashed across his mind, causing him to think, *That would be a wedding to see.*

# CHAPTER 56

FINDING THE PROFESSOR'S third-floor office, they walked in to a full house. Agent Leas was on the left, sitting on a weathered, deep-brown leather couch, staring across the room at two officers standing next to an oak desk. One he recognized from the Mount Pleasant PD; the other, in a grey-blue shirt, he associated with Charleston County Police. Jackie walked in with authority, as if to say 'this is my turf.' Their host was obviously missing. "So, where is this guy?" Jackie had little patience.

"He ran down the hall while waiting on you. Should be back in a second." Agent Leas looked tired compared to Cole's last visit with him just twenty-four hours earlier.

"Excuse me, sir." Still standing in the doorway, Cole felt a hand on his back. Turning in, he was faced with a diamond-faced man almost matching Cole's height. Hipster-styled dark hair emphasized the aquamarine, triangle eyes of man as he passed into the room. His tan suggested he was often shirtless, running some sidewalk on the Peninsula. Jackie flashed a huge grin at Cole who turned away to avoid being seen doing the same.

"Officer Mouzon, Cole, this is Assistant Professor of History Cash Calhoun." Agent Leas was acting liaison. Cole continued to take inventory of Cash as Leas introduced everyone. Cash wore a large-patterned pastel plaid fitted shirt, rolled at the sleeves and un-tucked to hang over a pair of navy shorts. A slight amount of chest hair was revealed between deep unbuttoning at the collar. Scruff from a few days of ignoring the razor accented the look.

Cash looked at his audience from behind his paper-covered desk as if to say, "And, how can I help you...?"

Agent Leas decided to start the conversation. "Mr. Calhoun, as I explained on the phone, we need to discuss your brother and the events of his kidnapping thirty-five years ago."

"Of course. But you do understand, I wasn't even born yet? So I don't know how much help I can be...well, not around for that! I was certainly around for the aftereffects." Cash looked down at his desk in heavy thought. Looking up again, he said, "I'll do what I can. That ruined my brother and ultimately, it took his life. I want to understand. I want to help."

"How much do you recall, Mr. Calhoun?" Leas was taking lead on the interrogation and the other officers were more than happy to sit back and just take notes.

Cash sat behind his desk and Cole followed in getting comfortable, leaning into the open door frame.

"Like I said, I was born almost a year after that, in 1983. Mark was five when that all went down from what I understand, six when I was born. I always remember him in therapy, and the outbreaks and tantrums. My parents tried their best, but he just seemed broken and damaged. Fights, cutting himself, and ultimately a lot of alcohol. That's how he died. Too much vodka and a jump off the Old Bridge." Cole's eyes were deep with emotion.

Leas was leaning up against the desk as the others

sat silent. "Mr. Calhoun, were you ever told of the event, what happened?"

"It wasn't like we talked about it much around the dinner table, Agent. But, did it get mentioned, yeah. Mark had horrible nightmares when we were young. We shared the same room and I would hear him going through it. It always ended in a scream. My parents stopped coming to check by the time I was ten. There was nothing they or anyone could do; he was stuck in a very dark, painful place. He would say it was like the event was stuck on a loop, playing out over and over again in his head. Any lifeline thrown out by therapy or my parents was never reached for. It was like he just couldn't see it, feel it... that he was safe."

"And, again, I'm sorry to have to put you through this. But, as I explained on the phone, there appears to be some recent activity that links to your brother's, and Mr. Mouzon's, kidnapping."

Cash looked over at Cole, taking his first moment to contemplate what had just been said. He was looking at someone who had been there with his brother, who knew what his brother had gone through and the pain he suffered. The look on his face said he was asking himself, 'Why has this person before him survived apparently unscathed?' His gaze made Cole uncomfortable and he looked toward the floor out of deference. Seconds went by before Cash turned and started talking again.

"Agent, from what I understand, from what I recall hearing growing up... Mark was snatched with Mr. Mouzon and his mother. Five days later, he was found with Mr. Mouzon, here, in the marsh behind a school over in Mount Pleasant. It's all in the police report that you sent over. Ms. Mouzon dead, them being half-starved and dehydrated, the brands." Cash was clearly upset at having to tell the story.

The officers bent their necks to relieve their obvious cricks and readjusted their stance to settle in for the conversation. Unlike Cole, there was no sign of sympathy, just blank stares.

Looking over to Cole as he began to speak, Leas asked Cash, "Did Mark ever talk to you about it...about what happened?"

"Not directly, no. But, like I said he would say things when he was in a panic, things that seemed to be playing out in his mind as if he was still there. Your report mentions a third boy. Mark mentioned him a lot. Called him 'Lake.' The file has all that in there, though."

"Are there any details not in the file that you recall?"

Cash thought hard as he looked down at the drawer of his desk. "Well, I mean, it's hard to say. I would really have to think about that and re-read that report. The only thing that stands out is that the report says Mark didn't remember much about the boy, no real description. But I definitely recall him saying in a dream or something that the kid was younger, maybe by a few years, and had a cut, a gash on his hand. Mark seemed worried about the Lake kid, a lot. I guess rightfully so, since he was never found. After he was about ten, Mark just stopped talking about it. Hell, he stopped talking about anything, just keeping it all in and reliving it over and over again. Agent, for him, he never got out."

# CHAPTER 57

COLE SHUDDERED AT what Cash had just described. He was being told he was held captive with this man's brother, forced to watch his mother be tortured and left for dead. But he had no memory of it. The dream, that horrible dream, had unknowingly been his only recollection of the event. His mind had put up a wall so thick, so high that the effects that ravaged Cash's brother had never materialized in his own mind. For the first time since hearing about his childhood he was thankful. But whether he wanted to or not, he needed a key to that dark forgotten place if he ever expected to understand and survive.

Mentally rejoining the conversation, Cole caught Leas talking to Cash, now standing to shake the agent's hand. "Please do that, Mr. Calhoun. You have my information and the others', too, I expect. If you do think of anything, please let us know at once."

"Should I be worried? Is the guy back?"

Wiping down his jacket, Leas responded. "You have no concerns Mr. Calhoun, but let me ask you, have you received any strange notes, letters with cryptic messages?"

Cash's mind showed shock and interest. "No, should I have? What kind of letter are you talking about?"

"Well, here, let me show you." Leas walked across the room to another officer and then back to the front side of the desk. Cole recognized the letter being pulled out of a clear bag with red taped top. Cash stood to inspect the item.

"May I?"

Leas nodded. "Sure."

Cash took the letter and inspected it further, turning it and then holding it up to the light. "Agent, I haven't received anything like this. Is this from the man that took my brother and Mr. Mouzon?"

"We can't really say. Perhaps someone connected to him."

"Poinsett? Sounds like a woman to me. But what I find more interesting is the name itself."

"What do you mean, Mr. Calhoun?" Cash had Leas' attention.

"Well, you know that name, right?" He looked around the room, to find no agreement. Cash rolled his eyes in apparent disbelief of the stupidity he had found himself surrounded.

Shaking his head, Leas asked, "Please fill me in."

"Well, the name Poinsett has history here in Charleston. You probably don't know this, but the poinsettia that we see at Christmas time is named after Joel Roberts Poinsett, a Charlestonian, who discovered it in Mexico. Like Mr. Mouzon here, Poinsett was of Huguenot decent, his family having fled religious persecution. They came to the Holy City after the renovation of the Edict of Nantes in 1685. In fact, I believe the families may have arrived around the same time, in the late 1600s." Cole knew about his Huguenot past from stories Granny told at holidays, but hearing a stranger discuss it so analytically felt uncomfortable, like he had been spied on.

Cash continued as though he were giving a seminar in some auditorium. "Born in March 1779, as a boy he lived back and forth between Europe and Charleston, learning military arts, culture, and history. This guy dined with Alexander in Russia, acted as consulate in Argentina and Chile, and worked with Andrew Jackson as a secret agent, acting as the proverbial 'fly on the wall' to Charleston's discussions of secession, which Jackson used to craft policies to avoid a civil war. He even co-founded the National Institute for the Promotion of Science and Useful Arts in 1840, what you and I know as the Smithsonian Institute."

Cole thought Leas was going to yawn when he first opened his mouth to speak. "Professor, do you know anyone who would have a link to this Poinsett person or why they would use the name?"

"Not a clue. Poinsett was a botanist; you are dealing with poisons. Not to be crass. But, poinsettias are red, like blood. And it's a familiar family name in this region. So, maybe a relative?" He shrugged his shoulders.

"Being the oldest museum in the Country, the Charleston Museum has a huge collection of materials on subjects like that. I'd recommend trying there. I can try to see what they have, if you would like."

Leas had already lost interest in the topic, turning back to the other agents in a sign to 'wrap it up.' His back turned picking up his files from one of the office's tables, he said, "If you could, that would be great. In the meantime, this has been educational, but you are a professor after all. Thank you again for your assistance and time, Mr. Calhoun. We all appreciate it. Again, you have our information should you learn anything about this Poinsettia link, please let me know."

Cash bent around the desk in an attempt to make eye contact with Leas. "Poinsett, agent. Not Poinsettia... that is the plant."

Turning, the agent nodded his head. "Poinsett. Just let me know what you find out as soon as possible."

"Will do, Agent." Cash appeared deflated by the Agent's lack of interest in history.

The agent and other officers left the room, leaving Cole to linger. He could hear Jackie talking to the officers in the hall. Walking over to Cash, Cole extended his hand. "Cole Mouzon, sorry we didn't get introduced under better conditions. Thank you for all your help. I'm sorry; I don't remember your brother. Hell, I didn't even know about all this until a day ago. But I promise, I will do everything I can to understand this, to understand what hunted your brother, and bring this person down before he or she takes down me or anyone else."

"What do you mean takes you down?" Cole looked slightly shocked; he had figured that Cash had been told why this was all kicking up now.

"They didn't tell you? Someone...a woman is back and killing all those who were kidnapped. From what the tea leaves say, I'm next."

"What!? I just assumed from what I was told earlier today that the guy was at it again kidnapping people. *Killing? You?*" Cash shook his head in remorse and shock. "Oh my god, I am so sorry. Well, what are you going to do? I mean they're going to get...you said *her*?"

"Yeah, 'her.' Seems it's someone new. And, just trying to live, man. Just trying to live." Cole's words were calm and patient. It was the truth. He knew it. He was still

detached from any sense of fear or pain as his cold analytical side stood guard, protecting him, and yet driving
him toward danger as he tried to understand and solve
this mystery.

"Here, let me give you my number. Putting aside all
of this, I would like to know your brother, who he was,
what he went through. My inability to remember was an
obvious gift, after listening to you. But whether I want
to or not, I need to remember…to understand before this
person comes. If you remember anything, please let me
know. I will understand if getting involved is the last
thing you want to do, though. Either way, I would like to
hear more about your brother, if you are at all interested."
Cole grabbed a pen from the desk and tore a sheet from a
stray pile of yellow Post-its. After writing down his number he shook Cash's hand and left to join his sister, still
chatting in the hall.

# CHAPTER 58

T HE CONVERSATION IN the car was short. Cole
 insisted that he stay at his parents' home. Things
were getting way too real and time was running out. If
Agent Leas was correct, the bugle of this fox hunt had
been sounded for the chase and he didn't want Jackie or
Billy anywhere near that. Cop or not, she was still his sister and if someone was going to die, it wasn't going to be
either of them. Jackie protested and it was only when a
call to Agent Leas and her captain affirmed the decision
was best did she agree. In exchange, Cole was to have a
twenty-four-seven hidden escort starting that night, no
arguing.

Cole arrived at his parents' home and opened their
cabinets for something to satisfy the heavy grumbling in
his stomach. Finding nothing, he zeroed in on the remaining half of the hummingbird cake on the counter. *Fuck
it. I can run in the morning.* Cole ran out to his Granny's
apartment and raided her beer stash, grabbing all available from the small, white refrigerator to complement his
meal. Back in the house, he put all but one in the main
home's brushed-steel refrigerator and moved to the living room, switching on the TV as background noise while
he read. He opened the file Agent Leas had given him the

night before and flipped to the police report as he shoved a forkful of cake in his mouth. He began to read.

*3/21/82 – 20:14. RESPONDED TO A CALL AT THE OLD ACADEMY. MOUZON AND CALHOUN BOY FOUND. MOTHER MOUZON D.O.A. UPON ARRIVING AT SCENE, MET BY OF.S HAMMOND AND RANDAL WHO LED ME TO BACK OF SCHOOL. TIDE WAS OUT. LED BY FLASHLIGHT TO MARSH TREES DIRECTLY BEHIND PLAYGROUND SWINGS, WHERE OFFICER BECKER WAS WAITING.*

*WALKING UP, A SMALL OPENING VISIBLE, THOUGH COVERED BY THICK BRUSH IN THE MIDDLE OF HAMMOCK. BODY STILL ON SCENE. OBVIOUS CONTUSIONS, LACERATIONS, AND BLEEDING. HANDCUFFS PRESENT ON LEFT ARM, POSSIBLY NEW. NO RUST. JOSEPH FRANKLIN – SON OF MOUZON BOY'S SITTER – FOUND THE CHILDREN / MOTHER IN MARSH. NO INDICATION HOW LONG THE CHILDREN WERE PRESENT AROUND BODY, POSSIBLY DAYS.*

*CHILDREN TRANSPORTED TO ROPER HOSPITAL PRIOR TO ARRIVAL. ADVISED MOUZON UNRESPONSIVE, APPARENT DEHYDRATION AND MALNUTRITION. CRITICAL. DRUGS POSSIBLE. CALHOUN*

*STABLE, ALERT. MEDICAL NOTED BURNS –
BRANDING ON BOTH. INCH IN SIZE SQUARE
WITH P INSIDE BOX.*


*AREA TAPED OFF UNTIL INVESTIGATION WAS
COMPLETE.*


It was one of the shorter reports in the file, but the one that gave the clearest picture of the scene. *I was marked, marked like cattle.* Cole could see the place. The report had filled in the space left by his dream. When darkness descended on his dream, it had hidden just what happened to him in that hammock of trees. Again, his mind had been protecting him, withholding the full truth that would have likely changed his life in a way not unlike Mark Calhoun's.

Cole glanced at the TV screen and took a deep swig of the Bud. Cole set aside the now empty plate and stood to walk back to the kitchen. *I need another beer.* His cell phone rang on the kitchen counter where he had left it to charge when first coming in. *Unknown number. 843.* Someone from Charleston.

Cautiously picking it up, Cole answered, "Hello?"

"Cole, this is Cash Calhoun from earlier today. I would like to take you up on that offer, if you're still interested." Cash's words came out rushed, like he had brewed on the decision to call and decided to act before the courage was lost.

Cole was surprised, but excited at the same time. "By all means...when are you free?"

"Are you available now?"

"I'm kinda under house arrest for the night. Killer out for me and all, you know…"

"Ah, I bet. You're probably as tense as the Charlestonians when Blackbeard blockaded the port and held the city hostage." Realizing his historic joke had landed with a heavy thud, he added, "I can come there."

Cole attempted to ignore the slip of intellect, but a small hiccup of a laugh escaped. Looking around to check the cleanliness of the living room, he said, "Uhmm, sure. Let me give you the address. Under one condition though. Well…actually two."

"Yeah, what's that?"

"That you don't kill me. And, and this is the important one. You grab some decent beer on your way. I can't deal with this Bud Light."

Cash laughed and spoke in a more relaxed tone. "The beer is a done deal. On the first request, we shall see."

"Ha, fair enough." Cole smiled to himself before ending the call.

# CHAPTER 59

CASH ARRIVED AN hour later, at almost midnight, to the Mouzon marsh-side home. Cole had previously warned his police escort and bribed him with a slice of the hummingbird cake and a beer. He had declined the beer, but the cake was accepted with gusto.

"Come in!" Cole shouted as he was placing the officer's plate in the dishwasher. "The door's unlocked." The futility of his security came to mind in hearing himself say that.

Cash walked in with the same navy shorts but now paired with a heathered grey t-shirt. His leather sandals clapped behind him as he shut the door. "Someone ordered beer?" From behind his back he revealed a six-pack of HopArt IPA.

"Thank god! I'm parched." Cole threw the bottle opener to Cash. "Open a couple of those bad boys, pronto." Cash grinned and obliged. "Uhm, you know it's probably not best to leave your door unlocked if someone is trying to kill you."

"Yeah, yeah. I just unlocked it for you. I figure if someone wants to kill me though, that flimsy glass door isn't really going to stop them."

Cash bowed in acquiescence. "Fair enough. Here is your beer, sir."

In the living room Cole introduced himself, his history, his life. He told him about the last couple of days, the note, the revelation of his childhood. Cash took it all in silence, absorbing the information like he was at a seminar.

Finally, Cole asked, "What was Mark like?"

Cash's face went grave as he spoke. "He was broken. That about sums it up...just broken. No amount of therapy, love, holding could piece him together. Sure, there were times that he seemed fine, but those were pretty rare, especially when we were young. In the last few years before his death, it seemed better. He didn't mention it. He had a steady job as a bartender and a part-time girlfriend. But, looking back. Well, I think he was just holding it in. And, then it popped. The sad fact is, it was kinda like watching an elderly parent sick in bed, out of it, just waiting to die... There was a good bit of relief by my parents and me when he died. The way, jumping off the bridge, was rough to take. But he was no longer in pain, troubled by it all." Cash's eyes were moist with tears fighting for release.

The statement 'holding it all in' stuck in Cole's head. He wondered if he was doing the same thing in always trying to keep up the wall...in not wanting to feel. The thought scared him.

Shaking off the thought, Cole said, "I don't know about you, but I think it's time for that second beer." Cole was again attempting to diffuse the serious mood.

"Deal." Relief filled Cash's voice.

Returning to the living room with two fresh beers, Cole plopped on the couch next to Cash. "Would you like to see the file? I know they gave you a report, but this has a good bit more."

"Uhm, I guess...actually yes."

COLE FLIPPED THE file open and proceeded to point out documents and pictures he found important. Cash listened intently, asking questions as they arose, though clearly uncomfortable with learning more. After about another forty minutes, "I think I need a break." Cash was overwhelmed by all this new information on his brother, his kidnapping and just what he went through. He had experienced the effect, sure. But according to him his knowledge of what had actually happened was limited by his parents' fears that if they probed too much they would injure Mark even more. So the event wasn't discussed, only Mark's behavior and thoughts about it.

Cole walked to the kitchen and returned with a bottle opener and two fresh beers. Without a word, he pointed to the screened porch on the back of the house, as if to say, "Join me?" Cash got up from his place on the couch and followed, collapsing into a patio chair overlooking the marsh.

The damp air took a moment of adjustment. Cole closed his eyes for a second before looking on the marsh being lit by an almost-full moon with the occasional cloud from the impending storm dimming its light. The dark butterfly shadows of bats chasing dragonflies and marsh gnats crisscrossed the air in their muffled flutters.

"Why do you think this is happening now...again, Cole?" Cash spoke without turning away from the marsh.

Cole took a deep breath. It was a question that had already passed through his mind many times. *What triggered this? Why now?* His kidnapping had been thirty years earlier; could it be that the kidnapper saw the end of his days coming and decided to act while he still physically or mentally could? Not likely since all the evidence was saying a younger woman was the one killing. So far he had been unable to come up with any plausible reason other than 'just because.' Cole finally responded. "You know, I really just don't know. All of this is so new to me. I haven't had time to digest it all. Hell, even the FBI is stumped at this point."

Cash nodded his head as a long howl was heard in the distance. A second one followed, as if they were saying, "Where are you?" "I'm here."

"Do you hear that? You know what that is, right?" Cole was full of worthless information and he knew he was about to show it.

Cash twisted his head in Cole's direction. "You mean those dogs?"

"Yeah, but those are wolves, not dogs. Red wolves. They were reintroduced back in the 1980s, but Hurricane Hugo all but killed them. They have just started trying it again. Pretty cool, huh? Wolves in Charleston."

"Yeah, I think I read about that in the *Post and Courier*. I am sure you wouldn't appreciate running across those in Francis Marion." Cole laughed and thought to himself, *No running into them in the national forest would not be fun.* But he had the feeling he was nonetheless being hunted by a wolf that he could not escape.

THE SIX PACK and the remaining Buds had all been drunk by the time the first yawn struck just past three a.m. "Thanks for coming over. I really enjoyed this. Just sorry it was under these conditions."

"Same here. I don't know who is doing this or why, but from a personal stance, it helps to understand what my brother went through. And, from what I know so far, Mark would have liked you, a lot." It was obvious Cash meant his words.

"Yeah, if I had gone to Bishop England, or ya'll lived over here to go to Wando, we would have probably stayed in each other's lives. I'd like to think so, at least." Cole stood up and yawned again. "So listen, we have drunk enough beers that you shouldn't drive back, especially with the po-po sitting outside my door. I'm in this house all alone and there are ample beds. So, you are crashing here for the night. Got it?"

Cash tried to wave off the invite. "Man, I am fine."

Interrupting before he could get another word out, Cole added, "Yeah, I know you are, but nonetheless, you're staying. I cook a mean breakfast Hot Pocket." A large grin crossed Cole's face.

"Well, when you put it that way, put me down for two." Cash stood up. "So where to, Captain?"

Walking inside the house together Cole filled him in on the sleeping arrangements. "You can stay in my sister's old room upstairs. Hope you like pink. Lots of pink."

"Ha. How did you know? That is 'like...totally me.'" Cash said the last three words in 'valley girl' talk and made Cole laugh.

"Okay, Regina George. Let me show you where the clean towels are and such before you get hit by that bus." Cole had seen Mean Girls one too many times with Ann and it had stuck. From the loud laugh he released, the reference was clearly not lost on Cash.

Cash settled upstairs, Cole crawled into his parents' bed. The silence of the house was unnerving and made all the emotions held back from the day crash through his mental wall. Anger, fear, and pain poured into his body and he wondered if he would survive this week. *Who was this Poinsett and why?* He knew, felt, that he would learn soon. Too soon. Jackie was here to help as she had always been. Standing strong against anything that threatened her brother. But he was still feeling alone in the threat of his impending death. There was comfort that night in Cash being in the house. Perhaps he wasn't alone in this after all.

# CHAPTER 60

*Day Six Ninety-Three*

COLE WAS BUSY with the electric griddle, pouring his second batch of pancakes, when he heard the shower start upstairs. *Ain't no Hot Pocket being served in this house.* The morning was cool enough to have the windows and doors to the screen porch open, letting the sounds of the marsh flood into the house, interrupted only by Etta James singing about needing a Sunday kind of love. Fifteen minutes later Cash came down wearing the same clothes as the night before, his hair still wet, slicked back, to be greeted to a pile of pancakes sitting in the middle of back porch's glass table. Cole took in the sight of him for a second. "Mornin'. How did you sleep?"

Cash responded as he grabbed the cup of coffee Cole had offered. "Well, if you discount the pink boogie monsters in my dreams, pretty well. Man you weren't kidding about all the pink."

Cole laughed, "No, I warned you. Ever since Jackie was little it was like one of those pink boogie monsters vomited in the room. Apparently Mom couldn't bring herself to paint over it when they turned it into a guest room."

Both men sat down at the table and admired the marsh view for a few moments. A red-winged black bird sung somewhere off in the distance as Cole noticed a morning dove cooing above the house. "You know, Granny always said it was bad luck to have a dove land on your house, it means someone's about to die." The statement caught Cash off guard as he reached in for a pancake. He retreated back into his seat with a puzzled look on his unshaven face, without his prize.

"Cole, you know that isn't going to happen. We're going to stop him, Cole. You'll see." The 'we' stuck out to Cole. How did it all of a sudden became a 'we?'

Cash continued, "Do you believe every old wives' tale you hear, Grandpa?" His wide smile crossed his face to reveal a perfect set of bleached teeth. Cole's random-fire brain sparked; he clearly did not grow up in Mount Pleasant, where the excess of natural fluoride stained children's teeth with white and brown lines for generations.

Rolling his eyes to exaggerate his response, Cole said, "No, Mr. Cash, I don't believe them all. But you know... the local hoodoo people seem to get it right most of the time. Whether it's throwing bones or what, I don't know. But I've seen my share of the unexplained and I'm not about to question centuries of African insight at this point in my life." He was playing devil's advocate, though he did tend to agree with his current stand.

"Lord, no wonder someone is after you. Sick in the head you are if you listen to all that mumbo-jumbo. Want me to pour some tea and you read the leaves, Miss Cleo?"

Cole playfully cut his eyes. "No, you can't afford my services, sir." They laughed at the game they were playing.

Reaching for a couple pancakes, Cole started again.

"So, a buddy of mine called this morning. That's what woke me up so early. I let him know the other day someone is running around with the name Poinsett and I needed any insight to see if there was a connection. He has apparently found something and wants to meet to show me."

Cash sat up in excitement. "That is great news! When are we meeting him?"

Cole silently registered what Cash had just said. *There's that 'we' again.*

"Where does he want to meet?"

Cole responded, "Actually, he said he can come here. He lives in Snee Farm just down the road. So he'll stop by on a lunch break. Must be nice to work from home, huh?"

"Can I attend? I mean… I'd like to know what's going on there. If this is in any way related to my brother, I want to know."

"Are you kidding? Of course! I don't know about you, but I'm excited to see what he has to say." With that, Cole wolfed down his third pancake and stared off into the distance. *We are on to you, Poinsett.*

# CHAPTER 61

CASH LEFT AFTER breakfast to head home and change while Cole showered. Security had been rotated with a new guard and Cole felt obliged to go out and deliver some sweet tea. Tropical storm Andrea was still in Florida but her winds were slowly arriving, cutting through the syrupy air, dense with moist heat. Summer was on its way and the area's only saviors were the coastal winds and storms that came like clockwork at three in the afternoon. The random tropical storm or hurricane was often seen as a mixed blessing, cooling off the unbearable summers, but wreaking havoc with its winds and tornados.

By ten-thirty Cash was back. The remainder of the 'team,' as Cole thought of them, was there within minutes. Agent Leas looked a little shocked when he walked in to see Cash in the kitchen adding ice to his glass of tea. Leas shook it off and focused on the task. He was followed by Daniel Page, who had agreed at dinner in Charleston to assist in digging up anything on Poinsett, now swaggering in with nothing in his hands but an iPad and some papers. Before Cole could press him on what he had found, his sister came rushing in, Billy in tow.

"I'm sorry, I'm sorry. I got stuck in traffic at the

connecter in front of the mall, and well, as you can see Hanna 'the miracle worker' is sick and my emergency babysitter flaked out on me. So...here I am." Jackie blew a piece of her hair out of her face, reminding him of Ava's disheveled moments when he was a child. "Billy, go upstairs and play with those dinosaurs Granny got for you last month."

"Awe, mom..."

"No, 'awe mom.' Upstairs, I need to talk to these people and then we will go, mister." Billy slowly crawled up the stairs and could be heard in the playroom above digging in the toy bin. A few "chomp chomps" and "arrs" later signaled it was all clear for adult talk.

"Okay Daniel, so, as you have been informed, someone is running around with the name Poinsett and we are just trying to figure out if it is important. Anything you can offer would surely be of help."

"Well, as we discussed, I called my contacts in D.C. to pull any records of Poinsetts around Charleston." Daniel paused to look over at Leas to see if there was any objection to a layperson using D.C. contacts but Leas just nodded him to keep talking. "Okay, I have to say, there are a hell of a lot of them around here and then out west. But, here... None seemed to really stand out but the one guy, Laurence Poinsett. And the only reason he stands out is because he disappeared around the time you and the Calhoun boy were taken. Cole, he worked for SCE&G back before it was SCANA, as a lineman or something."

"The electric and gas company? It makes sense, I guess. They work this area and every house and home. So they would know the best place to hide, to take someone so no one would know." Cole's mind turned to the suffering his mom likely went through; those days stuck in that make-shift cabin, dehumanized and knowing that her son was left to watch. Anger brewed up against the wall, threatening to frustrate Cole's ability to decipher all the facts he was hearing. "Where is this cabin?"

"Sorry, Cole. That has been gone for some time. After your mom and you were discovered, they bulldozed that thing. A few years later a developer put houses on it." Officer Hershel spoke for the first time in the two days he had been Cole's personal security guard. He seemed to have surprised even himself by speaking out.

Cole turned back to the printouts Daniel had spread across the dining room table. "What's this, his criminal record? Nothing really there, is there? Driver's license looks clean for those years. Georgia, Portland, Wyoming. He moved around, didn't he?"

Daniel responded. "Yeah, as you see, the South Carolina one didn't get renewed. That's the end of the trail."

Agent Leas looked down at the papers and then got a doubtful face. "Why do you think this is the guy? So the guy disappeared. People disappear all the time. Why is he the kidnapper?" Leas had once again lost patience with the information he was hearing.

Daniel leaned up, and spoke with irritated words. "Man, I have no clue. But, if someone with the name Poinsett kidnapped Cole and killed his mom, my money is on this guy. How that helps now, I don't know." Daniel wasn't impressed with Leas and his questions.

Ignoring the disagreement, Cole's mind kept brewing, *How was this person involved? Perhaps a relative?* He needed to figure out the connections fast before someone else died at the hands of this killer. Within thirty minutes it was obvious no answers were going to be found in that meeting. Daniel left what he had found with Cole. Agent Leas skulked off feeling his time had been wasted. Jackie was the only one still chipper. "We'll get him Cole, you wait. It's just not as easy as we'd like."

# CHAPTER 62

D R. WINTERS SAT back in her poolside chair at
MidCity Lofts on Spring Street. A young couple
was playing intimately in the corner of the pool while
another, much-older woman with too-red lipstick read a
cheap romance novel beside her. The doctor had moved
there several years ago for the view, of both Atlanta and
Rob Marciano, who'd lived there until getting hitched
and accepting his new position with Entertainment
Tonight. Sure, her frequent run-ins with Joe Manganiello
and other stars brought to town for the city's booming
movie industry were nice. But in her building... Rob's
departure had left the view mediocre at best, with little
more than Turner Studios complex across interstate 75 to
spark interest.

Her fantasy of having once rubbed his freckled back
down with sunscreen was interrupted by the buzzing of
her phone against the glass table beside her chair. "This is
Beth."

"Dr. Winters, uh...this is Agent Leas from the FBI. I
hope I'm catching you at a good time, and sorry to interrupt your day, but I have some questions if you have
time."

Watching the couple in the corner getting a little too

acquainted, she responded. "Oh, Agent, I'm out of the office today...just editing a toxicology article, but I've got time for you."

"Well, you see, a name has come up that, and this might be a stretch, but I wanted to see if you had any insight on this. The name is Poinsett. A Joel Poinsett, I believe." Still slightly hung-over from the night, Leas stumbled as he tried to read his handwritten notes from the meeting just moments ago at the Mouzon home. It was a stretch to him; but it was his job to follow any lead, even if he thought it was stupid.

The doctor took a sip of her Riesling. "By all means, Agent. Hmm, Poinsett, as in poinsettia, I believe. My specialty isn't botany, *per se*. But the poinsettia certainly fits with your case." As she finished her last sentence, the lipstick lady pushed the doctor's arm with her book for attention and then pointed at the couple, clearly sharing her shock as to what they were observing in the pool.

Leas continued talking on the phone. "And how is that?"

Shaking off what she was seeing, the doctor continued. "Well, poinsettias are in the plant family *euphorbia*. Plants that produce a milky sap that oozes when they're damaged. Almost all in the family are toxic to some degree, from mild irritant to deadly poison."

"Hmm, that definitely helps. Anything else you can think of?"

"No, not really."

"Doctor, let me ask you one last thing. Are poinsettias poisonous?"

"That's a common misconception. No. Other than being a mild stomach irritant, there is little toxicity in poinsettias. Why do you ask?"

"Oh, just curious. I've got some information here I'm tracking down. If needed, can you come to Charleston to assist? I know it's short notice, but…"

Dr. Winters sat up in her chair and interrupted with excitement, "Are you kidding? A chance to visit Charleston and enjoy your company? Sounds wonderful. Just let me know, okay?"

Leas was surprised by her excitement and grateful for her response. "Well, I will let you know. Again, thank you for your time. I'll let you get back to whatever you're doing. Perhaps we can grab that drink down here."

"Just let me know. Ciao."

Agent Leas withdrew the phone from his ear with a smile on his face momentarily before he refocused on his priority—*Find Poinsett.*

# CHAPTER 63

"JACKIE, LET ME take Billy while you get some work done." Cole looked down at his nephew and smiled. "You'd like that, wouldn't you, hanging out with Uncle Cole?"

On cue, Billy responded, "Can I, Mom? Pleeease." Billy played his mother with his large brown puppy eyes.

Mimicking his nephew's pitiful look, Cole said, "Sis, it's the safest place in the world. I have my own muscle thanks to the kind taxpayers of Mount P. And I haven't had a chance to hang out and whip his butt in LEGO Lord of the Rings." Cole stuck his tongue out at Billy, prompting Billy to respond with a waved fist and a smile.

Relenting against the pressure of two boys, Jackie smiled. "Cole, I don't want him staying in the house all day and playing video games. You hear me? He needs to get outside and do something." Jackie wagged her finger at both of the boys.

"Wow, you just sounded like Mom there…"

"I am a mom, if you haven't noticed." Jackie snapped her neck in a playful way.

"Sweet! Boys' time! I can't wait to take you down on the Xbox…" Looking back to his sister with Billy alongside him, he amended, "I mean...to hang out with you outside. Woo-hoo." Cole feigned excitement.

Looking around the wall into the living room, Billy located Cash on the couch texting. "Cash, you want to come?"

Cole felt awkward at his nephew's invite. "Oh, Billy, I don't think Cash wants to hang out here all day. He has..."

Cash interrupted, "Hmmm, I'd love to! But my bet is on Billy beating you."

Surprised by his acceptance and challenge, Cole playfully responded, "Uh, those are fighting words, sir."

Jackie decided she had seen and heard enough boy talk. "Okay. I should be back by six or so to pick him up. Cole, he better have been outside, mister, or the only person going down will be you."

"Ooooooh." All three boys responded simultaneously.

Throwing up her hands and turning, Jackie shouted out, "Boys!" Half-way out the door, they heard her repeat, "Cole, not all day, hear me?"

Cole waited until he heard the door shut before speaking. "Okay, before we get started, we need to eat. I'm starved. How about you, mister, are you hungry?"

Billy was twisting back and forth on one of the bar stools at the kitchen counter. "Yes, sir! Mom made oatmeal and it was cold."

Cole wrinkled his nose. "Oh no! Not cold oatmeal. What kind of craziness is that?"

"The worst, Uncle Cole."

"Oh I bet. Hey buddy, can you do me a favor? Yeah? Can you ask Mr. Cash over there if he would like a tomato sandwich and chips?"

Billy walked over to Cash who had now sat himself at

the dinette in the corner of the kitchen. "Mr. Cash, would you like a 'mato sam'ich and chips?"

Cash looked down. "Well, I think that would be wonderful. I love tomato sandwiches. Extra mayo and pepper for me, sir."

Clapping his hands together and looking around the counter for supplies, Cole said, "Then it's a plan; tomato sandwiches, then we better get outside before a storm runs through here. Don't worry, you aren't safe from your whipp'in in LEGO Lord of the Rings, Mr. Billy. You're going down." Cole channeled a WWE wrestler for his last three words.

Cash chimed in. "I play the winner!"

"I guess you're playing me then..." Cole's mouth dropped as Billy said the words. He admired the wit of his nephew.

Cole said, "Well, okay then. While you're planning your celebration, can you go grab some tomatoes off Granny's bushes out there? Nice and red, but not too crazy soft, please." Billy bounded out the back door and down the steps to his grandmother's garden.

Walking into the kitchen, Cash spoke. "That kid is crazy smart."

"Tell me something I don't know. He clearly takes after his unk Cole over here." Cole grabbed an imaginary shirt collar and tugged with bravado.

Cash laughed and pushed Cole's arm playfully with his elbow. "Ha, that remains to be seen."

Cole cut his eyes. "Oooh, rotten tomatoes for you, sir."

"Num num, my favorite."

"Figures," said Cole.

Billy had returned with three large, reddish-orange tomatoes. Sitting at the kitchen counter, Cash watched as Billy pulled up alongside him and the two formed an assembly line for the meal. Cole sliced the tomatoes as Billy laid out the bread on paper plates and slathered the slices with a thick coat of Hellmann's. Tomatoes placed, the three plates were dusted with pepper and salt before the sandwiches were closed, juices flowing out from the edges.

"Earth to Cash, uh, earth to Cash. Would you like some more tea?" He had drifted off and his mental absence had been caught.

"Oh, sorry, yes please."

"So are you in? We're going down to the dock to cast. Billy says he's cooking dinner. Game?"

Cole smiled as he tried to reconnect to the present. "Ha, for casting or dinner?"

"Both if you want."

Shrugging, Cash said, "Sure, why not."

Lunch was scarfed down quickly with the anticipation of play. On the back porch, Cole asked, "Billy, will you go grab the cast net out of the garage and a bucket for the shrimp?"

"You didn't say please."

"Ha. No I didn't, did I? Please."

Using Billy's absence, Cole asked, "So, what was that about?"

"What do you mean?" The two worked together to clean up lunch as they talked.

"That daze just a second ago. Everything okay?"

Caught, Cash awkwardly smiled. "Yeah, I was just thinking of Mark." He explained that though the good times had been rare, they were still there. Watching Cole and Billy was like watching Mark and himself, the *rumble from the jungle*, they called themselves. It was a name their father had given them because they made so much noise playing, "You would think two gorillas were outside." Mark had been his closest friend when they were really young. It was only when Mark entered his teens that he started to completely withdraw, to step away from the family. But, in this moment, Cash chose to remember their youth and how much he dearly loved his older brother.

The discussion ended when Billy returned quickly with a white net overflowing from a yellowed pail, thrusting the bucket in Cole's hands without notice and causing it to fall. "Mister, what do you think you are doing?"

"You carry it, Uncle Cole. I'm going to race Cash." Cole looked over and with a faux look of anger and matching hand movements proclaimed, "See my pinky, see my thumb, see my fist, you better run!" Both boys took off out of the kitchen and off the deck toward the dock as though the threat were serious.

# CHAPTER 64

"LET THE MASTER show you how to do this. Step back." Cash clasped the tangled white plastic mesh netting, shaking it until the weighted ends fell completely down. Billy stood on the dock, fixated, as Cash waded into the water slowly avoiding the sharp edges of oysters with his feet. Cole joined in on watching the show, sitting on the edge of the floating boat landing and dipping his feet into the milky brown water. Cash looked at home in the marsh as water wicked up the edge of his linen shorts. The sun beamed on his tanned, muscular back, causing small beads of sweat to blend with dark freckles along his shoulders and collect in streams where the ribbons of his muscles ran.

Wrapping some of the main line around his left wrist, he went step-by-step, instructing Billy just how to throw the perfect net. The net was airborne with an effortless sling of Cash's left arm, landing in a perfect circle on the rippled water's edge. A Carolina wren swept in and under the edge of the landing for a meal as though he hadn't noticed the fluid display. Slowly, Cash pulled the line and tugged at the weights now fighting against him. Inch by inch, the net was revealed at the water's surface, its captives flicking with shock of being extracted from their salty pool. Ravens called in adjacent loblolly pines as Cole let the moment wash over him.

"My turn, my turn." Billy was ready for his lesson. He jumped feet first into the water with his Wild Kratts green shorts. Cole cringed, fearing he would land on a bed of oysters hidden under the water. There were only screams of happiness as he swam, well, dog paddled, to Cash. Cash bent down and lifted Billy with one arm onto his shoulders and resumed his casting lesson, Billy absorbing his every word.

Cole pushed himself off the dock and slid into the water to partake in the lesson. The grey pluff mud held his feet, only to give way with a loud 'slurp' with every lift of his feet. Standing side-by-side, Cash impishly pushed Cole's shoulder in an effort to throw him off balance. "Oh, you don't want to start that, mister. You'll be the one with mud in your face, little man." Laugher engulfed all three of the boys.

FOR THE NEXT hour or so Cash had Billy hoisted on his shoulder, describing in detail the best way to cast the nylon net to perfect its flare into a perfectly opened circle just before entry into the tidal water. Long after Billy bored of the lesson and crawled back onto the dock, Cash continued netting the random creek shrimp and dumping them in bucket to flick around and occasionally escape to their freedom. Cole had grabbed a coloring book and crayons from the house and assisted his nephew in figuring out just what was the best color for Lightening McQueen's racing stripes. There was silence, perfect silence between them.

Eventually, Cash looked over and realized he had lost

his audience. Folding the damp net in large movements, he pushed through the soft bottom of the creek to where Cole and Billy were still coloring, leaned into the dock with his chest and folded his arms across the top of its weathered edge.

Cash asked, "What made you move away?"

With his head still down, Cole looked up with his eyes to find Cash inches from his face. The deep intensity of his sky blue eyes and their gold flecks felt calming and safe. Cole noticed a small, thin scar under his right eye. Working to ignore the turbulence trying to well up inside him, he looked back to the coloring book and said, "From Charleston? Oh, I don't know."

Cash craned his neck down and under Cole's gaze trying to reestablish eye contact. "I mean the South."

Cole paused and took a deep breath before he softly patted the deck next to him to suggest Cash crawl up and get comfortable for longer conversation. "Billy, I bet you can't land a crab!" Billy's eyes rose up from his waxy masterpiece. "I bet I can, too. Just watch me." Billy jumped up and shuffled over to the opposite end of the floating dock and dug into the bucket Cole had brought out earlier, withdrawing a raw chicken neck with a long piece of white string attached. He threw it in and dropped his feet in the water as he sat.

CASH AND COLE lay back on the dock's upper deck while Billy occupied himself with crabbing. Bands of storm clouds crossed the sky in fat, slow movements as they continued.

"Where were we, oh yeah…leaving the South. Yes. I miss the South terribly most days. What's not to miss?

But I have the luxury of making enough to fly wherever I want and I would rather wake up where I don't feel sticky from humidity. Have you ever been to Denver? It's a pretty amazing place. It doesn't mean I'm not still a Southern boy at heart. I still cook Southern and talk Southern. The only thing missing is other Southern folk."

"Yeah, I guess. Would you ever think of coming back?"

"Part of me would like to raise my kids here, but that's not really in the cards right now." Cole turned to Cash to see his response to that little bomb.

One brow was lifted. "Kids?"

"Tons of kids! Yellow ones, blue ones, pink ones, green ones."

"You getting abducted by aliens or something?" Cash returned the look and smiled.

"Perhaps... And you, sir? What keeps you here, family?"

"Nah, my folks moved up to Vermont after I went to college up at Dartmouth. When I landed a tenure track back here at C. of C., they decided they would stay. They come and visit in the winter for several weeks since I took over their place. But, other than that, there isn't much in the way of family around here... I can't really say what keeps me here. I mean, it is a great place. The people are so proper and mannered and such, like the magazines say. And life in such a beautiful city is pretty damn good. But I think it's comfort more than anything else. It's where I was raised. Memories of Mark, even if they are bitter, are still sweet, and I think if I moved anywhere else, I fear I would lose that tether that binds us. Sounds silly, doesn't it?"

"Uhm, not at all. My tether is just a little more elastic

than yours, but I am nonetheless fully and completely connected to this damn humid place." Cole smiled.

"I got one!" Billy shouted from the edge of the dock, providing a distraction from the otherwise serious conversation. "Well, where's the net? Let's scoop him up!" Cole walked over and immediately noticed that the crab was way too small to eat, but decided to scoop him up just for Billy's reaction. "Slowly now. Let me get the net under him." Cole dipped the net in and under the crab, still firmly clasping onto the pale chicken neck, lifting them in one large scoop.

"Wow! That sucker is huge!" Cash had decided to aid in the excitement. "But what are we going to do with just one crab? That might cause a fight between us, 'cause I can tell you I would eat the whole thing." Cash had clearly picked up on the need to release the crab.

"Yeah, Billy, that booger is a whopper, but let's let him go and we can catch him another time when we plan on cooking crab. Deal?" Cole was working at suggestion in hopes Billy wouldn't put up a fuss about abandoning his catch.

"Uncle Cole...Cash, you must be blind. That thing is tiny. I could eat ten of him. I'm letting him go." Cash and Cole burst out laughing at their clear misperception of Billy's intelligence. The crab released and sun-baked, the boys walked back to the house. Billy rode on Cole's shoulders and leaned down for a whisper. "Uncle Cole, I like him."

Cole looked over at Cash, trying to avoid being overheard. "Yeah? I like him, too."

# CHAPTER 65

L EAS PULLED UP to the powder-pink stucco home of Dr. Steve Christie and took a second to compose himself in his rented Camry. The stench of whiskey still lingered around him, though he'd attempted to cover it up with mouthwash. The three-story East Battery home overlooked the Charleston Harbor and Mount Pleasant. He buzzed the black wrought-iron gate's intercom twice before it was answered by someone who was clearly the maid or housekeeper. "Christie residence, may I help you?"

"FBI ma'am, I need to talk to the doctor please."

"Which one?" Leas hadn't picked up on the wife also being a doctor. *Keeping it in the family.* "Mr. Christie, please."

"He isn't home." The static-tinged voice responded.

"Is the missus in, then?"

"One second."

The gate cranked open and Agent Leas walked across the slate driveway to the back of a long triple-level piazza. The housekeeper was waiting at the top of the steps and escorted him towards the entrance of the home. Leas eyed a perfectly manicured garden behind the old slave quarters, now a garage. Walking in, he looked around and took in the opulence of the home with its dark mahogany woods and twenty-foot ceilings. The floors were wood, painted black, which made the ornate white crown molding stand out. The home was long and much larger than it appeared from the outside.

From the hall, heeled steps could be heard moving toward where he stood. He stared. *Christian Louboutins*. He had no clue about woman's attire, much less shoes, but he knew what the red-bottomed heels meant. His last year with Maria was marked by their tenth anniversary and he had splurged on the thousand-dollar shoes. He had never seen her so happy. God, he missed her.

The woman before him clasped her hands in front of her as she spoke. "I'm Dr. Christie, how may I help you?" Her words were short, uninviting. He had heard that extending a hand to a lady was considered rude in the older parts of the city, but he suspected she was intentionally sending a signal that she was not happy to see him.

Still looking around, he said, "Ma'am, Agent Leas from the FBI. Do you have a moment to talk?"

"Of course. We can talk in the parlor. Treece, please bring us some tea." Leas followed Mrs. Christie across several rooms, all perfectly fit for sitting in his opinion, until they reached one at the farthest end of the home overlooking a formal garden. Topiary filled its edges, with a black fountain in the middle. The equally meticulous room seemed composed to capture the best view, down to the letter opener in its proper place like a display.

Turning away from looking out the window, Mrs. Christie asked, "Now, what is it I can do for you, Officer?"

Ignoring the clear jab at his authority, Leas said, "Agent, ma'am, and I was hoping to talk to your husband. Would you happen to know when he will be home?"

"He is actually off on a business trip to Texas for a medical convention. I don't think he returns until next week. Is there something I can help you with?"

"Well, I really need to talk to him, Doctor. But let me ask you, have you seen any suspicious packages arrived in the past few weeks? They would be small and nondescript, likely in a brown or white box."

Her hands still tightly clasped before her as if she were about to belt out an opera, Mrs. Christie looked away in an obvious attempt to dodge eye contact. "No...no, not that I recall. Should I be concerned, Agent? What is going on and why should my husband be involved with this?"

"I'm not at liberty to say at the moment. But has your husband been to New York or California lately?"

Surprised, she said, "I don't believe so."

"Can I have his phone number to call him? I just have a few questions and I think I can resolve them if I can talk to him."

"Of course, but don't get frustrated if he doesn't immediately respond. As I said, he is in lectures most of the day." Mrs. Christie wrote down her husband's number on a piece of paper Agent Leas was certain was expensive, the heavy-weight kind. Escorted back to the door by Treece, he noted a cell phone sitting with keys in a bowl in the foyer. Outside, he withdrew his phone from his jacket, now damp from the humidity of the city, and punched in the number Mrs. Christie had given him as the door closed behind him. He could hear a phone vibrating back inside the home.

# CHAPTER 66

POINSETT WAS LIVID. Mouzon had disappeared and she couldn't figure out how to flush him out since the FBI agent showed up in Charleston. Without a lead, she'd had to stall the hunt. Her need to kill was spilling over violently like a boiling pot of water, making it more and more difficult to control her rage. She needed Mouzon dead.

Still brewing over the FBI's interference, she reflected back on when she learned about Mouzon and the others. She was in school in Charleston. A guy had mentioned the old event, saying he knew one of the victims. She'd started digging in the archives of the *News and Courier* and the afternoon paper, *The Evening Post*. It took weeks, but she found it there on the front page. From there the investigation splintered off. With help of the limited internet, she researched any kidnapping and murder that had occurred where the children were branded and released, their parents murdered. Slowly she found the others.

Somewhere during her search the realization grew that but for them, she would have never have been abandoned, abused. Why had the Taker chosen them over her? It wasn't as simple as her sex; Whitney Havex defeated that theory. She needed to know and the answer wasn't going to come from those he let go. If she was to ever get answers she had to lure him out.

Agent Leas and those around Mouzon threatened to frustrate her attempts to end their hold over her once and for all. It was Mouzon she wanted dead, not the rest. If she couldn't get him away from them she would have to draw him out to deal with this new contingency. *Bread crumbs.*

# CHAPTER 67

I T WAS FIVE till six when Jackie walked into the house. Without turning his head from the game he was play-ing on TV, Billy acknowledged his mother. "Hey Mom!" He was sitting on the floor next to Cash, deep into his next move. Jackie continued past the boys into the kitchen. "Well, hey! How was work?" Cole was standing over a cast iron frying pan full of small cornmeal-battered shrimp sizzling from the heated peanut oil.

"Someone went shrimpin' I see."

Billy shouted from the other room, "Mister Cash and I caught all those, Mom. Uncle Cole just watched and col-ored." Cole raised his shoulders with a sideways smile on his face and saw his sister look over her shoulder to pass a glance at Cash. "Watching, huh? I bet... Damn, I hate that I missed *that* show." A large mischievous smirk crossed her face revealing she knew *exactly* what Cole was actually watching.

"Anyway...whew, am I red?" She fanned herself. "What was it you asked? Oh, yeah, work... It was good, way too busy. I pulled the files of Cash's brother and plan to hit those tonight." Her head was still turned to watch Billy and Cash zoned into the TV. She leaned into the counter, resting on her forearms to get a better look into the next room. "Looks like someone has a new friend."

"Which one?" After taking the pan off the stove Cole joined his sister in taking in the view still sitting in the living room.

Jackie turned around and pressed her back into the counter's edge to engage her brother directly. Cole asked, "Any news on that Poinsett craziness?"

"Your guess is as good as mine. Your buddy Agent Leas locked himself in one of our spare offices for half the day and then bolted out of there like the place was on fire. Haven't heard from him since."

"Poinsett?"

"Likely, but no clue. As much booze as that guy smells like, I wouldn't be surprised if he is just using the office as his private bar." Jackie leaned her head back, staring at the ceiling. "Billy, get your things together, we need to get you home and in the tub. I can smell that stinky pluff mud from here."

"Here, take some of these shrimp with you. There are way too many." Jackie nodded thank you at Cole's offer.

"Awh, mom, but we're at Saruman's Tower trying to break the dams to flood the Orcs' fortress. Ten more minutes. Pleeease?"

"No, pause it or something. Your mom is tired and you still need to eat before your bath and bed."

"Awwwwh."

"Don't 'awh' me, now say goodbye." Cole stared at his sister, seeing her in new light since Billy was born. Gone were the tantrums and wild days of her youth when, at sixteen, she hid beer under the trailer out on Rifle Range. The woman before him was in no way associated with the girl dragged out of a boy-filled hotel room at seventeen by his father when she failed to come home after the prom. Motherhood looked good on her and changed her. She had always been strong and motherly to Cole. But that strength had only intensified with Billy in her life. The wild parties, the poor decisions had sloughed off like caked-on marsh mud, revealing the woman now before him.

"I guess I better go, too. It's getting late and I have gym in the morning." Cash nodded his head and exited the living room behind Billy.

"Wait! You aren't going to eat any of these shrimp I just slaved in the kitchen frying?"

Cash came alongside Cole, lightly gripped his neck from behind and threw a shrimp into his mouth. "Delicious. But, it's gotten a bit later than I thought and I do need to go. I have to work on some prep for a seminar I'm presenting at in two weeks and have nothing done. I promise I'll make it up to you, though."

Cole just frowned as the group walked out the door together. Gravel sounds dimmed into silence as their cars drove down the broken stone drive, leaving Cole alone again in the big house. *Well, fuck. What just happened?*

After eating alone on at the dinette, still slightly sad, he slumped down into one of the old leather living room chairs and cleared his head. Moments like this, of nothingness, passing through his head, recharged him.

After several minutes he wakened from his meditation. *Okay, let's do this.*

# CHAPTER 68

"COME IN. PARDON THE MESS." Agent Leas had called after everyone had left and requested Cole come to his hotel. From his voice, it sounded urgent, and Cole did not hesitate at the offer. The request to go to his hotel seemed unusual, but it was late. As Leas put it, 'She won't be looking for you here unless she's really dumb and I'd like your insight on some things.'

Thirty minutes later Cole pulled up to the old roadside hotel. Walking in, the room was dank with the scent of spent booze and musky carpet. Cole suspected the odor arose from the several empty liquor bottles that lay on their sides in the corner. One of the two queen beds was undone and a mess, the other apparently a makeshift desk.

Cole spoke without thinking. "This may be the first time I actually wish the government spent more. Did you find this place in the back of some seedy magazine or a bathroom stall?"

Leas grinned, liking Cole's candor. "The latter. But I didn't invite you over to admire my room. I've pulled all the files for the six children, including you, who were taken around the time of your kidnapping. All with brands. All released."

"Yeah, and what have you found?"

"Sit, sit. This may take a moment." Seeing no place to sit, Cole swept some old newspapers off the corner of the bed and caught an article from what appeared to be Texas with the headline, "Man Butchered In Dallas."

Several manila folders had been spread across the floor, each with a name and a date. His name was missing. "These are the three victims to date. Tony Patrick, Whitney Havex, and Phillip Neal. New York, Texas, California. The only things holding them together are the missing marks at this point." Cole picked up the Neal file and let it fall open in his hands. There were pages of police reports, but what caught his eye were the photos. There, lying face down, was a man associated with him by a common thread, a dangerous past that held them together like a web. That thread ran between all the kidnapping victims and now, like a spider, someone was waiting for vibrations on the thread to direct their attack. *What had these three done to be killed? What have I done to be next?*

"I suspect you've already cross-referenced their cell phone records, emails, and credit cards, correct?" Cole's days as a criminal defense attorney had taught him a tremendous amount about the crumbs we all leave when we go about our daily lives. With the right eyes, most people's activities read like a very tight schedule.

Leas sat down on the unkempt bed. "Yeah, there was nothing. Just static."

"And the coroners' reports? Anything of interest in there? There was poison in the Patrick case, right?" Cole had read the police for Patrick that Leas had provided at their meeting. He wasn't given the entire file now sitting on the bed, or the report in the New York case.

"Yeah, but we haven't any indication of that in the Havex case. But you're more than welcome to look." Cole pulled out the Havex report and began eyeing it for facts.

Lacerations, cardiac failure, contusions... Nothing stood out for someone who had been in a struggle, cut up from her navel to her neck and then spread open like the doors of a bloody bird cage. "Did you say she died from poison?"

Leas looked up from the file he was reading. "No, that was the other one. We have no injection site in the Havex case. But there is evidence her heart just stopped, so there is some suggestion of an agent. Of course, without any clue, it's almost impossible to isolate the agent if one was used."

Cole's brain began flicking through his metal library of images from book pages and medical articles he had seen over the years until it stopped on a particular page. "Have you looked into a poison, such as *belladonna*?"

Looking quizzical for a moment, Leas slowly took a deep breath. "Uhm, not sure. But, how would you know about poisons?" Leas leaned in.

Cole laughed. He often got this response when he spat out random information. "I worked a few murder cases when I was a PD involving poisons and otherwise have come across it handling toxic cases. The ME's report says dilated eyes and a bad heart. The tropane alkaloids in *belladonna*, or nightshade, cause sensitivity to light, blurred vision, loss of balance, confusion, elevated heart rate and ultimately death if not treated immediately. The tell-tale sign of *belladonna* is dilated pupils." Cole grinned at Leas. Cole's ability to recall everything he had seen impressed even himself on occasions. But, the revelation of his childhood had shaken his confidence in that skill until this moment. He liked that he was still a walking encyclopedia. It comforted him.

Leas wanted to laugh in amazement, but opted to just shake his head with a large grin on his face. "Hmm, that's interesting. Well, assuming poison was used, ingestion versus injection would clearly represent a swap in methodologies versus the Patrick matter and there is still no sign of poison in the San Diego killing."

COLE FLICKED FURTHER in the file, stopping at interior pictures of the scene. He stared at them for a minute or more and then looked up to the empty beige wall of the hotel room. Slowly, he pushed what he had just seen out and onto the wall, creating a mental transparency that existed in all three dimensions in his eyes. The mental space constructed, he mentally walked around in the crime scene of the Havex murder, maneuvering corners and furniture. Wine bottles lay next to her chair. Cole turned to the kitchen and saw a wine cart with a missing glass. He pulled one from the hooks and inspected it. Then he withdrew from the space, his vision going black before refocusing on the wall.

After several seconds he asked, "I don't see a chain of custody for the glasses. I saw where it said that Havex had alcohol, wine in her system at the time of death. Ten to one, she was poisoned by her chardonnay. There are stray wine bottles on the floor; so likely not by the bottles. Perhaps lacing of the glasses sitting on the wine cart, a wine goblet is missing?" Cole turned away from the wall to Leas, whose mouth was wide open.

"What the hell just happened?"

Cole sheepishly smiled, worried that he had exposed

himself to ridicule or judgment. "Sorry about that. It's… it's something *I do*. I can kinda make this photo real in my head, 3D and everything, and then manipulate everything in the space, analyzing it and such. It's called 'spatial intelligence.'"

"Spatial what? Is that like some special power or something?"

Cole slightly recoiled, feeling he was being judged. He tried to explain again. "No, no super power other than a very over-active imagination. 'Spatial intelligence' or so some Gardner expert says. I think it's also called 'picture smarts.' We all kinda have it as kids. Think about invisible friends and such. As a child, that person or thing is our imagination being projected across our vision so that we think we are seeing it, that it's there. Most people lose that mental skill early. But, some…like me, maintain it. I wouldn't be surprised if schizophrenics also have the skill, but unlike them, I know real from imagination and mine is not involuntary. I have to actually force it to happen. It doesn't mean I'm super intelligent or anything; it's just that I process everything by visualization."

Cole couldn't remember a time that the gift wasn't there, but he knew it wasn't something you talked about without being seen as a freak. He had always relied on it…trusted it in secret. But, emotions disrupted it like static. It lied to him in such moments, making accuracy impossible. That scared him now where emotions were constantly flooding against his wall since the revelation of being hunted and the story of his mother's last act of protection. To him, if there were ever a time he needed to be able to think clearly it was now.

"Holy fuck! What does it feel like? Can you see anything?"

Cole laughed, Leas wasn't judging…he was entertained. "I can't see anything. Ever see Star Trek, the holodeck thing they go into? It's just like that, but transparent. I see the wall that I am looking at. In that image I can walk, look under things, pick up things and such, as if I was actually in it. But it's limited by the information I have, the images I have. That's where having a photographic memory really pushes it to the limits. My mental images are very clear with all that information. So, for example, looking at this picture of Havex's kitchen, I can work that space in my mind up to the edge of the photo. My imagination can certainly fill in the visual gaps, but I try to avoid that because I've discovered I'm usually wrong about what lays off the edge of the photo. So, if I look at in my mind, in the space, I let it just fall off into darkness."

Leas shook his head and started laughing hard. "Damn man, what kind of attorney are you? You're like psychic or something. I would not want to be cross-examined by you. And, yes. Even the local detective missed that bit about the glasses. Of course, until Texas, we really weren't linking the poison to anything."

"Ha, well the glasses are in the picture. They are just kinda dark. It's my criminal background that made me pay attention to them. Working serious felonies like child molestations and murders I may have picked up a few things. Test any bottles or the wine glasses in that place and you will likely find poison."

Still chuckling to himself, Agent Leas was on the phone even before Cole could get the words out. "Yeah, Leas here. Is that crime scene in the Havex case still sealed off? Good, can you send one of your guys out there and collect any glasses that may be lying around or on a wine cart and test them for poison, specifically those that would cause immobilization. *Belladonna*, check for belladonna. Appreciate it."

Cole kept reading. According to the Havex file, a suspicious woman, like in Texas, had been identified in the security footage. The front desk security guard had messed up, buying the lady's story that she was surprising her boyfriend with a striptease for his birthday, but needed access to his floor to get the party underway. The price, a flash of her breasts, had been caught from the back on the video footage. Havex was seen entering the underground garage and accessing the elevators within twenty minutes after that, providing ample time for the killer to prepare.

FROM WHAT THE investigators could tell, the murder didn't happen for almost an hour, suggesting the killer hid and waited until Havex was likely drugged and unable to resist. In the bathroom, Havex's hands were bound by rope and she was dragged over the room's door until she hung by her hands against its back, the rope tied to the handle on the other side. That's when the cutting started.

Leas got off the phone with a slight smile "Sure you're not a psychic? That's some good stuff. Mind going through the rest of these and tell me what you see? A pair of fresh eyes may be what's needed. You can stare at my grungy wall all night if you want. I promise not to laugh...too much."

Laughing, Cole said, "Of course."

The video of the bars Patrick frequented had been pulled. He had been spotted at some Mexican restaurant the night of the murder. There was a female, blonde hair, slender, but she avoided the camera. *A pro.* From the notes, she played him like a fiddle, getting him to buy her a drink and then leaving with him within twenty minutes.

By one a.m., all the files were reviewed. It was apparent the Neal murder in San Diego was the first, based on the timeline, and the killer was still cutting her teeth on it. There was no evidence of poisoning, just pure violence— leading the investigators to initially believe they were dealing with a male suspect. Other than the removed singe mark on the back hip, there was nothing that linked it to the two other murders. It had occurred over two months earlier and then there was silence until three weeks ago. *Why the rush? Police pressure?* That remained unanswered as Cole left with his private escort.

# CHAPTER 69

AGENT LEAS HAD walked Cole out and then ran to his car for a fresh bottle he had picked up at the ABC package store around the block earlier in the day. As he slowly walked back to his room he noted the hotel appeared from its exterior to be abandoned. The few guests it did host were shadows, rarely revealing themselves to anyone. As he shut the door behind him he placed the brown-bag wrapped bottle of whiskey on the cheap table next to the bed. He stared at the bag. He knew once he started the bottle, it was unlikely he would quit until it was gone. Too many times he had lied to himself about his ability to stop, to control just how much was enough.

It hadn't always been this way. The drinking had come on fast, real fast with the death of his wife Maria. He could hardly think of her without craving a drink now. But, when she was alive, thinking of her was all he could do. She was beautiful. Not in the 'cover of some fashion magazine' way, but close. It was her spirit that really made her attractive and that made him fall in love with her. The day she died broke him like glass upon concrete, into a million shards of pain.

He wanted to kill him, her murderer. And, but for

six other agents in his way, he would have. He had been investigating George Kelley for a year, but he got too close. Kelley had discovered his pursuer and aimed all his evil at Leas. The vision stuck in his head, the Unmovable Post-it that, though frayed at its edges, refused to be torn away. Kelley had tortured her; that was the pain Leas could not let go, the thought of her calling out for him and him never rescuing her. The horror and sense of abandonment she must have felt in those final moments. He put himself through this mental exercise whenever he was alone.

Knee-deep in these thoughts, Leas twisted the cap off the still-wrapped bottle. The whiskey burned going down. He had hated whiskey before his loss of Maria. But now, it was the only thing he could stomach. Kelley sat in some dark cell, smiling at his success, while Leas toiled with the results. The death penalty wasn't an option, according to the DA. If he only had five minutes with his wife's killer, maybe then there could be some relief, some sense of closure to it all.

Leas lay back against the pillows of the bed and closed his eyes, savoring his second swig. *Everyone has their day,* he told himself over and over again. *Everyone has their day.*

# CHAPTER 70

I T WAS TEN a.m. Wednesday morning, and in all the excitement, Cole had forgotten to return one of Ann's calls. An hour and a half later, he had reached his limit of Ann advising him on what he should do or not do. She was naturally concerned. Who wasn't concerned? But it appeared he was safe for the moment. She had offered to come down, back to Charleston, but Cole refused to have her anywhere near the city while his hunter was still on the loose. He had already sent away his family and demanded Jackie follow, but she was having no part of that. By the end of the conversation he promised to keep her in the loop, even if just through texts.

Agent Lea's call had gratefully interrupted Ann's ranting about crazies. His voice was excited as he clicked back over to his line. "Cole, you were right. Belladonna was found in the glasses, even the clean ones. My expert tells me that such a dose would cause a rapid heart rate that would ultimately end in death. A scary way to die. So, the last two murders involved poison!"

"Wow, what's the source for something like that? It can't be too huge."

"Already on it, Colombo. Trying to locate ship-ments for the past twelve months to see if that leads us anywhere. I need to run, but I'll advise you if we locate anything." Agent Leas hung up suddenly.

Cole sat back against the couch, the TV humming in the background with some newscaster discussing the storm descending on the city. Eight inches of rain was projected in less than four hours, flooding and downed trees possible. The gloom of the storm approaching the city felt ironic, as he felt the doom of his hunter quickly approaching. He did not know from what direction, but his hunter's imminence was casting a fast shadow over his life.

# CHAPTER 71

"MR. CALHOUN... COLE, I'm not going to tell you this will be easy to watch. But, Cole, I need you to watch this and see if anything, *anything* sticks out. I'm going to turn on the video and then step out of the room for you two to watch. I saw it with your sister earlier this morning. So, just open the door when you're done and then we can talk. Deal?"

Cole took a deep breath and looked over to Cash. "Deal." The small room's walls were scuffed with black from angry heels and seemed ideal for its intended purpose of interrogation. But cramped in the makeshift theater, Cole felt claustrophobic and restrained, making it uncomfortable to breath.

Agent Leas had called and asked Cole to come in to the police station to watch the videos of his and Mark Calhoun's interviews back in 1982. Cole went cold at the idea that something like that existed. The thought of seeing himself at two, almost three years old was cautiously exciting. But what would be said, how he appeared, threatened to evoke the same mental carnage suffered by Mark. The choice was made to play Mark's first because he was older and would likely be conveying more useful information in Cole's mind. *I can't remember it now, but at two what really could I have said?*

"Now this thing is on VHS so it skips a bit here and there. I've turned up the volume as far as it goes, but you may have to lean in at some points to hear what he's saying." The two men scooted their chairs across the linoleum to get closer. The screen flickered on as a blue screen turned to a title frame. Leas walked out of the room as a small child, no older than perhaps five, appeared on the screen. Cole's mind momentarily flashed to Billy being four, close to Mark's age. The thought of Billy in this video unnerved him and made his squirm in the black plastic seat.

"Mark, my name is Patricia Boone. Do you know why you're here?" The brown-haired child nodded in affirmation. The too-short red tennis shorts and tube socks of the child aged the film. "Good, good. I'm here to talk to you about the past few days. Can you talk to me about that?" Again, his head nodded. Cole looked again at Cash, who was painfully transfixed by the screen, leaning in so as to not miss a word. The introduction between child therapist and patient went on for thirty minutes before there was any real headway.

"...I screamed, I screamed for Momma, but she didn't come. He told me he would hurt me...hurt Momma if I didn't stop."

Tearful, the child responded, "Yes, ma'am, Miss Libby was there, she told him...told him our names."

"Had you ever seen him before?"

"No, ma'am, never."

"What happened next, Mark?"

"Miss Libby started crying...telling the man to stop, to leave us alone, but he wouldn't. It was dark, ma'am, very dark." The young Mark looked around as if he was about to tell a secret. "The bad man, he…he hurt me, tied my leg with another boy. Miss Libby, he hit her."

"What other boy?"

"Mark, what was the boy's name?"

"Lake, miss. He was smaller than me."

"Was Cole there when you were tied?"

"Yes." Mark looked down, clearly upset. Cole watched this person he had no memory of speak of him, speak of the horror he could no longer recall, and felt connected through the screen. He leaned closer. "He…all he did was cry. I tried to stop him. I rocked him like Momma does, but he wouldn't stop. The bad man gave him some milk and then…then, he stopped crying."

"What do you mean he stopped crying?"

"He just stopped. He just slept."

"And Lake? What happened to him?"

"It was the day, the day he burned us." Mark started crying again, weeping. "Can I see my mother?"

"In just a bit, Mark. Can you tell me about Lake?"

"When the bad man came to burn us, he burned Cole first. He didn't wake up. He just laid there. I try to stop him miss, I did! I told him to get off Cole, to leave him alone. But he wouldn't listen." Tears continued down the child's face unabated, gathering in thick streams. "He burned me next. I screamed. It hurt bad, ma'am. I told him no but he wouldn't listen. Just kept saying I was number one."

"And Lake? What happened to him?"

"When the bad man stopped burning me he took Lake away. He took him away."

"Did you see him again?"

"No, ma'am. He was gone."

Cole processed what he just heard. Mark, a boy maybe five years old, had attempted to protect him, to ward off the 'bad man.' *A five-year-old boy*. But for Mark, he might have suffered more, possibly died. The clear drugging had been a blessing in disguise. It explained a lot, especially why he had no memory of what he was now learning about, as he sat there With the five-year-old's brother.

"Mark, can you describe the bad man? What did he look like?"

"He was a police man. But, then...when he came back...he was just with jeans. He had a black hat on; I don't remember his face."

"A black hat? Do you mean a mask, or could you see his face?"

Mark moved in close to the therapist. Cash and Cole responded in kind, creeping up to the screen.

Cupping his hand along the side of his mouth, Mark whispered something that sounded like, "He wasn't like Nita."

"Who's Nita?"

Simultaneously, Cash and his bother spoke, in different times, different places, but the same thing.

"She cleaned..." Cash sat back from the TV.

"You mean he wasn't the same color?"

"Yeah."

"Do you recall the trees...the marsh? Getting there?"

"Only behind the building. Miss Libby untied us, told us we had to run fast. The bad man was gone. But Cole couldn't move. She carried him in the dark. The grass hurt, but we ran...we had to run and hide like when we play. That's what Miss Libby said. The bad man was behind us, yelling for us, but we ran. Miss Libby stopped and told us to be quiet and stay still. Then she went to sleep."

Mark sat up and looked the therapist in the face. The tears were back. "She wouldn't wake up...she wouldn't wake up, ma'am. I screamed but no one heard us... No one heard us." Mark faded off with the last few words as though at that moment he felt alone and captive by his own mind from the fear of it all.

# CHAPTER 72

THE INTERVIEW WENT on for about ten more minutes with little more from Mark before the therapist concluded it and the white and black static filled the screen. Cole placed his hand on Cash's forearm. "Your brother was a good kid..." Cole let the last few works linger as Cash closed his eyes slowly, trying to keep back the tears.

After a few moments, Cash recovered. "You're not telling me anything I don't know. That protection that he showed you... he showed that to me every day, even when he was raging. There was always this side of him that could handle the internal anger and fear that consumed him. But if any such thing attempted to threaten me, he stepped in, like the big brother he was, and scared it away." With a pause, Cash looked up. "Thank you, Mark." The pain and longing wore on his face with deep sadness for a moment before he shook as a dog ridding himself of the dampness of rain, ready to proceed.

"You ready for this?" Cash had his hand on another tape, its spine marked in typewritten letters, "Mouzon, Cole – 3/22/82 Report No. 82-48921B"

Looking up, Cole asked with a slight grimace, "Do I have a choice?"

"Nope." Cash smirked, clearly trying to break the tension.

"Well, put it in already." It started like the first, just a blank screen.

"This is the interview of Cole Mouzon, March twenty-second, nineteen eighty-two." Cole saw himself being held. There, holding him, was not who he would have suspected. It wasn't Ava or Granny. *It was Jackie.* Tears welled up inside him and he fought them back. The salt that had accumulated in the corner of his eyes from a long day in saline air caused his eyes to sting. He felt an elbow in his rib as Cash knocked him out of an otherwise very emotional moment. Cole didn't hear most of what was being said as he stayed tethered to the moment and realization that Jackie, even then, had watched over him. She rocked him in her arms as, question by question, he provided no insight. By the end of the very short interview it was clear that he had known nothing or had locked it away so deep in his mental safe that even now he couldn't find the key.

The wall was down and Cole didn't care. He wanted to run to Jackie in that moment and hug her. Pushing the urge to the side, he relaxed. The men sat back in their chairs as the video went to static again. "Wow."

"You can say that again, Cole. Talk about memory lane, I feel…"

Agent Leas walked into the door. He had clearly been watching them as they took in the videos. Jackie was behind him, giving Cole a long look, and then closed the door with a pained, emotional smile. Just as now, she had always been there.

"So? Did that shake anything loose?"

Cash played protector in the tight space. "Man, give him some space. Let the man think."

Leas pushed further. "Think? Think? There's a murderer out there with his mark. Time is running out, and we don't have time to hold your hand, Mr. Mouzon."

"Why you..."

"Cut it out!" Cole jumped up and pulled the two apart, Cash having grabbed Agent Leas by the shirt. "Look, this isn't helping. Agent Leas, I know how serious this is. This isn't a carnival ride I'm on, it's my life! All these years I was thinking I was just another Charleston boy with nothing in the world to worry about, and then... well, then you came into my life. And, it hasn't been so much fun since then, Agent. I'm not blaming you, but let's not make it worse. You both hear me?"

The men retreated. "Agent Leas...nothing. Absolutely nothing. I'm sorry, but the only thing I apparently remember is the marsh."

# CHAPTER 73

COLE AND THE rest had moved to the main area of the police station, which was nothing more than a room full of flat-topped desks covered in paper and desktop computers. Cole looked around and wondered how any work got done in an area that cluttered the mind just looking at it. Leas piped in while Cole was still distracted. "Cole. Do you know a Janet Christie? Auburn-red hair, slender? Around thirty-four, thirty-five?"

The question caught him off guard for a second. He pinched his eyes to recall his memories of Janet at SNOB and Tommy O's, then slowly opened them as he responded with trepidation, "Uhm, I met her the other night. She had dinner with me and some friends. Why? Does she have something to do with this?"

"Cole, we aren't certain, but it may be her? It may be Poinsett." Cole's mind spiraled with the news. He had met his hunter and didn't even know it. How could he have been so stupid? *What a fool.*

"We matched her house to the order of belladonna. And, this is where it gets real interesting; we believe one or both were in Texas at the time of the murder of the Patrick guy. We pulled all the flights between here and Dallas for the day of and two days after. It was like a needle in a hay stack, but we found a name that appears to be one of them, one of the Christies. But we aren't certain yet. So we're tracking their movements."

"Why? Why wait? If they're the killers, they're going to act and act soon."

Dribbling his right hand up and down, Leas said, "We have to move cautiously here, Cole. The case is pretty circumstantial. Until we can get something more concrete, we are left just watching and waiting."

Cole was calm as he spoke. "What can I do?" If Janet or her husband was the killer, they were going to need something to tempt them, to draw them out to reveal themselves. "I can be bait." It slipped out without even thinking. But the idea of turning the tide on Poinsett was too much to decline. He was tired of running, and if that meant staring his hunter down in the face, so be it.

"Cole. You know I can't ask you to do that. But I also know that you appreciate the situation here. Unless we can get them to act, and soon, they will likely move on until the heat is off of you, only to then return again. I can't promise that we can track them if they move on... No more than I can promise you will be one-hundred percent safe."

Cole looked at Jackie as he spoke. "I understand, Agent. I know what I'm getting myself into. What's the plan?"

The plan called for luring Poinsett into finally pursuing Cole. Poinsett had proved patient in acting out her threats, watching the hands of time tick off while calculating her attack. Left to plan, she was likely to catch Cole off-guard and unprotected. Or, she would become frustrated by the constant protecting and seek an easier victim.

# CHAPTER 74

AGENT LEAS PLACED no further calls to Mr. Christie's number; he was convinced it was still in his Charleston home. Using his sources back in D.C., he canvassed every hotel in the Dallas-Fort Worth area for a booking by the doctor, but nothing had been discovered. More interesting, all credit card activity had stopped on his card at least two weeks earlier, in Dallas. It was like he just disappeared after that. Agent Leas decided to make another visit to the Christies' home and press the wife for information. Either she knew something and was hiding it, or she was in on this whole game.

Seated next to him in the rental was Winters. "Dr. Winters, thank you for joining me here in Charleston." He had called in his request for her to join him after receiving the toxicology reports in the Havex case and she jumped on a plane immediately. Whether it was for advice or company, he didn't know.

"By all means; it is Charleston, after all. If I have to do some work, I can handle that here. So, you didn't make it clear why you need me here. I received your samples and the reports are correct, belladonna poisoning on the second victim."

"Doctor, I need a second pair of eyes to help me on this and yours are keenly attuned to poisons."

"By all means."

"So here's the plan. The suspect is a Dr. Steve Christie; his wife is playing dumb at this point. I need you to help see if anything in the house can link her husband, or her, to these murders I have. Being the expert and all, perhaps you will see something my old eyes can't."

Winters looked out the window as they drove. "Of course; then that drink you promised me?"

"If I must." Leas smirked.

Leas returned to the pink home of the Christies and as before, waited to be buzzed in. Winters tugged at his sleeve as the gate opened. "Oleander, highly poisonous," she whispered, pointing to a large blade-leafed bush with white and pink flowers like large stars. "A single leaf would kill a child. A single suck on the flowers' nectar, a man. People put these in their yards because they're pretty, not thinking about how dangerous they can be if their child or dog get a hold of them. And, right next to it, that's poinsettia, it can survive the temperate winters here." Leas gave a pondering 'hmmm.'

Treece was at the gate and escorted the two into the home. Mrs. Christie was at the door this time and Leas could feel the tension when she noticed Miss Winters. For a moment he felt Christie might start in on some kind of a female pissing contest. With a clipped welcome, she spread the door open and invited her guests into the home. Leas noted that the phone from the hallway table was missing.

MRS. CHRISTIE STOOD in a bright green-and-brown

striped dress. She spoke impatiently as she said, "Agent, I told you that I know nothing about those packages you were inquiring about." She attempted to soften her displeasure, but it seeped through in spurts.

Noting Christie's eyes cutting away from Winters, Leas responded, "Yes Mrs. Christie, I understand that. But you see, I have a problem. Several packages of a certain chemical, or poison, were ordered by your husband and delivered to this address. Now, I've been unable to locate your husband in Texas. In fact, I can't seem to find him in any hotel there. Can you explain that?"

"Well, I don't... I don't know what to say. I haven't talked to him today, but I am sure there is a good explanation for all this."

"What do you know, Mrs. Christie? What are you not saying?"

"Nothing, I know nothing. This is all coming as a surprise. Let me try him now." She walked to the other room and returned with a phone. She was obviously locating her husband's number when Winters interrupted.

"May I see your hands?" Winters extended her hands to grab Mrs. Christie's.

"Excuse me!? No you may not." She recoiled, her arms now tight against her chest, hands tucked deep in her armpits.

Winters gave Leas a look that suggested she had noticed something of importance. "Would you mind if we have a look around the home, Mrs. Christie?"

Puffing, she responded, "I would mind very much. Am I under arrest or something?"

"No, ma'am. But I think it would be helpful if we could have a look around for those packages."

"Agent, unless you have a warrant, I want you to leave. *Now!*"

Bowing his head in good-bye and looking over to Winters, he said, "Of course."

Mrs. Christie almost pushed the two as she rushed to close the door. Walking back to the door, Leas looked at Winters. "Do you mind filling me in now on what that was about?"

"Her nails, Agent. She had indicators called transverse white striae, what people call Mees' lines, pale bands in the nail. Arsenic exposure. It disrupts nail plate growth when there are acute exposures, causing the white bands."

Leas scrunched his face, trying to understand. "But I don't have arsenic poisoning in this case. It seems to go against the MO displayed so far."

Winters' words were slightly irritated. "I don't know what you have, but she has been exposed to arsenic, Agent. And that is never a good sign."

"No, I appreciate it. Perhaps the killer has changed his pattern. It's not unheard of. Just another piece of the damn puzzle."

Leas explained to Winters his next steps. He couldn't arrest Mrs. Christie based on what he had so far, it was too circumstantial; no judge would issue a warrant. He would need to dig deeper and see if it was indeed the missus and not the mister that had been ordering the poison. Either way, the clock was ticking, but he could not act yet.

# CHAPTER 75

IT WAS SIX by the time he returned her to the Elliot House Inn off Queen Street. According to its street-side sign, the peach structure had been around since 1861 and likely had seen ample history. Leas attempted to be a gentleman and walk the doctor to her small first-floor room, which faced onto a bricked patio area. The doctor invited him in and he happily accepted. Inside, the room was almost entirely consumed by a large mahogany bed. "Beautiful, isn't it? It's a rice bed, unique to Charleston." She explained how the bed was a remnant of the area's plantation history and dated back to the 1700s. It was intended to capture the symbols of wealth at the time, tobacco and rice. So, each tall post of the bed was carved with a ring of tobacco leaves and rice seed heads. She ran her fingers across one of the ornate carvings and then looked up as if she'd had an epiphany. "Would you like to grab a drink? I saw this very rustic wine bar down the street that looked very interesting." Leas wasn't about to turn down the offer, though he wasn't much of a wine drinker and really needed a day off from drinking all together.

Winters wasn't kidding about rustic. Bin 152 looked like a country diner except for all the polished people sitting at its simple mismatched chairs. The raw wood floors were stained slightly black, and the communal tables added to the feeling of being in someone's grandmother's kitchen. They crawled up next to a young couple who appeared madly in love and ready to express it in front of the entire restaurant. Leas hoped that meant they would leave soon so he had more elbow room. It wasn't lost on him that though he was sitting three inches away from another person, there was no attempt to socialize, to engage, as though some glass wall had been raised and prevented even acknowledgement of another.

"So what are your thoughts on everything right now?" Two glasses of wine were ordered, a Goats do Rhome, and some Australian wine called Mount Pleasant Shiraz, both recommended by the waiter. Leas thought the second was fitting for the location.

After taking a sip he explained what he knew. The FBI was doing a complete background on Mouzon which was pretty easy since he'd had an FBI record since elementary school. So far nothing had popped up. They were also looking into Mark Calhoun's background.

"Didn't you say he died like nine, ten years ago? How would his background help you?" The waiter interrupted with a charcuterie and cheese plate mounded with meat; the waiter indentified each with of his hand: "Coppa, mortadella, and prosciutto." Leas waved the guy off and grabbed a slice before continuing with his mouth half-full.

"It's a long-shot really. It's highly unlikely that will result in anything. That's why we've handed that off to the Mount Pleasant PD. Their records are as good as ours on him. Let Mr. Mouzon's sister chase that rabbit down the hole."

"And what about this Poinsett thing? Any clue?"

"Well, that has us really concerned for Mister Mouzon. Whoever is killing under that name is likely from Charleston. According to the records pulled on all Poinsetts in Charleston around the time of Cole's kidnapping, there was one that seemed to just drop off the radar after the event. There wasn't much there, but it seemed just too much of a coincidence to not be considered."

He suspected it was highly unlikely at this point that the original kidnapper was involved. For one, it appeared from the video pulled at the restaurant in Dallas that they were dealing with a woman. The investigation files from the kidnapping were clear; a man had committed the original acts thirty years before. And, second, the woman in the video was too young to be the kidnapper. Though they didn't have a clear shot of the woman's face, the fact that someone was able to lure Patrick into taking her to his home suggested someone around thirty-five or younger.

What that left was that someone had learned of the kidnappings and decided to use the collection as their own to-do list. The kidnappings were publicized a great deal at the local level, but little was actually reported of the collection across the country. So, either someone had personal knowledge from knowing one of the victims or they grew up in one of the cities. There were four cities where kidnappings occurred. Charleston was the first, then Houston, White Plains, and finally Las Vegas. Whoever it was, they were working backwards on the list. There was the California murder that was connected to Vegas. Tony Patrick was the Houston connection. Whitney Havex was from White Plains. And now it appeared the killer was trying to finish the list, checking Cole Mouzon and Charleston off.

Winters shook her head in disbelief. "Wow, I have to say that scares me and I'm not even involved. Do you really think it's one of the Christies?"

"Everything is pointing in that direction. I've got the wife under surveillance now, and if she makes a move toward Mouzon, we'll see it. But enough about this craziness. What about you? Where are you from?"

Winters told Leas about her modest upbringing in rural Clyo, Georgia, outside of Savannah. She left home as quickly as she could get into school. Science had been her escape and it seemed natural to study it. Poisons, she fell into when she assisted a professor in college research project. From there her life was on auto-pilot. She had never married, choosing her work over involving herself in any some drama-laden relationship.

Leas pulled back in awe. "That's a shame; you appear to have it all together. I just figured someone had snatched you up."

"And you?" Winters turned the table on Leas and his personal life.

"Ah, me… That's one of those drama-filled relationships you avoid, filled with love, and lots of sadness. She died two years ago, murdered by a suspect in one of my cases. So, it's just me and lady whiskey at this time."

"I'm sorry to hear that." There was a pause in the conversation while both sides took in their discussions. An hour had passed and the waiter came over with a check, suggesting that their time at the table was done. Leas flipped open the black cover and swallowed deep at the check. No wonder they'd recommended the Mount Pleasant, at fifty dollars a glass he could have bought a bottle of Knob. Winters must have caught his reaction because she leaned over and pulled the ticket from his hand, demanding she pay. He could tell she was a woman that got what she wanted.

At the door to her room Leas told himself he couldn't, wouldn't sleep with her. She was an expert on a case and he didn't like mixing business with pleasure. A kiss into the exit that choice had been changed. Much like the check, the doctor took control. Leas liked this, even if it was just for the night.

# CHAPTER 76

"I HAVE TO DO this, Jackie. I... I have to." Cole sat on his sister's patrol car, contemplating everything he had learned over the past few days and doubt had seeped in like the tide on the marsh, threatening to seep under the wall that held back all his emotions. He knew he needed to do this, must do this, if his family was to ever be safe. But he felt helpless and insufficient for what was approaching and had no understanding of where to even start to tackle the riddle that was now his life. It had been three days since he learned of his childhood kidnapping, the murder of his mother and the intentions of someone to now kill him.

"Cole, you are the strongest person I know. But please don't do this alone. *Please*."

Cole spoke in rushed words. "I have to, Jackie! Dammit, I can't let this linger. I will not have you and Billy, or anyone else close to me, hurt. I won't be alone. Agent Leas will be there. Your people will be there. You've always been the strong one, not me. And, this... Well, this is my time to be strong, even if I don't know how. Sis, I *am* scared. Shitless."

"Okay, okay. Then fight, dammit. But not alone. I know you have the strength. Remember what Granny always says, 'God never gives you more than you can handle.' I don't know why all of this is happening, then or now. But, I do know that if there is one person who has the strength and ability to conquer this, it's you. Cole, you don't know how much strength you have in you. But just look at yourself. You have come through so much even before all this. The things you have gone through in your life are things most people could never survive. Every day I'm grateful to have had you in my life to give me the strength to kick my asshole of an ex-husband out of the house, to raise a strong man of a son, and to move forward. It is you who's inspiring, Cole, not me."

Cole's mind went awash with what his sister had just said. He had been through some rough times. The death in Atlanta, feeling absolutely helpless to stop it, having to accept himself and his lonely place in this world; life was not the easy sandy beach path most people saw when they looked at him. He had survived those moments, but not without bruises and the construction of a few emotional walls. Okay, more than a few. He knew he was the master of closing off the world when he felt under threat and he was doing it again, even if that was the worst approach to be taking right now.

"And, don't get me started on you accepting death. I was ready to wring whoever's neck that told you about dying when you were like four years old. Do you remember that? You cried straight for a day and then when mom tried to talk you through it and told you all things die including her, you bawled even worse for another two days." Cole laughed. Like almost every other moment in his life, he recalled the event with vivid detail. They lived in the trailer on Porchers Bluff and he lay on a mat pieced together with rags and woven by MeMe into a colorful collage, refusing to move. His only relief from the redness of his eyes was laying his head on the floor A/C vent to sooth the burn in his eyes when the air blew. Three days passed without eating before he stopped. That was the first memory he had of his internal wall going up, shielding his mechanics of life from the torment of his emotions. His sister was trying to break the seriousness of the moment, but it wasn't working.

"But, Cole... I know you. You think that the best approach is to work this alone so that no one else but yourself can possibly be hurt. I know you have tough skin. I know you are willing to endure. But, please understand, this isn't something you can do alone. Cutting out others who care about you, like what it sounds like you've done with Cash, just makes you weaker, not stronger. Let people help, Cole. We're already in danger, whether you want it or not. Nothing you can do will stop that. And guess what... we're still standing here and willing to risk ourselves for you. Don't lose sight of that fact. We choose you, Cole. And we've done that because we love you and you bring gifts to our lives. So stop locking people out, you ass!" Cole could feel his sister's smile come through the line with that last statement. He knew she was right, but his mind resisted the idea of permitting anyone else but himself to hurt, to grieve...to die for him.

"Jackie, I'm royally messed-up, aren't I?" He placed his head between his hands.

"No, Cole. You can be a pain-in-the-ass little brother sometimes, but you have it together like no one else. Just look at all your successes. I'm sure a lot of that was just a way to ignore and avoid your personal issues, but you channeled it and came out stronger. That's what you need to figure out how to do here. Channel all that fear, that doubt, that hurt, into defeating this bitch and coming out stronger for it."

"Yeah, I know you're right. I do. You know, for a cop you're pretty smart."

"Bite me, lil'bro." They both laughed, once again breaking the seriousness of the situation.

# CHAPTER 77

CASH HAD WAITED around in the station while Cole talked to his sister. Cole stabilized, they agreed to go where it all started. Twenty minutes later they pulled into the driveway of Mount Pleasant Academy after their meeting at the station and slowly exited the car as though dread had seeped into their thoughts. The school was a long cinderblock structure that appeared to end only because the marsh behind it would let it go no further. Several baseball and football fields ran along the depth of the school, though they were void of users. The sweet straw scent of asters filled the otherwise damp, salty air, and the sounds of sandy ground crunched as they passed through the corridor formed between the school and fence of the adjacent fields.

The green marsh could be seen from the front of the building, consuming more and more of the view as they continued toward the back. The hammock was still there, a thick tuft of trees, bush, and palmettos standing alone like an island amongst the green grass. Somewhere in the trees beyond the grass he had been hidden by his mother with Cash's brother. That past had been forgotten except for the memory that only appeared in the night, crippling him as a child.

The trees were dark, with thick branches that fought to forbid entry. Surrounding the island lay tides of green and brown grass, in serpentine waves, ebbing and flowing against the weedy, graded field. Cole looked over to Cash. "Are you okay?" There had been no words spoken since they exited the car.

"Yeah, I'm fine. I mean… I've never been here. Even though you can see the peninsula from here, we never crossed the river much unless it was to hit the Isles." Cole nodded; he knew all too well the bubble effects of Charleston, Mount Pleasant, and Summerville, another historic suburb of Charleston just north of the city.

With each step the marsh trees got more luring. The storm clouds darkened the sky, adding to the tension. The tingle along Cole's shoulders told him he had been here before though he had no memory of such a visit. Just yards from the island they stopped and paused. Cole took a deep breath. "I'm going in."

"Like that?" Cash looked down at Cole's bare legs and sandaled feet. "That grass will peel you like a paring knife. Have you ever walked through saw grass before?"

"I don't really care, Cash. I've walked sawgrass before, it isn't anything that's going to keep me from getting to that hammock, got me?"

Cash threw his hands up against the verbal assault. "I got you. I was just saying…"

"I know. But, no amount of stinky mud or sawgrass is keeping me off that island." Just then a lightning bolt cracked through the sky over the marsh.

Cole smiled. "Well, that might." Andrea was moving in from Georgia; they needed to move it if they wanted to do this. Cole continued dredging his way into the marsh as Cash slipped off his boat shoes to follow.

"You didn't think you were going alone, did you?"
*No, I don't want to be alone.*

The grass gripped at their legs with every step, drawing blood from bare skin. They looked at each other as if to say, "Should we go in?"


THE GROUPING OF trees was actually less dense than it looked when perceived from a distance. Small scrub and bush created a thin barrier to the heart of the island. Several layers of canopy prevented a clear picture of its contents from the outside. At its base were small clumps of saw palmetto and golden grass. Higher up were oak and wind-stunted pines, bent from the constant coastal winds and occasional hurricane. Highest were the palmettos, standing like frilled green pompoms atop weathered wood light poles.

Cole stepped in, pressing his weight against the resistant island. Branches broke or slipped with a *whip* as he mined through. At six-three, he had to dip and sway to keep from colliding into a branch. Deeper he went, with the world behind him going silent. At the only reasonably-sized clearing he stopped, looking up through the branches to the aubergine sky above. The clouds swirled slowly in anticipation of the impending storm. The only sound to be heard was the heavy tunneled wind sound racing through the trees. Looking down to the detritus and leaf-covered ground, he swept his feet until the tan sand below was revealed. And then he sat.

Moments turned into minutes before any thought came to Cole's mind. He turned to see that Cash had joined him and for a brief second he wondered if this was what it was like those years ago when it was Mark, not

Cash, who sat beside him looking into the woods and the school beyond. "I'm sorry that I don't remember your brother."

"Don't be. Though I have no doubt that you were there for each other, I saw just how powerful that memory could be played out day after day in my brother. I would never, *never* want that for you." Cash looked Cole in the eyes as he spoke those last few words. "I expect that he is up there somewhere now, looking down on us and proud that we're fighting back. I...I think that was the issue. He just wanted a chance to fight back, to take back control of the destiny that had been yanked from you both. That was denied to him. But somehow, that mind of yours. It figured a way to start anew, to deprive whoever did this of the power over you. Be grateful for that, Cole." It could have been a raindrop, but the slightest of tears appeared to enter Cash's speckled blue eyes before he looked away.

The sky unloaded with fat, cool drops landing on the hodgepodge umbrella formed by the canopy. The palmettos sounded like wind-beaten tarp as Cole and Cash absconded back to their entrance and into the marsh grass again. Drenched, they approached the car and looked at each other and their muddy, blood-caked legs. Cole raised his shoulders, "Whatever, it's a rental," and they jumped in. Cole drove in silence, grateful that the man beside him, like his brother before, was there in this dark time.

# CHAPTER 78

IT WAS NINE p.m. by the time he dropped Cash off back at the station and then returned to his parents' home. "Hey, Officer." From across the lawn, Cole waved at his detail for the night, but he clearly was having no part in of being cordial and refused to respond. As Cole walked into the back door of the house with its single lamp on, his phone vibrated with a text. "Had a great time." He responded back with the same and put his phone on its charger in the kitchen. It was truly a great time, but time for bed.

As he was placing his phone on its charger, he looked up and saw in the window's reflection a figure behind him. *Janet!* It appeared she had moved too fast for their plan.

Cole spoke calmly. "Janet, what are you doing here?" Playing coy in his question, Cole's finger slid across his phone and pressed the emergency 911 button while keeping his eyes on her.

She looked rabid as she spoke. "Oh, Cole... Let's not pretend. You know why I'm here. And let the police come. You'll be dead long before they arrive."

"They are right outside..."

She cut him off. "Ha. That officer in the car? Yeah, no.

He's been dead for about an hour while I waited on you. I've been waiting on you for a while. Nice date? He is a looker from what I've seen. I might have to visit him by the end of the night." Janet smirked as though she could see how she was going to kill Cash.

Panicked words escaped. "He has nothing to do with this. This is between you and me. I'm what you've come for, like the others."

"You really are clueless, aren't you? I don't understand why you were ever worth all this trouble." Halfway through her words, Cole hit the light switch and the house went dark. He was halfway to the front door when something solid caught him across the chest, throwing him on his back to the floor. He groaned as a second blow landed across his left shoulder.

"Why are you special? Why are you worth all this grief?" Her voice had come from behind him, full of anger and rage.

He yelled. *"What do you want?"*

*"Answer me!* Why are you worthy?" The voice was now in front of him.

Feeling around the floor, Cole shouted. "I don't know what you want! Worthy of what?"

"Exactly! You aren't worthy. That's why I'm going to kill you."

*"No!"* Cole twisted, sweeping his legs in the dark until they landed against something hard. He heard Janet fall while he tried to get up. She was on him again before he could regain his balance, now slashing his forearm with knife. Grabbing in the dark, he felt the sting of the blade as his hand wrapped around it; he refused to let go, kicking into the dark until it landed against her chest. The knife slipped through his palms as Janet was thrown

across the room. A groan in the dark told him that she was somewhere in the corner.

Reeling with pain, he reached for anything that could be used as a weapon, until his hand landed on the leg of the hallway shelf. Janet was charging when he pulled the shelf oak over, capturing Janet underneath. He got to his feet and ran across the room to turn the lights back on. Up and slashing the air as she charged, a shot rang out from behind Cole. Janet could be heard falling to the ground, howling in pain. Cole's turn was met by Jackie's shadow sweeping by him to pin Janet to the ground and handcuff her.

COLE HAD NEVER seen his sister as a cop. He understood she was one, but there had never been a thought or image of her actually acting like a cop until this moment. "Are you okay? Oh my God, Cole! You're cut! That fucking bitch!" Jackie looked back and was preparing to wield revenge on Janet when three other officers rushed in and discouraged her. "What happened?"

"She was in the house when I got home."

"What? Wait until I get a hold of Jameson."

"I think he's dead, sis." Janet's rage was deflated by the news. "She said she killed him." Jackie looked over at Janet again, now being carried out the front door by other officers, clearly pissed at the news and longing to act.

Another officer Cole had never met approached Janet. "Her name is Janet Christie. I met her like three days ago. I think she's been following me." Looking at his sister, he continued, speaking worrisome words. "Call Daniel Page, please. Make sure he is okay. She flirted with him the other night and then showed up with him when I had dinner with Ann. Please Jackie, make sure he's okay."

"I will. Promise. But you're the one I'm worried about right now. You're cut, Cole, bad."

Janet barked orders to one of the officers to get the EMT in the house, right away.

Cole's shoulder was almost bandaged up by the time Agent Leas arrived. The stench of whiskey and cigarettes wafted off of him like sulfur off a paper mill, making Cole hold his breath until he could escape the olfactory assault. His speech was slightly slurred as he attempted to catch up with the night's events.

Panicked, he said, "Shit, she moved too fast, Cole. Sorry about that. How did she learn where you were?" Cole wanted to shout at Leas, tell him that he was worthless for going on a drinking binge while he was being attacked. But he held it back, just staring at him with distain.

"I've said several times, I didn't know her. She was the date of a friend of mine the other night. He met her when we were having drinks. I'd bet money she attached herself to him to get closer to me. Maybe she figured it out when he visited the other day. Jackie, did you talk to Daniel?"

Jackie was in the living kitchen with other officers, but yelled out, "Yes, he's fine and can't say sorry enough. He said she flaked after that night y'all had dinner and he hasn't spoken to her since."

Cole threw his hand in the air. "So, there you go. That crazy was stalking me. She kept saying I wasn't worthy? Is that it, is that what this is all about? This Poinsett person is killing us based on some idea that we aren't worthy? Is that why the others died?"

"It's a bit early to say right now, Cole, but it's looking that way. Did she say anything else?"

"No...no, just that craziness about not being worthy, that I needed to die. So, you got her, right? It's over?"

"We got her Cole. You're safe now." The captain walked in and responded. "If your sister hadn't gotten here when she did, well... let's just say we're happy she did."

"Yeah, Sis. How did you know?"

"I didn't. I tried to call Jameson and he never picked up. I figured he was just ignoring me until the surveillance tail said they had lost him on the radio. So, I booked it over here. "Damn good work. We got her." The captain was going in for a pat on Jackie's back when Leas interrupted.

"Captain, I will agree it certainly looks like it's Poinsett, but where's the poison?" Leas looked around the room for a syringe or other item.

The captain wasn't buying the opinion. "Well, clearly she had to change her MO. We have had Cole here locked down like Fort Knox. It wasn't like she was going to be able to keep poisoning these boys with all that security. We will learn more once we get her back to the station and interrogate her properly. Don't you worry Cole, we will put her so far under a prison that the last thing she will be thinking about is trying to get after you again."

"I appreciate that, Captain."

Leas left the room to attempt to talk to Janet. Within an hour the house would be clear of everyone but Jackie. Cole, bandaged and wounded, started to pick up. "Cole, leave that. We can get that in the morning. Seriously, you've been cut. You're going to pop those wrappings they just put on you. And why are you insisting on staying here tonight? Please, just come back with me?"

"Jackie, I appreciate the offer. I really do. But we got her, Jackie. We got Poinsett. She isn't going to be coming after me tonight or any other night. I'd just like to have some peace and quiet. See that bottle over there, Tylenol PM. They and I are going to have a party tonight and I am going to sleep this off. I love you, sis, but I would really just like to be alone tonight."

"Okay, Cole. But please text me first thing in the morning so I know you're okay. Killer or not, you're still hurt. You hear me, mister?"

"Yeah, yeah. I hear you, you old nag. I love you, too."

Within minutes of Jackie leaving Cole was asleep in bed, feeling safe for the first time since returning to Charleston. The nightmare would not come tonight, in his dreams or in real life.

# CHAPTER 79

IT WAS LESS than thirty minutes after he had walked into Winters' room that he received the call. Mouzon had been attacked in his home and the attacker had been apprehended. Janet had struck sooner than expected and now he looked like the shittiest investigator out there. But for the Mouzon girl, Cole would have been dead. He had rushed over to the home still reeking of wine and the whiskey night cap he'd had back at the doctor's room. Mouzon was shaken but otherwise safe. He would survive. But this confirmed that the Christies were Poinsett, and now he needed to act to capture the second part of the couple.

Now midnight, it was Leas' third time in Mrs. Christie's home and he was still awestruck by the pedigree of the home. Mrs. Christie had been apprehended after attempting to kill Cole Mouzon. The warrant came swiftly and Leas was looking for anything that would help him find the man of the house before he sought retribution for his wife's capture. The mail-ordered poison was found within an hour of searching, hidden in the refrigerator crisper drawer. But there was no indication of where the husband had gone.

Standing in the drawing room of the house, Leas

was overlooking the dark garden lit by what moonlight was piercing the storm clouds above. *Appearances can be deceiving.* Janet and her husband looked like any other successful, well-connected couple. He was sure they were socialites of Charleston, going to fancy parties, drinking fancy wines. But at home in this nine-million dollar mansion overlooking the harbor, was a much darker reality.

Strolling out to the fountain he noticed the very large goldfish swimming around its base, lit by underwater lamps. Expensive, he was sure. Pedigrees, like the Christies. Everything he had seen so far indicated they both came from upper middle-class families, without any history of violence or suffering. He didn't know how it happened that a person slipped from sane to insane, but it did happen while the world was ignorant to the fact in front of them.

Agent Tifton walked up beside him and admired the fish as well. "Koi; huge ones, too. I bet they go for two or three thousand dollars each at that size." Leas looked at the slightly plump FBI agent with a puzzled look. "Are you serious? For fish? And how would you know?"

"What? A man can't like fish?" Leas shook it off as Tifton kept speaking. "And I think we've found something you need to see...really need to see."

Tifton led Leas back into the house and into the library. What appeared to be a bookshelf was swung open like a door, revealing a small corridor that wrapped around the back side of the wall. A light bulb hanging off a wire was a recent addition to the ceiling, which was otherwise slatted wood with grey plaster filling the gaps between. Walking in, Leas was struck by the smell of old wood and time. Tifton informed him that rooms like this weren't uncommon for the original homes of Charleston, especially after the great slave revolt of 1822, when a freed slave—Denmark Vesey—sought to execute slave-holders and free Charleston. But for two slaves leaking his plot, total anarchy would have ensued. Charleston's response was swift. Hysteria hit the minority white population, as the city was only one-third white, and laws were created limiting the movement off any person of color. Vesey and thirty-five others were hanged on the streets of Charleston to warn against any further mutiny.

AS LEAS LISTENED to the history lesson, he realized he was approaching a small, finished room. On the walls were pictures, hundreds of pictures of women in various states of torture. Leas couldn't be certain but it appeared there were five women in all, depicted in various poses, some of them likely underage. And that is what they were.

The lack of blood and the otherwise perfectly posed nature of the photos suggested the woman were volunteers in this horrific snapshot session.

What did stand out was a pile of photos spread out across a small metal shelf pushed against the wall. Leas picked one of them up after slipping on the requisite latex gloves and took stock of what he was seeing. It was Cole Mouzon.

Flipping through the stack, it was evident that someone had been watching him since arriving in Charleston. There were pictures of him inside a store, at a bar, and even walking into his family's home. Mrs. Christie and her husband had hunted him, waiting for the opportune time attack. The question remained, why? And where was Mr. Christie? From all appearances he was on the run, but his wife's capture could bring him back. Until he was found, Cole wasn't completely safe.

"Package all this up and that laptop I saw on the desk. If they took these, the files are likely on that. We need to move fast here, people. There may be another strike soon."

# CHAPTER 80

BEFORE LEAVING THE Christie house Leas had called the captain, who had agreed to double the guards on Cole based upon what they had discovered. He had left a message on Cole's cell phone, but there was no answer. Guards confirmed he had gone to bed promptly after the house was emptied, so Leas saw no reason to disturb him for the night.

Back at the station, Leas walked into the small interrogation room where Mrs. Christie had been placed after being released from the EMT at the Mouzon house. Janet Christie resembled nothing of the first impression Leas had about her just a couple days earlier. In the six by five white interrogation room she could be seen for the monster she was. Mascara ran down her cheeks and there were multiple cuts obviously gained during the fight. She looked at him with disdain, like an animal coiled in the back of cage...ready to strike.

FBI training called for establishing rapport with a suspect in hopes they would spill the beans. Under this approach he was to explore what pressures were experienced by the suspect, such as fear, confinement, relationships with any co-conspirators, or even with the interviewer. He was then to determine the suspect's perception of how strong the case was against him. Finally, he needed to feel out how important it was to the suspect to maintain respect. With these established, the manual told him he could leverage this information over time to collect information helpful to his investigation.

But Leas was never very good at being nice to those he suspected of killing someone. And he wasn't about to share what the agency called 'commonalities' with a murderer. His personal life was off-limits to suspects, a lesson he'd learned the hard way with Maria and had no intention of ever repeating again. Never leverage your personal life.

"Mrs. Christie, we found the room, the pictures." A smirk crossed her face.

"Which ones?"

"All of them, the girls and Cole. Do you want to tell me about them?"

"Agent, I want my lawyer. I think I already told your buddies out there that. I WANT MY LAWYER!" She shouted to the ceiling and laughed.

"Of course, you are entitled to that, but I was just hoping you could explain to me what those all were?" Janet sat back in her chair, staring at Leas. He wasn't getting it. He would never get it. She stared at him, puzzled by how stupid she thought he was.

"Let me help you out here, Agent. Those pretty little pictures of the girls, those aren't mine. Not my style, if you get my drift. Don't get me wrong, I suffered the reality of those photos played out in my bedroom. The bruises, the cuts, the whippings. But not because I wanted to. No, I suffered under that man."

"So your husband beat you?"

"Oh, beating doesn't even begin to describe what

he did to me, Agent. Have you ever heard of the Pope's Pear?" Leas had heard of the torture device, sanctioned in medieval times by the Pope, from a case he had worked on briefly in Washington State. It wasn't pretty from what he recalled. Reserved for those women who cheated and those men who had sex with other men, the device looked like a pear with a twist handle where the stem would otherwise be. There were three sizes, one each for the vagina, the rectum, and the mouth. The last was reserved for blasphemers who undermined the Pope's authority. The bulb of the device would be placed in the orifice, and twisted at its end causing the bulb to open, or petal. Thorns on the ends of each petal would cut and slice until death ensued from the loss of blood and excruciating pain. But, if Mrs. Christie was being honest, her husband turned it slowly, to cause prolonged, but nonlethal, pain and suffering.

"I can tell by the look on your face that you know what I'm talking about, Agent. Imagine that once, maybe twice a week. And those were the good times." She laughed and looked to the floor in thought, recalling the experiences. Life with her husband had been hard. She had met him in med-school and fell hard, too hard. When she discovered his taste for all things seedy and torture she stuck with him. She had invested too much. The first time he tortured her was when she announced she was pregnant. He never wanted children, considering them pests and a 'waste of good money.' She lost the pregnancy three days later. She was trapped, a fool who couldn't leave and was too afraid to stand up to him.

Leas could tell the woman before him was damaged in the worst way. He suspected Mr. Christie had discovered that the hard way.

He walked out of the room and immediately pulled

out his cell phone to call Tifton, who was back at the house, still processing it. "Tifton, Leas here. Have you found anything? Well, I think we're looking for a body, keep at it and let me know what you find."

# CHAPTER 81

"COLE, COLE, ARE you alright? It's all over the news. You were attacked? Why didn't you call?" Cole had woken to the phone ringing and answered it instinctually, without thinking. Cash was in a panic on the other end.

Groggy, Cole responded slowly. "I'm okay, I promise. They...they got her. I'm sorry I didn't call. With all the ruckus, I just forgot and I passed out as soon as everyone left. Please don't worry. Everything is okay."

By the tone of Cash's voice, the apology was insufficient. "Don't worry? A killer was in your house and stabbed you."

Cole was still groggy from the long night and in no mood to deal with unnecessary ministering so early in the morning. With his eyes still squinting to adjust to the light, he spoke, "Look, I'm starved. Would you like to do breakfast?"

"Breakfast? Cole, it's one-fifteen in the afternoon."

A howl out the window drew Cole's attention to the half bent trees. Tropical storm Andrea had finally arrived and the rain began pouring down, stinging the window pane with droplets, as grey swirling clouds brewed outside. *How could I have slept so long?* "What?! Shit, I must've taken too many of those damn pills."

Cash continued, "...But, if you're hungry, let's do a late lunch."

Leaning back into the king pillows of the bed, Cole murmured, "Perfect. Want to meet at Mamma Brown's? This fat boy could really go for some more bar-b-que."

"Wow, someone is really hungry. Didn't you have it like yesterday? Okay, yeah, sure... Does two give you enough time?"

"Yeah, that'll work. Okay, let me jump in the shower and I'll see you there."

After a few moments of lying still in the bed, Cole swung his body out over its edge and walked into the master bedroom's bathroom. Covered in floral wallpaper, the room was five times the size of his bathroom in Denver, with a double basin, garden tub and one of the three windows being a stained glass version of a snowy egret. Things are big in the South, even bathrooms.

RITUALISTICALLY HE LOOKED into the mirror and stared at himself to reflect on where he was, who he was. Halfway through noting the lines around his eyes that looked slightly healthier because of the tan accumulated in the past few days it dawned on him. Though he still woke to the feeling of being alone, he had stopped counting sometime after arriving in Charleston. *Was it day six ninety-five... ninety-seven?* He couldn't remember. That fact alone scared him. His memory was his safe harbor.

He had told himself that the habit gave him strength to move about in his daily life after Atlanta. The realization of its loss made him feel hollow and bare. The deeper acknowledgement of its purpose welled up, forcing him to feel. For almost two years the ritual had been unconsciously justified as a remembrance. Forgetting the ritual meant he forgot someone he loved and lost. He felt guilty, as if by not remembering he was forsaking all the memories, the existence…the death of a person he loved. *What kind of person am I?* His head spun in frustration. He could feel tears welling up from the base of his eyes and he fought to throw up his wall. Only red, irritated mist came as he gained control with the wall partially up.

Raising the wall further, he pushed himself forward. Jumping in the shower, he wondered why, when he had stopped counting. *Was it Charleston?* No, he had been back since the death and he recalled counting on the first few days of this trip. *When did you stop, when? Was it when you met Agent Leas and learned of Poinsett?* No. Flashing memory after memory like flash cards the flicking stopped when it reached one image… *Cash.*

# CHAPTER 82

B ROODING AND HALF-WAY soaked from the rain, Cole arrived at Mamma Brown's with Cash already waiting. Other than formal niceties and the faux cordiality mastered long ago by Southerners, Cole withheld from the conversation. He was still working it all though his head and didn't want to speak until he felt comfortable with what he suspected was the cause of his realized change. So, he focused on the food, speaking only when spoken to in hopes of avoiding the detection of his inner turmoil.

Cole had finished his platter of vinegar-pepper pulled pork with fried okra, collard greens, and field peas before he had barely sat—it kept his mouth too full to speak things he himself wasn't ready to hear. Cash watched in amazement at how fast the food disappeared. "Wow, do you want seconds?"

"Nah, I'm good."

"Ha, okay there chatterbox, I was joking." Cole stuck his tongue out at this comment and slid the last bit of collards on his fork and engulfed it with a dramatic, exaggerated bite. "Num, num, num. There is nothing like Carolina-style bar-b-que." He wiped his lips with the blue and white check washcloth a passing waitress had handed to him just before he finished.

Cash sat back and leaned sideways into the old yellow pine arrow-back chair. "Watching that was sexy."

Looking down, Cole grinned at the sight and spoke, "Yeah, I'm sure this massive gut will land me a keeper for sure." Cole placed his hand on his stomach and tried to stick it out as much as possible, beating it like a drum and then looked up.

Cash clearly wasn't falling for the Southern charm. He was immune to its effects. He pushed forward. "Ha. But, seriously Cole… Are you okay? They got her, right?"

"Yeah, they got her. There is still no understanding of why or if she is even Janet Christie. Agent Leas is looking into that and her husband based upon the message I received last night. But, it's all okay. It appears he has disappeared. So, I'll be heading back to Denver in a couple days."

There was slight shock in Cash's face. "Denver? But, so soon?"

"Well, there's nothing for me to stick around for. I'll have to come back for the trial, I'm sure, but nothing immediately. If Charleston criminal cases move anything like Atlanta, it could be years before that case sees the light of a courtroom." Cole was still trying to avoid direct eye contact as he spoke.

Cash pulled back at the 'nothing.' "Oh, well if there's *nothing*. Then that makes sense." His attempt to play it off failed. He wore stinging hurt and turned his eyes to the worn wooden floor in an apparent attempt to avoid showing too much.

Cole sensed the hurt he had just inflicted. Leaning in, "Cash, please don't take it that way. You know what

I mean. I was here for vacation. Not to get involved in a murder investigation, not to get involved..." And, then the wall went up completely.

Cole turned bitter without warning, trying to avoid a conversation that had been brewing for too long. Like overworked dough, the batch was bad and he just wanted to rid himself of the whole thing—to run. The idea of dealing with Cash and what he was looking for, what he wanted, was too much for Cole to deal with. The pain from Atlanta, the death that he could not escape, flooded against his wall, consuming any emotion other than flee. Snapping, he spoke, "Cash, why are you sticking around here at all? We just met." *Run, get away from him.*

Cash was thrown off by the question. "Cole, this happened to me too, you know. My brother suffered because of what happened thirty years ago."

"That's right Cash, *years ago*. She was after me, not you, not Mark." Throwing his napkin to the table, Cole added, "I don't need this right now. What you want, I can't offer."

Cash leaned across the small wooden table in an attempt to reach out to Cole. "Stop pushing me away!"

Cole withdrew his hand before Cash could grab it, turning his side into the table. But he kept contact with Cash's blue eyes. Looking into them, Cole just wanted to cry. The wall had abandoned him and he couldn't think with all the emotions flooding in. Instinctively he spat out, "You're not my protector. And I don't need one. They have her. And I've got a legion of FBI and cops surrounding me all day and night for the next two days if they don't. You being around, well, you're just another captor."

Cash pulled back from the table, still speaking softly. "I'm just concerned about you, Cole."

"What are you, my therapist now? I'm not Mark, Cash. Mark is *dead*. You can't save him and there is nothing you can do about that." Cole felt sick as those last few words left his mouth, causing his emotional wall to fracture. The sting was evident on Cash's face.

Standing up, Cash leaned over the table to look Cole in the eyes. "Fine, I'm going. But please stop and think about this." His words were thick with emotion even though his eyes said he was still stinging from the coldness coming off of Cole.

Slowly rolling his eyes away from Cash's gaze to turn off the flow of emotional torment, Cole could feel tears trying to break through. "I have, Cash."

Cash turned away after dropping a twenty on the table, only looking back as he paused to open the restaurant's door and put up his umbrella. Cole sat there, numb and nauseous over what had just happened. He hated himself in that moment. *How could you have done that to Cash? How could you have done that to yourself?* Like a flash in a pan, a desire to run after Cash extinguished as quickly as it came. Cole sat there for a moment, numb. He tried to justify it as unworkable, unattainable, and thus why try? He told himself Cash only offered pain and he didn't need more of that in his life. But he couldn't shake the feeling that he had just ruined something. He was the loser Ann mentioned in the battle for the 'good ones.'

# CHAPTER 83

B Y THREE P.M. Leas had his answer. Mr. Christies had been found buried under a new planting of pink hydrangeas in the back yard, from the looks of it dead for weeks. He had been stabbed repeatedly in the chest with an ivory letter opener found in the soil beside him. Samples were being sent to the local toxicologist for testing because it was suspected he, like the others, had also been poisoned. He wondered if it was the oleander Winters had eyed on their visit.

It appeared that it was Mrs. Christie, not mister, who ordered the poison. She was Poinsett. Leas wasn't comfortable with the decision to notify Cole of this finding; he wanted a closed file first. But pressure from higher-ups mandated it. A series of murders outside Atlanta had kicked up and they wanted him to get there. A message was left with Mouzon just saying he was cautious, but it looked like it was over.

Leas headed to the hotel to catch a few hours of sleep while waiting on the autopsy report. A fresh bottle of whiskey had his name all over it. Perhaps by tomorrow night he could be on a plane headed to Atlanta to torture himself with another group of murders. The springs in the economy hotel mattress dug deep into his back, making it impossible to sleep. Passing out from too much whiskey was his only option.


"HAMPTON, I NEED a review of those computer records we seized from the Christie house before you leave tonight, you hear me?"

"Yeah, yeah let me fill my coffee cup first." A skinny twenty-something officer was seated at the laptop Leas had previously seen in a room of the Christies' home.

"Agent, don't get your panties in a wad, we've got your killer. Why are you stressing so much? You're a whiskey man right? Go and get you one. We will dot all the 'I's and such, don't you worry." The Mount Pleasant PD captain had walked in with his Charleston counterpart.

"Captain, I'll get that drink when we know for sure."

"It's your time, Agent. As far as I'm concerned, this case is closed." The chief walked off into the other room.

"Nothing more is happening today, go home, Agent." Betsy passed by as she headed out the door to apparently grab lunch for the crew who had worked all night.

It was six p.m. by the time Leas returned to the station. Walking through the half-empty space, Leas dialed in the doctor's number. He had run out so fast he hadn't had a chance to explain. After two rings she answered, "Why hello Agent; is Mouzon okay?"

"Well, it looks like we're wrapping this up, and if you're still in town tomorrow I kinda figured we could finish what we started. After all I do owe you."

"Agent, there is something interesting here..." Hampton was seated behind him, still focused on the computer he had inherited in the morning.

"In a moment, Officer..."

"As I was saying, will you be around?"

"Awh, sorry Officer, I decided to catch an early flight back to Atlanta this morning. But if you are ever back there, let me know." A sound in the background jumbled her last few words.

"Sorry, I missed that, what was that?'

"Oh, just that I would like that drink if you ever get to Atlanta."

"Well, it's certainly my loss. But it looks like I'm headed to Atlanta after this. So, don't book that dance card just yet."

"Oh wonderful! Let me know."

"I certainly will. Night, Beth."

"Night, Agent."

"Now, what is it, Officer?"

Hampton began, "Going through our suspect's computer, I found something. Several files were deleted and then the hard-drive was defragmented to attempt to cover it." A puzzled look crossed Leas' face. He hated this geek-talk shit. "It's like having a file cabinet full of files and then pulling some out and pressing the rest to make room at one end. But, with computers, the file cabinet doesn't actually remove the files marked for deletion. Defragging won't do much though unless new files are saved to officially take up that space. There was some damage to the deleted files, but I was able to retrieve a lot of them."

"Well, spit it out."

Hampton perspired as he spoke. "Chats, lots of chats, Agent, to one person off what appears to be a battered women's board. See, Gmail caches your chats by default. And, well… There is a lot of discussion about what I take as a plan to kill her husband. But when I looked at emails after his murder, well, there is discussion about another murder… Mouzon's.

"What?" Leas moved in for a closer look at the screen.

"Look here, a chat dated 5/29/13 at 11 p.m."

> He needs to die, now

> How

> I know where he is, will you do it like u promised

> For you, yes, anything

> I'll text you, be clean. Like with Steve, tonight

"Who is she talking to?"

"Get this, 'PoinZett.'"

"Shit! If this is real, Mr. Christie was likely dead and the real Poinsett manipulated Mrs. Christie as a decoy. Who is that?"

"I've looked all over the computer, but the only references are 'PoinZett.'"

"Officer, call Agent Roger Goode in D.C.; tell him we need to find out *now* who that is and where they are."

# CHAPTER 84

"COLE, WHY THE hell did you do that? God, do you want to be single forever? Ugh, I can't really talk right now about this with everything going down last night, I am catching up. But I promise *we will* talk about your propensity to fuck a good thing up and I need to talk to you about Mark Calhoun. I think I found something. Let me get Billy to bed and then I'll finish up those files on him so I can understand what I'm seeing and let you know in the morning. Okay? I need to go; Billy is starved and filthy, again. I love you, too, bro. Chin up, we got this creep." As she hung up the phone, Billy rushed by her into the house, shouting, "Mac-n-cheese! Mac-n-cheese!"

"No, we had mac-n-cheese last night because we got home so late. I think I have some…ah, here we go. We still have grilled chicken from the weekend we need to eat, mister. Green beans or corn with that?"

"Awe, I want mac-n-cheese." A saying Granny always said popped into her head, *And people in hell want ice water, too*, but she wasn't about to tell her child that. "Corn or green beans?"

Billy responded with a sad, "Green beans."

"Now, go upstairs and jump in the bath. You can watch thirty minutes of TV once you eat. Go!"

The steps boomed with each rushed step up the stairs, followed by the sound of water running through the pipes. Jackie loosened her uniform top and proceeded to open a can of green beans, placing them on the gas range. There was a creak in the floor behind her as the gas range clicked and the burner went aflame. Turning, she was immediately surprised by the stranger in her kitchen.

"Who the hell...?"

"Hello Jackie." A mist hit Jackie's eyes; something had been sprayed. The pain was immediate, a deep burning sensation branching out in all directions that forced her to close her eyes. Jackie screamed out in pain and stumbled over something that felt like a leg. She fell hard, hitting her head against the sharp edge of the island's granite countertop.

"Mom?" Billy called out from upstairs.

*Oh god.* Jackie fought to open her eyes. A blurry figure stood over her. Fear passed through her entire body, not for her, but for her son. She had never been shot at, much less hit in the line of duty. Her closest encounter with violence was her husband who drank too much and then used her as a personal punching bag. *Who is this and why?* Jackie fought to maintain her vision as the figure kicked her in the ribs. Jackie would not, could not allow herself to be taken. She needed to stay conscious and fight for Billy.

*NOT BILLY!* Kicking out, she landed a blow on what she perceived as a knee. The figure was down. Jackie swung her body in its direction, swinging at the same time. Her fist landed solidly on a rib. She swung again, but it collided with a cabinet. Falling back again in pain, the figure was on her. Two punches into the assault Jackie went blind. The hot pain of her eyes had consumed her entire head; she could no longer feel the irritation of tears running down her face. With a final swing, the kitchen went quiet.

Poinsett couldn't resist taking on Jackie. She had stuck her nose somewhere it didn't belong and she was more than happy to teach her a lesson. The FBI was busy with Janet, thanks to Poinsett pushing her toward Mouzon. She knew that Janet wouldn't be successful. Mouzon had proved too resourceful and was covered in protection. But she did have to hand it to her for getting so close. The trap had been placed brilliantly and now it was time to spring it. *How could he resist not coming to help his sister.* The kid just made the performance that much more perfect. She slipped her hand into her coat and located a phone she had picked up at the gas station down the street. *Let the hunt finally begin.*

# CHAPTER 85

*79,52,23,74*
*32,47,3,69*

THE TEXT HAD come from an unknown phone with a local 843 number at six p.m. It made absolutely no sense. *Lottery numbers?* Cole called Agent Leas and forwarded the text just to be sure. A call to Jackie went unanswered, unusual for seven at night. Several texts went unresponded to before Cole started to get worried. *Where the hell is she?*

At seven-fifteen the phone rang. *About time.* "Hello?" A panicked voice met his. "Cole this is Mom, what is going on?! We just got a call from Billy. He's crying and said something about Jackie being gone."

Chills ran down his body at what Ava had just said. "What? When?"

"Just a second ago. Cole, is everything okay?"

"I...I don't know, but I'm going over. Call the cops." With that Cole ended the call.

"Cash, she has Jackie!" Cole was panicking with just the sound of what he had just said making him dizzy with fear.

"Wait, what? Who? I thought they had her, caught her last night?"

Cole's hand trembled as he spoke. "I don't know! I don't know! But Billy is alone and says someone took her."

"Where are you now?"

"I'm on my way to her house. Cash, what if…"

"Stop it. I'm jumping in the car and I'll meet you there, text me the address."

# CHAPTER 86

LEAS BARGED INTO the interrogation room where
Mrs. Christie had been returned.

"Mrs. Christie, I'm going to ask you again, why? Why did you do it?

"Do what Agent?" Janet smirked.

"Why did you target Cole Mouzon?"

"Because I wanted to, it felt good. Don't you like feeling good, Agent?"

"We found your husband."

She recoiled. "Piece of shit, he needed killing. You have no idea what that man did to me. The bruises, the cuts... The lies I told for that man. Nobody believed me, of course, until... Of course, they all knew, those piece-of-shit high-society ladies. But did any one of them help me? No! So... I helped myself. Steve won't be hitting me anymore."

"What did Mr. Mouzon do to you?"

"He looked at me wrong. He stepped on my toe. You pick."

Agent Leas sat back in his seat still looking at his suspect. "Here's what I don't get, and maybe you can help me out... Why the other kills? What did they do?"

"Don't I get a phone call or something?" Janet crossed her arms and looked away.

Agent Leas sat back and leaned into his chair until it was balanced on one leg. "We found the chats. Mrs. Christie, we know you have an accomplice. We found the messages, how you planned it out, killed your husband and then were told to go after Cole Mouzon."

"You really don't get it, do you, Agent. I guess it makes sense. You can't help yourself, can you...being so stuck on catching someone that you don't ask yourself if you deserve to catch them. Agent, you don't deserve to catch her. She was the only one who listened to me. She gave me the strength. You're not worthy of catching her."

"Worthy? What do you mean by that?" Leas was back on all four legs, leaning in.

She shook her head and grinned. "If I have to tell you, it would be no fun, now would it." The smirk was back, deeper and revealing deep smile lines across her otherwise Botox-frozen face.

"You didn't kill those others, did you? It was *her*." He watched as she stared with enjoyment at him. "We will find her."

*Bam bam bam,* the knocking at the hollow steel door echoed through the room. "Agent, you have a call."

"I'm in the middle of something here."

"Agent, it's Cole Mouzon... Jackie has been taken."

The agent turned on Janet. "What did she do to her? *Answer me!*"

"You'll never catch her; you're pathetic." Janet reached out to Leas, flirting with him for attention. For the brief second they were out, he noticed her hands. While he leaned in, she struck. Spit splattered across his face, like venom from a snake. Wiping his face, Leas stormed out the door praying that they had not made a horrible mistake and been played for fools; Jackie's life now was now at risk.

# CHAPTER 87

THE RAIN CAME down in sheets of thick, viscous water as Cole pulled up to the house, his heart beating through his chest, and was met with the wrenching sound of Billy crying in the house as he stepped out of the car. Cole bolted toward the house and onto the front porch, only to misstep on the slick, grey-painted surface, falling hard on his right hip. It ached with a throb. Up and opening the door, he screamed, "Billy! Billy! Where are you?" A pot was boiling over in the background, the burner still on, making a sizzling sound as the water overflowed onto the heated surface.

"Momma! Momma!" Cole rounded the corner of the upstairs bedroom as he caught a glimpse of Billy, seated on the floor at the foot of his mother's bed. "Momma!" Cole ran over to Billy uncontrollably weeping. Blood was everywhere, including on his pajamas. Jackie's phone rested in a pool of blood on the floor near his hand. He grabbed the child.

"Billy, are you okay...are you hurt?" Tears of anger entered Cole's eyes. "Where's Mom? Where's your momma?"

"Momma got taken. She's gone."

"What did you see, Billy?" Rushing words, Cole tied

not to interrogate his nephew but he felt time running out.

"I was at the stairs. Mom was screaming, she yelled 'run'! Someone was hitting her. But, she just kept screaming, telling me to stay back, to run. So I ran and hid under Momma's bed. I ran like she said, but screaming didn't stop. She was screaming, Cole." Billy broke down in deep sobs. "She screamed run and wouldn't stop. Then she did...the bad woman hit Momma and then took her away." More sobbing came as Billy finally released all his fear. "I wanted her to stop, but she wouldn't! Momma!"

"Shoo. Shoo. Uncle Cole is here. It's okay. Shhh." Cole sat on the floor holding Billy as Cash ran into the room. Cole looked up, his eyes moist and now red. The look on his face said it all. *Someone is going to pay.* Billy continued to whimper, calling for his mother, but it was softer now. Cole stood up with Billy still in his arms and walked past Cash, headed to the kitchen downstairs.

"'BOUT DAMN TIME!" Cash showed his anger as the police walked into the home, guns drawn. They looked past Cash into the kitchen and to Cole.

"All clear." Another officer had come in from the back porch and apparently realized Poinsett wasn't there.

Thirty minutes later the police were everywhere. One of their own was in danger and that meant emptying out the entire city if needed to find Jackie. Asleep, Cole had passed Billy on to Cash who was sitting on the couch, gently rocking him against his shoulder. Cole finished up with the officers, filling them in on the call and what they saw when they arrived. His patience was wearing thin. The police released him and Cash, explaining they were doing everything possible to find Jackie and to not worry. *Not worry? Right.*

Agent Leas pulled him aside outside the home. "Cole, I know what you are thinking, but don't do anything rash. Going out and trying to find your sister is just going to get you both killed. Let us handle this. You take Billy home and just sit tight."

"Right, right...like you've been promising since you showed up. The only things I know you've gotten to the bottom of are the empty bottles in your hotel room, Agent. So, go fuck yourself. That's my sister, Billy's mom. She wouldn't sit tight if that was me. So, you do what you need to do and I'll do what I need to do. If I find something out I'll let you know." The emotional wall had come crashing down at the sight of Billy and now his raw emotions were driving him into a frenzy for revenge. *Channel it, Cole. Channel it.* And then, clarity...

Leas looked at Cole with disapproval, knowing that the sudden calmness he just saw wash over his face was trouble. Cole walked away before he could say anything further.

# CHAPTER 88

COLE GRABBED AN umbrella from the stand next to the door and snapped it open to cover Cash and Billy as they walked to the car. Cole looked down at Cash and Billy as they maneuvered into the car; a word hadn't been spoken between them for the past hour. In the car, Billy was still asleep in Cash's arms when Cole slowly removed his hand from the wheel and placed it in his right pocket. He pulled out a white envelope he had discovered on the counter and glanced at just before the officers had rushed into the house, the seal broken, and handed it to Cash without a word. Cash looked in shock at what he saw. Taking the envelope in his free hand, he opened it and slid out the card.

79,50,22,70
32,45,36,85
2400

The numbers were in the same format as the text before, but clearly different, and with the added third line.

Cash looked at the card intensely and shook his head as he turned back up to look at Cole. "What the..." Cash spoke with whispered frustration. "Why didn't you mention this to the cops?"

"Dammit Cash, she has my sister. You saw how they were in there, they don't know anything. I know they're trying, but time is running out. Please, help me."

Cash caved in. Right or wrong, Cole's face wore determination and pain. "What does that all mean? It's like the last one, just gibberish."

"It isn't gibberish. She wants us to know something, to find her or do something."

"Cole, it's just a set of random numbers, nothing more. She's fucking with you."

"No, look. Let's think this out. They don't stand for letters because the numbers are too high. Letters only go to twenty-six. And there are three separate listings. So, each line is a separate meaning."

"I'm sorry, I don't see anything."

"What does she want? *What*?" Cole's voice was hushed to avoid waking Billy. Cole tried to flip through any image in his head that was relevant but his emotions kept getting in the way like stones sticking in the cogs of a clock. He pushed harder for the wall to go up.

Cash said, "She obviously wants you to find her."

"Exactly. How can I find her with this? Wait! The last number, look at it. That's like military time. I see that in medical records in my cases all the time."

"2400?"

"Midnight... Shit! Do you have GPS?"

"Like to track my phone or directions? Yeah."

Cole's mind finally sealed off his emotions and began working. Image after image flew by his eyes until one stood out. "Open up Google Maps.... Type this in: 79 50'22.70", 32 45'36.85", where is that?"

"Uh... the Arctic Circle."

"What? Let me see that. *Shit*. Put "N" after the first and W after the second."

"Yeah... thaaat's Greenland. Cole, I don't think these are coordinates."

"Dammit, they have to be, Cash, they have to!" Cole looked up to see Leas staring at them in the car outside the house.

"Okay, let's think about this. She's testing you."

"I've got it. Switch the two entries, renaming them north and west. She's fucking with us."

The screen flashed and the map came up. 'Charleston County School District.' Next to it was 'Edgar Allan Poe Library.'

# CHAPTER 89

"CAPTAIN, IF THERE is anything you need, you let me know. The FBI will offer what it can." Agent Leas had returned to the station knowing Cole and Cash were up to something. He called D.C. and asked them to get a phone tap on Cole's phone ASAP.

"Thank you Agent, but Jackie is one of us, we'll take it from here."

"Of course." Agent Leas pulled his phone out and checked his messages. Still no response from D.C.

The captain's door flew open and he stormed out to the agent yelling, "Dammit, I thought you had a leash on that boy of yours? What the hell. He's going to get himself and Jackie killed."

"What happened?"

"He dodged his tail; that's what the fuck happened! Somewhere off Dead Man's curve on Rifle Range. He's off the grid and likely going after her."

*Right into her trap.* Leas asked, "Have we heard back from your contact at the FBI about the profile of PoinZett?"

Hampton was walking by with coffee when he said, "They say there is no name attached to it."

"What? How can that be? We need a name, Officer." He shook the officer by his uniform.

"They would only say where the computer used is located." Hampton was wide-eye with the assault.

"Well, spit it out officer. Where?"

He straightened his uniform as he said, "Atlanta."

Agent Leas sat down at an old office desk in his make-shift operation in the station. A cheap plastic spray bottle, like the kind found on the travel aisle of stores, had been found on the kitchen floor of Jackie's home. It had been sent to the Medial University with the specific request that it be tested for chemicals.

He turned back to the strange set of numbers Cole had sent to him earlier. *What did they mean? A code?* But, what was the code saying? He had seen plenty of cryptic messages in his cases. It was always a mind game for those he was after.

BY ELEVEN HE had his answer on the bottle, a chemical was indeed found. The toxicologist had faxed his report; they had matched the poison in the bottle to an extract, *sapium marmieri Huber,* the tallow tree. The toxicologist had tagged it as a plant in the same family as poinsettias, the *Euphorbia* family, but this was a tropical variety, highly toxic if not treated immediately. He prayed Jackie was still alive. The department pulled up all sources of the plant and other than some botanical gardens; there was no readily available source for the extract. "Where is it from?" Leas looked back at the toxicologists report. Origin: *Upper Amazon.* The answer hit like a brick, with a flood of conversations and images flickering through his mind like cards. He knew who Poinsett was.

It all came flooding back to Leas, the history of bad relationships, poisons, plants, and the lack of white marks on Mrs. Christie's hands that had been suggested just to throw him off the trail. Now, this...a poison collected from the place she'd just returned from.

"Captain, it's the toxicologist from Atlanta. She's Poinsett."

"What?"

"I just got a call—the poison used in the most recent murder is only found in one place in the Amazon, the same place that Winters just got back from. It explains it all. The reason for the gap in murders was because she was out of the country, it aligns perfectly. How could I have missed it?"

"That doesn't tell us where she has taken Jackie and where Cole is heading to."

"Wait, there was a noise in the background on the phone when I talked to her earlier. A bell? No, a horn."

"Hell man, there are a million horns and bells in this city. It's called the Holy City for a reason, more churches per square inch here than any place in the States."

"No... A horn, like a boat." Leas walked around the room with his wrists pressed against his forehead.

"Agent, we have hundreds of miles of coast."

Calming down, Leas said, "No, she wouldn't take her far; she needs it to be close, to lure him in."

"Well, that would limit it to the inter-coastal and the harbor. Henning, grab that map." A young black officer went into another office and returned with a coastal map with Charleston at its center. Spread across an old pea green and aluminum desk, the three men gathered over it.

The captain worked fast. "Here's Mount Pleasant;

make a circle around it for fifteen miles out. She wouldn't have been able to take her much further. Now where is the inter-coastal in there?"

Another officer piped in. "Looks like Sullivan's Island. If you wanted to lure someone in, where would you go?"

"The lighthouse? Possible, but she would be trapped in there. Wait, what is this? That's where she would go."

Moments later Agent Leas was in his car with the others following. "Get me that damn GPS on Mouzon's phone, now!" *Dammit, why didn't I see it! She was right there in front of me.* Leas pressed the gas harder. He didn't know if where he was going was the place, but he had to get there fast before Poinsett collected another trophy.

# CHAPTER 90

"WHERE IS THAT?"
"Switch it to satellite mode. I know where that is. It's the old batteries on Sullivan's Island." There was a pause.

"Cole you aren't thinking about going, are you? Let the cops deal with this, please Cole, please. Don't do this."

Cole spoke with cold iron words, "I have to. It can all end. No more of this. It needs to end. I won't have my sister dying for me. I can't let that happen." Cole took a deep breath. "Now, I'm going to drop you off at the house with Billy. You can watch him, right?"

"Hell no I can't. If you're going, I'm going."

Still speaking with cold precision, he said, "Cash, this isn't your fight. She doesn't want you. This is all clear. Me and me alone."

"Fuck the text. And fuck you!" Billy mumbled and squirmed slightly as Cash's voice rose. Softer now, "Cole, I wasn't able to save my brother. I wasn't. Please, I need to do this. I need to help save Jackie and..." His voice trailed off, unwilling to say the rest.

"Dammit, man. If you show up she might kill her."

"There is no way you and she are going to come out of there alive if you go alone. Accept it, you need me."

Cole knew he needed him, even if he was willing to accept that he needed someone... needed Cash.

"Okay, okay. Let me call MeMe. I wouldn't trust Billy to anyone else; he'll be safe there."

Thirty minutes later Billy was in MeMe's large, homey arms on her family's wooded property. Cole remembered the feeling of that place... the warmth and safety of her chest, the soft but firmness of her breast against his head. Billy would be safe.

"Cole, go on now an' get Jackie. Mr. Billy and me be al'ight here till da morn." Love up-welled in Cole. MeMe was truly a mother, and he loved her for all that she was. He longed deeply to just grab her for one last hug, to have her tell him everything would be okay. But he had no time for such assurances.

"Cole, we need to get going." Cash was pointing at his arm; eleven-fifteen. Tears crossed his eyes for the second time in the night. He stole another hug from MeMe with Billy in her arms. "I'm going to get your momma, Billy. I love you. Please remember that."

The two men rushed back into the car and headed south towards the Isle of Palms Connector. They would come onto Sullivan's Island from Breech Inlet and South. From what Cole remembered from his childhood playing in the battery ruins, there was more cover from the North.

The old battery scared Cole as a child and ran fear through him now. The World War II ruins lay directly in front of the now-demolished Sullivan's Island Elementary School that backed up to dunes and the beach. The relatively new Edgar Allen Poe Library had consumed another battery a few yards down. Poe had been stationed at Fort Moultrie between 1827 and 1828, a Revolution-era fort further down the island. It clearly had made a mark because he used the island as the backdrop for several stories, including "The Gold-Bug" and "The Balloon Hoax." *Edgar Allen Poe? That dark fuck? What was Poinsett up to?*

COLE STOPPED THE car a few yards north-east of the battery. Cole filled Cash in. "In elementary school we used to dare each other to go in to play hide-and-seek. Ever seen the inside of an old navy ship? The *Patriot*, ever go inside that for a school field trip? Well, it's just like that. Old steel doors and concrete surfaces, painted black or dark grey from what I recall. There are only three ways in. It's otherwise buried in the dune. Scary as shit." Cole kept on, trying to describe the layout within.

Cash was listening intently. He thought to himself how the hell were they going to get in there and get out in one piece to get back to MeMe as promised. "I want you to stay here…"

Cash was caught off guard. "What!? I'm not staying here."

"Yes you are. End of discussion. I will not have you in there. She wants me. Not you. My sister is in there and it needs to be me. Stay out here in case you see her. Anyone else walks in there and my sister is dead. I can't handle that as a reality, Cash. I can't."

Cash knew all too well what Cole was feeling. He had felt it as well with Mark. "Cash, about yesterday… I didn't mean it. I'm just…" Cole was out of the car before Cash could respond. Within steps Cole had disappeared into the mat of oak and brush forming the north side of structure.

He was gone. Cash longed to chase after him, but he didn't. It was better that he play lookout and possibly catch Poinsett from the outside. The rain had picked up to a full thunder of water dumping so heavy that the soggy footsteps behind Cash couldn't be heard until the last second... Everything went dark.

# CHAPTER 91

COLE SLIPPED INTO the ruins from the north side entrance without noticeable detection, his feet and legs soaked through from the deep puddles now forming across the land. As he recalled, the walls were silted black, rivets forming a panel pattern on the walls and ceiling. Leaves and other debris covered the floor. Cole caught a cigarette package as he disturbed the covering. Twisting on a Mini Maglite until it filled the tight corridor with white light, Cole took a deep breath and focused on controlling his breaths so as not to be heard. Jackie was in there somewhere and he prayed she wasn't dead. She had been his protector all his life, warding off the dangers of a drunk father and bullies. Now was the time for him to return the favor, but it scared him to think that he might be too late.

Inside the tunnel, the left wall of the half-buried structure was solid and unbroken. The pouring rain from the outside was echoing down the corridor. Occasional lightning flashed outside, producing blue light from the small windows to the exterior. The right side was studded with numerous openings, doors to rooms. The one to his immediate right was open and empty.

"Jackie! Jackieeee! Where are you?! I'm here!" There

was no response. The thought crossed his mind that Jackie wasn't here, that the place was a decoy when he heard a faint sound from the very end of the corridor. "Jackie! Jackie. Are you here?!" Cole ran, his feet producing soggy steps, waiting for someone to jump out of any of the open rooms. But he didn't slow. "I'm here Jackie!"

The last two doors were closed. He reached the first and clasped the handle. It didn't turn. He tried again. Still nothing. Then he pulled; it slid open with a hollow metal creak. Its lock had obviously been long removed.

*Jackie, please be in there.* Mumbling came from a dark corner of the long room. There, gagged, bound with her arms behind her back and at her ankles, lay Jackie, still in her uniform. She was on her right side facing the back wall. Cole ran to her. "Jackie, Jackie, are you okay? Shit, you've been cut." Cole's hand was covered with blood as he removed it from his sister's left arm. He reached across her body and pulled down the gag, then rolled her onto her back. Her face was bruised purple and puffy. "Jackie, talk to me."

Weak but conscious, she spoke. "Billy, Billy." She could barely get the words out. "He's okay. I left him with MeMe. He's okay, Jackie."

"You shouldn't have come, Cole. You shouldn't have..."

"YOUR SISTER IS right again, Cole." The voice came from the darkness that had swept in behind him. Cole reached for the light. "Don't do that Cole. Not if you value his pretty little head. Say hi, Mr. Calhoun." *Shit.*

"Cole, I'm sorry. She snuck up behind me right after you came in here. I didn't know..."

"Shut the hell up. You know your brother was just as talkative, always yapping about his pain. Shit, you should thank me for putting him out of his misery."

"What? My brother jumped. You knew him? What the…"

Poinsett hit him with the hilt of her pistol and Cash went down hard, holding his head.

"I told you. Shut the fuck up! Yes, I knew your dear sweet brother. What a piece of work. We dated off and on for a year when I went to M.U.S.C. He started unloading on me about this crazy story about him and your boyfriend Mouzon and all. I thought he was crazy. But I looked it up. And, what do you know, he's telling the truth. It was you two. You destroyed my life."

"Fuck off." Jackie had regained some of her defiance. Cole looked over in surprise.

"Jackie, Jackie. Jackie you dug a little too deep into Mark's past. Luckily, a little bird tipped me off that you were snooping where you didn't belong."

"What do you want? We didn't do anything to you! You want me? Let them go. Take me. You don't need them any longer."

"Awh, isn't that sweet. But that won't be happening tonight. Now, can I finish telling Cash how his brother really died?" After a pause, "Thank you… Now, as I was saying, your brother wouldn't shut up about it, like I was his therapist or something. It was my father, Cole, my father that you escaped! Laurence Poinsett. My mom would always remind me a half a bottle into her vodka about the kids, the women he liked to diddle on the side. How we weren't good enough. How he left us because of you. But I never knew who they were. Why the fuck he let you live, I don't know. But, when your little whore of a mom got free, he ran. And, the shit went downhill from there. Mom went crazy, the meth, the drugs, the vodka. And I paid for it. *All because of you!*

"Right there in front of me was the source of all my problems. Mark... you... All of them. And then it just all clicked. If my father is still alive, I want him to feel my pain, to suffer the way I did. Maybe he would come, maybe he wouldn't. Just for good measure I used his name. Had it plastered over every newspaper to draw him out as I destroyed those he gave me up for, to hurt him the way he and you hurt me.

"Mark had been delivered to me, like a gift. Poor frail Mark. He was easy, a sleeping pill in one of his many night caps after work. Drive to the old bridge. And, plop. There he went over the edge. Whoops." Cole could see the shadow of Poinsett shrugging with indifference.

"You bitch!" Cash moved fast, digging his elbow deep into Poinsett's stomach, and then kneeing her in the head as she was bent down in pain. She fell over as the gun went sliding into the dark.

Cole turned to his sister, working to loosen the rope holding her tightly together. Cash ran over to help, tackling the knots at her feet. Free, Jackie sat up. "You little shit." Poinsett was back up somewhere in the black before them. Her hands raked the debris. *She's looking for the gun.*

Cash charged. Cole and Jackie instinctively followed into the nothingness. A spark, like a firework, went off with an echoing bang. A shot. *Cash!* Cash roared out in pain. He was down somewhere, hit by the shot.

Cole barely had turned his head in the direction of the yell when he and his sister collided with Poinsett. Cole immediately lost contact and his bearings. All three went to the cold steel ground. Jackie was on Poinsett and from what he could tell, was landing punches to her face. Then Jackie screamed. Poinsett had grabbed a hold of the large gash in Jackie's back rib. An elbow to the chin and Jackie was back in it, swinging with all her weight as they rolled around in the darkness. A series of hollow metal bangs told Cole his sister was knocking something hollow, like Poinsett's head, against the floor. He touched a leg. It was Cash. As he reached the thigh, another shot went off. He immediately recognized the scream. "Jackie!" Cole lunged over the leg. Lifting his hand to stand, the lamp light illuminated red. "Jackie!" There was no response.

"Get the fuck up." The gun had apparently been placed against the back of Cash's head. "You heard me. GET. THE. FUCK. UP!" Cash slowly got up.

Yelling out to Cole from somewhere in the dark, she continued. "Get over here. You know, you have been a real pain. You messed everything up. I have no clue why he let you live, but that is over. Know this, Mouzon. You would rather have me doing this than him. I just want you dead. He would keep killing long after you and your sister are gone. Perhaps your nephew, your family by the time it's all said and done."

Cole looked over at where he thought Cash stood with Poinsett in the dark, regretting his involvement. Regretting it all. Like the hand in his dream, Poinsett had come to drag him away into the darkness. It was the fear he had always held. The fear of that crippled him as a child into tears and rocking, alone in the dark. Whoever this 'he' was made it all that much worse.

He could feel his emotions channeling, tingling in his skin. The room was pitch dark and he only had one chance to take her down. Cole pushed out from his mind the image of the room that he recalled for his childhood.

In his mind the corners, the walls slightly glowed in the dark. He could see the entire layout now before him. He had to trust his mind again.

"Noooooo!" Cole leapt and tackled Poinsett, them both falling to the ground. She wrestled, crawling away as he held tight hold of her two legs. He could feel her trying to sit up and then, the click of a gun close to his head. A final shot rang out, echoing in around the room for seconds. Then silence.

# CHAPTER 92

"COLE! COLE!" CASH crawled across the floor, lame in his left leg. He called out for him again as he finally reached Cole just as he heard steps in the dark. A light was shined into his eyes; his eyes tried to readjust but saw only light.

"They're in here! Come on, get in here!" Leas' voice filled the room. He moved the light across the room until it landed on Cole. There, in the corner he was sitting up, Jackie's head in his lap. Blood was running down his leg. A drop fell to the floor in a faint wet thud. Cash pulled himself to Cole as Leas looked over from across the room. Jackie attempted to speak, but only thick, viscous bubbles of iron red came up. Lifting her hand to cup Cole's cheek, one word escaped, "Love," before going limp and falling into his body. Fighting to hold on to the salvation of his internal wall, he sat there for a several seconds before an EMT rushed in and Cole released her, grabbing Cash's neck for shelter. *Don't fail, don't fail…* He released, still cold from the moment.

Leas leaned down and pulled Cash's arm around his neck, lifting to pull him up. The three walked back through the corridor into the now misting rain outside. Lightening cracked miles away, shining its white and blue hue through the night sky. Cole stopped and looked up as Leas lead Cash to a flashing ambulance that had backed up into the flooded grass in front of the battery.

THE WALL CAME CRASHING down with a heavy internal thud, exposing his body to the rawness of his emotions. Like an old movie, images of Jackie flickered across his mind, starting at his earliest memory, working its way through youth, their strong connection, until the last slide… her lying dead in his hands. She was gone.

The tingling heat of sadness crept up from his temples and slowly consumed his face and throat. His mind swirled in dizzying, sweeping movements. He was helpless to fight the tide of loss that consumed him as he looked up into the dripping sky and collapsed onto his knees. Still looking up, feeling the drops colliding against his face, he succumbed to his tears, letting them flow across his cheeks and into the soggy ground beneath him. Another surge of emotion rippled across his body, forcing him to reach out with his right hand and lean into the ground, heaving up the bitterness of his loss in loud cries, the tannic acid of yearning for things taken. He was there, alone, as the tears seeped out of him like poison from a wound. Between them he cried out in painful sounds and sobs until slowly the flow of emotions returned to a trickle and calm came over his body.

Looking around with his red eyes, he saw Cash had been moved to the back of an ambulance and was getting checked as a covered gurney presumably carrying Jackie's body was wheeled out and placed in another truck. Cole looked away to avoid another flood. The tears had stopped, not because he didn't hurt, but because he had just run out. Looking back into the ambulance, Cash was laid on a stretcher being sedated for the ride to East Cooper Hospital. Having regained enough strength to lift himself and move, Cole walked over to Cash.

Agent Leas approached to check on both men briefly and to inform him that Beth Winters'—Poinsett's—body had been found, shot in the back. He was otherwise at a loss for words as the EMT stepped in. "Mr. Mouzon. We need to go. Will you be joining us?"

Cole looked to Cash, now laid out on a collapsible gurney, its yellow legs standing out amongst the white interior of the cramped space. Cash turned his head with slow, pained rotation to look behind him at Cole and mouthed, "Go…go." Cash caught Cole's hand as he stood to exit. Though they only held for seconds, the moment lingered in Cole's palm like the holding of a tight fist too long, lasting until he reached MeMe's place and knocked on her old wooden screen door. It was now almost six a.m. and the sun was rapidly pushing forward into the morning. MeMe opened the door and Cole didn't have to say a word. Tears flowed like ribbons across her soft wrinkled face. She turned and Billy stood behind her. Cole dropped to his knees and spread his arms while tearing up again and rolling down Billy's back.

# CHAPTER 93

JACKIE'S FUNERAL CAME quickly. Cole had picked up Cash from the hospital in the morning because he refused to miss the funeral. Billy had been quiet, with long bouts of crying in the week since that night on Sullivan's Island. But seeing Cash momentarily offered a break from his loss. Billy liked Cash's wheels, taking any opportunity to jump in his lap and ordering him to spin the wheelchair in circles. It was temporary, so Billy was advised to enjoy it while he could. Cole's family had turned the ceremony into a flower jungle. At least the flowers were pink. The entire police department had come out and most of Charleston County as well. If one's value to society is ranked by the number of people who show for your funeral, Jackie was very much loved. Jackie would have raised hell over such a production. Funerals aren't for the dead, but for the living.

The day before, Leas had briefed Cole on the investigation. Poinsett's real name was Beth Winters, or at least that was what she had it changed to after leaving Charleston. She had returned and attended MUSC, the Medical University of South Carolina, but dropped out her third year when questions arose about patient abuse in her eldercare clinic. By all indications she acted alone.

He was following up on her claims of being the daughter of the original kidnapper and killer of Cole's mom. The story was panning out so far, with witnesses confirming she dated Mark Calhoun immediately before his death. They had reopened his death but there wasn't much they could do ten years out. And, she was now dead, too.

Ava had lost her only daughter and retreated deep into depression in the days leading up to the funeral. She now sat quietly next to his father, lost in her emotions. Cole worried most for her. Jackie was her daughter but also her friend. Henry had come up from Florida and that seemed to provide some additional support to Ava. Cole's father was playing the support for the entire family, refusing to show the hurt he was certainly feeling. Cole worried this would throw his father back to the bottle, but that had yet to be seen. Granny was heartbroken by the loss, but seemed to be faring the best. When MeMe came over after the funeral they sat on the back porch laughing up a storm. Probably in no small part to the Bailey's Cole had picked up at her request before returning home. By the number of returns to the ice bucket, the bottle was half empty within the first hour.

The mood was broken momentarily when a shot rang out in the back yard. Every officer in attendance had drawn, only to see Granny yelling into the marsh. "You get out of my creek, you fool gator! This isn't your buffet." Granny had pulled out her old twenty-two and shot warning shots to scare off the six-foot gator, but he wasn't paying her any attention. MeMe girlishly giggled under her hand as the crowd looked on. *Jackie would have loved that moment.*

Looking out over the marsh and his Granny, Cole missed his sister deeply. Amongst all the other feelings, was dread of what had just become his life. As Billy's named guardian, he was an instant parent. He wanted children but when suddenly handed one, even Billy, he felt helpless and the questions to be answered seemed too numerous to tackle. How would he work and be a single parent? Where would he live? How would Billy handle all this change? There were no quick answers and that bogged Cole's mind down with doubt.


OVER THE NEXT several days it was agreed that Billy needed a break. For now, everyone needed to heal. He would take Billy back to Denver with him while his parents packed up his sister's house to put on the market. Charleston carried too many memories of Jackie. The family decided Florida was just a better place to recoup once the house was addressed. Cole had already promised to bring Billy down for a Disney week before school started at the end of the summer. But until then it was just the boys. They both needed time to heal and bond.

*Healing...moving forward.*

The realities of that hadn't set in as cole crossed over the ravenel bridge toward the airport. A song about giving up Manhattan came on the radio. Cole looked across to the steeples of Charleston on his left and then the mash far down on his right. The yellow morning sun caught the blades and danced on the river's waters. As a long note was held by the singer on the radio, he thought the song was fitting. He knew that sometimes healing is merely making the choice to take the step forward...to refuse to stand still...to step backwards. He had stood still too long since Atlanta. Looking at Billy in the back seat through the rearview mirror, he promised himself that even if just baby steps he *would* move forward.

One of those steps meant eventually dealing with Cash. It had been days since the funeral without more than text contacts from him. Cole was torn between wanting him close and also wanting him very, very far. *It is just better this way,* he told himself. Even without the events that led to their meeting, he already felt damaged. Though the mental counting of days had stopped, he still felt alone, empty…guilty.

"Are you okay?" In the end, Cash was there, against Cole's protests, looking over to Cole driving.

"Yeah, sorry…just a bit tired."

Cash looked at the man beside him and wondered if he were crazy…delusional for putting so much energy and placing his life on the line for someone he had never met and who, in Cole's opinion, was damaged goods. Cash just looked back with his blue eyes and smiled warmly.

Cole turned back to Billy in the mirror and continued his self-analysis. The dream was still there too, hunting his dreams every night. If the threat of Poinsett made it return, it should have gone away when she died in the battery on Sullivan's Island. Cole reasoned it was just his head trying to comprehend it all and eventually the dream would return to the darkness from which it came and never be seen again.

Stepping out of the car, the two men hugged. An overwhelming sense of longing washed over Cole as he felt the warmth of Cash's arms against his core. His skin tingled with sadness. Though he tried, the wall refused to go up, forcing him to feel the raw emotions of the moment as he forced a slight smile. Their meeting had been anything but ideal, and there were many more questions than answers. Standing in drop-off area of the airport was no place to start. Fighting back tears, they promised to stay in touch. Doubt crossed Cole's mind, he had heard that before, but he held out the slightest hope for being proven wrong.

# CHAPTER 94

GETTING OFF THE plane in Denver, Billy was quiet and subdued. Reality had hit hard that his mother was gone, he was in a new place and he needed to find a way to survive. Cole picked him up and held him against his shoulder, his teddy bear backpack flapping with each step. He could feel the tears soaking though his shirt at the shoulder as Billy finally unloaded his emotions. One of the gate attendants looked at them both with a concerned smile as Cole fought hard to maintain his own composure to avoid a total meltdown in the middle of DIA.

Catching a taxi, Billy laid his head on his uncle's lap, where he promptly passed out from his emotional exhaustion. Cole looked out the window taking in the vastly different landscape of Denver compared to Charleston and wondered if he would ever see again the city that was in his blood, that he had once craved. The time in Charleston had worn him thin and he didn't know if he could be the same.

Trying to just occupy his mind with the passing warehouse a text buzzed in and he retrieved the phone vibrating in his pocket. It was Cash. "I miss u. Hope ur flight was safe. DEN n a month?" For that brief moment a smile crossed Cole's face and a feeling of hope lingered that everything would be okay. Perhaps Charleston still held some happiness for his life.

# EXPLORE THE WORLD
# OF COLE MOUZON

*Maps and insight:* Robert-Reeves.com

*Locations, recipes, characters* @ Pinterest:
http://pinterest.com/crobertreeves/

*Sound Track* @ Spotify: http://spoti.fi/1cUM9nC

Connect with the author @

Facebook: https://www.facebook.com/a.robertreeves
Goodreads: http://bit.ly/161XAjI
Twitter: https://twitter.com/CRobertReeves
Web: Robert-Reeves.com

# ABOUT THE AUTHOR

Robert Reeves was born and raised in and around Charleston, South Carolina where his family still resides. He currently lives and practices law in Denver. Accompanied by his dog Cooper, Robert frequently treks the Rockies searching for inspiration for his next novel. To inquire about a possible appearance, please contact him directly at contact@robert-reeves.com or http://www.robert-reeves.com.

# BEFORE YOU GO

IF YOU ENJOYED this book, please spread the word. Review it on Goodreads and/or your favorite bookstore website including: Amazon, Barnes and Noble and Kobo.

# COMING SPRING 2014

WHEN ASPENS QUAKE. Cole Mouzon has returned to Denver to heal from the loss of his sister and learn to be the parent Billy desperately needs. As Cash Calhoun continues to chip away at Cole's defenses from Charleston, events in Atlanta cause Agent Leas to believe Poinsett was successful in drawing out the Taker, placing Cole in danger once more. Together, the three search for answers in Georgia before the Taker can finish what Poinsett started.

28589193R00234

Made in the USA
Lexington, KY
21 December 2013